PERIPHERY

PERIPHERY

By Michael Winter

For my wife Kathy and daughter Tess.

Table of Contents

"Whoever fights monsters should see to it that in the process he does not become a monster. And if you gaze long enough into an abyss, the abyss will gaze back into you."

—— Friedrich Nietzsche

Part 1: Revealed

One

T he negotiation team leader gripped Andrew Tate's shoulder hard and yanked against a strap, synching the Kevlar vest tight against the EMT's chest.

"Don't get any closer than you have to," Officer Brice told Andrew. "Reach out, hand him the water and back away. Don't engage him more than is absolutely necessary. Assess the woman's condition, come back. That's it."

Andrew nodded. He could feel the eyes of the other Tampa Fire Rescue responders on him, as well as those of the negotiation team members milling a few feet away, silent and skeptical. The blank-faced crowd-control officers were inscrutable behind their dark glasses. There was an uncomfortably childlike submission in being forced to stand here, arms outstretched, while Brice dressed him in protective gear, and he searched for something to say that would put them on a more equal footing.

"We know who the vehicle is registered to yet?" he asked.

"Tag check came back with a Gloria Fife," a team member offered. Brice shot the other officer a look and the cop stepped back, his eyes on the ground.

"Don't worry about that. Your job is to deliver water. That's it."

"And if he wants to talk?" Andrew inserted the radio's earbud, reached under the vest and began fumbling with the transmitter. "If he threatens to harm the woman if I don't stay and listen to what he has to say?"

Brice removed his sunglasses, his eyes two slivers beneath furrowed brows. "Look, I'm this close to pulling the plug here. You may be a first responder, but as far as I'm concerned you're just a half-step up from some random civilian plucked out of the crowd. Don't go over there thinking 'what ifs'. That's my job."

Brice reached under the vest and flipped on the transmitter. A loud crackle of static made Andrew wince and the officer dialed back the volume.

"It's just we have a history of sorts," Andrew continued. "Comanche's a regular. Homeless, alcoholic, diabetic. Twice I've pulled him out of comas with a glucose drip." He nodded toward his partner, Gary Wyatt. "A couple of other EMTs have done the same. It's amazing he's still alive."

"Comanche?"

"That's what they call him on the street. I don't know his real name. Point is, he obviously recognized me."

Brice bowed his head for a moment, long enough for Andrew to study the swirl of close-cropped gray hair spiraling out from the small bald spot at his crown.

"All right, if he's hell-bent on engaging you, say whatever it takes to keep him calm. Reinforce the idea that he's in charge, that he's controlling the situation. Don't contradict anything I've told him and don't agree to new demands. Just tell him you'll pass any requests on to the right people. Then get the hell back here."

And try not to get anyone killed, Andrew thought. Gary passed him the two condensation-slicked water bottles. They were still blessedly cold and Andrew gave them a hard squeeze, the plastic crunching in his palms.

He wanted to press one against the back of his neck, let the shock of its icy touch slap away the blood-soaked scenarios that had been looping through his mind since Comanche had pointed his chin toward Andrew and shouted, "Him. No one else but him."

The knife at the woman's throat flared with reflected sunlight every time Comanche twisted his wrist. Dipping under the crime scene tape, Andrew tried to avoid the glare, but the flashes were relentless, bursting like flashbulbs again and again, cluttering his vision with fading purple afterimages.

"Hold them up," Comanche yelled. "Over your head. I want to see them."

Andrew lifted his arms. The immense afternoon heat burned through the light overcast and radiated off the asphalt with a blistering intensity. When the blade flashed again he turned his head to avoid the glare and caught a glimpse of Gary standing cross-armed next to the idling ambulance from Station Three. Engines from four additional stations encircled the intersection, as well as a dozen patrol cars, a paddy wagon, a mobile crisis center and a pair of tow trucks, all but the crisis center pulsing colored lights into the torpid air. A fleet of television vans filled the parking lot of a nearby CVS, their raised antennas poking like masts above the idling traffic stretching unbroken in every direction.

"Now walk forward," Comanche said. "Slowly."

Brice's voice was in his right ear: "Just like we went over it. Slow and steady."

Andrew nodded. He heard a small sound from the woman, a stifled sob or a gasp as Comanche clutched her tighter. They were positioned near the rear bumper of the SUV, a balding man, deeply tanned, with a rutted face and a muscular, ropy build, and a disheveled young woman with mascara-streaked cheeks and sweat-matted hair. Andrew noticed her feet were bare, yanked out of her sandals, he presumed, when she had been pulled from the car. It must have happened quickly, a trap laid, a snare sprung, and yet for it to have gotten this far seemed more fate than plan. She must have been distracted, maybe fiddling with her phone as she waited for the light to change, ignoring the panhandler pacing the median with his cardboard sign and concealed butcher's knife.

Moisture from the bottles dripped down Andrew's arms, mingling with his sweat. If it would only rain. Rain would wash all this craziness away. But there hadn't been a drop since March, and now the heat and the drought were baking peoples' minds, melting their sanity. All of Tampa was roiling at a low boil.

When Andrew approached, Comanche's expression changed from strained scrutiny to satisfaction.

"It *is* you."

He was close enough to smell the man's sour clothes and unwashed body, a reek so strong it clenched his stomach.

"How we doing here?" Andrew asked, directing his question not toward the hostage-taker but to the woman. "Mrs. Fife, is it? Gloria Fife?"

She still held the roll of electrical tape that bound her and Comanche together with a dozen or more gray loops. How in god's name had he managed that? It had to have been a collaborative effort, but Andrew couldn't imagine the woman cooperating, even with a blade at her throat.

Although her head remained motionless, the woman's eyes slid toward Comanche as if seeking permission to speak. Comanche, however, was still focused on Andrew and now, Andrew noticed uneasily, he had begun to nod.

"My mother," the woman sighed after a moment, perhaps interpreting her captor's behavior as consent. The top buttons of her blouse were gone, the garment yanked up and back to expose a freckled shoulder and the sliver of a white bra strap, and this, more than anything else, epitomized her vulnerability, the unbearable precariousness of her situation.

"Your mother?" Andrew prompted.

"Gloria is my mother. I'm Katie."

"Hi, Katie. I'm Andrew."

"Open one of those bottles and hand it to her," Comanche ordered. "Slowly."

The blade pressed against Katie's throat creased her flesh. "CUTCO" was stamped into the metal near the handle. Andrew lowered his arms, set one bottle on the ground and twisted the cap off the other.

"Take it," Comanche said. When Katie did nothing he repeated the command, giving her a shake. She reached out, fingers splayed wide, the desperate flail of someone cast overboard in a storm. Pull me out of this, her eyes pleaded, grab hold and yank me back to reality. Instead, Andrew placed the sweating bottle into her palm and the fingers closed hard, sending a small fountain of water gushing from the open top.

"Just be cool," Comanche told her. "Take a drink."

Paranoid bastard. Worried we've drugged the water. If only they had. Twenty-five-hundred milligrams of Valium dissolved in each would have been enough to end the standoff. Why hadn't it occurred to him while he was waiting behind the line? Then again, even the most powerful oral sedative took time to work. Comanche would have felt the effects before being incapacitated, giving him enough time to inflict significant harm to his hostage before losing consciousness. Of course, Andrew could have lunged for the knife, but then...

"I know you," Comanche said.

Andrew nodded. "I've taken you to the hospital a couple of times." He wiped his slick forehead with the back of a hand. His sodden shirt clung to his chest beneath the tightly-cinched vest.

"You didn't do me no favors, man, bringing me back to this." Comanche jerked his head, a gesture intended to indicate what? The city? The weather? The cosmos? "And that's not what I meant. I know who you are. You're John's son."

Andrew inhaled slowly and deeply, his head tilting skyward as if following the trajectory of an incoming grenade. "My father's name is John," he said carefully. "It's a common name."

"John Tate. The Professor. The Mad Scientist. You're his son, right? He said he had a son who was a paramedic. You look just like him." The hand around Katie's waist darted up and snatched the bottle from her. For an instant, Andrew thought this sudden motion would trigger a sniper to take his shot. There'd be a pop, a backward jerk of the head, the rear door frame sprayed with atomized gore, the woman's screams. But nothing happened. Comanche poured half the bottle over his head and gulped the rest.

"You know about them, don't you?" He tossed the container away. "Probably been telling you monster stories since you were a kid."

Although Andrew said nothing, Comanche bobbed his head after a brief pause. " 'Course he has. I can tell by the look on your face. You worried people will think you're nuts, too? Shouldn't be. I used to think your old man was a whack job. Crazy fucker, handing out five-spots to homeless guys, asking them to keep an eye out for his creepy-crawlies. Shit man, he wants to throw his money away I'll take it like anyone else. Beats the hell out of standing in the hot sun with a cardboard sign. Only you know what?" Comanche leaned forward until the tape girdling his waist crackled, and in a fierce, conspirator's whisper said, "Turns out he's right. There really are monsters out there. And they're *everywhere*."

"Is that what's going on here? You want to tell people about the things you think you're seeing?"

"Let's wrap this up," Brice whispered in his ear.

"I don't *think* anything. These ain't hallucinations. They're as real as you. As her. As real as this fucking knife." Comanche twisted the blade; the white light stabbed out again.

"Okay." Andrew patted the air. "You're right; my father's talked about them. Started when I was twelve and hasn't stopped since. You want to discuss his monsters? Let Katie go and you and I can talk about it for as long as you want."

He could have heard Brice's "damn it" even without the radio.

"How long before you started seeing them?"

Andrew sucked in his lower lip and bit down hard, wishing this miserable afternoon had come with a pause button. He wanted to mull his options, consider the repercussions of each possible response. But Comanche wouldn't wait. His raised-brow look of expectation was already sliding into impatience and suspicion.

"I never did."

Comanche reared back as if Andrew had swung at him, forcing Katie to stand on tiptoe to keep the knife from drawing blood. "Not directly," Andrew quickly added. With her head canted up, he saw her carotid artery pulsing, a rapid flutter that was now matched by his own racing heart.

"But you've seen something?"

"Sometimes I'll catch a glimpse out of the corner of my eye. Just shapes."

"What kind of shapes?"

Andrew's partner was close enough to catch bits of the conversation. Brice as well. How could he stand here and admit the truth, confess just how far things had slipped over the previous year? How could he tell this knife-wielding vagrant about the patches of bark that appeared to shift? The motion on telephone poles like something coiling upward? Or coiling downward. The glimpses of things hopping through the grass in highway medians, springing away in an instant? It was always in his periphery, always just out of sight. When he bent to retrieve the second water bottle Andrew noticed a sticker on the SUV's rear bumper: "COEXIST" spelled out in a series of religious symbols.

"They're hard to describe," he said, twisting off the cap. "Shapes like something out of a deep-sea documentary. Twitching angles. Curves that ripple and heave. Dark spots opening and closing."

"That's how it starts." Comanche leaned forward, allowing Katie to sink back off the balls of her feet. "Subtle shit. Just a shadow. Just a swirl of leaves. Stuff you've seen all your life. And you *have* seen them all your life. Everyone has. That's what's so fucking hilarious. They've been here the whole time. Hiding in the open. Hiding in the light."

Andrew knew those phrases well. His father had repeated them dozens of times over the years, always with a warning to look away if he felt his gaze drawn toward something moving in the bushes, something too confounding to comprehend. He held out the second bottle and Comanche snatched it.

"Now break contact," Brice said through the earpiece. Andrew took a single step back.

"What does your old man call them?" Comanche drank without taking his eyes off him. "The something-ofalla? Should have listened better. Said they were refugees, castaways from a time when their masters *ruled the world*." He gave the knife a theatrical flourish, the tip spiraling skyward. "Oh yeah. I used to think your pop was one crazy son-of-a-bitch. But no more. No, no, no. Now I know he's a goddamn prophet."

"My brother," Katie said as if to herself, the words a barely audible sigh.

"Your brother," Comanche said after a moment, and although his tone was incongruously gentle, she pressed her eyes shut and turned her face away as if he had licked her ear. "What about your brother?" The blade touched her throat once more.

"Tate." Brice's voice cracked like a warning shot. "Break off contact. Make your way to the curb." Andrew took a second step back.

"He's been drawing things for weeks," Katie said in a rush. "Creatures. Weird things with too many legs or not enough. Floating balls with spikes. Something that looks like a cross between a centipede and an armadillo." She took a deep breath. Comanche whispered something Andrew couldn't catch and she shook her head. "He's autistic. Severely autistic. He doesn't talk. But he can draw." Incredibly, a small smile touched her lips. "He draws so well. But he doesn't want to go outside anymore. He spends all his time in his room. Drawing. Drawing monsters."

"You see," Comanche demanded. "You see. I've seen those things. Not just shit out of the corner of my eye, waving branches or shadows that point the wrong way. The whole thing. Something clicked up here." He raised the knife to his temple. "Something changed. And now I can't *not* see them. I can't go back to the way things were. I've tried. Getting high, getting drunk. It only makes things worse. What?"

Andrew shook his head. "I didn't say anything."

"No, but for a second you looked like someone gave your nuts a good yank. People need to know what's happening. Someone has to do

9

something. Bad shit is headed our way. The masters are coming. I can feel them getting closer, feel their minds, hear their words. Terrible words like maggots in my head. Squirming, burrowing, maggots. I don't understand the language yet, but I will soon. Won't be able to help it. Like catching a disease." His eyes darted about as if following the erratic flight of some unseen insect.

Slowly, pausing between each word and enunciating with the precision of someone trying to convey a simple direction to a small child, Brice said: "Get. Your. Ass. Back. Here. Now."

Andrew removed the earpiece. "A disease can be cured," he said.

Comanche's head drooped and his chin touched Katie's shoulder. Her body tensed; her breath caught.

"Why don't we talk to my father? That's why you wanted me to bring the water, isn't it? So you could get in touch with him?"

For a moment, Comanche appeared to consider the proposal. His gaze drifted past Andrew and out over the street before lifting toward the flat, pale lid of the sky.

"Come on, man," Andrew pleaded. "This has gone on long enough. Toss the knife away and I swear I'll do everything I can to help you."

When their eyes met again Andrew saw in them a willingness to be persuaded, a dawning realization, both appalled and ashamed, of just how far and how wrong things had gone. But a second later Comanche's glance darted to something over Andrew's right shoulder.

"Look," he hissed. "Over there."

Andrew turned and panned the street. The crowd of spectators had grown. They stood beyond the police lines in a silent throng, the stone-faced emergency personnel, the civilians eager and hungry, expectant. A sudden image of them all opening their mouths in unison made Andrew shudder as the vertebra in his neck and upper back began to pop.

"You see it?"

"Where?"

"Cross the street." Comanche's voice dropped to a ragged whisper. "The dumpster by the fence. You see it?"

"I see the dumpster."

"Look closer."

Something in Andrew's awareness quivered as he examined the trash bin, a perceptual straining he had recently come to understand was not an effort to see, but rather to not see. There was a beer bottle lying next to the dumpster. Its amber glass appeared to be softening in the heat, melting. The cracked and mottled asphalt around the bin stretched to a weather-beaten wooden fence streaked with burnt sienna sulfur deposits from a nearby sprinkler. A desiccated frond from an adjacent palm overhung the fence, reaching nearly to the ground.

"It's a *quintaloch*."

"What?" Andrew was teetering over a precipice he had been approaching for twenty years, ever since the day his father had returned from the police station still caked in dried blood and announced to his wife and son that he was moving out, that it was the only way to ensure their safety, although they had nothing to fear from *him*. All the scary stuff was out there, out in the light. Out in the open. It always had been.

"That's what your old man calls them. *Quintalochs*."

Andrew wanted to look away, but a feeling of inevitability had taken hold. In his mind, things were clicking and snapping, falling into a terrible alignment nothing could stop. The palm frond held his gaze. There was something unnerving about its size, about the way each long blade bent, then bent again, tapering to a barbed point. They jutted from the central stem like angled spokes that thickened every time he blinked. There were well over a dozen veins, running in twos all the way to the ground before curving toward the bin.

Andrew saw with a start that the frond wasn't connected to the tree at all. It was simply propped against the fence. What had made him think otherwise? And what about those discolorations on the pavement? Odd the way they continued up the side of the trash bin, as if the two marks were actually part of the same thing, a sweeping curve of antenna for instance.

Enough! He gripped his thighs hard, digging in his nails, relishing the dull, clarifying pain, and as he did the stains on the ground and the sulfur streaks on the fence shifted in unison.

Andrew had once seen a picture in a college psych book, a black-and-white illustration intended to demonstrate the way the brain incorporates bits of visual information into a coherent whole. At first, the image appeared to be nothing more than a random collection of splotches and lines. He stared at the page for minutes trying to discern some hidden connection among the elements. The caption claimed it was a cow, but he saw only visual static, a meaningless jumble of white spaces and shadings.

Just as he was about to slam the book closed in frustration, a dark spot near the center of the picture became an eye and suddenly it was there, complete and unequivocal. Not a cow as the caption said, but a calf, a Holstein calf staring at him with large, sad eyes. Comprehension came in a delicious instant of gestalt, followed a moment later by the realization that he would never be able to un-see the calf.

This was a similar experience, although far more profound. One moment there was nothing, the next moment, something. Some *thing* that, if drawn by an autistic boy, might resemble a nightmare amalgamation of armadillo and centipede. The crescent-shaped head rested near the trash bin. An elongated eye, shaped vaguely like a beer bottle, gleamed darkly from beneath a bony ridge of plating. One long antenna swept up the side of the dumpster, the other extended out across the pavement. The elongated body was composed of a dozen or more segments, each one boasting a pair of legs thick as broomsticks. Its length stretched from the bin to halfway up the fence, ending in a splay of overlapping discs arranged in a sort of fanning tail.

Despite the impression of being heavily armored, the creature was semi-translucent, its form revealing confounding internal structures, its surface swelling and contracting with a membranous flexibility.

As he watched, the eye began to bulge outward on a thick stalk, rising nearly a foot above the creature's head where it was joined by a second rising from the other side. For a moment they drifted, turning leisurely one way, then the other in opposing circles. Later, Andrew wouldn't be certain which happened first, whether someone, himself or Katie, had groaned "Oh, god," or those terrible eyes had suddenly locked on them.

"It knows I can see it." Comanche's voice was a high trill of panic. "It knows. It knows. And once they know you can see them, they mark you. Your old man never told us that part."

"When you look into the abyss…" Andrew muttered, finally managing to tear his eyes from the dumpster. Comanche was pivoting in a circle, the knife no longer at Katie's throat but sweeping the air, warding off unseen attackers. Andrew had to leap back to avoid the blade.

"Calm down. Let's all just calm down. I saw it, man. I saw it. I believe you."

"I believe you, too," Katie pleaded as she struggled to stay on her feet. "I saw it too; I swear I did."

Comanche staggered as he spun, Katie's legs tangling in his.

"I can't take this no more," he groaned. "I'm not…"

As they careened to the ground, the woman's left hand flew up and out. Andrew darted forward and caught her forearm, then leaned back with all his weight. Comanche went down on his back. Katie landed on top of him. She tried to slide off, but the electrical tape held her fast.

"Let go of me, you fucking maniac!" She jerked her head back, connecting with the side of her captor's face hard enough to bounce his opposite cheek off the asphalt. Each successive blow carried as much weight as she could lift before bringing it crashing down. "Let go. Let go! LET GO!"

Andrew straddled the sprawled figures and lunged for the arm still gripping the knife, but as he made his move Katie brought her head forward again, hitting Andrew squarely in the jaw, throwing him off balance. Comanche pivoted the knife around so the tip was pointed at his left eye.

"Not going out like this," he said. His focus wasn't on Andrew or the inrushing cops or the woman thrashing against him; it was on the dumpster across the street. "Not going to be run down like some fucking rat chased out of its hole. You hear me, you piece of shit? You can't have me." The knife flashed a final time and went out, three inches of blade buried in Comanche's socket.

Katie nearly dragged Andrew down on top of her as she struggled to rise. A cop darted in and wedged a knee between her back and Comanche's chest. Someone else fell on the arm with the knife, approaching at an angle to avoid the protruding handle.

"It's all right," Andrew said. He gripped the sides of Katie's head, entwined his fingers in her damp hair and pressed until she stopped her struggles. "It's over. It's all over. We just need to cut you loose." Her eyes, wide and vacant, found his. "It's going to be all right."

But before he could ask for something to cut the tape with, two burly cops yanked him to his feet and flung him back, nearly into the arms of Officer Brice.

"Quite a performance," he said, turning Andrew with a pressure on his shoulder that was more shove than tap. "Were you trying to get her killed?"

Andrew reached for the straps holding the Kevlar vest and yanked. "You heard him; he was delusional. I tried to keep him calm." The vest loosened but did not fall away.

"You let him draw you into a prolonged conversation. You ignored my orders."

"The radio was cutting in and out. Everything was garbled."

"Guess that's why you yanked it out of your ear."

Andrew released a final strap with shaking fingers and flung the vest and earpiece to the ground. A tremor shuddered through him and he balled his hands into fists as half-a-dozen officers worked to separate Katie and Comanche.

His partner Gary approached wheeling a gurney, followed closely by Jackson Thomas and Tracy Rodriguez, EMTs from Station Twelve who also had a gurney between them.

"All right," Gary said, positioning the stretcher in front of Andrew. "Let's get you back to the ambulance."

Andrew shook his head. "What?" He could barely hear his partner over the roaring in his ears.

"Tracy and Jack can transport the woman. I'll check you over. Need to make sure you're not injured." When Andrew continued to stare, he patted the gurney. "That knife was swinging all over the place."

The afternoon's oppressive heat ticked up to something nearly overwhelming, radiating not from the featureless sky but from his cheeks and neck and chest.

"This is for me?"

"Just a precaution."

"No. I'm fine. Hey," he called out to the other paramedics. "We'll take the woman. You two can take Comanche." The pair exchanged glances but moved on to the handcuffed figure lying motionless in an expanding pool of blood.

Andrew expected some move by Brice to intervene, but he said nothing as they hustled past. Katie was on her feet, a female officer assisting her to the sidewalk. He intersected them when they reached the curb, patted the gurney just as Gary had done, and without a word Katie sat.

"I'm going to check you real quick, make sure you're not seriously hurt. Then we'll take you to the hospital for a more thorough exam. Okay?"

Katie said nothing.

Andrew knelt in front of her and placed his hand over hers. "You're going to be fine, Katie. It's over." He wanted to reach up and sweep the hair out of her face like he used to do with Anna when she succumbed to some minor injury and needed reassuring her skinned knee or pinched finger would soon feel better, but even his hand on hers was a gesture bordering on inappropriate. He slid his fingers around her wrist until he found her pulse and began to count.

"It's not over," she said before he reached four.

"You can't think like that."

"How am I supposed to think?"

"This afternoon was a bad dream." His fingers probed her neck and jawline where the knife had pressed. He swept his hands down her shoulders, across her arms, turning her palms up before allowing them to fall back to her sides. "That's all. A dream you're about to wake from."

Finding no obvious injuries, Andrew eased the woman into a reclining position on the gurney before he and Gary wheeled her to the open doors of the ambulance bay. "You drive," he told his partner. "I'll get her vitals on the way." When they positioned the gurney to slide it inside, Katie clamped her fingers around Andrew's forearm.

"Is it still there?"

"No," he answered, glancing not at the dumpster behind them, but across the stretcher at Gary. They'd gotten along well enough in the eight weeks since they'd been partnered, had, in fact, quickly established a cordial if cool professional relationship—no small feat considering how his previous partnership had ended—but there was nothing of the rapport he had once had with Max. Gary's expression was a carefully composed mask of professional detachment.

"Is it asking too much for you to actually look?" Katie shot back.

"I'll go snag your bag." Gary trotted to where Andrew had left his medical kit. Once his partner turned his back, Andrew cast a reluctant glance at the trash bin.

"Well?"

He said nothing.

"You're hurting me."

"What?"

"Ease up."

Andrew realized he was squeezing Katie's forearm just as she had gripped his. He muttered a word of apology, stepped around to the foot of the stretcher, slid it inside without waiting for Gary, and climbed in after. His partner tossed him his bag and Andrew slammed the doors shut.

"Well?" Katie asked as he took a seat at her side, and when he still said nothing: "It's still there. I know it is. I can see it in your face."

The ambulance eased through the intersection. Inside this cool, orderly, rational space Andrew Tate went to work, falling into the familiar routine of recording blood pressure and temperature, checking pupil dilation and heartbeat.

"This isn't over," Katie Fife said again. "Not for either of us." She settled her head on the pillow and closed her eyes, allowing Andrew to work in silence.

But not in peace.

Two

"*There* he is," said Sid Langston. "Man of the hour." Engine eleven's hulking lieutenant rose from the rec room couch and swept his arm out with an introductory flourish. The other two firefighters remained seated, but both turned to track Andrew's progress as he silently crossed the room.

"Showing the cops how it's done," Langston continued. "Training? Who needs training? That's for pussies. All you need is a Kevlar vest and an attitude. Am I right?" He gave the others a cursory glance. "Marched right in there and talked that guy into sticking a salad fork in his eye. Or was it a steak knife? Point is, you saved the hostage. Fucking a. My man deserves a round of applause. Everyone." He began a slow, loud clap not taken up by anyone else.

Andrew pressed on to Captain Hamilton's office door. He knocked twice and twisted the knob without waiting for a reply. The last thing he heard as he shut the door behind him was Gary telling Sid to stop being such a dick.

"You wanted to see me, Captain?"

Hamilton motioned Andrew to the chair in front of his desk without looking up from his laptop. His fingers banged against the keys in sporadic staccatos as he tabbed from one field to the next.

Andrew sat and waited, eyes roving the floor as he tried to assess what he'd seen on that final glance at the dumpster: a defecation or a birth? The question was absurd, repulsive, insistent. Like an afterimage, it followed his mind no matter where it turned, and he doubted it would fade any time soon because whatever that thing – that *quintaloch* – had expelled from the orifice along its flank had started moving as soon as it spilled to the hot asphalt, its gelatinous surface roiling and heaving, a slime-covered sack of flies.

"You doing okay, Andy?"

"Captain?"

"Hell of a thing to get drawn into. Above and beyond, know what I mean?"

Andrew gripped the chair's armrest and slid his palms along its length, leaving a slick trail. "Didn't seem like I had much of a choice."

Hamilton raised his head for the first time. "We always have a choice."

"Yes, sir."

The station captain typed a last sentence and pushed the laptop back as if it were an empty plate.

"No need to 'sir' me, Andy. You're not in trouble. I just want to hear your side."

"You've already heard another side?"

Hamilton settled deeper into his swivel chair with a quarter pivot in either direction and folded his hands loosely over his stomach, only the fingertips interlaced. "I got a call from a Lieutenant Rodriguez at the Eighth Precinct. He got an earful from his negotiation team leader. Claimed you got the hostage-taker all riled up, something about your father." Hamilton paused a half-beat. "And monsters."

Andrew could barely remember a time when the mention of John Tate didn't prompt a tired shame. Until today, he'd managed to kindle a flickering hope he'd seen the last of the man. Since his mother's death, there was no one to prod him into checking up on the crazy bastard, no one crying into the phone at odd hours to remind him of his so-call obligations.

"He left us, Mom," he would remind her pointlessly again and again. "Three days before Christmas." And she, just as pointlessly, would insist that wasn't the case, that John Tate, former professor of biology, former department head at the University of Tampa, former husband and provider, had done what he had to do to protect his family. Her loyalty was unshakable and utterly baffling.

"Andy?" Captain Hamilton's thumbs had been turning leisurely circles around one another. Now they met.

"I didn't provoke him."

"Tell me what happened." Hamilton's tone suggested a desire to be on Andrew's side, but Andrew also noticed the way his captain's head ticked from side to side as he spoke, as if unconsciously negating what he said.

"I didn't insert myself into the situation. I was drawn into it. He demanded I bring him the water. Me, no one else. When I handed it over, he asked if I was John Tate's son. Said I look like him. At the time, I thought being truthful was the best way to keep from aggravating him further. At least he'd be focused on me instead of the hostage."

"And now? You still think that was the best course of action?"

"I wouldn't do anything different."

Hamilton nodded, what might have been the wisp of a grin tugging the corner of his mouth.

"I think what happened next," Andrew continued, "was a combination of plunging blood sugar, heat, dehydration, delusion. The man was a diabetic. I know that for a fact." He counted off each point with a raised finger. "He was an alcoholic. And I'm certain he was doing other shit, crystal meth, coke, something that pumped him full of paranoia and aggression.

"He was going to go off no matter what. If humoring him was the wrong thing to do, I am truly sorry. But I don't think it was."

Andrew turned to the office window, his glance sliding down the shuttered blinds. "And if Officer Brice thinks otherwise, he can kiss my ass."

Hamilton snorted. "Hell, Andy, tell me how you really feel." The captain leaned forward and rested his elbows on the desk. "I wasn't there, so I don't know what the dynamics were between you and this nut job. But from what I saw, you kept your head in a tense situation. You acted decisively when the shit hit the fan. And the standoff ended without the hostage being harmed. As far as I'm concerned, you did nothing wrong.

"Look," Hamilton settled his hands palm down on the blotter, "we both know you don't have a lot of friends left in the department after what happened with your previous partner. There are some who think you got off easy with a suspension and transfer. Slap on the wrist. Those people would like nothing better than to see you screw up enough to finally get the boot. But I'm not one of them.

"Whatever happened at your old station, that's ancient history. I only care about what happens at this one, and so far, you've given me no reason to think you're anything but a competent, professional fire medic. That's still my opinion."

Andrew nodded. " 'Preciate that, Captain."

"Now get the hell out of my office and go relax until the next bell. The way this summer has been going, that shouldn't be long." Hamilton centered the laptop before him once more and gave the mouse a shake. "I'm beginning to think this drought is affecting people's minds. The crazies are coming out of the woodwork."

Andrew's hand was on the doorknob when he paused and turned back.

"Captain, what did you mean before when you said 'from what I saw'? From what you saw, I kept my head. Someone take a cell phone video?"

Hamilton looked up from the computer screen with a lopsided smirk. "That's right; you've been on runs all day. Guess you haven't had a chance to turn on the news." The station captain pulled a remote from the top drawer of his desk and turned on the wall-mounted television. The image that sprang into focus was a still frame of Andrew taken from behind. His arms were raised, a water bottle in each hand. From the angle and poor resolution, it was obviously a zoomed shot from a distant camera. In the bottom left corner, a local news channel's logo was bisected by a frozen burst of static.

"I recorded your segment. They've been running it all afternoon." Andrew blinked up at the screen, his lips slightly parted. "You're in the middle of your fifteen minutes of fame, my friend. Enjoy it."

ANDREW FOUND GARY IN THE LOCKER ROOM WITH A suds-covered sponge in one hand and a bucket of soapy water on the bench behind him.

"Damn. Another thirty seconds and this shit would have been gone. Sorry, man."

Andrew approached, his elbow cupped in one palm, his chin in the other, the thoughtful posture of a museumgoer assessing a painting's artistic merit. Scrawled in red lipstick up the side of his locker door were the words: HOW ABOUT A GAME OF CRAZY TATES?

"It's mildly clever. I'll give them that."

"Don't let the lipstick fool you." Gary slapped the sponge against the metal hard enough to send a spray of suds across the adjoining lockers. "This is Sid's work. Clare has too much class to stoop to this." He began scrubbing, but the letters were thick and the first few swipes did little to erase the message.

"You don't have to do that. I'll clean it later."

"Jackson or Tracy must have started talking once they got back to their station," Gary said, ignoring the request. "The story's been making the rounds ever since. I swear to god this department is worse than a fucking sewing circle when it comes to gossip. Sid's a prick. I don't care how many citations he's earned or how long he's been here. He can't bully coworkers. You're going to the captain about this, right?"

"I'm not running to Hamilton every time someone tries to rattle me." The letters were disappearing in pieces, flecks of red suspended in the runoff pooling on the floor, a puddle of tiny hemorrhages. "This is nothing."

Gary shook his head. "It's not nothing. If he gets away with it once, he'll do it again."

"We don't know he did anything." Andrew understood he should be grateful for this display of support, but all he felt was a growing impatience with Gary to be finished and gone. He wanted in his locker. His cell phone was there. Maybe Grace had seen the news and left a message, a few words acknowledging his role in ending the standoff. "You did okay out there." That would be enough. And of course, there was something else in there as well, something secreted behind the back panel.

"The hell we don't." Gary wrung the sponge out over the bucket. "At the very least, we confront him, tell him we're not going to tolerate his bullshit. I'm not suggesting a physical confrontation." Color bloomed in Gary's cheeks and he turned quickly back to the locker. "Nothing like that. Just a quiet little chat out in the bay."

The letters were gone, only a few spots of red remained. Andrew pulled a handful of paper towels from the roll mounted next to the sink and began drying the door, forcing Gary to step back. "I appreciate the sentiment. Seriously. But I'm not in a position to make accusations. Long as nothing was damaged, I'm going to pretend you finished your cleanup before I got here."

"This isn't going to be the end, you know."

"It is for now. I'm letting it go. I'd like you to do the same. Can you do that for me?"

"If that's what you want, man."

"That's what I want."

Gary moved past him toward the exit, the soapy water sloshing heavily in the bucket at his side.

"Hey," Andrew called when he reached the door. "We cool here?"

Gary turned, his eyes focused not on Andrew but on the wall behind him. After a moment that stretched within a few heartbeats of becoming uncomfortable, his face relaxed. "Yeah, we're cool." He opened the door, took a step, turned back. "I have to know. Did you really see something out there?"

"You heard that part?"

"We all heard it. We all heard everything."

"No," Andrew said. "I didn't see a goddamn thing."

ANDREW STOOD FOR A LONG TIME WITH HIS THUMB poised over the phone, the light from the screen's display filling the inside of his locker with its blue glow.

His wife had left him no messages. He was neither disappointed nor relieved. His gaze alternated between the two photographs taped to the loose back panel. The smaller showed him and Grace at a department Christmas party. When? Two, three years ago? They both looked happy. His hand clutched her knee; her arm draped his shoulder. It wasn't a good photo, slightly out of focus and both sets of eyes red as stop lights, but the casual intimacy in their nearly identical smiles and the way they leaned toward one another suggested a quiet confidence in their happiness, an awareness that their love, like gravity, was something so constant and predictable as to be entirely unremarkable.

The second, larger picture showed Anna standing on the front porch steps in full cowgirl regalia: pink boots, brown vest, string tie, a miniature ten-gallon hat with a star centered above its wide brim. It was Halloween and soon she'd be off with a group of friends and parents, knocking on doors in the slanting evening light.

Andrew smiled despite the pang he always felt looking at his daughter this way, still perfect, without the skin grafts marring her right arm and hand. As he continued to examine the photograph, his grin faded. The bottom right of the image showed a portion of the azalea hedge fronting the porch, a dusty green wall that burst into fuchsia blooms every February.

But this photo had been taken in October. There shouldn't be any blooms. Not even the buds he now noticed for the first time, spots of color nearly concealed behind a profusion of leaves, six perfect spheres arranged in pairs up the length of a branch. He noticed an unusual luster in those buds, a wet gleam that gave them a decidedly un-plantlike appearance.

Andrew brought the phone's glow closer. The shadows around the buds appeared denser than anywhere else, so dense they formed a corridor of blackness. He removed the picture and in the flat, harsh light of the overhead fluorescents, the difference between the foliage around the buds and the rest of the azalea was far more striking, the dark swatch becoming not simply negative space but an object in and of itself, a black, compact body a foot thick and three times as long, split at one end like a forked tongue and covered with quill-like projections and red boils.

Or were those eyes?

Andrew traced the revealed shape with a forefinger as it swept from the edge of the photograph toward his daughter, a little girl in a Halloween costume who, if she had stretched out her left arm, would have touched something like a monstrous forked tongue covered with spikes.

"Fuck this."

Andrew shoved the photo beneath a Tampa Fire Rescue sweatshirt and, after a glance over his shoulder, pulled the barely-threaded top right screw from the back panel of the locker. He slid aside the metal plate to reveal a shallow recess created by the cinderblock wall notching around water pipes. The flask rested on the lip of a pipe fitting, wedged between the PVC and wall.

In the eight weeks since he had been transferred to Station Three, Andrew had taken three hits of Royal Crown. Once when Grace had canceled a planned outing because both she and Anna had come down with the flu. Or so she claimed. Once after he and Gary had responded to a hit-and-run involving a girl so like Anna in age and appearance his breath had caught as he removed her shattered bicycle helmet. And once after reading Max's letter, that fumbling, handwritten attempt to explain himself, to frame their current situation as a series of bad choices made by everyone involved.

Andrew pulled the flask out, relishing, as he always did, the way it fit his palm, the way his fingers molded around the stainless steel. Three hits. That was all he had taken, and yet the container was nearly half-empty. Three large hits, then, a few swallows each, just enough to settle his nerves without impairing judgment. Nothing like before. But after this afternoon, who wouldn't want a drink? It was entirely understandable.

Andrew ran a fingertip around the rim of the lid. "Who wouldn't want a drink?" he asked again, this time aloud. Just one swallow, a single mouthful to coat his tongue. Barely a taste. Hadn't he earned it?

"Hell yes."

The cell phone's shrill ring made him jerk back with a strangled gasp.

"Jesus Christ."

It trilled three more times as he fumbled the flask back into its hiding place. One more ring and his voicemail would pick up. Andrew had just enough time to scoop up the phone, see the incoming call was from Grace and hit the "talk" button.

"You sound out of breath," she said.

"I heard it ringing inside my locker as I came in."

"Ah." Grace fell silent. Andrew shifted the cell to his other ear and pressed his back and head against the lockers, his face tilted to the ceiling.

"So, what's up?" he said with all the contrived cheer he could muster.

"I wanted to talk about tomorrow."

Andrew raised his head off the locker. He was planning to take Anna to Clearwater Beach the following day, an outing that had required a month of cajoling and three weeks of outright pleading before Grace finally agreed. It would be the first time since the accident he'd be supervising his daughter on his own, the initial step in a long path toward eventual redemption. Or so he hoped.

"We're still on, right?"

From the other end, silence.

"Grace?" He heard the desperation in his voice and closed his eyes, trying to will himself to remain calm. If he got into an argument with his wife now, all hope of spending the day with Anna would be lost. "Talk to me, honey." When was the last time he had used such an endearment? The word sounded foreign in his mouth, calculated, but he pressed on. "What's up?"

Grace sighed. "It's just I'm not entirely comfortable with you driving all the way over to the Gulf. The sun is so strong out there and you know how sensitive her skin still is. There's no shade at all."

"But she loves the beach." This wasn't about the sun. The dermatologist had assured them the graphs had healed enough to tolerate a few hours of exposure, so long as they used a strong, moisturizing sunscreen. The real issue was the forty-minute drive across the Bay, the bridge traffic, the level of responsibly required to transport a child safely from point A to point B. The *sobriety* it demanded.

"I just think it would be better if you stayed closer to home. Why don't you take her to the playground in Hyde Park? There's lots of shade there and she can play in the fountains."

"Absolutely," Andrew said, surprising himself with his quick acceptance. What difference did it make where he spent the day with Anna? So long as they were together.

"Okay, then." Gracie sounded more off-put that relieved. Had she been expecting him to protest, hurl accusations, fly into a rage? Had she been expecting him to react in a way that would give her an excuse to cancel the outing entirely? There was a time, not long ago, when he could read his wife's intentions as easily as Anna's. Not anymore.

"Great." The alarm sounded and Andrew sagged in relief. "Duty calls. I'll see you tomorrow." He ended the call before she could reply, tossed the phone back into the locker, slammed and locked the door and exhaled into his cupped hands before hurrying to the door.

It wasn't until they were pulling out from the bay that Andrew realized his breath check had been unnecessary. He'd never taken the hit of Royal Crown.

27

***

THE NEXT TWO BELLS WERE ROUTINE: A STANDARD nursing home grab-and-go for a broken hip and a junkie trying to score a morphine fix by faking a kidney stone, a run Max would have called a "TDB": terminal display of bullshit. During these hours, Andrew threw himself into his work, and by early evening the day's events had scabbed over with a thin crust of perspective. Maybe the thing by the dumpster *was* just a product of heat and stress and his father's stories. Maybe he, Katie and Comanche had experienced some sort of shared hallucination. It wasn't unheard of. The mind was unreliable, easily fooled, vulnerable to suggestion.

Malleable.

Given enough time, people could convince themselves of all sorts of crazy notions, including living in a world where unnoticed monsters lurked in plain view.

By the third bell, Andrew had nearly persuaded himself what had happened during the hostage standoff was a sort of waking dream. And then the domestic disturbance call came in.

"Ah," Gary sighed as he pulled in front of the address dispatch had given them. "This looks like it's going to be fun."

A handful of neighbors were mulling along the street in front of a modest, cinderblock tract house. Two patrol cars were parked crookedly on the brown lawn, lights flashing, doors ajar. Even before exiting the cab Andrew could hear the thump-thump-thump of base notes buzzingly transmitted through the cab's metal and glass.

Outside, the din was thunderous, hip-hop music booming out the house's open door at chest-thumping decibels. Langston parked engine eleven behind them, the normal squeal of its airbrakes a thin whine under the percussive assault.

"Jesus Christ," he said to no one in particular. "Why don't they turn it off?"

A moment later the music *did* stop, prompting a smattering of applause from the crowd. "About damn time," someone said, but the relief was short-lived. The silence was almost instantly broken by a wail of protest.

"Turn it back on! TURN IT BACK ON! It was blocking 'em out. Oh god, they're still in my head! Turn the damn music back on!"

As Gary and Andrew pulled the stretcher from the back of the ambulance, his partner rolled his eyes in tired resignation. "Going to need the restraints on this one, I guarantee."

"Tweeker?" For once, Andrew was grateful of Langston's presence, his linebacker build and unflappable demeanor. If they were going to have to deal with a combative transport, he could think of no one else he'd rather have at his side.

"Huffer, tweeker, bath salt snorter. Who the hell knows?"

They pushed through the crowd, rattled up the flagstone path leading to the door and paused before the lanai. Langston and his partner Clare Humbert went in first, Andrew and Gary close behind. The screaming continued, now little more than a series of "na"s interspersed with guttural snarls that sounded like someone trying to cough up an enormous wad of phlegm.

May have to intubate, Andrew thought. This guy's on the far side of the moon.

They turned left down a hallway, following the noise to a doorway near the end. Although he had only been subjected to the blaring music for a few seconds, Andrew could still hear an echo of it at the edge of his perception, a lingering murmur deep in his ear that seemed to mimic song lyrics stripped of rhythm and harmony.

A red-faced and perspiring officer stepped into the hallway to meet them. "So, what's the story here?" Langston asked, pulling on a pair of latex gloves.

"Male, mid-forties, highly agitated. Been acting erratically for about sixty minutes now. Wife called nine-one-one after he started banging his head against the wall, ranting about voices in his head."

29

"History of drug use or mental illness?" Andrew asked, pulling on his own pair of gloves.

"Wife claims no." The officer was clearly unconvinced of this, but before Andrew could pose a follow-up question something large crashed to the floor inside the room.

"Could use some help in here," called a second officer. The first cop disappeared across the threshold, followed by Langston and Humbert.

"Here we go," Gary said.

Andrew stepped into the room last, leaving the stretcher in the hall. What he saw over the shoulders of the others was a bedroom in ruin. The mattress had been pulled off its frame and propped up against the far wall. Along another wall, a bookcase, chair, and numerous dresser drawers were piled in a heap rising nearly to the ceiling. The floor was scattered with the remains of a large, cathode-ray television—most likely the source of the recent crash—along with clothing items and bed sheets.

Thrashing on the floor amid the litter was a man in shorts and a torn tee-shirt. Andrew was mildly surprised by how slight the screamer was compared to the officers who were now on either side of him, each pinning an arm to the floor. Not that size was a reliable indicator of potential danger in a situation like this. He had seen octogenarians in the throes of dementia lash out savagely enough to break noses and jaws.

"He went lunging for the TV," the officer on the right said. "Knocked it off the dresser."

"I'll get the backboard and a couple rolls of gauze," Gary said, returning to the hall and giving Andrew a told-you-so grin as he passed.

"What's this guy's name? Anyone know?" Andrew asked, rubbing the indentation below his ear where his jaw hinged. The echo he'd been hearing since their arrival hadn't faded. Instead, it had settled into some sort of self-sustaining reverberation, looping over and over like muffled, indecipherable chanting.

"His name's Jeff. Jeffery Jackson." For the first time, Andrew noticed a woman standing at the bedroom's closet door, half in and half out of the threshold as if prepared to dart back and slam the door shut in an instant.

"Jeff," Andrew said.

"He goes by J.J." The woman offered.

"J.J. You need to calm down. We're here to help you."

"Yeah, we've been telling him that," the cop on the left said. "Hasn't helped."

"You think you know me?" Jackson demanded.

"No sir." But Andrew did not think the man was addressing anyone in the room.

"You don't know me! You don't have a right to be here. Turn on the TV. Turn it up loud! Goddamn you. Goddamn you!"

Jackson's struggles increased, his back arching and legs pinioning as he bucked. Sid fell on one leg, holding it to the floor while Clare did the same with the other.

Andrew placed a hand on her shoulder. "I'm going to prepare a syringe of droperidol. I doubt tying him to the board is going to be enough."

As his eyes swept across the bedroom, he noticed clothing stuffed into the air-conditioning vents along the ceiling. The mattress, Andrew realized, was positioned to block one window, while the bookcase, chair and dresser drawers were piled to block another. The room's disorder was obviously an attempt to shut out the voices in Jackson's head.

Hadn't Comanche also said something about hearing voices in his head? Jabbering voices in a language he couldn't understand yet, but soon would? What had he compared that inevitable understanding to? Catching a disease? Something he wouldn't be able to keep from happening?

Andrew trotted back down the hall. The masters were coming. That's what Comanche had said. The big bads. The nightmares behind the nightmares. The something-*offalla*. Andrew reached the end of the hall and froze. Suddenly, overwhelmingly, he wanted not just a sip of Crown Royal but the whole goddamn bottle. Because somewhere at the bottom of his mind something had whispered, only two words, a brief gurgle of syllables, but the sense of intrusion, of violation, was profound.

Vetro offalate.

Andrew suppressed a groan. The impression that shuddered through him was of a vast and alien presence poking its way into his awareness and slipping back out, leaving a hole behind, a bleeding gap he wanted to curl protectively around in a rocking ball.

"You okay?"

Gary was clutching two boxes of soft gauze, the backboard tucked under one arm.

"Going to snag the droperidol," he managed, wiping his sweating upper lip with the back of a sleeve. "Pretty sure we'll need to sedate him."

He needed to tamp this down hard. Get a grip. Get a fucking grip! Andrew took several deep breaths, resisting the urge to slap himself across the face. By the time he returned to the bedroom, the worse of his queasiness had passed. So, apparently, had the worst of Jeffery Jackson's agitation. He lay quietly on the backboard, allowing Gary and Sid to secure his arms, legs and head to the restraint with loops of gauze.

"What happened?" Andrew asked, although he already knew. The voices had stopped.

"He just suddenly went limp," Clare said. She was kneeling at Jackson's head, her fingers pressed against either temple. "We thought he might have passed out, but he was still conscious."

"They shut up," Jackson murmured. His eyes were closed, but beneath the lids, Andrew could see his gaze flitting about.

"Feeling better, Mr. Jackson?" Gary asked in the loud, mildly condescending voice Andrew recognized as the default tone of a professional pushed to the edge of anger. He was quickly wrapping one of the man's wrists to the board.

"Ain't never going to be better. Not after this." His lips trembled. "They fucked me up. In the head. Goddamn bastards!" Tears began leaking down the side of his face. "They left a hole in me. I can feel it. They tore a hole in my head they can keep coming back through. Liselle! Liselle, why they do that?"

The woman fell to her knees at his side. "J.J. you just lie quiet now." Her voice trembled on the verge of her own tears. "They're going to take

32

you to the hospital. You're going to be okay, baby. You're going to be just fine."

"Ain't no fine, woman. They'll be back. I know they will."

As they hoisted Jackson from the floor Andrew could feel Gary's eyes on him from across the backboard, wanting, most likely, a silent acknowledgment of the absurdity of the moment, a tilt of the head, a subtle shrug conveying their mutual recognition of how crazy people could be. This time, however, Andrew couldn't meet his partner's eyes. He knew Jackson was right. Sooner or later the thing that had penetrated his mind would be back.

The *vetro offalate* were close. And they were getting closer.

Three

They tried to kill John Tate a week after he was booked into the Orient Road Jail. Lingering in the yard near the basketball courts, he waited until his would-be assassin was nearly upon him before tossing a handful of sand in his face and dropping to the ground. The inmate's swing arched over his head and John kicked up hard between splayed legs. When the other man doubled over he kicked again, this time connecting in the center of his face. There was a satisfying crunch of cartilage and spurt of blood beneath his shoe. His assailant uttered a sort of honking snarl and swung again, striking John's still-upraised leg mid-calf. The hot sting made him hiss as he rolled out of the path of a third blow.

The weapon was a blur, but from the method of attack, he assumed it was some sort of blade secured to a handle, most likely a razor-headed toothbrush, the sort of shiv routinely confiscated during cell searches. Not a stabbing weapon. Not something that would be effective in close quarters. This assault required enough room to sweep an arm across an exposed throat.

John managed to loop around his attacker, but instead of running he leaped onto the guy's back and wrapped his arms around his neck in a sleeper hold. The inmate staggered forward, arms flailing. Something green fell from his hand and John shifted his weight higher, hoping to further unbalance him, maybe drive his broken face into the dirt. The maneuver only brought the assailant to his knees, but by then two or three guards were racing toward them across the yard. John leaned in close—a move that unexpectedly, preposterously, reminded him of the way he would sometimes approach Lindsay from behind to give the nape of her neck a playful nuzzle—and bit the top of the fucker's ear off.

Two days later they tried to kill him in the cafeteria. An inmate lunged across the table with, of all things, a candy cane licked down at one end to a spike. John caught him under the chin with his lunch tray mid-lung and followed it with a faceful of hot coffee.

The third attempt was more straightforward. A fat man covered in gang tattoos simply tried to toss him over the third-floor railing. John had secreted a tube of toothpaste into his underwear that morning. When the gang member charged, he found his footing compromised by a layer of Colgate. John didn't have the leverage or strength to turn the tables and upend his attacker over the rail, but a carefully placed kick to the seam of throat and collarbone ended the encounter with Mr. Tattoo gulping and gasping at his feet.

After that, they separated John Tate from the general jailhouse population. Now he spent most of his time in a top-floor cell, sometimes writing in a notebook purchased at the commissary, sometimes reading week-old newspapers, sometimes staring at the sky through the twin vertical slits that served as his cell windows.

Mostly, however, he listened. He did this not with his ears but with some keener, more fundamental sensor embedded deep in the center of his skull. Twenty, thirty times a day he would slip into a semi-trance, harkening for the knell of the *vetro offalate*. He no longer had to strain to hear them. Their thoughts had grown louder with each passing day, and what he discerned when they were being vociferous was usually a frenzied mental gnashing that reminded John of ravenous dogs straining against leashes to snap at a meal just out of reach.

Occasionally, however, their thoughts subsided to a low and strangely appealing rumble. It didn't take long to decipher these murmurs as a siren call for new recruits, a bubbling promise that any mind willing to submit to them, worship them, carry out their commands, would not only be spared the coming harvest but would be rewarded. Richly so.

Obviously, some had accepted the offer. But the *vetro offalate* had made the mistake of micromanaging their new foot soldiers. None of his attackers struck without first being ordered to, and so listening had kept him alive, alerting him in advance to each new attempt on his life. But such diligence was exhausting. And he was tired. Sick and tired.

John Tate eased off the cot and made his way gingerly to the cell door. The back of his calf ached, a warm throb indicative of a low-grade infection despite the antibiotics and twice-daily change of dressings. He doubted the wound would kill him outright, but it was a worrisome injury. The next time someone tried to take him out he'd be slower, less agile. More vulnerable.

Still, their proxy attacks suggested the *vetro* considered him a threat, and that, in turn, suggested his plan to prevent their return might have some merit after all. He could do little while in jail, however. He needed outside help and that meant putting others at risk, including the son he had spend two decades trying to protect.

Pressing his cheek against the bars, John listened for nearly ten minutes. In the common area below, the low echo of human voices created a simmering hum not unlike the roar of distant water cascading over a precipice. An occasional shout rose above the din, bounced off the concrete walls and fell back. He became aware of the buzz of cell doors opening and closing, toilets flushing, what might have been the polished narration of a television news anchor reduced to a faint, irregular murmur. As hard as he strained, however, he heard not a whisper from the *vetro*. For now.

It was only a matter of time before a guard simply walked up and shot him through the bars of his cell. Why hadn't they used a correctional officer as their assassin? It would have been more efficient. But then maybe the guards' minds weren't as pliant as the minds of the men who had attacked him. There were so many things he didn't understand. It was frustrating, considering how much he and Will had learned over the years about the *vetro's* lesser kin. Of course, the *bilantu offalate* were still here, literally underfoot, while their masters had vanished long ago.

John limped back to the cot, mentally ticking through the short list of things he was fairly certain of. The *vetro offalate's* reign on Earth predated the Yucatan asteroid strike. Probably not by much, maybe as little as ten or twenty thousand years. If not for the threat of global annihilation they might still be here. But they had retreated before the impact, scuttled back to the place they had come from and slammed the door behind them, leaving the *bilantu offalate* stranded. The *bilantu*, those that survived, had been here ever since, which meant they predated humans by sixty-five million years, give or take a million.

Grumbling in pain, John stepped up on his cot and peered through the nearest vertical slit. During the previous four days, he'd become familiar with this ribbon of view, the brown courtyard, the gray walls topped with black threads of barbed fencing and the pale blue sky above. No different than yesterday. Or the day before. As usual, the unaltered view disappointed him, but he was never quite certain what he kept expecting to see. The heavens turning red and poisonous? The ground breaking apart as black sludge oozed through the cracks?

John sat back down. What else had he learned over the years? Since their retreat, nearly all evidence of the *vetro's* cities had been erased. Only the stone-like outcroppings he called *xalanthracoils* remained. They were devices, relics of some unfathomable technology that had lain dormant for eons, awaiting the signal to awaken once more and tear a hole between the worlds. He was convinced they were alive in a way he could not quite comprehend. Not sentient. Certainly not mobile. Not even reactive in the way plants or microorganisms respond to environmental factors. But alive nevertheless. And inhumanly patient.

Other than the *bilantu*—God help him, he still got a shiver of exhilaration every time he recalled seeing his first *quintaloch*—the *coils* were his most fortuitous discovery. If he hadn't been tracking the *votasin* as it floated through the cemetery gates he never would have made his way to the overgrown corner where others of its kind were already amassed around an obelisk-shaped grave marker. In all his years of study, John had never witnessed such a gathering. His first impression was of a mating swarm, a supposition that gained credence when he realized the creatures weren't just mulling about. They were circling the marker and bobbing with the graceful synchronicity of merry-go-round horses.

He had watched in fascination for minutes, mesmerized by the dance, not even attempting to hide his presence. Granted, *votasin* weren't as aggressive as other species of *bilantu,* but they could still fire those six-inch quills with deadly accuracy. If they had attacked, he doubted he would have made it out of the cemetery alive. But they hadn't, and after some indeterminate span, they simply dispersed, drifting away in opposite directions, living pincushions taken up by the breeze.

Not a mating swarm after all, not unless their method of reproduction required no physical contact, and John doubted that. What then? Had they been attracted to the marker itself for some reason? Examining the obelisk proved exasperating, not unlike trying to see a star too dim to perceive directly, visible only as a vague speck of light in his periphery. Its shape kept changing, flickering back and forth between a granite spike covered in a strange, angular script (Sanskrit?), and a darkly marbled outcropping curving tusk-like from the ground.

Despite a growing desire to turn away, he edged closer, pushing through a sudden bout of nausea and dizziness until the illusion of the grave marker faded completely and only the sweep of marbled tusk remained.

And then he had touched it.

John limped to the polished metal rectangle bolted above the sink that served as his mirror. A lean, weathered and deeply lined face framed in long, unkempt gray hair stared back.

"Do I know you?"

The man staring back snarled. Or was that an attempt at a smile? Twenty years ago, he had been the dean of biology at the University of Tampa, published, respected by colleagues. He had Lindsey, lovely Lindsey, his muse, his inspiration.

And he had Andrew, the boy who loved model rockets and mutant turtles and looking through his father's microscope at drops of stagnate water, green and teeming with life. As a preschooler, Andy had delighted in speculating over wonderfully incongruous scenarios. Would a dinosaur enjoy listening to rock music? Could Superman beat himself up? If you were in a car traveling at the speed of light and you turned on your headlights, would anything happen? His boy wonder.

John had a question of his own: Would the man he once was, the father, husband, provider, recognize this hollowed-out relic in the mirror, someone capable of biting off another man's ear in a jail yard skirmish?

"Doubtful."

The click and buzz of the lock drew John from his reflection. Two guards he didn't recognize stood at the cell door, one with his arms crossed, the other with a hand on the grip of his holstered baton. He had time to wonder if this was it, if the *vetro* had discovered his eavesdropping and found a way to cloak their broadcasts from him. How many hits would it take to crack his skull or break his neck? Not many, not if the guards knew how to swing their cudgels. At least it would be over quickly.

"Can I do for you, gentlemen?" he said, holding out his hands for the plastic restrains the first guard had already removed from his belt.

"Doc's waiting to see you in the infirmary."

"So soon?" His bandages had been changed only an hour earlier. His second changing was usually after dinner, just prior to lights out.

"Yeah, I know," the second guard said as the first—Salvador his nametag read—approached. "You keep a busy schedule up here. Must be a huge inconvenience, cutting into your nine a.m. ball scratching. Tell you what, next time we'll call ahead."

John said nothing as the smart shit gave him a quick pat down in the hall, but during the procedure, he saw Salvador glance first to the left, out over the atrium, then to the right, into John's cell. Although both turns were deliberate rather than startled, there was something in the way the guard's eyes darted about that suggested an element of disquiet, a hint of uncertainty, as if he were searching for something he hoped not to find.

The smart shit—Brutrelli—declared John clean and with a man at either elbow the three proceeded down the hall. Descending the stairs, a new scenario occurred to John, one in which he thrashed against an examining table's restraints as the infirmary physician approached with a pentobarbital-filled syringe. He'd have to be alert, ready for anything.

He liked the jail's A-rotation doctor, a wryly unsentimental woman in her mid-forties who gave the impression of having seen it all during her twenty-year career. He and Dr. Cho had had two mildly engaging conversations, one about the relative intelligence of various dog breeds (border collies-sharp as tacks, afghans-dumb as posts), and one about the merits of multivitamins in preventing illnesses (not much). John got the impression she found him a refreshing change from the patients she usually dealt with. Under different circumstances, they might have been friends.

At the first hint of trouble, he would charge her.

And then what? Every possibility he could conceive of ended with him sprawled across the floor, dead, dying or incapacitated. He was certain of this much, however: if they were going to kill him, it would take all three to do it. As the good doctor probably already knew from patching up his would-be assassins, he wasn't going down without a fight.

"YOU CAN WAIT IN THE HALL, MR. BRUTRELLI," DR. CHO said without looking up from the chart. She clicked a pen, flipped through several previous pages and began scribbling something on the last sheet.

"You know there's got to be two of us here at all times."

"Mr. Salvador and I can handle things if Mr. Tate gets feisty." Although her voice retained the monotone of professional indifference, John thought he saw her glance flick from the chart for an instant.

"Sorry, doc. Last thing I need is another demerit. I'm on my second warning as is." Brutrelli turned to John with contempt. "The fuck you looking at?"

"Let me ask you this, Mr. Brutrelli. Have you ever had hepatitis C?"

The correctional officer snorted. "Hell no."

"Mr. Tate's tests came back positive for the disease and I'm about to change one of his blood-soaked bandages. Now, if you want to stick around and risk infection, be my guest. I've noticed several healing nicks on your hands and one on your cheek."

Brutrelli examined his fingers and ran a thumb over a scabbed knuckle.

"It's not like I'm going to be touching his bandages," he said after a moment.

"I'm sure as long as everything goes exactly as planned that's true. Suit yourself."

Brutrelli took a step back, still worrying the scab. "What about him?" he asked, nodding toward the other guard. "You don't care if he catches hep?"

"Mr. Salvador had an acute bout of hepatitis C twelve years ago. There's little risk of infection for him."

"Go on, man," Salvador said. "We got this. You're going to be just outside the door. We'll holler if we need you."

Brutrelli appeared to hesitate, but John sensed his reluctance was nothing more than theatrics. He was waiting for a final nudge, and when Salvador pointed out that no one in the room was going to say shit about improper procedures, the other guard nearly bolted for the hallway.

John watched the pneumatic door ease shut with a mixture of relief and dread. He had never had hepatitis A, B, or C. The story was obviously a ruse to get the other man out of the room. This was it then, attempt number four. At least there were only two of them. Maybe he could dart off the table, throw the paper sheet over Cho, smash something against

Salvador's head while she was distracted. He scanned the room, but saw nothing heavy enough to do any real damage.

"Relax, John." Dr. Cho waved her hand and Salvador retreated to the door, listened for a moment, returned.

"We're good for now," he reported. "But you need to make this fast. He's not going to stay out there forever."

Cho nodded. "Take those off him."

Salvador removed John's restrains and tossed them on a nearby counter.

"We're not sure about Brutrelli," she continued. "He could be under their influence. They seem to have more sway with… certain types."

"Idiot types," Salvador said.

"They?" John turned from the doctor to the correctional officer and back again, feigning confusion.

"No time for games." Cho pulled a large bandage from the drawer and a roll of gauze. "I'm going to slowly change your dressing and while I do we're going to discuss what's been happening inside and outside the jail."

"What would that be?" Looking down, John realized he had been gripping the sides of the table hard enough to rip two fistfuls of paper from the sheet beneath him. He forced his fingers open and the torn shreds spiraled slowly to the floor.

"Your son made the news yesterday."

John's throat tightened. "Andrew?"

"He's an EMT for Tampa Fire Rescue, right? He was involved in a hostage standoff with a homeless man."

"Jesus. Is he alright?"

"Your son? He's fine. The woman the homeless guy took hostage is fine. The hostage-taker apparently committed suicide. Newspaper story said he claimed he was seeing monsters and that it was your fault."

Cho gently tugged the bandage from John's calf and tossed it into the trash. The wound still gleamed with the prior application of antiseptic ointment. She unwrapped an iodine-infused towelette and began to methodically re-clean his leg.

"My fault? The article used my name?"

Cho nodded. "John Tate. They ran an entire sidebar on you. I wasn't living here in the '90s, so I didn't know anything about your history. Anyway, the story quoted an unnamed source claiming the hostage-taker had been looking for monsters because you paid him to."

"I'd never do that." John shot back defensively. "I'd never ask anybody to *look* for them. I might have asked a few people, a few homeless men, to report anything unusual they might see out there on the streets. But that's it. Of course, I had to give them *some* guidance. Their first question is always, 'what do you mean by *unusual*?' Maybe I get a little carried away at times, say too much."

John ran a trembling hand through his hair. "Jesus, he said he was seeing them? Actually seeing them?"

"He's not the only one," Salvador said. "I thought I was going nuts until this. I saw something last week that made my hair stand on end. Something out of a nightmare."

"Did it see you looking at it?" John reached out and grabbed the guard's arm, a move that should have earned him a baton to the gut. Salvador simply shook his head.

"Not that I know of. Believe me, I'm not going out of my way to look for them. Didn't want to see that one. Don't want to see any more."

"Listen, both of you..."

Dr. Cho raised a finger to her lips and tilted her head toward the door. John took a long breath and began again in a lower voice. "Don't ever let them catch you watching them. If they know you can see them, they'll attack. We learned that the hard way."

"You and William Phipps?" Salvador asked.

John raised an eyebrow. "That in the sidebar, too?"

The guard nodded.

"You seeing things, doctor?"

"Please, call me Emily. I think we're all on a first-name basis at this point. Have I been seeing them? Not yet. But my friend mentioned seeing something in the bushes the other day. She tried to make a joke of it. Said

43

it must be all the airplane glue she's sniffing. But I could tell she was scared." The doctor applied a thick layer of ointment to the pad of the bandage and pressed it against his calf. "And now the voices."

"You've heard them?"

"Again, not me personally, but in the last few days I've had seven or eight people say they have; too many to dismiss. In fact, all the inmates that have attacked you later claimed they were compelled to do so by voices. Alien voices. Demon voices. Mr. Salvador here is the one who suggested we talk to you." She began wrapping gauze around his calf, the bandage slowly disappearing under the thickening layers.

"Figured if anyone knew what the hell was going on."

Cho nodded. "We discussed the current weirdness a few days ago and how you seem to be at the center of it. We were planning this meeting for later today, but considering what happened yesterday with your son and what Hector—Mr. Salvador here—found this morning in the yard, we decided not to wait that long."

"What did you find?"

Cho raised her finger to her lips again and bobbed her head at Salvador. The guard went to a cabinet, opened a door and removed a medical tray covered with a hand towel.

"Apparently, we're not the only ones who read the paper," he said, removing the cloth. John stared for a long moment as the room's temperature seemed to plunge. His calf throbbed dully under the new wrapping, an ache that radiated down to his ankle and up to his crotch. Finally, in a low, quivering voice he said, "I need to make a phone call."

When Cho, without a word or moment's hesitation reached for her cell phone, he nearly sobbed in gratitude.

"What is it?" Salvador prompted.

With shaking fingers, he began punching in numbers. On the tray was a copy of *The Tampa Bay Time's* metro front, dominated by a grainy close-up of Andrew kneeling next to a young woman with her head in her hands. Piercing the newspaper through the exact center of his son's image was a barbed stinger, six inches long and thick as a finger.

"What *is* it?" the guard repeated.

John put the phone to his ear as the called connected and Andrew's cell began to ring.

"A message," he said.

Four

They were surrounded. Andrew thought there were six, but the number changed every time he blinked. There might be six, or sixty or six hundred.

"Daddy, hold this for me," Anna said, passing him a sodden paper airplane. "It needs to dry out."

"I don't think it's going to fly again, honey," he said, but she was already racing back to the center of the water jets, on for the first time in more than a week due to increasingly severe water restrictions. Anna retrieved her plastic bucket from another little girl and together they took turns soaking one of the stone lions bordering the fountain.

She appeared unaware of the bulbous-headed creatures clinging to the trunks of several nearby trees like tumorous growths. Andrew kept his eyes on the fountain, but it was nearly impossible to ignore the monstrosities around him, especially the one mewing softly from the live oak a dozen yards to his right.

These weren't like the thing by the dumpster, the *quintaloch*. They were smaller, rounder, more compact. In his periphery, he caught some sudden motion, the spasmodic twitch of an appendage, the swelling and contraction of an air sack or bladder, and his gaze tugged in their direction.

His father had warned him repeatedly over the years that the slightest suggestion of awareness was enough to provoke an attack. So far, he had managed to stop himself from turning. But it was hard. Christ, it was hard. Like an intense itch, it required a monumental effort to resist. Would a quick peek be so bad, just a glance to determine what he was up against?

In the duffel bag at his feet was a change of clothes for Anna, a towel, a bottle of SPF 50 sunscreen. Every twenty minutes he was supposed to call her over for a reapplication. It was important to keep her scar tissue moisturized to prevent the skin from tightening and impairing dexterity, or so claimed her physical therapist.

At the bottom of the bag was a tea bottle filled with single malt Scotch. Andrew had been startled to find it as he was packing that morning, a forgotten relic lying like a landmine at the bottom of the bag. He should have tossed it in the sink, but something had stilled his hand as he reached for it. He told himself it was fear, a superstitious reluctance to touch such a toxic reminder of past mistakes, but he couldn't fool himself for long. The real reason he'd kept it was the reassurance it provided, the secret knowledge that if things got truly bad (and what did *that* mean, exactly?) he could re-center himself with a quick swig.

Not that he *would*, of course, but knowing he *could* provided a festering sort of comfort.

Now he wished he'd thrown the damn thing in the trash. Because a drink would help him keep his mind off the things around them. Because a drink would settle his nerves. Because a drink would make things just a little bit better.

And so much worse.

"Andrew Tate."

Andrew flinched and squinted guilty up into the face of a tall, lanky, bearded man dressed in baggy khakis, a threadbare shirt, and ancient sneakers, one of which was held together by duct tape. A green canvas knapsack hung from a shoulder, its free strap dangling nearly to the ground.

Andrew's eyes darted to Anna and back. "I don't have any change."

The man smiled, reached into his pocket and pulled out a handful of coins. "That's cool, I do. How much you need?"

Andrew said nothing. His first thought was of Grace, that in her suspicion she had hired a homeless man to keep an eye on him, make sure he was toeing the line. It was ridiculous, of course, paranoid shit, but he was already scrambling for some sort of defense. It's not what you think. It's just tea. Herbal tea.

"You holding up okay?" the man asked finally. "Hard to keep the old peepers off them."

Andrew shaded his eyes with one hand and scrutinized the man's face more closely. There was something familiar about him, something in the sharp nose and high cheekbones that made him wonder if he'd seen those features before. In a picture, maybe, or on TV. With a belated start, Andrew realized the man had called him by name.

"Do I know you?"

"Na." The vagrant took a seat next to him on the bench. Andrew tensed, expecting to be overwhelmed by a stench like the one that had been steaming off Comanche, but the only thing he smelled was a faint whiff of sweat no stronger than his own. The man nodded toward the group of children in the fountain. "Which one's yours?"

Andrew hesitated. What was going on here? He felt like he had somehow missed a crucial exchange that explained who this person was and how they knew each other. What had this guy said about keeping your eyes off them? Off the creatures?

"The girl with... The girl in the purple bathing suit," Andrew finished. He had been a breath away from saying, "the girl with the skin grafts."

"Cute kid. Looks like you."

"Thanks." Andrew caught himself reaching for the tea bottle and froze, his fist clutching the bag. Jesus Christ, what the hell was the matter with him? He retrieved the towel instead and mopped his face. Off to the right, something began inching down the oak, gripping the trunk with enormous, finger-like digits.

"Okay, Andrew Tate, quick introduction. I'm Will. Most people call me Little Billy. I'm a friend of your dad, and this is what we're going to do to get out of here alive."

THE FINAL MINUTES IN THE PARK WERE A JUMBLE. ONCE they were up and moving everything became a slideshow of frozen moments: Anna's puzzled but happy face looking up into his, Little Billy's bony shoulders as he walked in front of them, a boy with a water pistol at the top of the slide, a basketball on a picnic table, all glimpses of an unremarkable world no different from the one he had known most of his life.

Except for the mewing, flailing things dropping from the trees like massive globs of Spanish moss, paralleling them on either side, keeping pace as they narrowed the gap. Tightening the noose, Andrew thought. They must hunt in packs.

And still, incredibly, no one paid the slightest attention. At one point, he thought he glimpsed one of the creatures pass directly in front of a woman on a bench while two more scuttled behind. Her phone conversation never wavered, and in the last few moments before their real flight began, Andrew experienced a pang of envy at her ignorance so strong his throat closed.

When they reached the place where the path forked, Little Billy abruptly turned and pointed. "I see you," he sneered. "I see you and you and you. So, let's just cut to the chase." And with that, he took off down the right path. Although they had discussed the simple plan before calling Anna back from her play, Andrew was still taken by surprise. He bent, caught his daughter up in his arms and raced down the opposite walkway, toward the parking lot and the presumed safety of the car.

"What's wrong, Daddy?" Anna asked. Her grip around his neck was a stranglehold.

"Nothing, honey. I'm a dragon. I just scooped up the princess to take her to my mountain lair."

"What's a lair?"

"Where I live." Within seconds his breath was coming in ragged heaves. He was carrying too much and moving too erratically, already on the verge of toppling. "They'll go for your hamstrings if they get the chance," Little Billy had warned. "Try not to run in a straight line."

Andrew spun to the right. His daughter was laughing, her arms held out, her head flung back so that her center of gravity shifted away from him. He lurched in the opposite direction and pulled Anna closer. For an instant, the impression of something within close proximity, within striking distance, raised goose flesh across his arms and neck. The next instant he was crashing into a wall of snapping branches, tumbling through a hedge bordering the parking lot.

"Daddy!" Anna exhaled into his ear.

He managed to twist as he went down, turning his back and shoulders toward the boxwood, enclosing his daughter in his arms, plowing through the brush, emerging on the other side and hitting the ground hard enough to bounce his head off the asphalt.

For several moments, all he could do was stare into a swimming blue haze of sky. He couldn't breathe. He couldn't hear. The ringing in his ears was a fire alarm overwhelming everything else. They were down. They were vulnerable. If the creatures attacked now it would be over quickly and all he could do was flounder and gasp. Anna was squirming off his chest. He tried to put her back to him, drape his body over hers, but she squirted away as he struggled to roll over.

His breath returned in a series of small hitches, each a little deeper than the previous, and as the ringing began to diminish, he swept his arm out and around, hoping to hook Anna.

"What happened, Daddy?"

Andrew sat up. His daughter was next to him once more, unharmed. He swallowed and tasted blood. He had bitten his tongue.

"Are you okay? Are you hurt?" he asked.

"I'm okay. It was like we were flying. Did you fall? Did I get away?"

"Get away?" From around the demolished hedge, a face appeared, the woman from the bench he had seen talking on her phone. She came running with her hand to her mouth.

"From the dragon," Anna said. The woman knelt next to him. "Did I escape?"

"My god, my god. Are you all right? Please tell me you and your little girl are all right. I saw the whole thing. You went right through."

"Just a few cuts and bruises." He probed the back of his head. A lump was forming, but he found no blood. His exposed arms and neck had taken the worst of it. "I'll be fine."

The woman appeared unconvinced. Her hand kept reaching and pulling back from his arm as if she were trying to gauge the temperature of a stovetop burner.

"You should get yourself checked out. Some of these cuts might need stitches."

Andrew looked past her toward the park and saw nothing but trees and playground equipment.

"It's okay," he said, fishing his keys from his pocket. "I'm a paramedic."

THE GLOW FROM THE TINY KITCHENETTE'S OVERHEAD lamp cast a cone of watery illumination across the table. Except for the slivers of late afternoon sun filtering through the closed vertical blinds, it was the only light in the room.

He'd been living at the motel for eight weeks and even the meager glow from the lamp's single, sixty-watt bulb revealed too much. The dingy walls of the kitchenette, its battered microwave and Seventies-era, avocado-green stove filled him with a quivering despair. The yellowed linoleum floor reminded him of deodorant stains on the armpits of an old tee-shirt, and the veneer on the particleboard cabinets had bubbled in places, giving the doors a blistered appearance. The overall effect was one of squalor held feebly at bay, something that had appealed to Andrew in

51

the first days of his self-banishment. Because when you were falling, there was something bleakly satisfying in falling as far as possible. Anything less would seem incomplete.

And this was certainly the sort of rock a father would crawl under after failing his child so monumentally. This was the hollow a firefighter would hole up in after disgracing his badge, his brothers, his station. For a week, he had wallowed in his threadbare incarceration, relished it, and then even that masochistic satisfaction faded under the realization the motel was nothing more than a stage for his indulgent self-pity.

On the table in front of Andrew was the empty tea bottle from the duffel bag. The Scotch was gone. So was every other drop of booze in the place, the gin and the Jack, the Smirnoff, even the mini-bottles of tequila and rum, emptied into the toilet bowl and flushed in a cocktail swirl. Maybe somewhere beneath the streets of Tampa, the sewer rats were getting stewed.

How could you? Grace had demanded. How *could* you? If only she'd slapped him. Then maybe he would have snapped out of it, found the words to explain some small piece of what had happened, at least enough to deflect the worst of her anger and disappointment. Instead, he had stood there offering implausible explanations and half-truths (quarter-truths? one-eight-truths?) while she checked Anna for injuries.

"It was only a game," his daughter said, looking from one parent to the other in a tick-tock of deepening confusion. "We were playing the princess who got scooped up by a dragon. It's not Daddy's fault he fell."

"Did you bump anything when you hit the ground, honey? Your head or your shoulder?" His wife's hands probed Anna's head and neck.

"I landed on Daddy. I didn't get hurt. Not one bit. The other man ran away. I think he pushed Daddy."

Grace sat back on her haunches and turned to him.

"A jogger. I guess that's who she means. He ran past us as I fell."

It might have ended there, his abrasions and Anna's lack of injury enough to provoke at least a pang of sympathy. And tripping over a curb, falling into a hedge, those things did occasionally happen, even when

52

sober. But then her eyes had fallen to the duffel bag at his feet, and as if drawn by some whispered clue she had snatched it up and unzipped the top.

The reek of alcohol sprang at them like something out of a jack-in-the-box. The bottle must have cracked in the fall.

"Anna," Grace said in a flat, uncompromising tone. "Go to your room, please."

"But I want a glass of chocolate milk."

"Now." He and Grace stood in silence as their daughter's footsteps retreated down the hall and her bedroom door clicked shut.

"How could you?" His wife hissed. "After everything you've already put her through. How could you?"

"Grace." But what explanation could he possibly have offered? It was at the bottom of the bag? I forgot it was there? I never touched it? It was all too preposterous. And so, he said the only thing he could think of. He told her he was sorry.

"Did you drive our daughter home drunk?"

"No, of course not. God, I would never do that. I saved her today."

"Saved her from what?" she demanded, springing to her feet.

Andrew stared back.

"From what?"

"From anything bad that could have happened to her," he managed at last. "From anything that would do her harm."

Grace shoved the duffel bag into his chest. "That would be you, Andy. You're what she needs to be saved from."

"I'm sorry," he told her again. "I screwed up, okay. I'm still a work in progress. It's been a hell of a year. I've got a lot to recover from."

"All your wounds are self-inflicted. It was your decision to move out."

"After you made it clear you didn't trust me with Anna anymore."

His wife's mouth tightened, but she did not lower her eyes.

"It's not even that." Andrew knew he was only making things worse, but he was powerless to stop. "What happened to Anna was inexcusable. Is inexcusable. You're right to be skeptical about me. I'd be skeptical about me too. What bothers me is that you never once talked to me about any of this. Not once. You shut me out and had Max do all the talking for you. He knew our marriage was dangling by a thread before I did."

"That's not what I intended. I was afraid of how you'd react." Her tone was calm now, reasonable in the manner of an adult explaining to a raging preschooler why ice cream was not a viable choice for breakfast.

"What did you think I'd do, Grace?"

"I don't know, Andy. That's the point. I never know with you anymore."

In the dank kitchenette, Andrew placed the cracked tea bottle on its side and gave it a spin. "She wouldn't have me back now if I begged her."

He gathered up the empties and carefully positioned each in the trash, as if the small clink of glass might wake someone sleeping in the next room. Every part of him ached. His head throbbed. His shoulders and arms stung, the back of his legs felt hot, as if sunburned. He still hadn't cleaned up.

Andrew crossed the darkened main room and flicked on the bathroom light. The face that squinted back at him from the mirror appeared bloated, the skin under the eyes dark and puffy, the cheeks heavy, jowly even. Not an old face, not yet, but certainly one in decline, softened by punches self-inflicted or otherwise.

As he leaned over the sink cupping water over his head, Andrew noticed once again the warm ache across the back of his legs. He'd been feeling it on-and-off since the park, a minor discomfort he hadn't had the time or inclination to investigate. Running a hand down the back of his jeans, he found a horizontal rip just above the inside knee. Above both knees, actually. He twisted and tentatively probed the gaps, wincing as his fingers discovered the wounds beneath. When he dropped his pants, Andrew found the back of his calves caked in dried blood from two shallow but precise gashes across the tendons of his thighs.

"They go for the hamstrings," he muttered, reaching for the damp washcloth hanging over the shower curtain. Before he could grab the bar of soap his cell began to ring. He had intentionally left it behind that morning, not wanting to provide Grace the opportunity to continually check up on him throughout the afternoon. The phone's display showed an unfamiliar number. Normally, he would let it go to voicemail, but he was still feeling masochistic. Ending the day listening to a sales pitch for timeshares would be the perfect capper for the evening.

"Hello?"

"Is this Andrew Tate?" a female voice asked.

"Yes." Timeshares, or maybe life insurance. You always think you have enough, but what would your family do if you were suddenly unable to support them? His chest heaved with silent laughter. Celebrate! That's what they'd do.

"You're a hard man to get a hold of, Mr. Tate. We've been trying to reach you all day."

"I bet." Andrew swept a pile of clothes off the bed and rolled onto his back. He intended to play this out as long as he could before telling the bitch to go fuck herself.

"My name is Dr. Cho. I'm an infirmary physician at the Orient Road Jail."

Andrew pushed himself up on one elbow. "You're who?"

"My name is Dr. Cho. I'm calling on behalf of your father, John Tate."

"My father? My father's in jail?" Andrew swung his legs over the bed and sat up.

"Yes, and he needs to see you as soon as possible. Can you be here tomorrow morning at nine?"

"What's this all about? Why is he in jail?"

"I'd rather not say over the phone. Can you be here tomorrow or not?"

Andrew stirred the air with his free hand. "Why not? I've got nothing better to do on my day off. Might as well visit my old man in the clink."

"Good. I'll let him know you're coming."

She hung up before he could offer a parting quip. Andrew tossed the phone onto the pile of dirty clothes and flopped back across the mattress. Not a sales pitch for life insurance, but as shitting endings go, discovering your estranged father was in jail was none too shabby. All he needed now was the motel to catch fire.

Andrew ran his tongue over dry lips and wished he'd kept just one of the mini bottles. Plunging toward rock bottom was apparently thirsty work.

Five

The jail's visiting room was packed. He had to wait forty minutes before John Tate's name was announced and his father was ushered to a chair behind the transparent acrylic divider. Andrew began speaking before the other had brought the phone halfway to his ear.

"Why are you in here, Dad? What the hell is going on?"

"Are you and Anna alright?"

"Yeah, we're fine. Why?"

"I had reason to believe you were in danger. I tried to reach you all day yesterday. Grace told me you and your daughter were spending the afternoon at the park. She gave me your cell number, but you never answered."

Something Grace had failed to mention.

"You knew I was in danger? From the creatures? *Your* creatures?"

"They're not *my* creatures."

Andrew slowly raised an index finger at his father. "Did you send that homeless guy to check up on us? Calls himself Little Billy?"

"I know him as William Phipps. Yes, I asked him to try and track you down."

A pulse of anger flared and died, replaced by an image of Anna screaming at his feet as he swung a branch at the first of an endless onslaught of attackers.

"I guess I should thank you, then. He probably saved our lives." The muscles of his father's face betrayed the struggle between keeping silent and asking the next obvious question and Andrew allowed the conflict to continue for a second or two before ending it with a huff of tired resignation. "Yeah, Dad. I can see them."

"Shit."

"Shit indeed."

"How many were there?"

Andrew shook his head. "Not sure. More than a few. Seemed like the whole park was infested. Dad..." He cleared his throat, slid his chair up until his knees struck the wall and pressed his upraised forearm against the divider. "Dad, I'm sorry, okay? I'm sorry I doubted you all these years. You were right. There *are* monsters out there hiding in the light. What the hell is going on?"

John Tate inhaled deeply and rubbed the side of his face. "I can't go into the details now. It would take all afternoon."

"Can you at least tell me why you're in jail?"

"Someone at the storage facility found out I was storing three hundred pounds of black powder in one of their units and called the cops."

Andrew stared back through the pane, waiting for more. His father had aged considerably in the two years since their last face-to-face. In the orange Hillsborough County Correctional Facility scrubs he looked gaunt, jaundiced, his cheeks and eyes sunken as if his features were sinking into a void that had opened beneath the bones of his face. His shoulder-length hair, faded to the color of yellowed teeth, was brushed straight back, emphasizing the changes. Only his irises were the same, two brilliant green chips shining with malarial intensity. The overall impression was not, however, one of sickness or defeat but rather a hot, radiating defiance, the righteous resolve of a defrocked street preacher determined to reclaim his flock.

"Why would you keep three hundred pounds of black powder in a storage unit?"

"I didn't want it in my apartment."

Andrew pinched the bridge of his nose. "You know what I mean."

"I was going to blow something up."

"Of course you were. Do I want to know?"

"No, but I guess that doesn't matter anymore. I heard what you did by the way," his father added after a moment of silence. "The other day with the hostage thing. They're calling you a hero."

"Depends on who you ask."

"Find that hard to believe."

When Andrew said nothing, his father edged forward until his forehead was nearly touching the divider. "How'd Comanche know you were my son?"

"Apparently, we look a lot alike."

"You don't think so?"

"Never thought about it before. What are these homeless guys to you, Dad? The ones you're paying to be lookouts? Canaries in the coal mine? Expendables?"

His father's gaze never wavered, but his free hand curled into a fist. "I never taught them how to see the damn things. All I did was ask them to report anything out of the ordinary."

"The thing Comanche pointed out next to that dumpster was definitely that."

"How long have you been seeing them?"

The crowded visiting room was getting warmer by the minute. Andrew wiped his sweating face with the back of a sleeve. "That was the first time. Comanche said you called it a *quintaloch*."

His father slammed his fist against the phone shelf. "A word. It was just a word! Never a description."

"Does a *quintaloch* look like a kind of mutant centipede?"

His father's eyes closed, head listing toward his left shoulder.

"I'll take that as a yes. So somehow, he managed to associate the name with the creature. Thing is, Dad, I've been seeing flashes of things out of the corner of my eye for almost two years. Two years! If what you've always told me is true, then Anna and Grace are going to be in danger every time I'm with them from now on. *Is* that true? Am I toxic to them?"

"I'm afraid your wife and daughter are in danger for bigger reasons than that. We all are. Something's coming, Andy. Something very, very bad."

"What? More of those things in the park? More of what was next to the dumpster?"

"Worse."

"Dad, I don't know if I can bail you out of here, not if they've charged you with some sort of terrorist-related act like bomb making."

"I didn't ask you here to bail me out."

"Then why? To make sure Anna and I were okay?" Andrew swallowed, fighting an abrupt wave of nausea. A soft buzz began to fizz at the bottom of his mind. "I'm sorry. What was that?"

His father was speaking, but the words bounced off the divider and tumbled back at him. Andrew became aware of the woman sitting two chairs to his right. She'd been having her own phone conversation with a bearded man Andrew had briefly noted for the cobra tattoo coiling around his neck and over his bald head to sink its fangs into the flesh of his forehead. Her voice had risen to a sharp bark, a single word repeated over and over: "Dennis? Dennis? Dennis!"

Andrew turned as a uniformed officer began to make his way across the room.

"Dennis, you're scarin' me now. You doing drugs in here, too? Say something."

The officer angled his way to her chair and asked if there was a problem.

"Hell yes, there's a problem. My boy's having some sort of seizure. He's gone all white and won't answer me. Dennis. You see? He's just sitting there staring off. Oh, god. Now what?"

The man she called Dennis had dropped the phone to raise both hands to the side of his head, his eyes wide in terror or pain, his lips pulled back in a rictus that bared a mouthful of ruined teeth. Andrew pivoted to survey the room. Three or four others had assumed identical poses. It was as if somewhere an excruciating alarm was sounding, one only a select few could hear.

"Who's that?" a man behind him cried. "Who's that? Who's that? Oh, no, no, no. Goddamn you. Goddamn you!"

The man tilted his head and slapped the side of his face hard, as if trying to dislodge water from the opposite ear. A thump drew Andrew's attention back to the tattooed inmate, but it wasn't until Dennis drew his head back and slammed it against the divider once more that he understood what had produced the dull boom. The man's mother, her hands now clamped across her mouth, watched as a third blow crumpled his nose, spraying blood across the pane. Three officers swarmed him, one as pale as the inmate.

"What's this?" Andrew asked, although he knew. The static from the hole in his mind had condensed into the faint echoes of an ancient, guttural, jabbering language.

The voices had returned.

His father waited until Andrew turned back toward him to say, "It's getting worse." He touched the divider with an index finger. "Now listen closely. If you want to be able to protect your family, there's something you need to do."

"Something legal?"

His father's smile was sharp as a scythe. "Perfectly."

ANDREW STOOD AT THE EDGE OF A WEED-CHOKED LOT, empty except for a billboard promising a Mediterranean-style duplex "Coming Soon!" The letters had faded from what might have been a vibrant turquoise to the color of an old bruise, the sign's wooden scaffolding weathered gray and tangled in dead vines. "Soon" was apparently a relative term.

This couldn't be right. He took a step closer to the broken finger of concrete poking up from the tangle of weeds a few feet from the sidewalk. His father's directions had been meticulous, but somewhere Andrew might have taken a wrong turn. This was just an old property marker, a relic from the '20s or '30s when a house had stood at the site.

He re-read his notes, tapping the page as he checked off each turn. The intersection one block south. Check. The retention pond off to his right. Check. The apartment complex across the street with its bright yellow security booth and the convenience store one block north. Check and check. Everything matched. This *must* be the right place. Andrew stared sourly at the marker. All this urgency over a three-foot column of weathered concrete. He had driven from one end of Tampa to the other for this?

"Jesus."

And yet, something wasn't right here. A thrumming had begun somewhere near the center of his mind, a deep, cyclical vibration that resonated the same way the voices had.

"You go there," his father said after watching Andrew scribble the directions. "You'll see a pillar of stone. It might be hard to find at first because it'll look like something bland, the base of an old lamppost, a cement planter, a chunk of retaining wall."

"Which is it?" Behind Andrew, people were blowing their noses, coughing and clearing throats, wiping away tears. The voices had stopped abruptly, seemingly in mid-utterance, as if some critical alignment had slipped out of phase, but those affected were still struggling to recover. Two stalls over, the trio of guards were pulling Dennis to his feet, the lower half of his face masked in a smear of blood that continued to pour from his shattered nose.

"I don't know. Their real shape is like something sculpted out of bone, an enormous rib poking from the ground. But that's not how you see them at first. I think those initial impressions are different for everyone.

The first one I saw looked like a grave marker. It takes a few encounters before you learn how to push beyond the illusion."

"Dad," Andrew sighed.

"Andrew, listen closely. Go there. Touch it. That's all I'm asking." The guards led the bloody inmate from the room. "After what just happened here, after the park, after Comanche, I think I deserve the benefit of your doubt."

Now, Andrew edged closer to the property marker, noticing for the first time the way the drought-withered vegetation diminished as it approached the concrete, growing lower and sparser until it stopped altogether a foot from the base. The earth around it had a baked and powdery appearance, ash white, as if scattered with crematory remains. He glanced around, saw no one, and sank to one knee, wincing as the wounds across his thighs flexed.

Something bland? It was certainly that. If he'd been strolling along this sidewalk he wouldn't have given the thing a second glance. But wasn't that what it wanted, not to be seen? Andrew frowned. What had given him that impression? It was inconspicuous, yes, but so were telephone poles. So were mailboxes. So were a thousand other things passed daily without notice.

Still, he could feel his eyes yearning to veer away to the left or right. It was an effort to keep them centered on the pillar. His thoughts wanted to turn away as well, to focus instead on the empty bottles in the kitchenette's trash (replaceable), or the look on Max's face after dodging Andrew's swing, or the pot of water boiling away on the front burner of the stovetop next to a forgotten box of macaroni and cheese. It was as if the marker and his mind were identical magnetic poles. His attention deflected around it, circled back, slipped over and past it once more, following the contours of an invisible bubble of deterrence.

Andrew concentrated harder.

Here was something else: the air around the marker wavered slightly, as if the concrete radiated heat. It was barely visible, but it was real. Its surface was pitted and scarred, the corners eroded, the top third broken off completely. Particles of maroon speckled the gray rock, giving the concrete the appearance of mottled skin, coarse, flaked, and scabbed. As he studied the marker, he thought he noticed subtle motion beneath the lightly wavering air, a slow flexing as the sides of the pillar gradually expanded and contracted.

Andrew made a low sound at the back of his throat, turned his head and spat. His nose was running. He wiped it across a sleeve and rose to his feet, leaning back with both hands pressed against the small of his back until the vertebra of his lower lumbar began to pop. Touch that thing? How was that going to help him protect his family? Protect them from what?

The *vetro offalate.*

Gibberish. Made-up words like something out of a children's book. But he had heard them in his thoughts, syllables pushed into his mind and uttered by a lipless mouth that yawned wide and puckered closed with a wet, viscous snap.

A nursery rhyme trilled suddenly through his head, a little four-line verse Anna would sometimes ask him to read, climbing into his lap and flipping through the pages of *In Your Own Back Yard* until she found the drawing of the big, bright insects:

> "Beetle, butterfly, ant and bee,
> In my garden, but so hard to see.
> I need a clue, where can you be found?
> Just open your eyes, we're all around."

A week ago, he would have also dismissed *quintaloch* as babble-speak. Now a new rhyme occurred to him with an effortlessness that seemed to suggest he was remembering a long-forgotten favorite rather than inventing a new one:

> Quintaloch, quintaloch hiding in a tree,
> Quintaloch, quintaloch coming after me.

Periphery

I'll close my eyes and sit real still
and hope it passes by.
"Don't fool yourself," said the quintaloch,
"We both know you will die."

Andrew reached out and grasped the marker. In the instant before his arm went numb to the elbow he felt the concrete yield under his fingers, a muscular and reflexive pliability, rigid yet supple, like touching a bladder taut with fluid. Revulsion closed his throat, but before he could yank his hand away crimson light flared around him, blinding and hot. His weight doubled as if an invisible, leaden cloak had crashed down across his shoulders. It pressed him lower, compressed his spine, tugged at his arms. He lifted a heavy head to behold distant black mountains silhouetted in an enormous red sun and opened his mouth to scream. Sulfurous air rushed in, coating his tongue, clawing his throat while a booming moan so deep and resonant it was nearly subsonic erupted nearby. A huge and confounding shadow fell over him. It stretched across the hardpan plain toward the distant foothills, a writhing mass of protrusions furling and unfurling in a lunatic frenzy.

Under the swollen, bleeding sun, Andrew thought: *This is how...*

Under the familiar yellow sun: *... I die.*

He spun, took a single, lurching step, and smashed into a plaid chest. His legs crumpled. Hands were on his shoulders, pushing him away while holding him up. He hung limply in the man's grip like a garment pinned to a clothesline, and blinked up into a smiling, bearded face.

"It's okay," Little Billy assured him. "I know exactly how you feel."

TWENTY MINUTES LATER THEY WERE SITTING IN THE shade of A coffeehouse veranda. Had it been any farther than two blocks, Andrew doubted he would have made it, but Little Billy kept him on his feet long enough to stumble here and sink into a chair. The vividness of the vision was fading, but the smell remained. Andrew could still detect a faint, acrid odor with every inhalation, a baked pungency, vaguely sweet, that gave the hot, still, afternoon an unsettled quality, as if everything, the trees, the fence posts, the hedges, wavered on the verge of combustion.

"Used to be, you could touch a *xalanthracoil* and all you'd get is a mild yuck, like sitting on a public toilet seat still warm from the last guy. Now." Little Billy extended his hand palm out, eased it forward, then yanked it back and shook it vigorously.

"*Xalanthracoil?*"

"Your dad's name for them. I wanted to call them *initiators*, but he said that was too *prosaic*." Little Billy repeated the word again silently, as if gauging the feel of it on his lips. "Claimed there was a Greek or Latin reason for the name, but he never bothered to explain it."

"How do you two know each other?" Andrew stared into the other man's face, struck, as he had been the day before, by the familiarity of his features.

"We go way back."

Andrew held his gaze for a moment before dropping his eyes to the glass of iced tea sweating on the wrought iron table between them. The awning provided only a thin band of shade, but it was enough to knock the early afternoon heat back a notch or two. For some reason, the thought of sitting inside the coffeehouse's over-cooled interior made him uneasy. "You obviously know a hell of a lot more about these things than I do. My father and I haven't talked much over the years. And never about his... research."

"So, here's the deal." The abrupt irritation in the other man's voice pulled Andrew's eyes back to his face. "I can see this playing out two ways. Me sitting here all afternoon trying to convince you you're not crazy, and me just getting up and telling you to follow if you want to learn what the hell is going on. How about we agree to not waste each other's time and get on with this?"

Andrew said nothing.

"Look," Little Billy said in a more conciliatory tone. "I've been on the streets a long time. I'm not used to talking to people the way I once did.

You tend to be more direct when you're trying to convince some douchebag not to stick you and steal your coat. So I'm sorry if I seem," his gaze rose, as if searching for the right word in the air above their heads, "abrupt? Abrupt.

"I understand how overwhelming this shit is. You think I woke up one day and said, 'I'm going to start believing in hidden monsters lurking around every corner?' You think your dad did? All we set out to do was count the local squirrel population. Squirrels, for Christ's sake."

Andrew snapped his fingers. Some mental flutter had erased the beard, shortened the sun-bleached hair, smoothed away the crows' feet and tightened the features to that of a man years younger, and with an 'oomph' of recognition, he realized why Little Billy looked so familiar.

"William Phipps. Of course. My dad told me your name but it didn't register until this instant. You're *that* William Phipps."

The man across the table raised his arms with a theatric flourish. "One and only."

"Christ, almighty." Andrew glanced around and saw they were alone. Still, he lowered his voice to something barely more than a whisper. "I know it's been a long time, and I know the charges were eventually dismissed, but you're taking a risk coming back. If someone recognized you."

Little Billy snorted, threw an arm over the back of his chair and pulled his mug of coffee clattering across the table. "What? They'd run me down in the street? Beat me to death with the first club they could find?" He took a sip, made a face and tossed the rest of his coffee into the planter at his side. "I've spent the last twenty years dodging things that would make a cage fighter piss himself. You think I'm worried about being harassed by someone who remembers me from all those years ago? Besides, there's not many who *would* recognize me. Not anymore."

In the silence that followed Andrew mulled a number of questions, rejecting each as either too big, too personal, or too absurd. *Did you do it? Did you kill them all? Or did something jump out of the bushes and tear them to shreds?* He sighed and asked the only question that didn't feel like an invasion: "So why *did* you come back?"

"Your dad asked me to. Time's almost up." He stood and slung his knapsack over a shoulder. "John and I had to learn things the hard way. Some of it was brutal. You, on the other hand, have the great good fortune of getting me as a teacher."

"Where are we going?"

Little Billy made for the exit and Andrew followed. The afternoon smelled of parched vegetation and the first whiffs of some coming conflagration, a firestorm that Andrew was beginning to suspect would reduce his world to ash and cinder.

"On a little field trip. Consider this the first day of class. I suggest you take notes."

THE ANSWERING MACHINE PICKED UP YET AGAIN AND THIS time Andrew left a message, something casual and unconcerned and painfully forced. Just touching base. There's a sale on school backpacks. Did Anna need a new one this year? Let me know and I'll pick one up. Talk to you soon.

What he needed was reassurance his family remained alive and well. After yesterday, Grace believed Anna's safety depended on keeping her father as far from her as possible. After today, Andrew feared she might be right.

He slipped the phone back into his pocket and turned what he hoped was a blank face to Little Billy. Or did he prefer William? He was following his father's assistant(?), partner(?), acolyte(?), across a parking lot four blocks southeast of the *xalanthracoil* Andrew had touched.

"Thank you for yesterday," Andrew said. "I should have said that earlier. I don't want to think about what would have happened if you hadn't shown up."

"Just glad you and your little girl made it out of the park alright." Little Billy glanced over his shoulder. "You *were* both alright?"

Andrew seesawed his hand in the air. "Anna was fine. Me, not so much. Ended up plowing through a hedge and cracking my head on the pavement."

"I've never seen *squim* act that way before, moving as a pack. Your dad was right to be worried. It was as if they were being directed."

"Squim? That what you call them, *squim*? Not very Greek-sounding." They crossed into an alley bordered by a tall backyard fence on one side and a row of scrub pines on the other. There was trash under the pines, beer bottles and Coke cans and candy wrappers and Andrew wondered briefly if this shaded ribbon of shelter, padded in a bed of fallen needles, was someplace Little Billy hunkered when he wasn't doing his father's bidding.

"That one was mine. We've named everything we've found. Dozen species so far. Who knows how many more out there waiting to be discovered."

"Jesus. It's like an entire ecosystem hidden right under our noses."

"We use the term shadow biosphere. Collectively, they're called the *bilantu offalate*."

Andrew flipped open the small notebook Little Billy had given him upon their arrival at the parking lot. "This lesson number one?"

"Why not?"

Andrew kept his eyes on their shadows stretching ahead of them. Things were flittering in his periphery, but he did not turn. Keep talking, he told himself. Focus on Little Billy's voice. Don't let them know you know they're there.

"*Bilantu offalate*. Not the *vetro offalate*?" Andrew noted with a small mental cringe the words no longer sounded made up.

"They're two different things. The *bilantu* are lesser creatures. Think of them as vermin stranded here after the *vetro* retreated back to their universe."

"You mean like the rats and cats left in the New World after the Conquistadors went home?"

"Sure. They're mindless for the most part, all instinct and appetite. The *vetro* on the other hand…"

"Okay," Andrew stopped him with an arm against his chest. "Before we launch into some sort of sensei/grasshopper thing here, I need you to answer one question."

Little Billy smiled. "Just one?"

"My father told me if I wanted to protect my family I needed to touch that thing. So, I have. I've touched it. Now you tell me, how am I better prepared to defend my wife and daughter against whatever is coming?"

"Touching the *coil* has changed you up here," Little Billy pointed to Andrew's temple. "Not a lot. Not yet. But it's a changed that needed to start today. Look," he gripped Andrew's shoulder and squeezed. "Getting you caught up with all of this, it's like drinking from a fire hose. Before I say anything else, let me show you what I dragged you out here to see. It'll help you understand."

Andrew thought of Anna and Grace running from something in the backyard, barricading themselves in the bathroom, the scratch of teeth or talons across a door too flimsy to hold back the terrible things determined to get inside.

He lifted an arm as an invitation for Little Billy to proceed, and together they walked down the alley past a dumpster (don't turn, don't look, not every trash bin has a *quintaloch* curled around it), past the back wall of a Laundromat, to the edge of a shallow slope that bottomed out in a dry drainage canal. A line of kudzu-entangled trees ran along the other embankment, screening the pair from the street. The withered vines hung in brown nets from the branches, giving the foliage the appearance of old women hunched under tattered shawls. After glancing behind them, Little Billy made his way down.

"It took your father four years to identify every *xalanthracoil*. As you've probably already noticed, they don't want to be found."

"How many of these *coil*-things are there?"

"Eighteen. They form a perfect circle 1.8 miles across."

"Like a big Stonehenge?"

70

Little Billy mopped his face with a cloth pulled from his back pocket. "They were intentionally positioned, but they're not a calendar."

"What then?"

"They open doorways. Show me where this one is."

"A *coil*? There's one here?" The culvert was a dumping ground, littered with discarded furniture, car parts, electronics, items that couldn't be shoved into a garbage can and dragged to the corner. A battered dresser lay overturned to his right, one drawer extended in surrender. A mattress. A television. A bicycle frame. There was even a pot-bellied stove buried in the sandy soil up to its cast-iron door. Rotted bedding. Discarded toys. Broken lamps and legless chairs. And shining hotly between it all, the glint of broken glass.

"I wouldn't know where to begin." Andrew took a tentative step toward the dresser. A faded and bubbled Spider-Man sticker appeared to be the only thing holding it together. "I'm not going to go rooting through all this shit."

"You shouldn't have to."

Andrew sighed. A headache was coming on, the kind that would settle into the base of his skull and sink its roots deep into his jaw. If he didn't take something soon he would spend his evening lying in bed, riding out the waves of pain and nausea and wishing for his friend Jimmy Beam to drop by and keep him company.

He scanned the litter once more. Was this how his father had spent the years after resigning his position at the college, traipsing through the moldy corners of Tampa looking for something that was trying hard not to be there?

"I don't see it."

"Tell me what you *do* see. Saying it out loud sometimes helps to highlight what you're missing."

Andrew extended his arm and, working from right to left, inventoried the debris. "I see a dresser. I see a mattress. TV. Bunch of rusted paint cans. What's left of a bike. Couple of chairs. A couch. A broken mirror. Seven years' bad luck for somebody. Wait."

71

He cocked his head as if listening for the repetition of a low peal of thunder. Something had happened during his inventory. He had felt it, the same diversion of attention he'd experienced with the other *coil*. Only this time it had worked. He'd jumped right over something in the center of the clutter without pause.

What was it? Andrew concentrated harder and started over, speaking each item slowly. "Dresser. Television. Paint cans. Bicycle frame." It was there, next to the bike. "The pot-bellied stove," he grunted, cupping the base of his skull. "The *coil* looks like a stove."

Little Billy gave him a thumbs-up, then frowned. "You okay?"

"Headache."

"A side effect, maybe? Let's sit over here in the shade."

They edged their way under the canopy of a nearby Brazilian pepper and sank to the ground. Little Billy took a water bottle from his knapsack, handed it to Andrew, opened a side pocket and fished out a bottle of aspirin. "Living on the street, you learn to carry everything you need on your back." He shook three tables into Andrew's palm.

"Like a turtle." Andrew gulped the water and leaned back against the trunk with his eyes closed.

"Something like that. So," he clapped his hands together. "Answers."

Andrew eased his head forward, took another long swallow of water and fumbled the cap back on. "What happened to me when I touched that thing? Was I really there, in that other world?"

"Part of you was. You're consciousness. Part of your consciousness, I should say. Physically, you were still here."

"And the place I saw, that was where they come from? The *vetro offalate*? The *bilantu offalate*? A world with a giant red sun and black mountains and monster gravity?"

"We think they've spread across many worlds, but that's their home base. Not exactly a vacation spot."

"How did going there help me? How am I better prepared to save my family? Save them from what, exactly?"

72

Little Billy plucked a blade of grass and split it down the middle with his thumbnail. "Once upon a time, the best way to protect your loved ones after you started seeing these things was to stay the hell away from them. That's the way it is with the *bilantu*. After they know you can see them, they mark you. It's part of the reason the *squim* honed in on you at the park.

"You were holding up pretty well, I'll give you that, but they could sense something, your awareness edging toward them. And like I said before, they may have had another reason to target you."

"What do you mean?"

"Your father tell you why he was concerned for your safety yesterday?"

Andrew shook his head, the tendons at the base of his skull protesting even that minor motion. "We didn't have much time to talk. They broke up our meeting right after the shit hit the fan in the visiting room."

"The voices."

"You're hearing them, too?"

"Just whispers. You?"

"Just whispers. For now."

He took a sip of water and listened as Little Billy told him about the skewered newspaper photo. Andrew waited for the implications to sink in and stir some emotional reaction, but all he could do was stare dully at the tips of his shoes.

"Andy?" Little Billy prompted after a moment.

"So, these things have me in their crosshairs?" How close had he come to getting Anna killed? "I thought you said they were mindless."

"They have been. But with the *vetro* so close, things seem to be changing. They're slaves to their masters' will."

"And the *vetro* want me dead?"

Little Billy raised his hands. "Or they want your father to know they can get to you. A warning, maybe? Fuck with us and your boy dies."

"How do I protect my family?"

"Our minds, they're kind of like guitar strings. They can be tuned up or down to an extent. The *xalantracoils* are like tuning forks. Every time you touch one your mind is brought a little more into their frequency. Now that you've had some exposure, you'll be more aware of both the *coils* and the *vetro,* and not just when the bastards are hollering the way they were this morning. When they're quiet, too, trying to lay low."

"Why is that good? You just said ignorance is bliss when it comes to these things."

"With the *bilantu,* yeah. We think our brains have evolved not to see them. Some kind of a defense mechanism. Keeps them from targeting us." Little Billy raised a hand as if attempting to stop traffic. "Don't ask why. We don't have all the answers. But the *vetro,* they're different. Ignorance won't protect you from them. This is going to sound batshit crazy, but they were here before." He paused, seeming once again to search for the right word.

"Eons. Eons ago. Their cities were everywhere. But they had to retreat. Must have been the asteroid. They knew it was coming and hauled ass back to that shithole you saw, and while they were gone the gap between their world and our, their *universe* and ours, it widened too much for them to get back. That's what John and I figure.

"Now the gap's shrinking again. Fast. And if they make it back here, they'll digest every last one of us before we know we've been swallowed."

Despite the headache, Andrew had been attempting to take notes as Little Billy spoke. Now his pen rose from the page. "Tell me that's just a figure of speech."

The man who had once gone by the name William Phipps stretched out his legs and turned his face to the sky. Andrew waited. The still afternoon was eerily quiet. No dog barked, no air-conditioner hummed. He heard neither bird nor insect. Even the traffic had vanished.

Slowly, Little Billy's head sank as if the silence had lulled him to sleep. Andrew remembered the shadow stretching across the baked hardpan, the unfurling protrusions whipping and fluttering, spasmodic, eager, reaching for him, for the world he came from.

"How much time do we have?" he asked finally, no longer able to bare the answer to his previous question.

Little Billy shook his head. "Days, probably. When the gap is thin enough, they'll punch through. That's what those things are for." He nodded toward the culvert. "The *xalanthracoils*. They can twist reality, manipulate... spacetime?"

"You're asking me?"

"Spacetime. Einstein. Shit, I don't know. They're scalpels. When they all turn on, when they *activate*, they'll open a breach large enough for the *vetro offalate* to come pouring through."

Andrew leaned forward, his eyes on the pot-bellied stove that was not a stove. "It's glowing. You see?" A faint orange light, no brighter than the ember of a lit cigarette, pulsed in veins across the surface. If the glow had corresponded to the dark recesses of the stove—the gaps between the door slats, the circle of the empty exhaust pipe coupling—it might have given the impression of a fire smoldered within. Instead, the light ran in jagged fractures from one end to the other, as if escaping through the cracks of something shattered and carelessly pieced back together.

Little Billy watched for a moment. "Humming, too."

Even in the deep silence, the sound was nearly unperceivable, a low moaning both mechanical and organic, rising and falling in syncopation with the glow.

"Have they always done that?" Andrew whispered. The stillness had taken on substance, enclosing them in a cathedral of hushed expectation. A tremor passed through him and he turned to glance over his shoulder before he could catch himself. There was nothing, only the brown slope and the straw-like weeds and the motionless things they concealed or did not conceal.

"No." Andrew took some comfort in that Little Billy was also whispering. "They're starting to wake up." He stood, shouldered his pack, dusted off the seat of his pants and pulled Andrew to his feet. "Let's get the hell out of here."

The two men made their silent way back to the parking lot. As they exited the alley Andrew felt a subtle easing of pressure. When he swallowed, his ears popped and the outside world with its droning traffic, its rumbling life, came rushing back in.

"I think that's enough for today." Little Billy squinted into the hazy sky as if seeking some confirmation there. "Definitely enough." He turned back to Andrew. "Go home, rest."

"Not yet." Andrew wiped his face with the back of a sleeve. "You just told me some sort of apocalypse is coming. What am I supposed to do now? Pack up my family and run?"

"Running won't help. You'll never be able to get far enough away. No one will."

Andrew tore the pages he'd scribbled from the notebook and tossed them at Little Billy. They struck his chest and scattered at his feet. "Then what the hell good are you? What the hell good was any of this? You're telling me the world as we know it is coming to an end and there's nothing we can do about it?"

Little Billy scooped up the pages and took the notebook from Andrew's shaking hands. "That's not what I said. There is something we can do. May be a long shot, but your father thinks it could work."

"What?" The parking lot was listing slowly to the right. Andrew shifted his balance to remain upright.

"We were almost ready to try it when he got arrested. Now that you're on board, you'll be able to take over for him."

Andrew watched his arm float out to hand the pen back to Little Billy. "What do you think I'm going to do for you?"

"Help me blow one of the *coils* to kingdom fucking come."

Andrew canted forward. Little Billy braced him with a palm against his chest.

"Go home and rest, Andy. Before you fall over. We'll talk again soon."

"Rest." The word felt fat in his mouth, something that had to be spit out in a wad.

"Rest. Do you have to work tomorrow?"

Did he? Andrew thought for a moment. The answer rose slowly, a cognitive bubble in mental syrup. "Yes. B shift."

He was retreating from the world once again, sinking beneath waters tinged pink with pain. His head throbbed. The back of his thighs throbbed. He planted his legs and fought the sway rocking him from side to side.

Little Billy had asked him a question. He blinked hard. "What?"

"Where do you live?"

Andrew mumbled the name of the motel, the room number, maybe a street name. He couldn't be sure. The words dribbled down his chin and dripped to the pavement.

An arm was around him. No, wait. Andrew's arm was around a shoulder. He couldn't remember when that had happened. He was in front of his car, and he couldn't remember that either, how he had gotten there. Were there keys in his hand?

There were.

He dropped them and stared into a white, featureless sky. There was another sky somewhere, one with an infected, blood blister sun, hot and swollen. The world brightened, dimmed, brightened, dimmed, and as he spiraled downward, he heard a faint moaning, both mechanical and organic, whispering from a hole at the bottom of his mind, a hole a little larger than it had been just a few hours before.

Six

Little Billy swung awkwardly through the motel door with Andrew Tate dangling at his side. John Tate's son had regained consciousness twice during the drive, each time glancing around groggily to mutter a few syllables before drifting off again. Little Billy had a deepening suspicion the man was suffering the effects of *squim* toxin. Andrew hadn't told him he'd been injured, but his rapid slide into delirium, the twitching in his arms and legs, the purple rash blooming across his neck, all matched Little Billy's own symptoms after being slashed.

If he was right, Andrew was in for a long, ball-twisting night. The timing was right, assuming he had been wounded at the park. *Squim* venom took effect slowly but relentlessly, cranking up and up and up. Thankfully, it dissipated quickly after reaching peak toxicity. If Andrew's experience was like his own, he would be back on his feet in twelve hours with little more than a lingering headache and low-grade nausea. *If* this was *squim* venom. And *if* everyone reacted the same.

Big ifs.

Little Billy kicked the door shut behind them and together he and Andrew shambled across the room to the unmade bed. He lowered the other man face-down onto the tousled sheets and eased a pillow under his head.

First thing first. If this was a toxic reaction, he probably got swiped across the back of the leg, where his own, long-healed scar ran in a puckered diagonal from the nook of his left knee to a few inches above the ankle. Had he warned Andrew about the *squims'* fondness for targeting the tendons of the hamstrings? He was pretty sure he had, but in the panic of flight, warnings were seldom enough.

Gently, Little Billy lifted the cuff of Andrew's right pant leg, exposing a bandaged calf. The wound had been covered with an antiseptic pad held in place by tightly wrapped medical gauze. The dressing looked professional, something a paramedic would do. He lifted the left cuff and found an identical bandage. An inch or two higher, and the bastards would have succeeded in bringing him down.

Although the flesh around the wounds was obviously inflamed, Little Billy saw nothing seeping from the bandages, no blood, no puss. He touched the skin with the back of his fingers. The flesh was warm, but not hot. Of course, infection wasn't the main danger.

"Andy. Andy, can you hear me?"

Andrew's eyes fluttered open briefly.

"Andy, you've having a reaction. From the cuts along the back of your legs. *Squim* toxin."

Andrew's head rocked against the pillow. Little Billy wasn't sure if it was an indication he had heard and understood, or simply a shudder of pain.

"I've gone through the same thing myself. Not going to lie to you, you're in for a hell of a night. But if your experience is anything like mine, you'll come out on the other side with no permanent damage." William ran his hand slowly down the back of his leg.

"'Cept for the scars, of course. I think maybe this toxin is intended to incapacitate rather than kill. Could be their prey is usually much bigger than themselves."

Little Billy blew out a long breath of exasperation and raked his fingers through his hair. He was beginning to slip back into his old way of thinking, back before The Great Divide. When was the last time he used the word "incapacitate"? On the street, you didn't incapacitate shit. You kept pounding until the fucker stopped coming at you. Or stopped moving altogether.

Stepping into the bathroom, Little Billy found a dank washcloth draped over the towel rack. He soaked it with cool water from the tap, wrung it out and pressed it against the back of Andrew's neck.

At least the professor's son wouldn't have to face this alone, as Little Billy had, moaning and groveling in the litter-strewn embankment beneath a highway overpass as the fever took hold and the dead came drifting out of the night to stand in silent accusation around him, first Bobby with his missing left arm and his unspooled intestines dragging in the dirt, then, Mr. and Mrs. Felton, their throats opened to their sternums, their faces a ragged mass of dangling flesh, and then...

"Christ."

Little Billy returned to the sink and splashed water onto his face until his beard dripped and the runoff soaked his neck and chest. He knew the memories of that gore-strewn backyard couldn't be washed away, but they could be submerged, push beneath the dark mud of thoughts sloshing thickly against the inside of his skull. At least for a little while. He wiped his face with a towel that smelled faintly of booze and returned to the bedroom.

"I'm going to stick around for the rest of the night. Try and keep you as comfortable as possible."

If Andrew heard, he gave no indication. His breathing was shallow and rapid, and beneath purple lids, his eyes darted, following whatever dark visions the toxin had conjured from his past.

"Good news is, you only have to go through this once. You should be immune to their venom after this." Little Billy dragged a chair from the kitchen and placed it next to the bed. He eased into it with a grunt and stretched his long legs out in front of him. "Bad news is, it's going to cost you. Quite a lot. But that shouldn't come as a surprise." Glancing around the dismal rooms, his eyes fell to the kitchenette's small trashcan heaped with empties. "I got a feeling you already know everything comes at a price."

THE MAN WHO HAD ONCE THOUGHT OF HIMSELF AS William Phipps still remembered his life before The Great Divide, but he was finding it more and more difficult to convince himself *those* memories were real. He was fairly certain he'd had a normal childhood growing up in Temple Terrace with Mirabelle, his younger sister, and an older brother, Oscar, named after a beloved great-uncle on his mother's side. He remembered attending St. Lawrence for eight years, Tampa Catholic for four more. As a child, he'd had a passion for soccer and baseball, lettering in the latter during high school, although he hadn't been quite good enough to attend college on an athletic scholarship—the scouts agreed his fielding was great, thanks in part to his six-foot-six height and ninety-two-inch reach—but his batting average was middling at best.

He remembered taking his parents' advice and staying in town for college, attending the University of Tampa on a partial academic scholarship where he majored in zoology and minored in psychology.

He'd had a vague notion of someday becoming the next Jane Goodall, only maybe specializing in crows or pigs instead of chimps. Pigs were extremely intelligent, ranked fourth among mammals right after humans, chimps, and dolphins. And crows were right behind them. William liked the notion of such common creatures possessing unexpected capabilities, of the extraordinary lurking just below the everyday, staring out from the seemingly mundane, awaiting discovery.

He remembered the first time he'd laid eyes on Laura, how she had paused in the doorway for an instant to survey the classroom, how her glance had passed through him without pause before turning to the chalkboard with the words BIOLOGICAL DIVERSITY 201 written in block letters across the center. And yet she had sat in the desk next to his, even though the room was still nearly empty. He'd doodled in his notebook for several minutes as the chairs filled, feigning indifference while attempting to study her out of the corner of an eye. Auburn hair pulled into a ponytail and tumbling to the seatback. A freckled shoulder. One long leg, bare, ending in a white sneaker.

He wanted more than the brief glance of her face he'd caught from the doorway and was thinking up some casual question he could ask her that wouldn't come across as creepy or pathetic, when she leaned over and said, "Tell me your name isn't Tim."

"My name isn't Tim." The blue of her eyes could not be contained. It seemed to reflect off her pale cheeks and shimmer over the bridge of her freckled nose. His first impression of her features was glacial, an Arctic landscape of snow-softened details accented by the ethereal cobalt glow of ocean ice. The room pitched lightly and righted itself, and William gripped the desktop to keep from sliding to the floor.

"Good," she said. She pulled the band from her hair and gathered the strands again with her fingers. "I couldn't stand sitting next to someone whose frat brothers called him Tiny Tim. What is it with tall guys and nicknames?"

William watched, fascinated, as she re-tamed her hair and cinched the band once more. To have those locks fall around his face as she hovered above him, tenting them both in a private place of lips and whispers and unbroken gazes. He pressed his back against his chair and reminded himself to breathe.

"Or short guys," she added after a pause. "If you were five-three and a hundred-and-ten pounds soaking wet they'd call you Bruiser, or Stilts, or Bull, or Big Al."

"Most people just call me Will. And I'm not in a fraternity." He didn't mention that since overtaking his brother in height, Oscar had started calling him Little Billy.

On an intellectual level, Little Billy understood all these things had happened. He understood he had met Laura on the first day of class in his sophomore year and that they had dated throughout college. He remembered the scare in their junior year when she was a week-and-a-half late and the mixture of relief and disappointment when it turned out to be a false alarm.

He understood he had excelled in his classes enough to attract the attention of the dean of the school of biology, that Dr. Tate had taken him under his wing and encouraged him to apply to the nation's top universities for grad school, promising a letter of recommendation that would make any admission board swoon.

He understood he'd been accepted at Duke, that his father bought him a used Audi with low mileage as a graduation gift, and that he and Laura had driven up to Durham one weekend in May to scout out apartments.

And he understood that Dr. Tate had offered him the opportunity to participate in a little summer project he was planning, a CV builder with minimal leg-work, a job right here in Tampa that wouldn't take more than a weekend or two of fieldwork.

He remembered all these things happening, but they were on the far side of The Great Divide, and the more he tried to solidify the details, the more unreal they became. To feel the satisfying punch of a baseball hitting the center of a mitt, to drive a car—one that he actually owned—to a supermarket, a movie theater, to sleep every night indoors, to have a family he could visit, parents he could talk to, a woman he loved and planned to grow old with. For years, he would dream about what he had lost, every morning waking somewhere new, somewhere a little farther from Tampa, until he was no longer certain where dream ended and reality began.

If it weren't for the faded picture of Laura he kept in his wallet, he doubted he would remember the details of her face. The snow would have erased everything, even the iceberg gleam of her eyes. Little Billy had decided long ago if that ever happened, he would tie a cement block around his neck and walk into the nearest body of water.

Until then, however, he would have to live on this side of the Divide, the side where otherworldly gastropods denned in the flowerbeds of public libraries and living pincushions floated unnoticed in the grassy

83

mediums of four-lane highways. The side where everything that mattered most—a new fiancée, grad school, a future free of guilt and toxic nightmares—could all vanish one bright summer afternoon in a backyard drenched in blood.

FOR NEARLY AN HOUR, ANDREW'S MOANS HAD BEEN LOW but constant, soft exhalations of discomfort escaping between the seams of an unquiet doze. Now they rose in intensity, sharpening into exclamations of protest, cries of anguish. There were words as well, no longer a mush of syllables but a series of pleas and angry negations. One word, in particular, called over and over, sometimes with a tremble of tears, sometimes in alarm, but mostly in a long wail of despair: Anna. The first few times Andrew's agitation crescendoed, Little Billy had attempted to wake him, but there was no breaking through the delirium. He was locked in his own hell now, and the most Little Billy could do was make sure he didn't harm himself as he flailed and thrashed.

Anna. He remembered the girl in the purple bathing suit. Chestnut hair braided down her back, green eyes like something off a magazine cover, dimpled chin an exact miniature of her father's. Did he realize how much she favored him, especially around the nose and mouth? The type of child whose adult features were already apparent, lurking just beneath the soft contours of pre-adolescence.

And of course, the scars. He remembered those as well, covering her right arm up to the shoulder, still pink and shining. Skin graphs. The girl had obviously suffered severe burns recently. Maybe within the last year. He was beginning to suspect those injuries had something to do with her father.

Guilt.

Little Billy rose and crossed to the window, lowered a blind with a fingertip and peered out at the mostly-empty parking lot. Everyone has their share. He'd come to understand that very well over the years. Most of the time it's kept hidden, the little acts of cruelty: the classmate tripped on the schoolyard, the coworker blamed for our own screw-up, the candy bar slipped into a pocket at the convenience store. But sometimes the guilt is too big, the wrongs too monstrous to hide. Sometimes everyone knows what you've done.

Or thinks they do.

After all, when the policed arrive at a crime scene and find a man covered in blood ranting about monsters amid the shredded remains of four bodies, it's fairly obvious who the guilty party is. And if you somehow manage to survive their accusations, avoid their reprisals, it's not because you're innocent. It's only because you've played the system well enough to squirm out of the noose you so richly deserve. But what then? Crawl away on your belly. Crawl, because that's what murdering worms do. They burrow through the filth until they're buried, until not a single piece of them is visible to the respectable, civilized world.

Little Billy let the blinds fall back into place, reducing the late-afternoon light to a few thin ribbons slanting across the threadbare carpet. It would be dark soon. And then the long night would begin. Andrew was quiet for the moment, but that wouldn't last. The *bilantu* were diurnal. Little Billy smiled. The word had bubbled up effortlessly.

"Diurnal," he said aloud, relishing the feel of it in his mouth. Active during the day. During the bright hours monsters were supposed to shun. But there were *other* things in the dark, worse things maybe. A daughter with burn scars across her arms, for instance. Or a fiancée who drags herself from the grave to stand silently under a highway overpass as the man she once loved and trusted, the man who got her entire family slaughtered on a cheerful, cloudless Saturday afternoon, writhed in the grip of his toxic dreams.

THE DAY WILLIAM CROSSED THE GREAT DIVIDE WAS HOT and bright, a typical August afternoon in Florida. There would be rain later, there always was this time of year. The storms would drop the temperature ten, fifteen degrees and wring some of the moisture out of

85

the air, but for once he wasn't thinking about the stifling heat and the promised relief of late-afternoon thunderstorms. He was too restless to feel the sweat soaking his shirt and stinging his eyes.

No, that wasn't quite right. He *could* feel it, but he savored the discomfort, relished it. Didn't every great discoverer experience some kind of distress in the field? Darwin was seasick during most of his eighteen months on the *Beagle*. Amundsen lost a good part of both heels to frostbite during his trek to the South Pole. Hell, Marie and Pierre Curie eventually died from their pioneering research with radiation. Sweating in the August heat was laughably trivial compared to those, but he would make note of the temperature in his journal, a document he had come to believe would one day be held in the same historical esteem as Darwin's *Voyage*.

"How long?" Dr. Tate asked. They were both lying on their bellies in the grass at the Lowry Park Zoo band shell. Across the street, families ambled from the parking lot toward the zoo entrance, happy and oblivious of the things lurking unseen all around them. William doubted he would ever get used to the juxtaposition of the mundane and the exotic, the blandly every-day and the breathtakingly bizarre. If they only knew the true nature of things, those moms with their strollers, those dads finishing their Cokes and fishing for their wallets at the ticket gate. Would they still be so complacent? So indifferent to their environment? Would they even dare step foot outside their front doors?

"Will?" John Tate lowered the binoculars and glanced toward William, one brow raised.

"Sorry, professor." He checked the stopwatch ticking in his hand. "Two minutes, forty seconds. Forty-one. Forty-two."

"Stay focused, Will. I want this data to be as accurate as possible. I have no intention of being out here all afternoon." He returned to the binoculars. "And for the love of Christ stop calling me 'professor.' Firstly, it makes me feel like the guy from *Gilligan's Island*. Secondly, I have a goddamn Ph.D. If you're not going to call me John, I'll have to insist you call me doctor."

Over the summer, William had gained a keen appreciation of Dr. Tate's wry and usually understated sense of humor. "Sorry, *John*."

"You really are a rather impertinent lad. I often find myself questioning your commitment to this project. Your personal hygiene as well."

William squinted toward the patch of sandy earth near the picnic shelter. The two gray squirrels were still there, one moving in twitches, digging, darting, digging some more, behaving so typically squirrel-like as to be effectively invisible. The other was up on its hind legs, diligent as a prairie dog, watching, always watching, ready to sound the alarm if it was fortunate enough to see the threat before it was too late. In the four weeks since they had begun their observations, he and John had witnessed thirty-four hunts. They seldom ended well for the squirrels. One in five might get away. The rest ended up a meal for any one of the eight new species they had discovered over the summer. Eight! And they were still finding more. It was getting so easy to see them now. He hardly had to strain at all. How could he have been so blind before? How could any of them have been so blind?

"It's happening!" Tate shifted forward on his elbows. "The guard's agitated. It's doing the spin. Mark the time."

William checked the stopwatch again and penciled 3:32 in the notebook next to the words "SPIN STARTS". The spin was what they called the whirling immediately prior to a strike, as if the squirrel knew something deadly was approaching but not from which direction.

He shielded his eyes with his free hand and strained to witness the kill. It would be fast. That never varied. Sometimes it came from above, a blur of undulating, flange-like wings as an *ectokete* plucked up its dinner. Sometimes it came from a nearby tree when a *fidelax* used its yard-long flagellum to lasso a victim. And sometimes it came from beneath the ground, although he and John had yet to glimpse whatever was burrowing through the soil.

Even from this distance, he could hear the spinning squirrel's sudden chirps of alarm, but though its foraging companion darted toward the trees immediately, it didn't make it past the nearest picnic table before vanishing in a puff of fur and blood.

"Time!"

William checked the watch. "Four minutes, seventeen seconds. What was it?"

"*Apperix*. Big one. Three, maybe three-and-a-half feet long. Took the second animal with a flick of its uropod."

"Hard to believe squirrels haven't gone extinct by now." He wrote the time in the notebook. Four minutes, seventeen seconds from leaving the tree to being devoured. Dr. Tate's theory appeared to be correct. At least so far. If a kill was going to be made, it was going to happen in the first five minutes of exposure. They had never witnessed a strike taking longer than—William riffled quickly through the notebook—four minutes, forty-seven seconds. If the squirrels made it to the five-minute mark without being taken, they were safe. Why this was, was still a mystery, but he had no doubt they would ferret out an answer sooner or later.

Their research was only just beginning. They both had the rest of their lives to study this vast, unsuspected ecosystem, this *shadow biosphere* covertly coexisting within the natural one.

William closed the notebook thoughtfully. The natural one. The thought had been so matter-of-fact he was a little surprised it had given him pause. The natural ecosystem. *Our* ecosystem. It implied a fundamental differentiation between the everyday world of people and parks and squirrels and birds and everything else we considered part of life on our planet, and *them*. That these creatures, which both he and John had begun referring to collectively as the *bilantu offalate*, were not of this planet was becoming increasingly obvious, at least to William.

It wasn't just their unheard-of morphology with its often confounding locomotion, their tendency toward epidermal translucency, their seeming defiance of gravitation constraints (how did the damn *votasin* manage to float like that, were they filled with helium?). It was their aura of otherness, their complete disconnection from everything around them, as if they were four-dimensional creatures hovering a few inches above our three-dimensional world. William could actually feel their alienness as a subtle pressure against the hollow places of his skull, his sinuses and inner ear, the corners of his eyes, the gaps between his teeth. He knew Dr. Tate felt it was well, although he claimed otherwise.

"I think we've done enough today," John said, rising to his knees with an exaggerated groan of exhaustion. "I promised my wife I'd be home by four. If I'm late for my kid's Little League game one more time, she's going to change the locks on me."

When they had begun their study of the local urban squirrel population at the behest of Tampa Electric, John had described it as a few weekends of surveying, getting a sense of their numbers and distribution, especially around particularly vulnerable utility assets. Three substations had been damaged in the previous nine months due to chewed-through cables, the perpetrators' remains nothing but blackened husks by the time the linemen arrived, and the company wanted a better sense of what they were up against. The two of them would be noting dietary trends, foraging habits.

It was kid's stuff, really, nothing particularly taxing, but how often did you get the chance to poke around the urban/suburban environment while getting paid for it? And who knows, they might even end up with enough original observations to get a paper published. A minor paper, mind you. They were studying squirrels after all, but it would be another line on his CV.

He'd have been foolish to turn down the opportunity to do field research the summer before starting grad school. But he almost had, weighing the benefit of the experience against several lost weekends with Laura and finding the scale tipped decidedly toward his new fiancée. In the end, of course, he had accepted Dr. Tate's offer, but he should probably mention his near-refusal in the journal. It would add a nice element of early precariousness to his later fame, a recognition that he had very nearly missed the boat.

"Let's sit in the shade, do a quick review of last week's data and call it a day." Tate pointed toward the picnic shelter.

Halfway across the park, William cleared his throat. "Summer's going fast. Hard to believe it's August."

John grunted, but did not look up from his own notebook filled with drawings and hastily scrawled observations.

William hesitated until they had reached the shelter and settled onto a picnic bench before adding, "Only a few more weeks before I'm off to Duke."

"Your next adventure begins. But no stories about your summer exploits."

"No. No." They had agreed early on not to say anything about their astonishing discoveries until Dr. Tate was ready to formally announce their findings, a promise William had promptly broken, making Laura a sort of silent partner in their pursuits.

John would flip if he knew he had been telling his fiancée everything, even teaching her how to see the creatures (she was nearly as apt at finding them as William was), but the truth was, he didn't entirely trust that Dr. Tate would make mention of his undergraduate assistant when he went public with one of the biggest scientific discovery of the century. John had assured him they would be partners in all subsequent announcements, that both their names would appear on the papers they would publish, the books they would write. But William found it a little hard to believe a doctor of biology and department dean would be so gracious as to elevate a lowly undergraduate to the rank of partner, even a junior one.

Laura was his insurance policy if John decided to take full credit for everything. She had come up with the idea of mailing herself letters describing each week's discoveries and depositing the sealed envelopes in a safety deposit box at her bank. Hopefully, the postmark date and the bank's deposit records would be enough to convince anyone he had been in on the discoveries from the very beginning. He wanted to believe it wouldn't come to that, but now that he was going off to grad school...

"It's just." William tapped his notebook against the tabletop. "I can't help wondering if leaving when we're making so much progress is a good idea."

90

Dr. Tate removed his floppy-brimmed sunhat and mopped his face with a handkerchief. "What are you saying? You don't want to go to graduate school?"

"More like a postponement. I could always start next year, after we go public."

"Will, it's three weeks before the start of the semester. You think you can just call them and say you want to push everything back a year? It doesn't work that way."

William said nothing for nearly a minute. Off to the right, a *fidelax* clung to the trunk of a sprawling live oak, pulsing in that unnerving way they did before a strike. He watched as it slowly pivoted around its central stalk. He could almost have reached out and grabbed it, it was so close. Another squirrel was about to bite it. Or a bird. Or a lizard. A monster had to eat, didn't it? Thing was, the eyes appeared to be staring back at him. He shifted slightly to the left and could have sword the orbs drifted to follow his motion.

"You're serious about this?" Tate had been writing something in his notebook. Now he looked up with a puzzled frown.

"I can't imagine learning more in a classroom than I am out here with you. I mean," he slid his own notebook back and forth between his hands. "This is revolutionary work we're doing. It's going to change everything. I don't want to walk away from that."

Something flittered at the corner of William's eye, Dr. Tate fanning himself with his hat, maybe, but he kept his gaze on his own slowly drumming fingers. What did John expect, that he would just march off like a good grad student and put all this on the backburner? Would Darwin have done that? Would Linnaeus? Mendel?

"You won't be walking away, Will. We'll be in constant contact. And don't forget, there'll be more research to do in North Carolina. We have no idea how widespread this ecosystem is. Is it just a local phenomenon? Regional? Global? You'll be our eyes and ears up there." The fanning slowed, then stopped altogether. John tossed the hat on the table and

William felt a slight puff of air as it settled next to his arm. "Or is this about something else?"

So here we are, he thought. He hadn't realized until the moment was upon him how much he wanted this confrontation, how much he needed to voice his concerns. He would be addressing Dr. Tate as an equal for the first time, and it gave him a giddy sense of self-worth. He was about to cross a line that would fundamentally change everything between them and it felt right. Overdue, even. But as he squared his shoulders and began to turn, something whipped his cheek hard enough to send him careening off the bench and crashing to the ground.

LITTLE BILLY WOKE WITH A START. FOR A LONG, confounding moment he had no idea where he was. Somewhere inside, obviously, and that was odd. He hadn't slept with a roof over his head for two, maybe three weeks now. But this wasn't a homeless shelter. He glanced around the dreary room. A motel then. Not a very good one.

Think, damn it. Think! He had been dreaming about the day everything came crashing down, but that was years ago. Now he was ... here.

But where was here? Cement-block walls stained yellow from years of cigarette smoke. No help. Battered, Seventies-era furniture. Nothing. A faded print above the bed of mountains nearly lost in a gray haze of accumulated dust. Zip. Then his eyes fell to the trash, filled with empty liquor bottles and everything came back with a hot jolt.

This was Andrew's place. Andrew Tate. Son of John Tate. John had called him back to Tampa last month because the shit was about to hit the fan. The *bilantu* were getting more and more aggressive as they sensed the approach of their old masters. The *xalantracoils* were pulsing back to life. And Andrew had been wounded by a *squim*. He was...

Little Billy glanced at the bed and jerked to his feet with a breathy "oh." Just sour sheets and flat pillows. No Andrew.

Turning on his heel, he went to the window and yanked back the blinds. It was dark now, the parking lot bathed in the amber glow of sodium-vapor streetlights. Andrew's car was still where Little Billy had parked it, one of the few in the lot. He let the blinds fall back and checked his watch: ten forty-five. He'd been asleep for nearly three hours. Could Andrew have left the motel without waking him? It didn't seem likely, and yet here he was, alone in a room silent except for the buzzing ceiling lamp, the soft thump of an occasional insect striking the door and the faint drip of water.

Little Billy crossed to the bathroom. The drip swelled to the steady hiss of the shower. He eased into the dark room and after a moment of patting blindly at the wall found the light switch. Andrew was lying fully clothed in the tub. When the overhead fluorescents pinged to life, he threw an arm over his eyes and groaned.

"You scared the shit out of me. Thought you might have wandered away while I was dozing."

Andrew slowly eased his hand away from the top of his face and squinted at Little Billy through the stream of water. He appeared to be locked in some sort of internal debate, his head ticking ever-so-slightly back and forth. After several seconds, he wiped the water from his eyes with a trembling palm. "Are you real?"

Little Billy offered what he hoped was a reassuring smile and eased down on the closed lid of the toilet. "Real as you."

"Should that relieve me?" He tilted his head and blinked though water-beaded lids. "You *seem* real. What about Anna?"

"You saw your little girl here tonight?"

Andrew sniffed wetly. "She seemed real, too. But she couldn't have been. Her arm and neck. They looked like they did the day she was burned, skin hanging in tatters. Her arm." He covered his face again, this time with both hands. "God, it was swollen. I thought it would split down the middle."

Little Billy reached over and turned off the water. "Your daughter wasn't real." He held out the booze-smelling towel and waited until Andrew took it. "You were hallucinating. From the *squim* toxin. The wounds on the back of your legs."

"I heard this before." He rubbed his face and draped the towel over his head. "Thought I was dreaming."

"No. You still have about six hours until the effects wear off. At least, that's the way it was for me."

"You mean she could come back?"

Little Billy hunched, rested his elbows on his knees and stared at the grimy black and white tiles between his feet. "What's the line from that movie everyone used to quote? 'I see dead people?' When I was in the grip of this shit, I saw dead people all night long."

"Anna's not dead."

Little Billy was encouraged by the anger in Andrew's reply. It suggested he was, for the most part, in the here and now. But for how long?

"Sorry. Bad choice of words. I didn't mean to upset you."

The silence stretched out for nearly thirty seconds, each man lost in his own dark memories, or so Little Billy assumed. He rubbed his cheek, feeling the raised flesh of the scar beneath his beard. Had the *fidelax* struck two inches higher it would have taken out his eye. His body was a canvas of battle scars mapping out two decades of life on the border of the *bilantu's* awareness, a threshold he never crossed without paying a toll.

John Tate had his share of scars as well. But neither of them had ever paid a price as high as Laura and her family. Even as he and John had been cowering in the park's men's room, waiting for dark and the retreat of the *bilantu*, his fiancée and her family were being cut down. He had imagined the scene over and over, adjusting the details until it fell into some sort of mental slot and solidified into a memory as real as any other.

She had shown them how to see the *bilantu*, just as he had shown her. Must have. The four of them would have been in the backyard, her dad at the grill, her brother kicking a hacky sack under the big magnolia. Mom would have been reading under the pergola, a glass of sweating lemonade in one hand. And Laura in the porch swing, bored and playful, deciding this lazy afternoon was the perfect time to share her secret. It would be fun.

And her family would keep the secret once she explained how important discretion was until Dr. Tate went public with the big announcement. She couldn't wait to see the look on their faces when she casually pointed out the *quintaloch* crouched against the fence, the *polyglanite* wrapped around the flagpole. They would stand amazed as she showed them all the incredible creatures sharing their own backyard. So many. Look. Look! They're just as curious about us. They're coming to investigate.

"It was my fault."

Little Billy shook himself out of Laura's yard.

"Sorry?"

"Anna's injuries. My fault. I was supposed to be watching her. Instead, I let her pull a pot of boiling water down on herself."

Little Billy inhaled slowly and leaned back until his shoulders touched the toilet's tank. "Accidents happen. You can't watch kids every second."

Andrew snorted in contempt. "I was drunk. Passed out on the couch. I'd put the water on to make her some macaroni and cheese for lunch and forgot all about it."

"At least she's alive. And she seemed happy enough in the park." Little Billy tilted his head back and contemplated the ceiling tiles. "It could have been worse. Much worse."

"You know I actually blamed my father for a long time. Blamed him for my drinking. If he hadn't filled my head with his monster stories." Andrew rubbed his forehead and dragged his fingers down the side of his face. "Kept warning me they were out there. Kept telling me to stay vigilant. Stay vigilant, but don't go looking for them; don't stare too long at the tree line, or a telephone pole with odd shadings, or a puddle rippling on a still day.

"What kind of shit is that to feed a twelve-year-old? There are monsters out there, son, and the best way to avoid them is to pretend they don't exist. Thanks, Dad. And by the way, you're clearly out of your fucking mind."

Little Billy brought his hands together between his knees. "He was afraid total ignorance would be worse. Lots of people go missing every year, just disappear off the face of the earth. We think many of them may have learned how to see what's really around them. And then they can't stop seeing. They look and look and look and sooner or later, the *bilantu* look back."

"Well, it didn't work for me. His warning. Or it did." Andrew settled deeper in the tub, the shower curtain crinkling around him. "I don't know. After twenty years of thinking he was a nut case, I started seeing things myself. Out of the corner of my eye. Something would move. It'd turn. Nothing. Something in front of me would change, somehow, and for the life of me I couldn't figure out what it was. It kept getting worse. If I never drank I might have worried I had a tumor growing in my head, making me hallucinate.

"But I've been drinking since high school. Never thought I had a problem. Guess I did, though, because my first thought was the booze. The booze fucking with my vision. So, what did I do? Swear off alcohol? Turn over a new leaf? Hell no. I started drinking more."

Andrew waved his hand through the air in front of his face as if shooing away an insect.

"Yeah, I know. But it seemed to work. At least at first. A few extra nips helped me ignore all the things I was almost seeing. A little later, drinking stopped me from worrying that I was losing my mind. And after that…" Andrew slapped his sodden thigh. "After that, it just helped me. To relax after a shift. Forget the things I saw at work. Helped me see my wife like I used to see her, when we were first dating and she was the most beautiful damn thing in the world."

An image of Laura as he had last seen her flashed before him, and Little Billy flinched. He needed the picture in his wallet to remember her as she had been in life, but how she had appeared in death was seared across the inner lining of his eyelids.

"If my old man hadn't filled my head with monsters, maybe I never would have started drinking in the first place. If I'd never started drinking,

I never would have fallen asleep on the couch and left the water boiling on the front burner. If Anna hadn't been burned, my wife would still think I'm a good father. A good husband."

Andrew pulled the towel off his head and tossed it against the opposite wall.

"A good man. And if she still though all those things, she wouldn't have turned to my former partner for help getting through to me. He wouldn't have felt obligated to confront me about the drinking, threaten to go to the chief if I didn't get help because, let's face it, a drunk EMT is a threat to everyone around him, not just his family."

Andrew closed his eyes and rattled off the rest in a rapid, sing-song lilt, his hand swaying from side-to-side, revealing each new step of his decline with a magician's flourish. "I wouldn't have gone off the deep end and accused him of fucking Grace, or at least wanting to. I wouldn't have made such a scene half the station gathered around to watch. I wouldn't have taken a swing at a man who, five minutes earlier I considered my best friend. I wouldn't have been put on probation and moved to a new station. And I wouldn't have moved out of the house so I could hole up here and drink and feel sorry for myself."

Andrew opened bloodshot eyes to regard Little Billy. "And it all started with my father. You see the logic in that, right?"

A cold, merciless smile yanked Little Billy's mouth up and to the left, pulling his scarred cheek taut. For a moment, he thought he might leap across the bathroom and clamp his hands around Andrew's throat screaming, "I lost everything; your father lost everything," over and over, each word punctuated with the dull thump of Andrew's head striking the lip of the tub. Instead, he squeezed his hands until the cords of his forearms ached and waited for the red wave to pass. When it had, he plucked up the towel and tossed it back into Andrew's face.

"This thing isn't over. You may want to hold on to that until morning." Andrew pulled the towel off his head and gave Little Billy an unfocused frown. He was sliding back into delirium. Already, his breathing had shallowed and quickened. Little Billy hadn't realized how quickly the turns came. Lucid one moment. Ranting the next. So like the schizophrenics he had met on the streets, the broken outcasts living on the fringe, there but not there. The *bilantu* weren't the only things the modern mind had learned to un-see.

"Whyareyouhere?" Andrew slurred. The trembling had returned in his hands. His dilated eyes studied Little Billy steadily, but who was he seeing? His scarred daughter? His wounded wife? Or maybe his father, the man who had filled his head with all those bad thoughts and then stayed away so his son would have at least a chance of surviving into adulthood? Little Billy slid off the toilet lid and knelt next to the tub, leaning in close, forcing Andrew to retreat against the shower curtain.

"I'm here, Andy, because your dad asked me to come. You and me, we have a mission."

"Mission." Andrew repeated, his chin sinking toward his chest.

"Mission," Little Billy agreed.

Andrew's eyes fluttered.

"Your dad hoped destroying one of the *xalantracoils* would break the circuit, keep them from opening the door." Little Billy couldn't help breaking into a broad, vicious grin as he brought his lips to the other man's ear. "Now," he whispered, "we're going to finish what he started."

Part 2: Detonation

Seven

The meeting was already in progress when Andrew slipped into the common room the next morning with his duffel bag slung over one shoulder. Fifteen minutes late for B shift, he'd hoped to make a quiet entrance through the bay, dart into the locker room, gulp a few migraine-strength Excedrin and lay low until the worst of the nausea and headache passed. Instead, he nearly plowed into his station captain presiding in front of a semi-circle of firefighters. Hamilton stopped mid-sentence and gave Andrew a terse nod.

"Good of you to join us, Andy."

He felt the rake of a dozen set of eyes on him and mumbled an apology as he edged around the gathered squad and settled in the back of the room. Sid Langston made a show of slowly turning to regard Andrew with uncloaked contempt before turning back to Hamilton. Gary touched his shoulder and mouthed, "You okay?"

Andrew waved him off.

"So basically," the captain resumed after a few calculating seconds, "we're in a wait-and-see situation. As of now, the DOF guys feel they have things under control. A thousand acres may sound like a lot to us, but from what I've been told it's no big deal when it comes to wildfires. If the winds pick up and shift our way, however." Hamilton surveyed his audience. "Things could go south fast, and I mean that literally. We're talking Lutz. We're talking New Tampa. With the tree canopy we have in this city, we're even talking downtown in a worst-case scenario."

Andrew resisted the urge to give his head a clarifying shake. He'd heard nothing about a local wildfire during his days off, not that he had been paying much attention.

Now he was standing in the back of the room, feeling as if he was tardy for class on the day of a pop quiz. From behind his sunglasses and without turning his head, he surveyed the firefighters to either side of him. Clare Humbert was on the left, listing to Hamilton with her hands clasped behind her back, her legs slightly apart in the "at ease" pose typical of so many of the station's ex-military.

To his right was Gary, eyes on the floor, head tilted as if the captain's words were spiraling into his brain via a funnel in his left ear.

Andrew struggled to absorb what Hamilton was saying. Something about possible joint training operations with DOF and county firefighters. Something about urban firebreaks. Didn't have to worry about those yet, but special ops were in preliminary planning stages. Something about the *vintumalu ab'ha fintos*. About the har'uu *cosh rhysillus Yog-Sothoth. Iä! Shub-Niggurath!*

Andrew's head jerked, sending a silver sliver of pain down his neck and into his shoulders. But even as he realized the voices had returned, he understood the last utterance had been howled through a rapidly closing aperture. This time the connection had lasted only a few seconds, but the throats that had uttered those burbling exclamations, throats like sewer pipes lined with downward-pointing spikes, had been closer.

So much closer.

He pressed his lips together to keep from groaning and reached up to massage the tendons at the base of his skull. Although it had been less than a dozen words, this communication was different from the previous one, more concise, more focused. No, that wasn't quite right. It was more directed, as if the things his father and Little Billy called the *vetro offalate* were not bellowing to anyone who could hear, but rather speaking to a specific individual. Even worse, Andrew was almost certain the word, "*Iä*," meant "quickly." How the hell did he know that?

"Yes, Andy?"

Andrew glanced up. The room had fallen silent once again.

"Captain?"

"You have a question?"

Andrew realized Hamilton had misinterpreted the movement of his hand to the base of his neck as an arm raised in question. If he begged off now, he would appear distracted, indifferent. He could already hear Sid's snort, his unspoken confirmation that yes, Andrew Tate had staggered to work hung over and barely functioning.

Yet again.

In desperation, he flung out the first question he could think of: "Evacuation timetables?"

Hamilton shook his head. "Still too soon to think about that."

Andrew pressed on, sensing more was required if he wanted to avoid appearing caught off guard.

"My in-laws had a little summer cottage just north of Sedona. Five years ago, they lost it in the Slide Fire." Grace's parents lived in Virginia and had never, so far as he knew, set foot in Arizona. But a hot exhilaration swelled as the lie began to coalesce before him, and the more the ruse thickened and set, the more his confidence grew.

"Twelve hours before the fire swept down the valley they asked the authorities if they should evacuate and were told they still had days before the front reached them. *If* it reached them." He carefully removed his sunglasses before addressing not just Hamilton, but the entire room. "They barely made it out. If the dog hadn't gone ballistic..." Andrew raised his hands.

The captain gave him a small nod. "Which is why we'll be getting regular updates. Can things change in a heartbeat? Of course. But for now, we carry on as usual. Alright?" He clapped once, bringing the meeting to a close. "Good, now back to work."

102

As the other firefighters dispersed, Andrew shuffled slowly toward the locker room, reviewing his morning conversation with Little Billy. His father had been planning to blow up one of the stone pillars, one of the *xalantracoils*, before his arrest, or at the very least damage it enough so that it couldn't turn on. "Fatally wound," was how Little Billy had phrased it.

"When John called last week, he said he was nearly ready to try. All he had to do was rent some excavation equipment and move the explosives. He sounded strange, though."

Andrew had been shaving as Little Billy spoke. Now their eyes met in the medicine cabinet mirror. "Strange how?"

Little Billy tsked. "Jittery. A little paranoid. Didn't want to say exactly what he was planning out loud. I had to guess most of it."

"Worried his phone might be bugged?" Andrew asked as he resumed shaving. "Considering he was arrested a few days later, he may have been right."

"Or maybe he was worried something worse than Homeland Security was listening in."

Andrew slipped down the hall past Station Three's tiny gym (a rack of free weights, a Nautilus machine, two treadmills) and ducked into the empty locker room. It took several attempts to open the combination lock. From a nearly empty bottle, he shook three aspirin into his palm and dry-swallowed them, saying a silent prayer no bells would sound for the next twenty minutes.

Little Billy said he didn't know how long they had before the shit hit the fan. Days probably. A week at most. If they were going to do something, it would have to be soon.

"John thought maybe since you're a firefighter, you'd know where they stashed the black powder they impounded from him."

"No clue. That would be the Feds, not Tampa Fire Rescue."

"In that case, I don't suppose you know where we can get our hands on some high explosives?"

He'd shaken his head, told Little Billy he would have to chew on that one for a while, but he had immediately thought of the department warehouse at the Port of Tampa. He'd been there often on supply runs. The building held nearly everything used by the department other than special op's heavy equipment and the Schedule II narcotics, which were kept under lock and key at each station. On one of those runs, he'd noticed a number of crates under plastic sheeting sequestered to a far, dim corner. While Max loaded the pushcart with bandages and alcohol wipes, Andrew strolled over and lifted the plastic, revealing the pale blue writing stamped across the top of each box: Trenchrite.

"Got a stump you want to blow into your neighbor's yard?" Max asked.

"Strong stuff?"

"Stronger than an M-80. Not as strong as C4. Oil companies use it mostly. For seismic exploration. Didn't you pay attention during training?"

"That was many moons ago, my friend."

The warehouse was locked up tight and monitored by security cameras, but there was no on-site security, something that had mildly surprised Andrew the day he'd discovered the explosives. Of course, what firefighter in his or her right mind would steal Trenchrite from the department warehouse? Such an act would be an unconscionable breach of trust and a criminal theft that would not only end a career but also send the culprit to prison for years.

Still, if he stayed out of the floodlights, went in through a window, wore a mask. If he got in and out quickly, how long before anyone even notice a box was missing?

"I just have to know; do you even give a shit anymore?"

Sid Langston stood in the locker room doorway with his arms crossed over his chest, back pressed against one side of the threshold and legs stretched across to the other. A human barricade. Andrew wondered how long he'd been there.

"Cat got your tongue?"

Andrew continued to unpack his duffel bag, stowing his bunk gear with a deliberateness he hoped would pass for indifference. In the months since his transfer to Station Three, he'd exchanged perhaps four words with engine eleven's lieutenant. Their introduction had been brief and one-sided, Gary presenting Andrew with the mildly contrived cheerfulness a grade-school teacher would assume introducing a new student to class.

"I know who he is," Sid had responded, staring him down until Andrew lowered the hand he had raised between them. Since then, their conversations had amounted to a few muttered "excuse me"s in the break room. Even on runs together he refused to speak directly to Andrew, instead directing his remarks to Gary, a tactic that would have been laughable had it not hampered their ability to work effectively as a team. There was no place for personality conflicts when people's lives were at stake. Sid's tirade the other day was the longest commentary he had offered on the topic of Andrew Tate. At least the longest in Andrew's presence.

"I bet you think that little performance with the wacko earned you a few brownie points in the department, that somehow you're a model fire medic now. Mr. Hero. Mr. Take-Charge."

"I don't think that, Sid." He shut the locker and moved to the sink, where he washed his hands for no other reason than to delay squeezing through the exit.

"I don't think that, Sid," the other mocked in a warbling falsetto. "You fucking crack me up. You really do. I've watched you since you weaseled your way in here. Always gulping aspirin, always at the sink gargling with mouthwash. Trying to mask the smell of hooch on your breath. You think I have it out for you because you took a swing at your old partner? I don't give a rat's ass about that. Hell, if I thought someone was sleeping with my wife, I'd probably do the same.

"What pisses me off is that you can't be trusted.

"What pisses me off is that your I-don't-give-a-shit attitude puts the rest of us at risk. Us and the people we're trying to help. Does somebody have to die before you realize you need to find another line of work?"

With Sid stretched across the threshold, they were nearly the same height. Andrew approached and leaned in until their noses were inches apart. "Here's the reality of our situation," he said in a soft, even cajoling tone. "You don't like me? Fine. Don't like me. But you know what? The captain trusts me. My partner trusts me. And I don't really give a shit if you don't. I'm here and I'm here to stay. From now on, when we're out on a run I expect you to treat me with the same professional courtesy you'd treat anyone else."

"Or what?" Sid lifted his chin. "You'll take a swing at me?"

Andrew smiled. "You'd like that, wouldn't you? The last straw. The final screw-up. But it's not going to happen. You're not worth it."

Sid's expression did not change, but a minute shift of his head indicated the confrontation had ended for now. Andrew took a step back, satisfied with this minor victory in the same fleeting way he would have been had he made it through an intersection on the yellow light.

"Now get the hell out of my way."

AT THE CRASH SITE, ANDREW REALIZED THAT WHAT HE'D been smelling since the previous afternoon—a vaguely musty aroma like a hot closet filled with old clothes—wasn't a lingering memory of the *vetro's* alien atmosphere after all.

"Smell that?" Gary asked as they rolled the stretcher toward the nearest vehicle, a late model Corolla wrapped around a utility pool, steam hissing from the crumpled hood and radiator fluid pooling beneath.

"I thought I was imagining it."

"I've heard you can smell a wildfire from a hundred miles or more if the wind's right."

Off to the right, an overturned minivan blocked the road's northbound lane. Next to it, a pickup with its rear axle lying thirty yards from its demolished bed sat with its nose angled toward the sky.

"Who's our first priority?" Gary asked an approaching officer.

"Guy in the car's banged up. He's still conscious. Complaining of leg and neck pain. Got a bump on the head, too. Other drivers are standing over there in the shade. They say they're fine, but you might want to give them a once over."

The officer was about to motion them forward when a second cop approached, whispered something in his ear and nodded toward the sidewalk where the two drivers and a small gathering of onlookers lingered.

"Both of them?" the first officer asked.

"And two of the bystanders."

The cop pulled what looked like a dishrag from his belt and mopped the sweat from his face. "This is going to turn into a paperwork clusterfuck, I can see that already."

"Anything we need to know?" Andrew asked. Behind them, Sid and Clare were already dragging some of the larger pieces of debris off to the side.

"Other than people in this city losing their minds?"

"I'm blaming the heat and drought," the second officer offered. "Good an excuse as any."

"I'm beginning to seriously wonder if we're not under some sort of terrorist attack. Don't roll your eyes, Evelyn, even you have to admit the level of crazy has been off the charts for days now. That smell might not be the wildfire. They could be releasing some sort of hallucinogenic into the air from the back of vans or something."

"Gerald, you need to lay off the conspiracy websites. Next thing you'll be lining your hat with aluminum foil to keep the CIA from beaming messages into your brain."

"What's going on?" Gary angled the stretcher toward the steaming Corolla but waited for a response.

"Lot of people seeing things," Evelyn said in a low voice. "That guy," she pointed to the driver still in his car, "says he swerved into a pole because, and I'm quoting here, 'giant grasshopper creatures were jumping across the road.' We assumed drugs or alcohol, but then the woman in the van said she hit the pickup because children in monster costumes ran into the street and now the pickup driver and a couple of pedestrians are claiming a pack of deformed dogs came tearing out of that wooded lot, caused all this, then disappeared behind the strip mall."

"Well, goddamn." Gary turned to Andrew with a smile. "Maybe we *should* be wearing gas masks."

"Don't think I haven't considered it," Gerald said. "I've been seeing weird shit out of the corner of my eye for the last two days."

As Andrew and Gary wheeled the stretcher forward, a second fire engine and ambulance pulled up, followed immediately by a flatbed tow truck. The injured driver was still behind the wheel, staring out the cracked windshield with pain-glazed eyes, the deflated airbag drooping from the center of the steering wheel like a collapsed parachute. Mercifully, the air-conditioning was still laboring away, exhaling a steady current of cold air out the open driver's side door.

"Do we know his name?" Andrew asked.

Gerald pulled out a notebook, flipped it open. "Tanner. Joseph Tanner."

"Mr. Tanner," he said, taking a knee next to the door—the road's asphalt almost unbearably hot even through the cloth of his pants—and opening the cervical collar Gary handed him. "We're going to assess you real quick and get you out of there. You holding up okay?"

Tanner reached out and grasped the steering wheel, but did not turn toward Andrew. "I'm not drunk. I might be losing my mind, but I'm not drunk. You give me a breathalyzer, you'll see."

"We're just here to help, Mr. Tanner. You told the officer you're experiencing pain in your neck? How about your back?"

"They just appeared out of nowhere. One minute nothing. Then they were right in front of me. It was like they were decloaking or something. You know what I mean? Like those ships in *Star Trek*?"

"I'm going to put this collar around your neck, Mr. Tanner. Just keep still."

Tanner's gaze roved across Andrew's face as he worked. A wound above his left eye had dripped blood down his temple and cheek, but appeared to have coagulated to a gummy red fissure. When he was finished with the collar, Andrew performed an abdominal check before asking for an antiseptic bandage.

"What'd they look like?" Gary asked, crouching next to Andrew and passing him the dressing. Andrew shot him a look, but his partner ignored him.

"Like I told the cop: nightmare grasshoppers. Big legs in back, smaller ones up front. But with heads like wedges and eyes on stalks. Big as pit bulls."

"Scary."

"You have no idea."

Throughout the extraction, Andrew had to fight the urge to glance toward the wooded lot across the street or the strip mall behind them. By focusing on the task at hand, he managed to keep his eyes on his work, although he noticed both officers turning again and again toward something Andrew hoped wasn't there. As they wheeled Mr. Tanner to the ambulance, his thoughts circled back to the warehouse and the case of Trenchrite.

The first outlines of a plan were beginning to coalesce. It would be risky, of course, but waiting until his shift ended the next morning was no longer the best option. Things were moving too quickly. And too many things could go wrong attempting to break into the facility after dark. Better to enter on legitimate business and find a way to secret the Trenchrite out the front door. And that would mean...

"Andy."

He had been about to jump into the back of the ambulance after the stretcher. Gary was already behind the wheel. For an instant, he was tempted to simply leap inside and slam the doors, pretend he hadn't heard Max's voice. He'd been so preoccupied with Mr. Tanner, he hadn't noticed which station the second ambulance had been dispatched from. A confrontation with his former partner was one more complication he didn't need.

"Make it fast," he said.

"I wanted to give you a head's up. Something's brewing at your station. I don't know what, but there are a lot of rumors flying around that the hammer is about to fall there. On someone."

"On me?"

"I didn't say that. But whatever it is, it's serious. The union reps have already been called in. And legal. I'm not going to lie. There are people who expect it has something to do with you. Who *want* it to have something to do with you. Watch your back."

Andrew stepped up into the ambulance.

"And Andy."

He paused with his hand on the door.

"I thought you did good the other day, with the hostage thing I mean. You've got ice water in your veins, man."

Gary gave the air horn a blast and Andrew swung one door closed. "Max."

The other man turned back.

"Whatever's up at my station, it has nothing to do with me. But thanks for the warning."

"No problem."

"Maybe we can grab a beer sometime."

Although his eyes were unreadable behind sunglasses, the lift of Max's brows conveyed enough. "Absolutely."

Andrew swung the second door closed and slid down the bench as ambulance twenty-three lurched forward. Through the rear windows, he saw Max pivot suddenly toward the overgrown lot, his hand rising to shield his eyes from the glare. Then the ambulance turned left onto Hillsborough Avenue and Max, the accident scene and whatever else lurked there was lost behind a brown wall of desiccated scrub pines.

Eight

When they got back to the station, Andrew grabbed an inventory sheet and clipboard from the office.

"I'm going to do a quick storeroom check," he told Gary. "I poked my head in there earlier and noticed we were running low on a lot of things."

"Already? We just did a check Monday."

"You know how crazy it's been." Andrew began scanning items as an excuse to keep his eyes on the invoice, afraid his partner would read some falsehood in his expression. "That was the last cervical collar, for instance. And we're low on cotton swabs, inflatable leg splints, alcohol rubs, couple of other things."

Gary snorted. "Knock yourself out."

"Would you be up for a warehouse run later?"

"Long as you're not planning on bringing back a dozen oxygen canisters. I have no desire to drag those fuckers around on a day like today."

"We'll leave those for C shift."

In the storeroom, Andrew was relieved to discover the station really was running low on a number of items. He had been prepared to clandestinely trash supplies to make the warehouse run necessary. Now, at least, that deception was unnecessary. His relief, however, was short-lived.

As he surveyed the shelves his mind kept pin-balling between recent incidents, each one flashing and clanging before sending his thoughts off in a new direction. Max's warning: was it legitimate? Was there something about to go down at the station, and did it have something to do with him? The message that had been scrawled across his locker, for instance. Maybe the guilty party had been identified. But he'd told Gary to keep quiet. He wouldn't have blabbed. Something else then. Nothing he could do anything about, whatever it was. Waste of time dwelling on it.

The *bilantu* were becoming more aggressive. Could Tanner's "mutant grasshoppers" have been anything other than one of their breeds? How much time did they have left before the shit hit the fan?

And the voices that morning? During Captain Hamilton's briefing. Had the *vetro* been talking to someone specifically? Andrew thought they might have been. A collaborator. But who would willingly cooperate with such monstrous wills? And if he could hear their thoughts, was it possible...

Andrew's pen hovered over the sheet. Slowly, the tip sagged until it touched the paper. If he could hear their thoughts, could they hear *his*? Was he even now broadcasting his plan to them, providing all they needed to stop him? The walls and ceiling of the storeroom appeared to bow incrementally inward, the overhead lamps dim slightly as a spotlight beam of awareness swept across him. Searching. Turning their attention this way and that. Seeking his consciousness.

No. Andrew shook his head. The temporary alignment that had allowed them to broadcast earlier had slipped out of phase. He didn't know how he knew this, but he did. The *vetro* were currently unable to see into this world. Or receive anything from it. Like a child cowering under the sheets, he was spooking himself with ghost stories. He inhaled through his nose and exhaled out his mouth. Keep it together, Andy. You're only at the beginning of this.

A brisk rap on the storeroom's open door nearly launched him into the air.

"Damn, you're jumpy." Terrance Jackson stood in the threshold, watching him with mild bemusement. Terrance, a six-year vet, had recently transferred to Tampa Fire Rescue from the Hillsborough County system. Andy considered him a neutral presence at the station, a rare colleague who had yet to form any strong opinions about the infamous Andrew Tate. Or so he wanted to believe.

"Sorry, man. You caught me in a daze."

"Inventory duty can do that." His eyes flitted across the shelves and returned to Andrew. "Nothing but boring shit in here."

Andrew tilted his head in puzzlement, a faint but deep note of misgiving thrumming beneath his sternum. Nothing but boring shit? What did that mean?

"So, what's up?"

"You've got a visitor. She's waiting in the lobby."

His immediate thought was that Grace had dropped by, maybe to offer an olive branch. Maybe to serve him divorce papers.

"Tall woman? Early thirties? Shoulder-length blonde hair?"

Terrance shook his head. "Younger. Curley dark hair. And I should warn you, she's upset. Obviously been crying. Hamilton said you can use his office to talk if you want. I don't think he likes having an upset lady in the front lobby. Makes him nervous."

"Makes me nervous, too. And she didn't give you a name?"

"Cathy maybe? Kelly? Sorry man. I'm no good with that shit."

Following Terrance down the hall, Andrew mentally rifled through the women he knew, trying to place the name. When they turned the corner into the small lobby, Terrance presented the visitor with an outstretched arm before retreating back into the common room.

Andrew stared for a moment, fighting a momentary, powerful urge to follow Terrance and flee into the innermost reaches of the station. He recognized her instantly, her swollen, tear-streaked face exactly as he remembered it from the hot intersection.

113

"They got him," Katie Fife choked out. She closed the gap between them in three quick steps. "They killed Bobby." She stifled a moan with the back of her fist. "Those bastards killed my brother."

HAMILTON'S OFFICE WAS DARK SAVE FOR THE LIGHT FILTERING   through the pulled blinds. Still, it was too bright to cloak the naked anguish crumpling the woman sitting at the other end of the couch. She appeared to be retreating into herself, disappearing beneath the folds of her clothing.

Andrew wanted to pull her to him as he would if Anna came to him in this condition, Anna or Grace, wrap his arms around her shaking shoulders and let her head sink to his chest. But such intimacy was impossible, and so he sat two cushion-lengths away, leaning forward every so often to pass her a tissue and bob his head in pantomimed sympathy.

"He couldn't stop looking," Katie said. "That's why they attacked. When I would drop by the house, I would catch him staring and staring. I tried to warn him. I remembered what the homeless guy said, you know? About them marking you if they knew you could see them. But Bobby didn't understand. I couldn't make him understand." She blew her nose and tossed the tissue in the wastebasket Andrew had placed next to her. "Autism fucking sucks."

"I'm sorry." Andrew winced at what sounded to his ears like the hollow clang of artificiality in his words, but Katie simply nodded and plucked a fresh tissue from the offered box.

"I didn't know who else to talk to. I thought you might be going through the same: seeing these things, like I have, since that day." She looked him in the eye for the first time. "You *are* seeing them, aren't you? You weren't lying when you told him you saw that thing next to the trash bin."

"I wasn't lying." He shifted closer, drawn by her close-eyed sigh of relief. "My daughter and I. We were at the park." He cleared his throat to mask the hitch in his voice. "There seemed to be creatures everywhere. We were lucky to make it out alive."

"I feel like I'm stuck in a nightmare I can't wake up from. Everything's so unreal." Katie tilted her head. "No, that's not right. Everything's too real, like someone's pulled back a curtain and now I see all the awful things that have always been around me.

"My mother's in St. Joseph's, under observation and pumped full of sedatives. She found him. Bobby. Ran out to the porch when she heard him screaming. I don't want to think about what she saw.

"My dad's taken a leave of absence from work to be with her at the hospital. He told me all she could say until they knocked her out was 'horrible' over and over."

"Katie…"

"Why is this happening?" she demanded. "What in the name of god is going on? I can't talk to anyone, not my friends, definitely not my parents. Either they'll think I'm suffering post-traumatic stress from what they keep calling 'the incident,' or worse, they'll believe me. Because if they believe me I'll be putting them in danger, won't I?"

His father's constant warnings: be cautious, be diligent. But don't look at them directly. Don't give yourself away.

"My father spent the last twenty years trying to find a balance between ignorance and information. Telling me just enough to keep me safe. I didn't realize that until just a few days ago."

"Guess he didn't find the right balance, huh?"

"Guess not."

They said nothing for several long moments, and as the silence turned uncomfortable Andrew struggled to find a way to conclude their meeting without seeming impatient or dismissive. His eyes flitted to the clock on the wall. Only eight minutes had elapsed. When he turned back to Katie, he realized she had seen his glance and understood its meaning. Her face became a mask of composure, her postured stiffening to an attitude of formal detachment.

"Well, I'm sure you need to get back to work." Katie wiped her nose a final time and stood. "Thank you for listening. Sorry for taking up so much of your time. I won't bother you again."

"It was no bother."

She extended her hand and he shook it, reminded suddenly of the way Katie had reached out to grab the water bottle on their first meeting, the desperation in her eyes, the water gushing from the open top as her fingers clamped around the plastic.

"Hold on." He fished out his wallet and flipped through it on the way to Hamilton's desk. He found what he was looking for, copied the name and number to a fresh sheet and handed it to Katie. "There's someone else you can talk to, a friend of my dad's. He knows a lot more about what's going on than I do. He's the one who made sure my daughter and I made it out of the park."

Katie held the sheet up to the window to read the name. "William Phipps?"

"You don't have to worry about what you say to him." Andrew slipped the original scrap of paper back into his wallet. "You won't put him in danger."

"Why not?"

Andrew opened the office door and followed her out into the hall. "He's already lost everything that matters."

LITTLE BILLY WAS TORN. HIS GUT TOLD HIM HE HAD HUNG around too long, circled the block one too many times to remain unnoticed. Someone even now might be calling the cops to report a suspicious character casing the neighborhood. After nearly twenty years on the street, he knew the routine. It didn't matter how well-groomed he appeared. Fresh hair cut, clean clothes, new shoes. People didn't like strange men prowling their sidewalks, especially sidewalks like this, bordered by manicured lawns fronting Mediterranean-style mini-mansions and sprawling bungalows, shaded by century-old live oaks, the utility lines hidden away beneath the streets.

His sister had obviously done well for herself.

He should be content with what he'd already seen: the tasteful and tidy house, the immaculate yard, the detached garage with the basketball hoop mounted above the door, the carriage house (or was it a cottage house?) tucked neatly behind. Surely the lives lived here were happy ones. Secure. Content. He could walk away now and convince himself that putting as much distance between himself and his family had been the right choice.

His brother, Oscar, was the marketing v.p. for a Silicon Valley software startup, at least according to the company's website. Maybe someday he would make his way out to California to lurk in the pleasant, shaded corners of a neighborhood a lot like this one, waiting to catch a glimpse of the man his brother had become.

Little Billy checked his watch. He had no idea what his sister's daily routine was, but if Mirabelle picked her children up from school and drove straight home, it was reasonable to estimate a return sometime between three fifteen and 3:40, give or take ten minutes. It was now quarter to four and the driveway was still empty.

What was he hoping to accomplish here? What could he learn from spying on her as she shuffled her sons from car to front door that he hadn't learned from her Facebook page? He should be researching ways to obtain explosives, since he had only the slimmest hope Andrew would be able to get any. But every time he tried to turn his thoughts to the task, they swerved again and again to the house number he had jotted down shortly after his return to Tampa. From the beginning, the Palma Ceia address felt equal parts invitation and invasion.

What if he simply knocked on her door? Would she recognize him, throw open her arms in welcome? Throw a punch for dragging the family through hell and then disappearing? Or would she peer through a blind, see a strange man on her stoop and pretend no one was home?

Waiting for the city bus, he thought he had the guts to find out which it would be. Upon making his way into her neighborhood, however, he realized the most he could manage was a distant, voyeuristic peek at her life. He tried to convince himself he couldn't risk putting his sister and nephews in jeopardy. If the *vetro* had directed the *bilantu* to target Andrew as a way to strike at John, why not target Mirabelle and the boys to strike at him?

Possible, he supposed. But the truth was, he simply couldn't stomach the thought of facing her hurt and her anger. They hadn't spoken in eighteen years, not since the day the judge had dismissed all charges against him.

Like his brother and parents, Mirabelle had stood by him throughout the ordeal, endured the looks and whispers, the anonymous phone calls and notes slipped through the slats of her locker door. Her brother was a murderer, a psycho killer. He had chopped up his fiancée and her family with an ax, cannibalized the male bodies, done worse things to the women. They'd found him covered in their blood. He was a sick, sick bastard and he would burn for his sins.

She'd been so fragile that autumn, balanced between defiance and despair. Her pale, weary face always managed a feeble smile when he caught her eye, but she couldn't keep from flinching if he got too close. Of all his family, Mirabelle had suffered the most. She had none of Oscar's defensive anger or his parents' righteous indignation. She was a thirteen-year-old girl who still had posters of *New Kids on the Block* and horses on her wall.

Yet she had endured. And when the judge dismissed all charges, agreeing with the grand jury there was not enough evidence against him to proceed to trial, she had embraced him in the court hallway, kissed his cheek, told him she had always known things would turn out okay because she had said a rosary every night for his acquittal.

And how had he repaid her? The same way he had repaid all of them, by slipping out of the house after dinner and disappearing from their lives. Professor Tate might have been content hiding out on the far side of town, but Little Billy knew the true extent of what the *bilantu* were capable of. Across town wasn't far enough. If he wanted to prevent more deaths, if he wanted to keep Mirabelle and Oscar and his parents safe, he needed to put as much distance between himself and them as possible.

Distance. That was what he had chanted as he began his long walk north. Distance, distance, more distance. And when the chanting finally faded, he was somewhere in Tennessee, so far across The Great Divide, he couldn't remember what, precisely, that border represented.

Little Billy decided to circle his sister's neighborhood once more, despite his misgivings. It was the knapsack that gave him the most concern. It branded him a transient, but he had been reluctant to leave it behind in Andrew's motel room. He felt vulnerable without it. The olive-green pack contained nearly everything he owned, and yet it was only half-full. A couple of change of clothes, a few personal hygiene items, some over-the-counter medication. A water bottle. Notebooks and pens. A battered paperback potboiler he was reading in miserly snippets. The most expensive thing he owned was his cell phone, and he kept that in his shirt pocket, next to his heart.

Little Billy still felt an odd mixture of pride and shame knowing he could inventory all his possessions in less than ten seconds. At first, this lack of belongings had left him feeling rootless and adrift. He'd met through-hikers on the Appalachian Trail laboring under enormous backpacks, their possessions towering over them and bulging from bright nylon compartments. What did they consider vital that he was missing? A hell of a lot, apparently.

Later, as memories of life before The Divide began to fade, the lightness of his knapsack became a blessing. He was unburdened, free to go wherever he wanted. Self-contained. What had Andrew said? Like a turtle, everything he needed on his back.

Little Billy turned the corner.

Only once in eighteen years had there been anything more in his life than the knapsack and his regular calls to John Tate: a half-starved terrier-mutt who had adopted him one bitter winter day as he huddled in an Atlanta alley under a bakery's exhaust fan, the warm air filled with the aroma of baking bread. The pooch approached with its tail between its legs and its belly scraping the ground. But it didn't dart away when Little Billy stamped his foot, driven, perhaps, into the same delirious yearning as he by the maddeningly wonderful smell. Soon they were sharing a box of saltines, and when the dog followed him out of the alley, he didn't have the heart to chase it away.

For a while Little Billy resisted naming it, figuring the mutt would slink off sooner or later. But as the days turned into weeks, it became clear it had no intention of leaving his side. When he realized the dog was beginning to respond to "Hey, boy" as it would a name, Little Billy had finally given in, modifying "hey, boy" into "Highboy," thus formalizing their relationship. For the next year-and-a-half, they crisscrossed the Southeast together, roaming as far west as Memphis, as far north as Ashville.

Then one morning, Little Billy woke to the sounds of a struggle, Highboy and a type of *bilantu* he'd never seen before, locked in battle. By the time he found a branch large enough to beat the thing off, it was too late. The creature had expelled some sort of sack (a stomach?) from an orifice along its flank and the only part of his dog still visible was a twitching rear paw that disappeared inside as he ran up.

An instant later the creature appeared to turn itself inside out once again and vanished below ground amid a shower of loose dirt and fallen leaves. He had knelt at the spot for a long time, waiting, watching the small puddle of blood soak into the soil. And then he had broken camp and push on.

Little Billy turned the corner.

Three days later John, had called to tell him he'd seen an obituary in the now-defunct *Tampa Tribune*: Samuel Phipps had passed away after a lengthy battle with cancer. Little Billy thanked him for the information and politely declined his offer to wire money for a bus ticket home. The thought of watching his father's burial from some dark corner was too bleak. And when his mother died four years later, John hadn't offered a bus ticket home, instead warning him to stay away, at least until he had a better idea of what was going on in Tampa.

"What do you mean?" By then, Little Billy had begun noticing subtle changes during their conversations. John was increasingly distracted, often trailing off in mid-sentence until Little Billy gently nudged him back on topic. At first, he worried John's prolonged contact with the *xalanthracoils* might be causing some sort of dementia. As far as Little Billy was concerned, it had taken a huge amount of suicidal courage to find all eighteen pillars, knowing each new discovery changed awareness in ways they were only beginning to suspect, bringing thoughts, *John's* thoughts, ever-more into alignment with the *vetro's*. That shit had to take a toll.

"Things are changing here. I've been trying to convince myself it was just my imagination. How do you quantify something that's only in your head? Hard to be objective. But I'm certain of it now. They're closer."

"The *vetro offalate?*" A pang of dread plucked at his throat as he pronounced the words. He usually avoided even thinking the name.

"Their minds are getting clearer by the day. I can almost hear words now. Sometimes I turn on music to drown them out; it's that bad. And the *xalanthracoils*. William, I think they're starting to wake up."

"Christ."

"There's more." John paused long enough for Little Billy to wonder if they'd lost the connection.

"John?"

"Will, I've done something I thought I'd never do. I've put people at risk. Homeless men. I've been giving them money and telling them to call me if they see any monsters."

Little Billy transferred the phone to his other ear. It had been raining that day, and he was sharing a Dothan bus shelter with another vagrant, a man wrapped in plastic garbage bags against the weather, his head bowed in sleep, his bicycle—its basket filled with aluminum cans— propped against a nearby pole.

"Did you teach them how to see?"

"No. No, of course not. But I have a strong suspicion the *bilantu* are becoming more aggressive. I can't verify that without more eyes."

"And if they are?"

121

"Invasion."

Little Billy turned the corner.

Of all the things he'd discovered during his long exile, the most unsettling was how ubiquitous (now *there* was a word he hadn't used since college) the creatures were. The *bilantu* weren't a local phenomenon. He had hoped each step north would take him farther and farther from their range, and at first, it appeared that would be the case. Their numbers began to drop significantly after fifty or sixty miles.

But while they became scarcer, they never disappeared entirely. Sooner or later he would see a *quintaloch* curled around a tree trunk, a *malta* fastened to the side of a building. In Valdosta, he'd seen a multi-jointed arm reach up from a pond to snatch a duck from shore. And what the fuck had *that* been?

There were no safe zones, no sanctuaries. They were everywhere. Cold, heat, rain, drought, nothing bothered them. Only the night offered relief.

"Diurnal," Little Billy said aloud, rolling the word around in his mouth. Active during the day. That's what the *bilantu* were. So much so he sometimes wondered if they might be solar powered.

It was one of the few comforting discoveries he'd made during his years of fieldwork. The night became his friend, his security blanket. Occasionally, when the weather permitted, he would make camp far enough from town to build a small fire without fear of attracting unwanted attention. The bugs didn't bother him. The raccoons and opossums peeking at him with their gleaming eyes from just beyond the fire's glow didn't bother him. The mat of damp foliage slowly soaking through his pants and jacket didn't bother him.

Even the occasional snap of branches as something large moved under cover of darkness didn't bother him. All the real monsters were asleep, and Little Billy would lie with his head propped on his pack and stare at the stars pivoting slowly above him and almost never wonder if around one was a planet where creatures of vast and malevolent intelligence plotted their return to Earth.

Eventually, he would drift into a deep, untroubled sleep, the fear slumbering with the *bilantu* until the first light of dawn awakened it once again.

Little Billy turned the corner.

He had expected his return to Tampa to be an emotional roller coaster. At Laura's grave, he stood waiting for the tears to come, but he was unable to connect her marker to the woman he had loved. It was just a stone. Laura was only real when she came to him in his dreams or in fevered, toxin-induced hallucinations. There was nothing left of her at the gravesite, and when he left he knew he would never come back.

It was the same at his parents' graves. He had nothing to say to polished granite. Either they had forgiven him or they hadn't. Excuses and apologies were lost on the dead. Maybe on the living as well.

Little Billy slowed. Across the street and four houses up, Mirabelle stood next to an SUV. He recognized her from her Facebook photos, a slight woman with bobbed black hair, sunglasses perched atop her head. She wore shorts and a pale blouse and was fanning herself with a stack of mail she had evidently retrieved from the mailbox.

A moment later, one of the rear doors of the SUV opened and a boy about ten emerged wearing a bathing suit, a large beach towel draped over his neck. A second, smaller boy followed, also dressing for the beach, and as Little Billy whispered their names-*Caleb, Darren*-he realized he had missed the obvious. He'd based his scheme on the assumption his sister would be picking her boys up from school. But it was mid-July, summer break. Was he that out of touch with the world of semester calendars?

His sister said something to the older boy, to Caleb. She reached inside the vehicle and removed a duffel bag. Little Billy strolled slowly down the sidewalk, not daring to stop, willing himself to be as inconspicuous as possible. He watched from the corner of his eye as Mirabelle locked the SUV and told her sons to move their trucks before their father ran over them again.

Happy. They were most certainly happy. But don't stop. Don't slow too much. Keep moving. Never stop moving because up on the left, in the yard of a yellow house with trim so white it seemed to glow, an *apperix* was inching across the front steps toward a tabby asleep in the shade. When his cell rang, both he and the cat started. The tabby darted under the porch as he read the incoming name and number. No one he recognized. But then, with the exception of John Tate, that would include pretty much everyone on the planet.

"Hello?"

"William Phipps?" a female voice asked. William Phipps? He pulled the phone from his ear and re-read the name. Kathleen Fife? Who the hell was Kathleen Fife?

"Yes."

"Andrew Tate gave me your number. I'm sorry to bother you, but I need..." her voice wavered and she cleared her throat angrily. "Sorry. Last thing you want is a call from a hysterical stranger." She took a watery breath and started again. "My name is Katie Fife. I was the woman taken hostage a few days ago. Maybe you saw me on the news?"

Little Billy shook his head, then silently cursed for making such a useless gesture. "Not on the news. But I read about you in the paper. You say Andy gave you my number?"

"Something killed my brother this morning. Something horrible. Mr. Tate said you know more about these monsters than he does. Please, Mr. Phipps. I need to talk to someone. I need..." Her voice broke. "I need to know what's going on. I need to know how to keep the same thing from happening to my mom and dad. Can we meet?"

Little Billy stood on the curb watching his sister mount the front porch steps, Caleb and Darren trailing behind. Nothing interfered as she unlocked the front door. Nothing surrounded them as first one boy, then the other dashed inside. Nothing came slithering or flopping over the porch rail as she turned briefly to glance over her shoulder. And nothing came swooping down from the trees as she stepped into the house. She shut her door on nothing except the stranger loitering across the street.

"Mr. Phipps?"

"Call me Will."

Little Billy turned his back on his sister's tasteful and tidy house and began moving again.

Nine

There was a moment when Andrew thought the whole plan was going to shit. Everything was taking too long. Gary would be back soon and all he had managed to do was make a mess. It was the packaging. He hadn't anticipated how intricate it would be. The box contained thirty sticks of Trenchrite bundled five each inside molded plastic sleeves. The plastic was thick and apparently seamless. The only way to open them was to cut through the material. All Andrew had was his set of car keys. He'd never be able to saw through the plastic in time.

In addition to the explosives, the box also contained a coiled length of detonation cord, thirty blasting caps and a small, handheld master control box about the size of a television remote, all encased in their own confounding packaging. He had been planning to pocket the detonation cord, blasting caps and control box and shove four or five sticks of Trenchrite beneath his belt, pressed tightly against the small of his back and covered with his shirt.

All that was out the window. He'd deliberately left the inventory sheet in the ambulance's cab so he could ask Gary to retrieve it. The walk from the vehicle to this aisle of the warehouse had only taken two minutes, forty-seven seconds-Andrew had timed it-which meant he had approximately five-and-a-half minutes to do what needed to be done.

But the box of Trenchrite had been moved since the last time he'd seen it, and it had taken just over two minutes to find it again. Pulling the box off the shelf, opening it and sorting through the items inside had taken another forty-five seconds. Now he had two-and-a-half minutes left to come up with a new plan. Less if Gary was a fast walker.

Andrew's impulse was to abandon the attempt at stealth altogether and simply wait for his partner's return. If he explained the situation, told him how desperate things were, perhaps Gary would understand. Andrew knew others were seeing the creatures. Katie was proof of that. Gary might have had his own encounters.

It wasn't all that outlandish. In fact, after hearing claims of hopping monsters and alien voices and Comanche's desperate pleas, wasn't it likely his partner would, at the very least, be wondering what the hell was going on? Wouldn't he be trying to fit the pieces together?

Of course he would. Even now Gary might be puzzling over a way to broach the topic himself. What better time than now? Andrew repacked the opened Trenchrite box and carried it to the aisle where they had left the pushcart. All this sneaking around was ridiculous. Better to be honest and open.

The soundness in this line of reasoning lasted long enough for Andrew to start gathering some of the items he remembered from the inventory list. Inflatable splints. Check. Box of syringes. Check. It was too late to do anything now anyway. He could hear Gary's footsteps approaching. Yes, better to be honest. Gary would understand.

Cervical collars. Check. He transferred the box of collars to the pushcart. It was a large box, four feet by four feet, and only half full. When he noticed this, something bright and hot flared in Andrew's chest and without pausing to consider what he was doing, he upended the container, dumping the dozen or so collars to the floor.

Gary's footsteps grew louder. Only seconds away now. Andrew slipped the smaller box of Trencherite into the larger box and began tossing the collars back in. Five, six, eight.

"What happened here?"

Andrew scooped up the remaining four collars and threw them in with a huff of exasperation.

"Overturned when I grabbed it. Collars went everywhere."

Gary glanced in the box with mild curiosity. "You're taking all of them?" He reached in and plucked one up.

Andrew held out his hand and Gary handed him the clipboard holding the inventory sheet. He pulled a pen from his shirt pocket, clicked it open, made a mark on the paper. "Yeah."

His partner tossed the collar back in the box. "Expecting a rash of neck injuries, are you?"

"Never know," he said, finally remembering to breathe. "The world's a dangerous place."

Gary pulled two boxes of tongue depressors off the top shelf. "No truer words were spoken."

JOHN TATE SLAMMED HIS FIST AGAINST THE TABLE HARD enough to bounce the box of tissues to the floor.

"Not the reaction I was expecting." Dr. Cho said, retrieving the tissues.

"You've no idea what you've done. None. I never should have mentioned the damn things. What the hell was I thinking?"

"If it'll soothe your conscious, you were pumped full of antibiotics and sedatives at the time, one of which has been known to make people more, pliant shall we say, when it comes to their inhibitions."

"What? Sodium pentothal? You gave me a dose of sodium pentothal?"

"That would be highly unethical, a breach of my Hippocratic Oath, and grounds for revoking my medical license."

"Is that a denial?"

"Besides, you sent your own son out to touch one."

John hissed as Cho removed the bandage across his calf with a sharp yank. "That was different," he said, turning to the guard standing at the door, the one he was beginning to think of as "Hector". "He was already in their crosshairs, thanks to me. I was trying to give him a chance to defend himself, an alarm bell in his head so he wouldn't be taken by surprise."

"And we don't deserve the same chance to protect ourselves? Our families?" Hector asked. The guard had escorted him to the infirmary alone, a breach of protocol John assumed under normal circumstance would result in serious disciplinary action. It was a risk made moot, however, considering Hector was also wearing his gun. And *that*, John was almost certain, would result in immediate termination if discovered. Both the correctional officer and Cho were risking their careers with this meeting.

"By touching that thing, all you've done is made yourself a target. You weren't that before."

"It was my choice, John," Cho said, probing the flesh around his wound with unkind fingers. "I needed to know you weren't just spinning some elaborate fantasy. I wasn't hearing the voices. I wasn't seeing the monsters."

"And now?"

Cho removed her gloves with a brisk snap, sending a small puff of talcum into the air. "And now I am."

"Dr. Cho…"

"I told you before to call me Emily. Don't make me tattoo it across your forehead."

"Emily, why did you and Hector get involved with any of this? There's no going back. Not anymore."

"I can't speak for Hector, but I got involved because I'd rather know the world for what it really is than continue living with blinders on. As a fellow scientist, you can understand that, right?"

"I can't protect my wife and kids if I don't know what I'm protecting them from," Hector added.

"Wrong!" John's vehemence surprised him into a moment of silence before he pressed on in a low, angry growl. "Wrong, both of you. Ignorance of these things is exactly what's kept the human race from extinction. Our goddamn brains have evolved to not see them. Do you understand the implications? Not seeing them was an adaptation that ensured continued survival.

"Why? Who knows? There's no terrestrial equivalent. If the brains of gazelles evolved in a way that caused them to perceptually erase lions from their awareness, they'd be extinct by now. But that's how it is. And all those people who go missing every year? Thousands? Tens of thousands? I'm betting a lot of them somehow stumbled on a way to see the *bilantu*, either through drugs or changes in brain chemistry or maybe just by learning to see in a new way."

"You mean like with those 3-D posters that were popular back in the day?" Hector said. "Cross your eyes and focus in some weird way and a space ship or tiger pops up out of the dots."

John nodded, warming to the topic despite his effort to remain angry. "Yes, like that only far more complex."

"I never was able to get that shit to work," Hector said with a dismissive wave. "Never saw anything but dots."

"Point is, once you see them you spend the rest of your life pretending not to. That or risk getting yourself and everyone close to you killed."

"I understand your concerns," Emily reassured him, quickly re-bandaging his calf. "But you need to stop living in the past. What happened to that family in the '90s was terrible. Maybe they'd still be alive if your assistant had kept his mouth shut about the creatures. I don't know. I don't care.

"What I care about is what's happening now. My partner's an E.R. physician at Tampa General. Over the last week, she's treated nearly a dozen people for injuries like nothing she's ever seen before: crescent-shaped serrations the size of dinner plates, abdominal gashes deep enough to disembowel, seeping puckers left by god-knows-what kind of projectile. The victims are all telling similar stories.

"They started seeing monsters everywhere, and then they attacked. Let me show you something." She stood, pulled her cell from her pocket and touched the screen. "I took this on my way in this morning."

She handed him the phone and John saw a picture of the concrete slope beneath a highway overpass. Spray-painted across the surface were angular designs scrawled in overlapping patterns, filling every blank space with frenzied hieroglyphics inscribed with lunacy.

"And don't tell me it's gibberish," Emily said. "I can read this, John. I can *read* it."

"So can I." Although it had been twenty years, he'd recognized the writing instantly. It was the same script etched across the grave marker the *votasin* had been circling, the marker that was really a *xalanthracoil*. He hadn't been able to read the markings then. Now he wished he still couldn't.

"I'm not going to like this, am I?" Hector asked.

Emily raised her hand and John reluctantly translated. "It says, 'We will all dissolve within the folds of their glory.' Over and over again."

Hector edged forward to examine the phone's display. As he did, something bellowed in John's head loud enough to curl him into a fetal ball on the table, hands clamped over his ears. Through watering eyes, he saw Emily do the same. It was only a single word, a phlegmy trio of syllables too jagged and dichotomous for human pronunciation, something between a gurgle and a snarl. But though it was a single word, its meaning was both vast and terribly specific. The *vetro*, John suddenly understood, had many words for killing. This one involved the insertion of heated metal into the...

"Bitch!" Hector fell to the floor, clutching his left bicep. John jumped to the floor himself and shimmied until his back was pressed against a filing cabinet. There was a hole in the door that hadn't been there before. A second hole appeared below and to the left of the first, leaving a small volcanic pucker in the metal, while above his head, something hit one of the cabinet doors with a sharp ping.

Emily crab-walked up to him with her hands over her head and pointed toward a far corner, where a second door stood.

"Not without him."

"I'll get Hector," she answered. "Get in the closet."

The knob of the infirmary door rattled.

"I locked it after we came in," Hector told them. He pulled his walkie-talkie from his belt and began shouting their situation into it: "10-74, 10-74, shots fired in the infirmary. Man down. Need assistance, goddamnit. Need assistance now!"

The handle shook again, then something slammed against the door hard enough to buckle the upper frame.

"Christ, that had to be more than just a man," John said, sliding up to Hector and placing a hand on his shoulder.

"Deadbolt's holding for now," he said, attempting to wave John back. The radio crackled a garbled response and he repeated their situation. A second jolt separated one of the frame's corner joints from its housing, the strip of metal unfurling amid a cascade of falling drywall.

"It's going to take the door right off its hinges." John grabbed Hector's collar and tugged him into a sitting position. "Emily."

She circled around to the officer's other side and looped his injured arm over her shoulder. Hector's lips pulled back in pain, but together John and the doctor managed to hoist him to his feet.

"That's Brutrelli out there," Hector protested. "Ain't no way he's gonna bust in."

A third blow bowed the entire metal door inward.

"Who says it's Brutrelli?"

"If any guard is working for those things, it would be him. Who else would be shooting at us?"

The three retreated across the room to the far corner. Emily opened the closet door, and together they stepped inside. It was a small space, barely enough room for them to squeeze into, but this door appeared far sturdier than the outer one, more like the entrance to a bank vault than an infirmary alcove.

"The narcotics are kept in here," Emily said, interpreting his look. "This thing is built to withstand a lot of abuse." She slammed the door behind them. "And I'm the only one with a key."

"He's not getting in," Hector repeated. "There's cameras everywhere. Right now thirty officers are headed this way."

"*If* the cameras are working," Emily said. "And *if* you were able to get through on your radio."

Through the closed door, they heard the infirmary phone start to ring.

"I got through," Hector said. "That's them now."

A tremendous crash seemed to shudder through the entire wing of the jail. There was a bouncing, scraping thud that ended in the crunch of splintering wood. The phone rang three more times before it was silenced with a clatter of shattering plastic.

"Down!" Emily hissed, grabbing the collar of John's orange jumper and yanking him to the floor with her. There wasn't enough space to take any further evasive steps. The room was less than eight feet wide, and all three walls were lined with shelves. Four shots dimpled the door in a tight cluster, but they did not break through.

"Brutrelli, is that you, you fuck?" Hector was easing himself gingerly to the floor, his gun now drawn and trained at the door.

For a moment there was silence, then John saw the shadow of feet block the light beneath the door. He thought he heard a series of faint taps, like the drumming of fingernails. The taps continued for several seconds, and with each passing moment, the impression of a slavering presence pressed against the other side of the door increased. The notion grew not with a steady swelling, but in distinct stages, as if the thing was somehow assembling itself piece by piece.

"You feel that?" he whispered to Emily. She said nothing, but in the gloom of the closet, he saw her nod. The sense of a consciousness, deliriously inhuman, just feet away had become nearly overwhelming. John realized he was taking deep gulps of air, as if he were something dredged from the sea floor and tossed, gasping and writhing, to shore.

"Brutrelli!" Hector's voice was half-an-octave below panic. "I swear to god, I've got my gun pointed straight at your head. You try and step foot inside here, your fucking brains are going to paint the fucking wall."

"WE APPROACH."

In unison, the three shimmied back from the threshold to squeeze against the far shelves in a jumbled mass.

"Shit!" The gun in Hector's hand began to shake wildly. "Was that the *door*? Did the door just talk to us?"

"WE ENGULF."

The words were an insect buzz of vibrating metal as the door reverberated with the utterances.

"They must be using the metal as a resonator," John whispered. "There's something in contact with the other side of the door, and it isn't Brutrelli."

"Or it's not *just* Brutrelli," Emily said.

"WE DIGEST."

They groaned in unison as the buzz wormed its way into the hollows of their skulls. For a moment, an unsettling stillness settled over the room. The shadow beneath the door did not move. The door did not speak. Even Hector's gun was motionless, as if the guard was caught between one terrified heartbeat and the next.

And then the door began to melt.

LITTLE BILLY GROANED AND WOULD HAVE SLUMPED TO the floor had Katie not steadied him.

"What's wrong?"

The *vetro's* howl faded and the world began to reemerge from a gray fog.

"Something just shouted in my head. You didn't hear it?"

Katie shook her head. "No. I mean, I thought I sensed *something*, like a whisper. Kind of made the hairs on the back of my neck stand up, but nothing like a shout."

"Lucky you." Little Billy pulled a handkerchief from his back pocket and mopped his face. "That was the loudest yet." Glancing around, he noticed an ashen-faced woman standing motionless next to her cart, a packet of light bulbs clutched in one hand.

"What?" Katie asked, following his glance to the other shopper.

"I'm not the only one who heard it."

After a moment, the woman appeared to regain her bearings with a slight shudder and a deep breath. She dropped the light bulbs into the cart and began moving off in a slow shuffle, glassy eyes fixed straight ahead.

Despite his misgivings, Little Billy had agreed to meet with Katie that afternoon, although his choice of meeting places had been greeted with a moment of confused silence.

"You want to meet me at a Home Depot?" she had repeated. "That's what you said, right? Home Depot?" Hearing the unease in her tone, Little Billy imagined her considering the possibility that Andrew had saved her from one lunatic only to pawn her off on another.

"I have an errand there that can't wait."

Now, as he and Katie worked their way toward the gardening section, he wanted to say something that would put the young woman at ease. She'd been through a lot in the last forty-eight hours, shit that would leave most people reeling. Although she appeared shaken and desperate, her grip when they shook hands outside the store had been firm, her eyes unwavering as she searched his face for something he suddenly hoped was there.

"This errand I have to do, it's part of a plan to fight these things."

"You're going to kill them, right? Wipe them out?"

Little Billy stepped through the sliding glass doors into the outdoor garden section, the heat smacking him like a breathy kiss. The smell of the wildfire was sharper.

"Nothing short of sterilizing the planet would do that. But we might be able to stop something even worse from punching its way into our world."

"The *vetro offalate?*"

Little Billy nodded as he approached a long shelf holding various gardening tools. When he turned, there was no one at his side. Katie was several feet behind, her bewildered eyes scanning the space between them.

He backtracked to her. "Katie?"

"How did I know that? How did I know what they're called?"

He touched her elbow and gently guided her into the shade of a nearby overhang.

"The closer they get, the more our minds sense theirs. And vice-versa."

"Is that what you heard a few minutes ago? *Their minds?*"

"Eventually, I think, everybody will."

"Then you have to stop them. You *have* to. Even those two words are too much. I can feel them burrowing in my head. Trying to take root." She reached out and grasped his shirtsleeve. "I want to help. Whatever it is you're planning, I want to be a part of it. My mother's in the hospital losing her mind because of these things. My father is worried sick about her and trying to make funeral…"

The muscles of her face tightened. Little Billy struggled to find words of comfort, but before he could offer some awkward and insincere assurance that things were going to be okay, she stopped him with an upraised hand. Katie sniffed angrily, blinked back tears and appeared to swallow her anguish in a single gulp. "What did you come here to get?" she asked after a moment.

Little Billy pointed to a nearby shelf. "An auger."

She looked from him to the row of tools and back again. "You're going to stop these things with a garden drill?"

"It's a little more involved than that." He began inspecting the tools to keep from having to face Katie's disbelieving look. He needed something big enough to drill down at least twenty feet, but small enough to carry on the bus. And of course, there was the cost. He had sixty dollars left of the five hundred John had wired him last month. That eliminated all but the hand augers, which was probably for the best considering the noise of a gas-powered tool.

136

"How much more involved?" Katie ran her hand over a box holding a two-hundred-and-fifty-dollar model boasting a forty-three cc engine and a drill rpm that seemed ridiculously fast.

"I'm not even sure we'll be able to come up with the other... component. Without it, the plan's worthless. I'm an optimist, though."

"So you're going to dig a hole?"

"The deeper the better."

Katie turned her back to the shelf, crossed her arms and planted herself in the line of Little Billy's progress. "Rent a backhoe," she said when his eyes met hers.

He laughed before he could catch himself and lowered his glance, afraid she would think he was mocking her. Instead, she joined him.

"I'm serious. If this is worth doing, it's worth doing right."

"Two things. One, this job is going to require a good deal of stealth, and a backhoe isn't going to be easy to sneak in and out of a cemetery."

"Cemetery?"

"Secondly, I couldn't afford to rent bowling shoes, let alone a piece of industrial equipment."

"Cemetery?" Her deadpan tone was inflectionless, but a smile, genuine if asymmetrical, continued to broaden as he sheepishly nodded. She leaned in close and whispered, "Are we going to dig up a grave, Will?"

"With an auger? No. *We* aren't going to do anything. Tonight, *I'm* going to dig a hole with this," he plucked up the nearest hand auger without bothering to check the price tag, "drill down as far as I can. Then I'm going to cover the hole with some brush, hope no one notices my handiwork and pray like hell it wasn't a waste of time."

"Wow," Katie said with feigned admiration. "You've really thought this through. So let me see if I can grasp the intricacies of this plan of yours. You're going to take that drill—which, by the way, looks like it's made for digging fence post holes—sneak into a cemetery, drill down, let's see," she framed the top and bottom of the auger shaft with her hands, "about four feet," and call it a night. Is that about it?"

"Well, when you put it like that."

"And how are you getting to the cemetery?"

Little Billy ran his palm over the auger's metal handle. "Bus."

Katie's laugh chimed across the gardening department, prompting a woman at a nearby seed rack to turn and smile.

"I'm sorry, Will. I'm not trying to be mean, but that is so incredibly pathetic. I can just picture you trying to get on a bus with that thing. 'Don't mind me, ma'am. Just going to squeeze in next to you with my giant *augur*. Can you let me know when we reach the cemetery?'"

"It's not that big."

"No driver in his right mind is going to let you get on a bus with that thing. I'll drive you. And I'll pay for something that will dig a real damn hole. Aup," Katie raised a finger between them. "No arguments. I'm doing this and that's, that. And I'm going with you tonight. You're going to need someone to keep an eye out while you punch holes in sacred ground."

Little Billy knew what he should do next: remind this young woman of the risks in offering a man she had just met a ride to an undisclosed cemetery so he could perform an act of vandalism. The absurdity of the situation was, well, laughable, and he was on the verge of asking if her mother hadn't warned her about offering lifts to strangers with garden tools, when he remembered where Katie's mother was. And why she was there.

"Don't you have better things to do than chauffeur me around town?" he asked.

"No," she said, all levity drained from her tone. "I don't think there's anything more import than this."

Little Billy couldn't argue.

Ten

Andrew clutched the baseball bat and watched through a sliver of open door as his father stuffed clothes into garbage bags as fast as he could. When one bag was full, he shook open another and continued. Socks, underwear, tee-shirts, jeans, sneakers. Andrew stood in his parent's closet, surrounded by his father's ties and dress shirts. When John Tate came for those, Andrew would swing as soon as the door opened.

He didn't think he would kill his father. He might not even knock him to the floor. But he was going to make damn sure he didn't miss. And when the bat connected, he knew what he was going to say: "Go then, you piece of shit. Get the fuck out. Mom and I don't need you." Because even though he was twelve, he was the man of the house now and that's what men did, they told their good-for-nothing, family-abandoning, crazy-ass fathers exactly what they were. And exactly what they weren't.

"You're not my dad," he would finish, hopefully as John Tate squirmed on the carpet clutching his stomach or a shin or a limp arm.

His mother stood at the foot of the bed, and although he couldn't see her, he could picture her clutching the collar of her blouse the way she did whenever something bad was about to happen on television: a murder, a gross-out discovery, a plane crash.

"Isn't there any other way?" she asked. Andrew was mad at her, too, but in a different way. Why wasn't she pissed? Why wasn't she screaming and throwing things? Why wasn't she tossing his crap out the window? You want help packing? Here! She could start with the guitar case he'd taken—no, *stolen*—from Andrew's room. He had no idea what was in it. Not his guitar. The instrument had been left on Andrew's bed. He'd seen it from the hallway as he'd crept into his parent's room. Once he was done smashing his father, maybe he'd take the bat to whatever the son-of-a-bitch had inside the case.

"You want the same thing to happen here? Jesus, Lindsey, it was like something out of a horror movie. Every second I stay I'm putting you and Andy at risk."

"John," his mother moved into view, placed a hand on his father's shoulder. For a moment, he continued stuffing clothes into the trash bag. Then his hands fell still.

"John," she repeated. "Can't you tell me anything else? What if we take precautions? What if we're careful?"

How could she believe any of this? From the very start, Andrew had known something was wrong. From that first day when his father had come home after an afternoon of what he called field research, flushed and excited and talking about some major discovery that would change the world, Andrew had stood apart, watching from the doorway as his father paced the kitchen and his mother tried to get answers from him. New species? Undiscovered ecosystem? Perceptual disparities? It wasn't what his father said that had made Andrew uneasy. He understood none of it. It was the wild-eyed heat coming off him, the glee so weird in a man that had always been cool and a little distant. Over the summer, *that* father had evaporated, and now all that was left was this nutcase running from things even a twelve-year-old knew didn't exist.

"I can't *not* see them, Lindsey. Not anymore. Everything up here," his father pointed to his head, "has changed. They're everywhere. Sooner or later, they'll catch me looking, or worse, you'll catch me looking and you'll look, too. And what if you see? No," his father resumed stuffing clothes into the bag. "This is the only way."

"Will we ever see you again?"

His father moved out of Andrew's line of sight, but he could track his progress around the bed and toward the closet by the sound of his voice.

"I'm not going far. Just across town. I'm moving out of the house, not out of you and Andy's lives. We'll keep in touch, and I think he's starting to come out of it..."

Andrew clutched the bat tighter. The room beyond the closet was an expanding sliver of white.

"Andy? Andy, can you hear me?"

Even his father's voice was different now. It had acquired a reedy, southern twang. The sliver of white continued to expand. Andrew tried to pull the bat back for a stronger swing, but it must have gotten entangled in hangars because he couldn't move it, not upward or backward or forward. It was stuck, as was Andrew, immobilized in the expanding column of light.

"I don't think we'll need those, Clare. He's coming to now."

Andrew's back was pressed against the far wall of the closet, but somehow the closet had rotated. The wall was under him and it was cold and white and there were feet sprouting from it. Feet and legs. And beyond those the legs of chairs.

"Andy."

"What happened?" He tried to push himself up, but was restrained by a hand on his chest.

"Whoa, whoa, whoa. Let's just take this slowly. You may have hit your head when you went down. I want to check you first."

Gary flashed a penlight in his eyes.

"I fainted?"

"We were on our way to the kitchen. Follow the tip of my finger with your eyes."

"I remember."

"I didn't see what happened, but Clare said you suddenly clutched your head and went down."

"Looked like you heard something agonizing," she offered. "You covered your ears and just kind of ... swooned."

"How long have I been out?"

" 'Bout a minute." Gary's fingers fluttered over the back of his skull, finding the lump from his previous fall with Anna in the parking lot.

"Looks like you did hit your head."

"No. That's from a few days ago. My head's fine."

"Debatable," Sid quipped, and Hamilton fired back, "Can it, lieutenant." Was the entire station gathered around him?

"Help me sit up."

Gary eased him into a sitting position, but continued his examination. "Just being thorough."

"How you feeling, Andy?" Hamilton asked.

"Better, captain. Not sure what happened there." Although he did know. The *vetro* had bellowed a killing command and the world had flared white.

"Here. Something to sip." Clare was at his side, a bottle of water in one hand.

"I'm fine," he said, but accepted the water with a grateful nod.

"Slowly," she advised. "You know, this may sound crazy, but I swear I heard something at the exact instant you grabbed your head, like voices echoing from the other end of a long metal pipe. Crazy, huh?"

"I don't know," Terrance said. "Might have noticed something myself. Not a voice. Nothing like that. More a change in air pressure, a sudden whistle and then a whooshing."

"Help me up."

With Gary on his left and Clare on the right, Andrew regained his feet. A moment of gray vertigo passed quickly. He pointed to the common room couch and moved toward it, shedding the hands offered to steady him. When he reached the couch he sank into it, feigning the businesslike sniff of someone relishing a moment of calm between customary bursts of activity.

"Sorry for the drama. I'm fine. Probably just dehydrated." He took another gulp of water to reinforce the point. "Is that necessary?" Gary positioned the portable EEG next to him and placed the leads on his shin and chest.

"You already know," he said.

"Heart's fine." He didn't realize Clare was next to him until she pricked his finger. "Blood sugar's fine, too. I told you, I'm just dehydrated. It's the heat."

"Sure, sure," Hamilton agreed, a little too quickly. "Been hard on everyone. This just re-emphasizes what I've been saying for months: you can't take care of someone else if you don't take care of yourself first. It's easy to overexert in these conditions. None of us are superhuman."

Andrew gave him a thumbs-up but noticed Terrance's head angle toward Sid as he muttered something under his breath. Let them whisper. He had bigger things to worry about. But sitting here with all eyes upon him was an intolerable situation and his gaze drifted about the room, avoiding other faces as he mentally scrambled for anything he could say to shift their attention elsewhere.

Out of habit, Andrew glanced up at the television mounted on the opposite wall and leaned forward on the couch.

"Could someone turn that up?" he said, pointing.

Terrance plucked the remote off the table and increased the volume as the other firefighters, to Andrew's tremendous relief, turned and watched.

"...hampering firefighter's efforts to contain the blaze." The camera pulled back from a tight shot of a wall of flame to reveal a line of dusty Department of Forestry firefighter's digging breaks through the kindling dry brush. The dust rising from the ground and the smoke from the fire seemed to combine in a choking fog, and Andrew took another sip of water as his throat closed in sympathy.

The news report switched to a head-and-shoulders shot of a woman standing before a glass wall etched with the logo of the Hillsborough County Sheriff's Department.

"Sheriff's spokesperson Annette Fitzpatrick says there are currently no plans for either voluntarily or mandatory evacuations, although nothing is being ruled out."

"Obviously, we are carefully watching the situation and are constantly re-evaluating the threat level. Lots of people are working very hard to contain the fire, but as you all know, we're in the middle of an unprecedented drought. Our advice is the same as it would be if we were under a hurricane warning: be prepared and stay informed. If evacuation orders become necessary, we don't want to have to go door-to-door telling people to get out."

The report switched to an aerial shot of the fire, Tampa's skyline an irregular collection of blue-gray blocks on the hazy horizon.

"Officials say the wildfire has burned three thousand acres to date and is less than two percent contained."

"Three thousand?" Andrew said. "This morning it was only one. Can a wildfire burn through two thousand acres in a single afternoon?"

Hamilton shook his head. "Maybe my intel was outdated. A thousand was the figure they gave me and that's what I passed on to you. No use worrying about it. If they lose containment, we'll be the first to know."

Andrew slapped his thighs and stood. "I'm ready for lunch. Ziti, right?" The thought of food turned a sour fist in his stomach, but he had to rebuild an aura of normalcy with his fellow firefighters, something he'd been struggling with even before the *vetro's* howl. His thoughts circled back to the box of cervical collars now sitting on a shelf in the station's storage room.

The fainting spell might have actually done him some good, providing a momentary break to his fretting over whether or not the Trenchrite would be discovered before he could secrete it from the building. There was no use obsessing about it. All he could do until his shift ended the next morning was act as if everything was fine. It shouldn't be that hard.

He had plenty of practice with deception. And although others would probably disagree, Andrew had come to believe he had at least a small talent for feigning normal.

THE CIRCLE OF BUBBLING METAL CONTINUED TO EXPAND, A sizzling, smoking corrosion that would soon chew its way through the door. To John, it resembled a brown stain soaking into a paper towel, a puddle of old blood absorbed by a gray mesh of disintegrating fibers.

The smoke was thick, greasy, yellow. It sank and accumulated in a vaporous mat, creeping across the floor. Even if the door somehow withstood the onslaught, death from smoke inhalation appeared a real possibility.

Instead of panic, however, a profound calm was settling over him like a caul, slick and membranous. The things on the other side of the door were not the *vetro offalate*, only their vermin. As such, they could do nothing more than kill them, a fate far kinder than what their masters would do upon arrival. Death: an end to worrying. An end of guilt. To finally, *finally* be able to let it all slip away and sink into the peace of oblivion. No, there were worse things than death, even death beneath the claws, teeth, talons, barbs of the *bilantu*.

"Let them come."

John turned to his right. Emily's head was resting against the shelf behind them, her eyes nearly shut. "Let them come," she repeated in a syrupy sigh as her head lolled toward his shoulder. On his left, Hector was no longer pointing his gun at the door. His hand rested in his lap. The officer's finger was still within the trigger guard, but his grip had relaxed to such an extent that the handle had slipped from his palm.

Something bucked beneath John's sternum and he shuddered. There was spittle at the corner of his mouth. He wiped it away and with a monumental effort staggered to his feet. As soon as his head was elevated, the fugue began to dissipate.

"Get up. Get up!"

He reached down and grabbed Emily's left arm. The limb rose languidly in his grip, but she made no effort to follow it.

"We're being gassed. There must be a neurotoxin in the smoke. Get up, damn it!"

He redoubled his efforts and managed to lift Emily a foot off the ground. Her legs wobbled under her and for a moment the two swayed in a teetering waltz. Bent over as he was, with his head near the floor, John's will to fight ebbed once more. Emily took a groggy swipe at him and he let her go.

"The point? We're going to die no matter what."

"Maybe," he said, straightening to gulp the fresher air above. "But I'm not going down without a fight."

"Me either." Hector was inching slowly upwards, sweeping boxes and bottles off the shelf behind him as his hands sought purchase. "I didn't drag myself out of a Mixco slum to die in a supply closet. Fuck that shit."

John held his breath, grabbed Hector under his armpits and lifted him to his feet. The correctional officer stood with closed lids, breathing deeply for three or four inhalations. His left shirt sleeve was tacky with blood, but the flow didn't seem substantial. It appeared the bullet had only grazed the muscle.

"Better," he said as his eyes fluttered open.

"Help me with her, but hold your breath."

Hector holstered his gun and together he and John managed to pull Emily to her feet. The yellow fog had spread to cover the entire floor, so thick their feet were invisible beneath. John thought he felt his skin beginning to prickle and lifted a foot to reassure himself his jail-issued slip-ons weren't canvas rags dangling from blistered flesh.

"Shoot whatever comes through," he said, scanning the shelves for anything that could be used as a weapon.

"Count on it."

"Do they keep scalpels in here? Bone saws? Anything like that?"

Emily snorted. "Bone saws? No. No cranial drills either before you ask. We've got scalpel blades in one of these boxes, scalpel handles in another, but it would take me a few minutes to find and assemble them, and I don't think we have that long."

The metal within the expanding circle of corrosion was boiling wildly, ribbons of steel curling off the surface in dark petals that fell, hissing, into the rising fog below.

"Here," she pulled something long and slender off a high shelf and handed it to him. "This is the best I can do."

John hefted the crutch, trying to gauge its balance. Emily grabbed one for herself and when their eyes met, both smiled.

"Ain't we a couple of warriors," she said.

"Give me a target, Brutrelli." Hector's gun was again pointed at the door. There was no tremor in his grip. "Stick your face right in the center of the hole."

Something in the infirmary bellowed, and with a dull boom the circled of degraded metal flew inward as if punched. The first thing to appear in the resulting space was not, however, Brutrelli's head. It was a bristled tarsus hooking itself to the lip of the opening.

"Don't fire until you see the whites of their eyes," John advised. A second tarsus joined the first, followed by the flutter of antennae.

"They even have eyes?" Hector asked.

"Quite a few."

In a blur of motion, something came hurling through the opening with beating wings. Hector shot it from the air, the sound of the gun deafening in the enclosed space. John darted forward and brought the crutch pad down on the shape thrashing in the yellow fog. There was a crunch of exoskeleton, felt rather than heard, a spurt of viscous ichor, what might have been a squeal. He managed a second blow before Hector fired again.

John couldn't make out what was sagging through the opening this time. It appeared an amalgamation of several *bilantu*, as if an *apperix*, *malta* and *quintaloch* had fused into a single creature. A maw rimmed with needlelike teeth dilated wide and Hector put a bullet through the center. The thing spasmed but continued to ooze its way into the room, tentacles whipping like unmanned fire hoses. Two more bullets dropped it in a heap at the door's threshold, where it continued to twitch and buck.

"How many bullets you got in that?" Emily asked.

"Eleven now."

A form, vaguely man shaped, flitted past the opening and Hector fired another round. To John, it was a confounding riot of textures and flailing appendages, an upright heap of *bilantu* acting in concert. An image flashed and faded in his head with a phosphorescent *phiff*, a troupe of costumed Chinese acrobats assembled into a towering human mimic, lumbering across the stage in a marvel of strength and coordination. The form shrugged a segment of its shoulder through the opening, and for a fraction of a second John thought he could make out the blue of a uniform before the mass re-coalesced around it.

Jesus, could there be a man under all that?

Hector shot again. Emily darted forward and swung her crutch down. Once, twice. John could hear nothing over the roar in his ears. Each new round sounded more distant than the last. He'd lost track of the number of shots. Six now? Eight? The floor was littered with carcasses. His footing was becoming treacherous. Every time he moved forward to smash something, John's shoe came down on an irregular surface. He nearly slipped on a slick patch and would have gone down had Emily not grabbed his flailing arm. How could there be so many of them?

Pop went Hector's gun. Pop. Pop. He was nearly deafened now. It no longer sounded as if the shots were coming from inside the closet. They seemed to issue from the infirmary or the hall beyond. Hector was shouting, but like the gunshots, his voice was a distant echo.

Pop. Pop. Pop-pop-pop-pop.

What was he shooting at? Nothing had come through the hole for several seconds. Hector's gun, a Glock, John noted dully, was still pointed at the door. Must be hot, he thought absurdly. Pop, pop. But wait. He wasn't firing after all. No flash came from the muzzle, no buck of recoil. John swallowed, stuffed a finger into the canal of his left ear, shook it vigorously, and swallowed again.

Pop.

The shots *were* coming from outside the closet, as were the shouts.

"About fucking time," Hector said. "Calvary's finally here."

When John took a cautious step forward, the guard pressed a restraining hand against his chest.

"Let's just hang back here until things settle down. Or haven't you had enough excitement?"

John eyed the hole in the door, resisting a sudden, maddening desire to poke his head out. What had trapped them here? Man? Beast? Brutrelli? *Bilantu*? He wanted to know. He *needed* to know.

"What if they don't get control?" Emily asked. She was clutching the crutch against her chest like a soldier presenting a rifle for inspection, the pad thick with gore. Her face was a pale oval in the glow of the single overhead bulb, bloodless lips pressed tight below dimly shining eyes.

"They will. We're trained for this sort of thing."

"You have *got* to be kidding."

"You know what I mean. Trouble. We're trained to react when the shit hits the fan."

The commotion in the next room intensified with a staccato of gunfire and confused shouts. Something overturned with a metallic clang and John realized, belatedly, that an alarm was pulsing in a continuous warble. The entire facility was probably under lock-down by now.

"I hope you're right, because the shit is most certainly hitting the fan."

The shooting continued for what seemed an inordinately long time but was probably no more than twenty or thirty seconds. The crack of gunfire slowed from a flurry to individual rounds to a smattering of bangs punctuating increasingly lengthy breaks. John couldn't help picturing a bag of nearly-cooked popcorn spinning slowly on a microwave turntable. A final shot rang out and for the next minute, they stood listening as the alarm droned on.

"Don't move," Hector said. "I'm going to check things out."

The guard moved to the door, picking his way over the fallen *bilantu* as if he were high-stepping through a minefield. When he got to the hole he bent to peer out.

"Well?" Emily demanded after a moment.

The guard waved her silent. "Martin!" he called through the opening. "It's me, Hector. You guys done? We'd like to come out without getting shot to pieces."

Someone responded and Hector hitched a mirthless chuckle. "Yeah, tell me something I don't know. So, can we come out or what?"

John heard nothing, but Hector gave the person on the other side of the door a thumbs-up before motioning them forward. They advanced slowly, plowing the way clear with their crutches. When they reached the front of the closet, Emily gave a nod and Hector swung the door open.

The room they stepped into was a detonation, broken furnishings, shattered glass, debris everywhere. Half the overhead fluorescents were dark. The hallway door rested at a forty-five-degree angle directly across from the smashed threshold, propped against the remains of a low bank of cabinets. Bullet-hole constellations peppered the walls, while plaster dust and gunpowder smoke hung thick in the air.

Littering the floor in a profusion of convoluted shapes were a dozen or more *bilantu*, their carapaces already softening and sagging in death. In another hour, all that would remain of them would be a thick, translucent slime, a glaze of decomposing viscera that would disappear completely when it dried.

And at the center of the chaos, lying in an expanding pool of blood, were the remains of a man as broken as the rest of the room, his limbs angled unnaturally, his head punched through by at least two bullets, leaking a wet scramble of gray matter.

John saw a gleaming finger of clavicle poking through the guard's collar, a shard of humerus through his sleeve. Both femurs had erupted from the flesh. Brutrelli, and it *was* Brutrelli, still recognizable despite the damage, had been reduced to a shatter-boned mush, a crash test dummy sprawled amidst the twisted heap of a failed tolerance trial.

"He demolished himself breaking through the door." John's own bones felt as though they were being ground together. "They used him like a scaffolding."

The room began to fill with officers. They crept forward with drawn guns and eyes darting, skittish as feral cats. John considered raising his hands to show he wasn't a threat, then decided against it, fearing even that gesture might trigger a sudden round of nervous gunfire.

"He was wearing those things," the nearest guard said. His face was so livid the pallor appeared to have been powered on with a makeup sponge. "Like a suit of armor. We didn't even know a person was under all that until they started dropping off him. Christ, it was like something out of a nightmare."

Along a far wall: a twitch of motion. Someone hollered and pointed. A volley of renewed gunfire reduced the carcass to smaller and smaller pieces.

John decided he would remain perfectly still until told to move.

"But was he the driver or the vehicle?" Emily asked. She glanced down at the crutch she was still holding as if noticing it for the first time. "Who was controlling who?"

"We won't be getting any answers from him, that's for sure." At some point, Hector had re-holstered his gun. He flexed his left arm experimentally, fingering open the bloody tear in his sleeve. "But I'm guessing those things alone wouldn't be able to take shots at people."

The alarm cut off and a thick silence filled the infirmary. Like Emily, John still gripped a crutch. Slowly, he lowered the tip to the floor, but as his fingers began to relax from the shaft a new shout drew fire to a *bilantu* already decomposed to the consistency of skinned-over pudding. When the bullets hit they raised mud-pot eruptions in the flattening puddle.

John remained perfectly still.

The lead officer's walkie-talkie crackled. With a dreamy sort of indifference, he reached down and plucked it off his belt. The voice on the other end, a supervisor demanding updates, only partially roused the guard out of his stupor, answering each barked question with hesitant monosyllables. One down. Safe. Here. No. No. No. No clue. After a final, shrill demand for specifics, he simply returned the walkie-talkie to its clip and flicked it off.

"Dick," he offered to no one in particular.

During the exchange, the strength had drained from John's legs. He would have sagged to the floor if not for the support of the crutch. He lifted a head that felt like a bag of drying cement and found Emily's eyes. She nodded, but he had no idea what unspoken question she was responding to.

"Can I go back to my cell now?" he asked. Sleep, his mind chanted. Sleep. Sleep. Sleep.

The guard stared at him as if he hadn't understood the question.

"Doctor's orders," Emily said. When the man still did nothing she added, "Now!" barking the word. The command did what the walkie-talkie exchange hadn't, snapping him back to some semblance of professional focus.

"Right. Hograms, Swydorsky, escort this one back to his cell."

As they stepped out of the room and into the hall, someone shouted, "Right corner!" and the echo of gunfire accompanied them all the way to the steps and up to the next floor landing, where a new phalanx of rifle-toting officers squeezed past in a rush to join the fray.

Eleven

"Fossils!"

"What about them?" Little Billy paused to mop the sweat from his face, wishing they had thought to buy a good pair of gloves this afternoon. After only twenty minutes of twisting, his palms had begun to blister. He'd pulled his windbreaker from his pack and wrapped the sleeves around the handles in an effort to pad the grip, but it provided only marginal protection.

"Why aren't there any? If these *bilantu* have been here for millions and millions of years, why haven't scientist discovered their fossils by now?"

"Because fossils need physical remains to form: bones, cartilage, teeth, that sort of thing. After death, the *bilantu* just sort of melt away, liquefy to goop that evaporates completely in about twelve hours. A puddle of jelly isn't going to leave a fossil."

In the dim illumination from distant streetlights, Katie was a vague outcropping in the near darkness. If it weren't for the glowing tip of her cigarette arcing periodically to her lips where it flared, faded, and returned to her knee, she might have been mistaken as just another gravestone, a marble angel sitting cross-legged in some forgotten family plot.

"I just don't get it. Why do they play this, 'don't look at me' game? It makes no sense."

Little Billy slowly pulled the auger up with a laborious, hand-over-hand effort. The soil was so dry the shaft continually filled with falling debris each time he removed the drill to clear dirt from the blades. But he was making progress. Slow progress. After forty-five minutes, he'd managed to dig out a twenty-foot hole next to the *xalantracoil*. The *coil* did not pulse or glow. Like the *bilantu*, it slept at night, although its ability to disguise its appearance continued. To Katie, it still looked like a grave marker.

"I have a theory about that."

Katie's cigarette hissed faintly as she took a drag. "Do tell."

"You're not going to like it."

"Shocking."

Little Billy wormed his fingers through the packed soil until they touched the auger's metal shaft. Taking care not to cut his palm on the blade edge, he began prying dirt clots free.

"There seems to be a correlation between intelligence and the ability to perceive the *bilantu*. The less intelligent the animal, the more likely it can see them. Cats can see them. Most dogs. Nearly all birds. Rodents. Squirrels. Most definitely squirrels. But I've seen elephants parading down main street as part of a circus promotion. They walked right past a cluster of *squim* without a flicker of awareness. And believe me, elephants are incredibly perceptive. They *should* have seen them. They didn't."

Little Billy tapped his temple.

"Too smart. John says pigs can't see them, either. How he figured that one out I have no idea. And most of the smarter dog breeds, the standard poodles, the shepherds. Invisible to them."

"Glad to know my brother was smarter than a squirrel." Katie's voice wavered. "Ha!"

The exhalation descended into a series of quite hitches, and before he quite realized he had dropped the auger, Little Billy was at her side, his arm across her quivering shoulders. He said nothing, allowing her to regain her composure in her own time, but as she sagged deeper into his embrace he was acutely aware of his sweat and stink, the dirt caked on his hands. His filth.

But she didn't pull away, even after the hitching had stopped and she'd grown still. His own stillness deepened to something almost excruciating, the breathless immobility of an ornithologist (the word came back to him with a mental "pop") whose subject suddenly lands on the rim of his binoculars.

"So," she said after some minutes, easing her head off his chest. "Your theory."

Little Billy undraped his arm from her shoulder and stood, thankful the darkness would likely mask anything Katie might otherwise have read in his expression. "Intelligence seems to correspond to an inability to see the *bilantu*, a sort of blindness that protects." He made his way back to the hole and resumed digging. "As long as a species can't see them, they're not viewed as prey. You'd think it would be the opposite, right? Something that can't see them coming should be their easiest targets, sitting ducks."

"Absolutely." Katie rose, took a last drag on her cigarette and carefully rubbed the butt out on a nearby gravestone. A ping of disapproval tugged Little Billy's lips to one side. *Show a little respect, young lady.* But it died quickly, snuffed by a decidedly stronger desire to not view her as a child. She was a woman, after all. What had she told him, twenty-three, twenty-four? Definitely, a woman, although one young enough to be his daughter. Technically. If he had started having kids as a teen. A young teen.

Little Billy fell silent as he did the math.

"Sitting ducks," Katie prompted after a moment.

"Right. Instead, they prey on species that *can* see them. Harder targets. Much harder. The squirrels around here have developed some incredible defensive strategies. What John and I witnessed was amazing. They have a permanent bunker mentality. And their breeding practices, holy crap."

He knew he was getting off topic but was helpless to stop himself. The old excitement had taken hold, relentless and deeply satisfying, the urge to explain, to share their discoveries. *His* discoveries. "To maintain their numbers in the face of such aggressive predation, they've become incredibly prolific. They're like naked mole rats. They have colonies and queens. Queens, for Christ sake! That doesn't happen overnight. They must have adapted over eons."

Little Billy had stopped auguring during his sudden burst of enthusiasm. He sighed and began twisting once again, but before he had completed three turns Katie placed a hand on his forearm.

"You've been doing all the work since we got here. Let me take over for a spell."

"I'm fine."

"I insist." When he shook his head, she squinted up at him. "Oh, I get it. This is *man's* work, is it? Wouldn't want the little lady breaking a nail."

Her tone was mildly playful, but Little Billy detected an undercurrent of real annoyance. With a flourish, he presented the augur poking upright from the hole. Katie re-wrapped the windbreaker's sleeves around the handles and began twisting.

"Anyway, the question is: why do the *bilantu* protect intelligent species until the moment of discovery? What benefit could there possibly be in such a strategy?"

"Maybe they know if we discovered them, we'd wipe them out."

"Would we? We haven't wiped out rats or cockroaches or tapeworms. Haven't even tried. If everyone knew about the *bilantu,* we'd probably just accept them as one of the many creatures out there with the potential to harm us."

"So what then?" Sweat already sheened her face and arms, but her motions were fast and forceful. She was making quicker progress than he had been. Little Billy would need to add another shaft extension to the auger soon.

"I think, maybe, their instinct, their *biological imperative,* is to give intelligence a chance to ripen for as long as possible."

Katie blew a damp strand of hair from her face with a huff. "Ripen? You make it sound like they're waiting until we're juicy enough to harvest."

"For their masters to harvest, the *vetro offalate*."

"Squeeze our big brains out of our heads and slurp them up through a straw?" She lowered her voice in imitation of a cartoon ghoul. "We want to suck your braaaaiiinnnsss."

"Not our brains. Our intelligence. Our self-awareness. Our..." His fingers fluttered about his temples. "Essence."

Katie's motions were mechanical, tireless, and despite a shudder of revulsion, uninterrupted. "Like leeches, then? Drinking our superior I.Q.s? Please tell me that's not what you're suggesting."

Only it was, and the clearer the *vetro's* thoughts became, the more he was convinced of this. Over the previous twenty-four hours, images had flitted through his mind, murky at first, then gradually clearing as if multiple layers of sheer curtains were being pulled aside one by one: sinuous machines that gleamed like flayed muscle as their collectors telescoped toward victims immobilized on slabs of blackened stone. Bulbous terminals that puckered and swelled while the sentience was guzzled from deflating consciousnesses.

"It's just a theory."

"Oh, my god. You are such a lousy liar. Theory my ass. You've seen something. A vision? A premonition? Whatever you want to call it."

"Flashes. Just flashes. I could be misinterpreting them."

"Don't do that."

"What?"

"Backtrack. Decide you have to soften things, spare me the worst. You know what? This actually makes me feel better. If having our consciousness sucked dry by cosmic leeches is what we're in for, I'm glad Bobby isn't here to face it. And I'll make damn sure my parents won't be here either, even if it means smothering them in their sleep with a pillow."

"We can't let that happen," Little Billy said, breaking the momentary silence.

"No. That's why we're-whoa!"

157

Katie had been pushing with all her weight as she worked the auger. Now the tool plunged, meeting no resistance until the handles hit the ground. Katie fell with it, striking the protruding T-bar with an 'umph' that left her rocking in pain.

"Jesus!" Little Bill leaped to her. "Are you alright?" An idiotic question. Of course, she wasn't alright. Her face was a quickly evolving montage of hurt, annoyance, embarrassment and feigned recovery. He realized he was rubbing his hand between her shoulder blades in a "there-there" gesture of fatherly concern a moment before she waved him away.

"I'm fine," she wheezed. She pressed a palm against her chest. "Just got the wind knocked out of me." Katie drew a ragged breath and blew it out slowly. "What the hell happened?"

"Looks like you hit a void of some kind, an empty space."

She clamped a hand over her mouth. "Oh my god, Will. Did I just drill into somebody's *coffin?*"

"Thirty feet down? No. More like you hit a cavity of some type. A cavern. A... a bubble. I read we're in the middle of the longest drought on record. Not surprising there'd be some subsidence. Water table's probably lower than it's been in who knows how long."

"Will, what exactly is your plan? I want to know. You come out here, dig a hole in the middle of the night next to a grave marker, and somehow this is going to prevent the end of the world. It's time you shared the big picture." She gave him a cock-headed look of appraisal. "Provided there *is* a big picture."

Continued secrecy was pointless now. The previous eight hours had been a non-stop Q and A. He'd already told her so much, more even than he'd shared with Andrew. At first, his answers were sketchy summaries of how he and Dr. Tate had met, their unlikely discovery of the *bilantu*, the *xalanthracoils*, the *vetro offalate*. But as the stifling afternoon slid toward a sticky evening, he had begun to speak of other things. Fears and regrets.

Loss.

Haltingly, he told her about Laura. Highboy, too. He probably shouldn't have run on as he had; she was already dealing with her own loss. Why heap his sorrows on her fresh wounds?

Still, what was done was done. And wasn't holding back this last bit of information a little like slamming the lid on hope after all the other evils had escaped into the world?

"Okay, the big picture."

She said nothing as he explained what the *xalantracoils* were and what they could do. She remained silent as he confided his expectations, slim as they were, that somehow either he or Andrew would be able to obtain explosives to lower into the hole they had just dug and blow the *coil* out of the ground, or at least wound it enough to keep from activating when the time came.

She kept quiet when he recounted his and John's attempt, six years earlier, to yank down a *coil* using a steel cable attached to the hitch of a rented F-350, how the truck had jerked when it reached the end of its tether, bucking and straining like a mad dog, tires spinning, engine roaring, John behind the wheel trying to coax every last bit of torque out of the screaming V-8 while the *coil* stood unaffected, moving not an inch under the assault.

Eventually, Little Billy found her continued silence more disturbing than comforting. She had seemingly accepted so much already. It was hard, after all, to deny what your own eyes, your *newly opened* eyes, revealed about the previously unknown world. But maybe this was more than she could believe. Gateways to other universes? Cosmic convergences? Crazy schemes involving explosives? Katie had reached her limit.

Little Billy wound down, his last sentence trailing off rather than concluding. In silence, he reached for his pack and rummaged through it until he found his water bottle. He drank half and wiped his lips dry before realizing he should have offered Katie a drink first. Damn. Damn, damn, damn! He held the bottle out to her.

After another moment, she stood and brushed the dirt from her shorts, then clapped her hands in a "that's that" display.

"Well, then." She turned and strode to the *xalanthracoil*. "Let's get this over with." She raised her palm to the black stone.

"Katie, don't!"

She turned to him with a rueful smile. "Sorry, Will. I have to. Whatever's coming for us, it's already marked me. Like it's marked you and Andrew and his father. Like it marked my brother. What's the expression, in for a penny? Besides, I'm not going to let the guys have all the fun."

For an instant, Little Billy considered rushing over and wrestling her away from the *coil*. *Don't be a fool! They'll tear your mind to shreds.* But something held him back. It wasn't hard to define. He wanted her on his side, not as a sympathetic observer but as an equal, a partner like Andrew and John. A member of the team. God help him, Little Billy wanted this woman, whom he had known less than a day, at his side when the endgame began, however it might play out. Besides, once you learned how to see the *bilantu*, you couldn't unlearn it, could you? As she had said, in for a penny.

Without taking her eyes from his, Katie Fife went in for a pound.

Twelve

It turned out to be alarmingly easy to leave the station with the Trenchrite banging at his hip, concealed by a few shirts and a bath towel at the bottom of his overnight bag.

Andrew hadn't slept well, spending most of the night blinking up at the bunkroom's drop-tiled ceiling and listening to the snorts and snores of the rest of the men on B shift. Each time he began to drift off, a bell would ring or a firefighter would haul himself out of his cot, coughing and absentmindedly scratching his ass, to use the john.

Try as he might, he could conceive of no scenario that would allow him to simply waltz into the supply room, remove the explosives from the box of cervical collars, and sashay back out again without drawing attention. Someone would notice. With his luck, it would be Sid Langston. In the dim light filtering in from the hallway, he could envision the exchange with a neon brilliance, Sid's bulk blocking his escape, his expression changing from suspicion to a "gotcha" smirk. *What's in the bag, Tate? Oh, man, you really fucked up this time. No squirming your way out of this one.*

Even if he made it out of the storeroom without being noticed, he would still have to exit the station, and that would mean going through the common room and passing at least half-a-dozen firefighters. Of course, many of them would be the C crew arriving for their shift. There'd be the usual exchange of greetings and gossip.

He might be able to slip out quietly while the rest chummed it up. Actually, wasn't that the way things usually turned out, with Andrew slipping away after a vague wave to an indifferent crowd? But how to conceal the Trenchrite? He couldn't just throw it in his overnight, could he?

Could he?

What choice did he have? He couldn't hide the explosives under his clothes. He couldn't toss them out an open window and nab them on the other side. Maybe the simplest plan had the best chance of success. Wasn't that the way they approached every fire? Every medical emergency? First responders didn't have the luxury of elaborate schemes and convoluted strategies. That was for engineers and architects.

Even as these considerations looped wearily through his thoughts, Andrew came to realize on an almost subconscious level that over-thinking his plan might be more than just counter-productive. It might be dangerous. He did not believe his thoughts were entirely his own anymore. Others might be listening in, their ears-if they had such things-pressed against the outside of his skull like a drinking glass to a closed door. In the hours before dawn his exhaustion settled in an obscuring white drift over the outlines of what he would do the next morning, and with that Andrew had slept until morning.

He woke in a sort of anesthetizing fog, knowing on some level what he planned to do but giving it little, if any, conscious thought. Andrew showered and shaved. He brushed his teeth. He went to his locker and dressed in his civilian clothes. With his bag over his shoulder, he strolled down the hall to the storeroom. His heart beat slowly and steadily as a collision of voices drifted out from the kitchen. Breakfast. Eggs and bacon. Laughter and pancakes.

He felt nothing as his hand drifted out to insert the key into the lock on the storeroom door. Andrew could not remember having removed it from its peg on the office wall, yet he must have. He stepped inside. He was a piece of driftwood, moving effortlessly on a current sweeping him into this eddy before swirling him out again into deeper waters. Slowly, methodically, he removed the collars, gathered the Trenchrite, stashed it away, returned the collars, returned the box to its shelf and exited the storeroom.

He felt nothing as he relocked the door, replaced the key on its peg. He did not rush. If anything, he moved slower than usual, almost defiantly sluggish. No one stopped Andrew. No one saw him until he crossed the common room and even then no one took notice except Gary, who slapped him on the shoulder, gave him a questioning look and wished him a good day.

In the car driving back to his motel, the bag sat next to him on the passenger seat. Gradually, the fog lifted and the reality of what he'd done rushed in to take its place. He was a criminal now. A thief. There was something naggingly familiar in the way surrender and resignation swirled sourly in his stomach, and for several blocks, Andrew puzzled over the tug of déjà vu until it came to him. This was how he had felt the first time he'd taken a drink before work, the shameful realization that he was now a man who couldn't keep the booze from spilling into places it should never go.

Now he had become something new yet again.

You had to appreciate the irony, Andrew thought as he turned into the motel parking lot. He'd started drinking in earnest to keep from seeing his father's monsters (hadn't he?), and now he had stopped drinking (hadn't he?) after accepting they were real. Maybe this was what sobriety looked like. Andrew had always assumed it would arrive gradually, a slow accumulation of dry days that would solidify into something substantial, a border dividing *then* from *now*. But maybe, under extreme circumstances, sobriety came all at once, like a wall, a tree, a guardrail bringing an abrupt stop to a long skid.

Andrew rounded the motel's back wing and hit the brakes. Grace stood outside the door to his room, and she wasn't alone. Her brother James was with her.

After a moment, he eased forward and crept into a parking space. He considered leaving his overnight bag in the car, afraid that Grace would somehow sense the Trenchrite concealed inside. But he quickly rejected the notion. It probably wasn't a good idea to keep high explosives locked in a hot car.

"I didn't want to bother you at work," she said, taking a step back as he approached. Andrew could feel his pulse in the inner lining of his mouth, hammering so hard his gums felt inflamed. All the fear he had kept a lid on earlier sprang up with a Jack-in-the-box release of uncoiling dread. James held an envelope in one hand.

"Jim," he said, giving his brother-in-law a nod that was mechanically returned. "What brings you to my humble abode?"

Grace cleared her throat. "Andy," she said, not taking her eyes from the pavement, "Andy, I'm sorry. I never wanted… I never thought it would…"

"Grace?"

She let out a watery breath and shook her head. "God. I don't know how to…"

"She's taken out a restraining order against you, Andy." James thrust the envelope at his chest. His tone was businesslike, the brisk, unsympathetic professionalism of a man with a job to do. "Take it," he said. Andrew's head tick-tocked between Grace, still refusing to meet his gaze, and James, whose face was an expressionless mask, his eyes invisible behind the black ovals of his sunglasses. "Take it," he repeated. "Don't make this difficult. She's already doing you a favor. A cop normally does this. Grace asked Natalie to keep things just between us. She wanted to protect your privacy."

Natalie, James' wife, was a Hillsborough County family court judge. Numbly, he grasped the envelope. Yes, she was definitely a judge. A judge for the county. He couldn't seem to move beyond this simple fact. Natalie Couter was a judge. He was holding a restraining order from his brother-in-law's wife and she was a family court judge.

164

"It's only temporary," Grace said. She wiped her cheek with the back of her fingers.

"Until a permanent one can be issued," James added. "Thirty days."

"I haven't decided that yet."

"Grace, what's this all about? What does this thing say?"

She tried to speak, but managed only a series of clicks and gulps.

"It says you've lost your right to have unsupervised visits with Anna." An edge of impatience gave James' words a sharpened precision. "From now on, you want to see your kid, you do so in the presence of Grace."

Presence of Grace. Presence of grace? Isn't that what he had always tried to do?

"Is this about the other day? I wasn't drinking, Grace. I swear to god, I would never put Anna at risk."

"Since when?"

"James, stop." His wife placed a hand on her brother's shoulder.

"Fine. I did what I came to do. I'll be at the car." He turned without giving Andrew another glance and marched off across the parking lot, his heels clicking like distant gunfire across the asphalt.

"I'm sorry, Andy. I had to bring him. Legally, I'm not allowed to serve you the order. It has to be someone else."

"Grace, please. Don't do this." His throat clamped shut.

"You didn't give me much choice, did you? You think I like this?" She was crying freely now, gasping out words between sobs. "You think I want to keep you and Anna apart? She loves you so much. Even after everything that's happened. This is going to break her heart."

"Mine, too. But it's not too late." He grasped the envelope in both hands. "We can tear this up, start over. I'm not the same man I was six months ago."

"I don't know who you are now."

"Sober."

"Then I'm happy for you." She pulled a tissue from her pocket and dabbed at her eyes. "I am. But for now, I think this is best. I'm not forbidding you from seeing Anna. Visit whenever you want. You just won't be taking her out on your own."

"What about us, Grace? Where does this," he waved the envelope between them, "leave us?"

"You're the one who moved out."

"I'm ready to come back."

She leaned forward and gave Andrew a peck on his cheek. "We'll see. I have to go now. Anna's with my sister and I promised I'd be back before lunch."

Grace turned. *Stop her*! a voice screamed. *Take her inside. Tell her everything. Make her see the truth.*"

He reached out, grasped her hand, interlaced his fingers with hers, and although she did not turn to face him her fingers tightened around his.

"Grace, there's something I need to tell you." She said nothing, but her head turned slightly, as if she were watching what their hands would do next.

Andrew imagined leading her into the motel room, sitting her down at the table, falling on his knees and begging her to believe what he was about to say. In the next instant, he saw the room's squalor, the unmade bed, the yellowed walls. The wastebasket still filled with empty liquor bottles. It would be the first thing Grace noticed and no words would convince her he hadn't drunk them dry.

And yet, he was willing to push on despite his misgivings, when the impression of movement drew his glance over his wife's shoulder to James, standing next to his car and tapping away on the screen of his iPhone. Something floated over his brother-in-law's head, a living ball of spikes. It hovered for a moment, rotating slowly. Little Billy would have a specific name for this thing, but "monstrosity" was good enough for Andrew. It swelled, the folds of its translucent skin stretching taut before a spasmodic constriction sent the creature drifting toward them with the soft hiss of air jetting from a valve.

"What?" Grace whispered.

Without taking his hand from hers, Andrew pivoted to position himself between his wife and the approaching *bilantu*. He leaned in and kissed her hard, pulling her close with a fierceness that startled them both. He felt her stiffen as she tried to back away, but he followed, keeping his lips on hers even as he sensed the creature directly overhead. Andrew's tongue probed across lips pressed tight. The struggle went on for an unseemly amount of time. His testicles drew up in anticipate of an imminent knee to the groin, but just as he was about to relent, he heard another hiss of expelled air. A shadow drifted over them, and as it did Grace suddenly relaxed, although whether in resignation or empathy he couldn't tell. He held her for another two seconds, three seconds, four, then released her. As she stood with her head tilted up to his, the *bilantu* disappeared around the corner of the motel.

"I wish you hadn't done that."

"Because it was so horrible?"

"Because it wasn't." She waved off James, who was halfway across the parking lot, his hands balled into fists. "Is that all you wanted to say?"

"Tell Anna Daddy says 'hi'. Tell her I love her very much and I'll see her soon."

"Of course, of course."

Of curse? No, that wasn't right. He was losing it.

"And you. So much, Grace. I'm sorry for everything. Everything. Give me a chance to prove it."

"Thirty days. Then we'll see."

LITTLE BILLY JUMPED WHEN HIS PHONE BEGAN TO RING. The apartment had fallen into thick silence after Katie left, and although she'd urged him to make himself at home while she attended Bobby's funeral, he couldn't bring himself to turn on the television. Even using the toilet felt invasive. Two nights of sleeping under a roof had left him jittery and claustrophobic.

At least in Andrew's motel room, he had taken some comfort in its cheapness. There was nothing there he could ruin or corrupt with his presence. But this tidy one-bedroom with its shelf of family photos, wall of Monet prints and little bowls of potpourri made him nervous. He didn't want his presence to change a thing, not even the couch cushions. He'd slept fitfully on the couch, afraid his snores would wake Katie as she slept—or so he assumed—behind her closed bedroom door.

Little Billy wished now he had refused her offer, but she'd been so adamant he return home with her after the cemetery he hadn't had the heart to say no. What she'd seen after touching the *xalanthracoil* had scared the hell out of her. He couldn't blame her for not wanting to spend the night alone.

Little Billy pulled the cell from his shirt pocket and glanced at the display.

"Andy."

"Got what you want."

"What we talked about the other day?" He understood Andrew's reluctance to speak openly. Even thinking the word "explosives" felt dangerous.

"Boom, boom."

Little Billy winched. "You free tonight?"

"Free as a bird."

Little Billy pulled the phone from his ear and checked the display again, as if reconfirming who he was talking to. "You okay? You sound... tired."

There was a pause during which he thought he heard a faint slosh, the clank of glass against a countertop. "Didn't sleep well last night. Too much going through my head."

"I know how you feel."

"Do you, now?" A gulp. The smack of lips.

Little Billy nodded to his faint reflection on the dark television screen. "I'll come tonight at eleven. Why don't you get some sleep in the meantime? You sound like you could use it."

"Yes, *sir*! Sleep, sir. Count on it." The line went dead.

Little Billy sat for a long time with the phone in his hand, perched on the edge of the couch, listening as the clock on the wall relentlessly ticked down to a terminal event, one represented by a long series of glowing red zeros.

"HOW MUCH SHOULD WE USE?"

Andrew leaned back on his haunches and ran a finger over the molded plastic capsules enclosing the packets of Trenchrite. He hated being this close to a *coil*. He could feel its aura as an unpleasant tingle in the nasal lining beneath his eyes, a low-grade irritation that left him on the perpetual verge of a sneeze. They might sleep at night, as Little Billy claimed, but even now he could tell their potency had grown since his last encounter.

Of course, being hung over was probably exasperating its effect, but that was the cost of doing business with Mr. Beam. At least his afternoon sleep had been dreamless. If the *vetro offalate* had been listening, all they would have heard was the hollow drone of a brain sloshing in an alcohol bath.

"If I'm remembering right, two coils of this can knock over your average-sized tree. The entire packet can blast a firebreak twenty or thirty yards long and five feet wide."

"I say we use everything," Katie said. "If we're going to do this, then let's *do* it. Go big or go home."

Her presence still annoyed Andrew. He had answered the knock at his motel door in his tee-shirt and boxers, expecting only Little Billy. Instead, he had come face to face with Ms. Fife, who had given him a bright smile and sighed, "My hero." What the hell did that mean?

"Katie's the all-or-nothing type," Little Billy offered. "She wanted to bring a backhoe in here to dig the hole."

Andrew removed the top blister pack of explosives and set it next to the detonation cords, blasting caps and orange control box already on the ground. "How far down did you say you dug?"

169

"About thirty feet."

"And the *coil*? How far down does *that* go?"

Little Billy's lips fluttered as he exhaled. "Hard to say. Deep. Your dad and I found that out the hard way. I think Katie's right. Use all of it."

"I have absolutely no experience with this stuff. Using it all could mean downed trees, downed power lines." Andrew surveyed the houses and backyards abutting the small cemetery's chain link fence. "Not to mention property damage. Broken windows. No matter what, we're going to be waking the neighbors."

"Maybe they'll think a transformer blew," Little Billy suggested.

"Or some kids set off fireworks," Katie added.

"More like a couple sticks of dynamite. I'll use five feet worth. That should give us a big enough bang. Then we'll need to get out fast." He gave Katie a sidelong glance. "Ever fantasize about being a getaway driver?" They had all come in Katie's CRV, the same vehicle she had been driving on the day Comanche took her hostage.

"Ever since I can remember."

Andrew cut open the plastic using Little Billy's pocket knife. It only took a few minutes to set the charge. Packaged in ropey folds, the putty-like Trenchrite uncoiled to a single long segment which he double-braided around the detonation cord before threading down the hole.

"What prompted you to dig this?" Andrew asked as he worked. "Don't get me wrong. I'm glad you did. But there's no way you could have known I'd be able to score a box of high explosives. I didn't know until the minute I walked out of the station with it."

Little Billy handed him a second braid of Trenchrite, which Andrew attached to the first by squeezing the ends together.

"Hope, I guess. And not wanting to sit around waiting. Clock's ticking."

Once the explosives were in place, Andrew connected the blasting cap, synching one end around the detonation cord and the other to the control box's looped ignition wire. He removed the plastic ties holding the loops together and began unspooling the wire, Katie and Little Billy following as he retreated its full length of forty yards.

Andrew would have preferred twice that, but kept his thoughts to himself. They hunkered behind one of the cemetery's massive live oaks and Andrew held the controller up to Little Billy's flashlight beam. It was nothing more than a plastic rectangle boasting an on-off switch, two indicator lights and a safety pin.

"So this is it?" Little Billy asked.

"Guess so." Andrew hefted the controller a few times. "It's light. Reminds me of the ignition boxes I used to launch model rockets with."

"And I was picturing a big red thing with a handle," Katie whispered. By some mutual and unspoken agreement, they had all begun speaking in lowered voices.

"Keep your heads down," Andrew advised. He flipped the switch to "on" and frowned.

"Shouldn't one of those lights have come on?" Little Billy asked, echoing Andrew's own thought.

"Pretty sure."

"It has batteries, right?" Katie asked.

Andrew's shoulders dropped. The box's heft had already answered the question. Turning it over, he thumbed open the battery door. "Of course not. Why would it?" He angled the empty compartment toward the light. "I don't suppose anyone has two AAs?"

"I do. In the car." She shook her head in mock dismay. "What would you boys do without me?"

"I could tell you were pissed when you opened the door," Little Billy said as they wait for her return, "but she insisted on coming. And she's not someone you can say no to. Not easily. Plus, she's had a rough day. They buried her bother this afternoon."

Andrew was finding it hard to reconcile the frightened girl at the mercy of a raving hostage taker with the confident, competent woman now saving their scheme from an unforeseen setback.

171

"Don't worry about it." He slapped him on the back. "We're obviously incapable of pulling this off on our own. I wonder what she does for a living."

"Teaches second grade at Egypt Lake Elementary. She's on summer break."

"Ah."

After a moment, Little Billy cleared his throat. "Get any sleep this afternoon?"

"Plenty."

Another pause. "It's just that tonight we should all be as... focused... as possible."

"Agreed."

"Look, if you ever want to talk. Not that I'm a wealth of wisdom. I know a hell of a lot more about monsters than men. But I can lend an ear, if it helps."

Andrew stared into the branches above them. "I've found that most people can't see the big picture until they step far enough back from it. Maybe your unique perspective has given you some unique insights. I might take you up on your offer. When this is all over."

Katie materialized out of the gloom, presenting the double-AAs with a flourish. "I return triumphant."

Andrew installed the batteries and turned the box over. The red indicator light was aglow. He removed the safety pin and the green indicator lit.

"Maybe we should have the car running," Andrew suggested, crouching down with the others. "To save time."

"How much time does it take to turn a key?" Katie already had her fingers pressed to her ears. "I'm not going to miss this. But if you insist, I'm sure Will will be more than happy to keep the engine running."

Little Billy snorted. "Fuck that shit. I'm not missing this either."

Andrew nodded. "On three then." Peeking around the edge of the tree, he had a clear line of sight to the *xalantracoil*, an obsidian claw blacker than the surrounding night, curving up from the bone dry earth.

"One." Andrew's thumb slid over the fire button.

"Two." Little Billy followed Katie's lead, plugging his ears with his fingers.

"Three."

The detonation wasn't as loud as he feared, more like the crack of an enormous whip than the deep-throated boom he had expected. The ground around the *coil* heaved upward in a brown plume that was immediately obscured behind a cloud of white smoke. A gust of hot air ruffled his hair, bringing with it the acrid smell of rapid combustion and the cries of birds startled from their roosts. Andrew reinserted the safety key and turned the controller off as a rain of leaves and Spanish moss fell around them.

"That was impressive," Katie said. She stood and peered around the tree. "That thing's history. Pieces of it are probably landing in people's yards three blocks away."

"I'm going to check." A chorus of dogs was barking alarms throughout the neighborhood. A light flicked on in a second story window across the street, a porch light a few doors down. They would have to move quickly. "Wait here."

"I'll take that under advisement," Katie said, matching him step-for-step as he edged into the smoke. Little Billy was at her side, his flashlight beam sweeping through the air in rapid arcs. There was something in Andrew's hair. He ran a hand over his head and removed a clump of moss. A small lizard landed on the back of his neck and wiggled beneath his shirt collar. He scooped it out and tossed it away, imagining a dozen 911 calls reaching dispatch in the next few seconds. Which fire station would get the call? Fifteen? Or maybe sixteen. Go, go, go, he chanted under his breath; the clock is most definitely ticking. Still, Katie was probably right. The coil should be nothing but...

"Holy shit," she said.

A puff of warm breeze had parted the smoke enough to reveal a crater ten feet across descending into darkness too deep for the flashlight's beam to penetrate.

"What a hole." She punched Andrew in the upper arm. "None too shabby, Master Blaster. I just hope no graves were... Oh, you have *got* to be kidding me."

Through the dissipating smoke, a sweep of black stone appeared like the prow of a ship emerging from a fog bank. The crater exposed another fifteen feet of the *xalanthracoil* corkscrewing downward, widening in places to bulbous knuckles before narrowing once again. To Andrew, it resembled a petrified taproot burrowing toward whatever bedrock lay below the sandy topsoil.

"It was worth a shot." Little Billy sighed after a moment. "Maybe it was pie-in-the-sky to think we could destroy something that's survived millions of years."

"It's leaning more."

"Katie..."

"I'm sure of it. Not by much, but we definitely loosened it."

"We need to go." When Andrew turned, Katie grabbed his arm.

"Go? We can't *go*. We need to try again. Use everything that's left."

"No time." Andrew thought he caught the faint warble of sirens over the clamor of barking dogs, maybe the rumble of a patio door sliding open. "You saw how long it took to set the first charge. We have to go. *Now*."

"This might be our only chance." Katie blocked his path, both hands pressed against his chest. The desperation in her face wasn't quite as intense as it had been when Comanche had ordered her to reach out and take the water bottle, but it was close.

"Getting arrested will guarantee that. We go now, fall back to plan B."

Katie's hands curled to fists, twisting the fabric of his shirt, pulling him down until they were nose-to-nose. "My brother's in a place just like this now. You want the same thing to happen to your family?"

Sirens. He was sure. Blocks away but approaching fast. Closing his own hands over hers, he squeezed until her fingers untwined from his shirt. "We're done for now."

174

"Discretion is the better part of valor," Little Billy added, approaching with outstretched arms, as if attempting to herd them both back.

Katie yanked her hands out of Andrew's. "We quoting Shakespeare now? How about this one: 'et tu, Brute?' You two need to grow a pair and finish what we started."

"You're not thinking straight," Little Billy shot back. "Andrew's right, we can't risk getting arrested. I'm leaving. He's leaving. And if you still want to be a part of this, I suggest you snap out of it, get behind the wheel and drive us the hell out of here."

Without another word, Katie spun and began trotting toward the exit.

"Grab your stuff. She might leave our asses behind."

"*Do* we have a plan B?" Andrew asked, gathering up his paraphernalia.

"Convince the military to bring in a few tanks and blast the shit out of every single *coil*."

"Brilliant."

"In the meantime, I have a more immediate plan."

"What's that?"

"Run."

Thirteen

Little Billy and Katie spent most of the next day working their way in a slow circle from one *xalanthracoil* to the next, trying to determine the best candidate for a second, bigger assault. The cemetery *coil* was no longer an option. It had been cordoned off with yellow police tape and flashing barricades. Little Billy wondered if the people who had erected the perimeter had experienced any odd sensations as they worked, a sense of disorientation maybe, or an unpleasant tingling across exposed skin, as if invisible insects were attempting to scuttle under collars and cuffs. And what about the hot glow pulsing from its fissured surface like methodically stoked coals? Had they noticed that? Christ, how could they not?

"Of course," Katie slapped her forehead. "Tampa!"

Little Billy pulled his handkerchief from a pocket and mopped the back of his neck. They had surveyed six *coils* so far and rejected each as too exposed. The one they stood before now, rising from a triangular patch of landscaping in the center of a strip mall parking lot, wouldn't do either. Security cameras kept surveillance from at least three locations. And there was a busy street not twenty yards away. He wondered what this *xalanthracoil* looked like to passersby. A birdbath? The base of a streetlight?

Or nothing at all, erased from awareness not by a trick of mental manipulation but by the triviality of its location, just another dusty green island in an ocean of gray asphalt.

Little Billy was beginning to doubt they'd find another *coil* isolated enough to plant explosives around. He'd never scouted them all himself. That had been John's department. Now he was relying on a map the senior Tate had given him shortly before his arrest.

"Hello? McFly?"

Little Billy turned. "Sorry. What was that?"

Katie's mood had improved dramatically from the previous evening. Unwilling to spend another night in Andrew's den of self-pity, he'd been prepared to curl up on a park bench, especially after their silent ride back to Andrew's motel. As the other man exited Katie's CRV, Little Billy, who was riding shotgun, opened his own door.

"Call tomorrow if you want," he told her, one foot already on the pavement.

"Don't be stupid," she responded flatly, not taking her eyes from the front windshield. Little Billy met Andrew's glance as he passed and they exchanged smiles, his sheepish, Andrew's sympathetic. At her apartment, Katie banging through the front door without a backward glance, leaving it for Little Billy to close after slinking inside. And yet at breakfast, she had been pleasant and talkative, as if their relationship had reverted overnight to a prior emotional setting. He had no idea if she'd had a real change of heart, or if she was just playing mind games with him.

"Think, McFly. I just made a major discovery here."

"Were you even born when that movie came out?"

"You sure like reminding me about my age."

Little Billy refolded the map he'd been consulting and tucked it in his pack. "Do I?"

"Yes. It's annoying. Knock it off. Anyway, my discovery." She motioned him to lead on, having apparently rejected this *xalanthracoil* without need of his counsel.

"Your discovery."

"I just figured out how Tampa got its name."

"'Sticks of fire,' right? That's what 'Tampa' means in the Seminole language. Or was it some earlier dialect? It's been a while since middle school." Little Billy pulled his water bottle from the pack, took a gulp, offered it to Katie.

"Who knows? Point is, everyone thinks 'sticks of fire' refers to either lightning or the guns of the Conquistadors."

"Sounds right." He pointed to the other side of the street and they crossed at the intersection. Their next target was three blocks north and two east. Hopefully, it was tucked away at the back of an overgrown lot and not smack in the middle of somebody's front yard. The *coil* he had shown Andrew the other day in the litter-strewn ditch was far from ideal, but it was looking more and more like their next best candidate. At least it wasn't visible from the highway.

"It's not. That's not what the Indians were referring to."

"Native Americans."

"Jesus, would you just listen? They weren't referring to lightning bolts or guns. They were talking about the *xalanthracoils*!"

"Say what now?"

"Think about it. Sticks of fire. That perfectly describes what they look like when they're firing up, big glowing sticks poking from the ground." Katie stopped him with an arm across his chest. "Which means this isn't the first time they've come to life. This convergence thing, whatever, must have happened before and somehow primitive natives found a way to stop the invasion! If they can do it, so can we."

"First, we've got no proof 'sticks of fire' refers to the *xalanthracoils*." Katie opened her mouth to protest and he hastened to add, "but let's say it does. And let's say the *Native Americans* could see through the illusion, saw them powering up. Just because they started to glow doesn't mean a convergence was about to happen. Maybe the conditions weren't quite right. A near miss. There's a shitload we don't know. We're talking about alternate universes and parallel realities and things that make wormholes seem ho-hum. I doubt they could have stopped a full-blown invasion with bows and arrows."

They set off again. Little Billy had made his own discovery today. As they surveyed more and more *coils,* their power to repulse had become more and more obvious. Nothing had been built over or around them, no building or bridge, no cell tower or, as they had just observed, parking lot. In some cases, the spacing between utility poles changed dramatically in order to leapfrog them. Otherwise straight roads veered and veered again in avoidance. Walls notched around them. He doubted these adjustments, subtle or otherwise, had been conscious decisions, and in their discovery, he felt like an archeologist unearthing the underlining principle of the city's design. The *xalanthracoils* were unmovable outcroppings around which centuries of development had flowed.

"So how do we know this isn't another near miss," Katie asked. "Maybe we're getting all worked up for nothing."

"If it wasn't for the voices in my head, I'd say you had a point. Or if the voices were fading. But they're not. They're getting louder. Every day. Every hour. Haven't you noticed?"

"Ever since touching that thing," she said after a moment. "Yeah, I've noticed. But maybe they won't be as loud tonight. Or an hour from now. Maybe this is as close as they'll ever be. You never... What?"

They'd crossed into a neighborhood of modest cinderblock homes, chain link fences, canted mailboxes and doghouses whose residents were too heat-dazed to do more than pant at them. Rounding a hedge of dying bougainvillea, Little Billy had come to a sudden halt, his lips parting in bewilderment.

The *xalanthracoil* was in the corner of a backyard, nearly buried beneath a heap of deadfall. Something was swelling from its tip like a soap bubble. It grew until it was about three feet across, then detached and rose, undulating, into the air. It lasted only a second or two before imploding with a soft "whoosh," but it was long enough for Little Billy to glimpse within its membranous surface a brown sky ablaze with hundreds of ancient red stars, a vast, hardpan plain stretching to black mountains and the spires of a distant city clawing at sulfurous clouds.

"What would the name of the city be if the natives had seen *that?*" he whispered.

"Loosely translated: 'we're fucked.'"

ANDREW WOKE THE FOLLOWING MORNING FEELING better   that he had any right to. The empties were gone from the kitchenette's wastebasket, tossed into the motel's outdoor bin. The refrigerator was cleaned out except for an ancient box of baking soda. His clothes were all freshly laundered and folded in his suitcases. Before leaving for work he dropped by the front office and checked out. He wasn't sure where he would stay after his shift ended, but it wasn't going to be in this damp armpit of a motel. That phase of his self-exile was over.

The booze was over too. How many times had he told himself that? Hundreds? In the car, rushing Anna to the hospital on that horrible day he had sworn off drinking so vehemently he had to fight the urge to pull over and bash his head repeatedly against a wall screaming 'never again' at the top of his lungs. But two weeks later 'never again' turned into 'one last time,' just to prove he was capable of stopping after a single longneck. A few days later he had another Heineken to verify his previous success hadn't been a fluke. Before long he was reassuring himself three or four times a day.

This was different. He had nothing to base that on other than the profound clarity and sense of purpose he now felt in the aftermath of Little Billy's text, although initially, the message had filled him with queasy dread: *Need to sound the alarm. Will explain face-to-face. END IS NIGH.*

Words worthy of a sandwich board.

Surrender followed dread, fatalistic and profoundly draining. It didn't last. After ten minutes of staring at the stained ceiling tiles, a warmth had kindled in his chest. Propelled by the beating of his heart, it spread to arms and legs, twitching fingertips, tingling scalp, steadily building into something close to exhilaration. Maybe it was simply the relief of knowing the burden of preventing the end of the world would soon rest on more shoulders than theirs alone.

Or maybe this was the other side of terror, when all the neurochemicals responsible for fear were exhausted and the only thing remaining was a few lingering endorphins.

He even had a plan of sorts. First, recruit Capt. Hamilton. Others must be hearing the *vetro's* call by now. Others must be seeing the *bilantu*. Maybe Hamilton was one of them. He would convince his station captain to go to the chief, the mayor. Anyone. Everyone. There was enough Trenchrite in the warehouse to plant charges around all eighteen *coils*. Big charges. Twenty times bigger than the one they had used in the cemetery. With heavy machinery, they could dig down far enough to blow the things out of the ground like rotten molars. And if that didn't work, there was the military. Little Billy was right. Time to enlist the big guns.

There was something else as well, another factor that could potentially increase their chances of success. He didn't dare mull it for long, unlikely as the possibility was. Something urged him to keep it buried, secret, hidden from the things gibbering and clawing at the edges of his mind. They were always seeking a way in and if this turned out to be a card up his sleeve he did not want the bastards reaching under his cuff.

Andrew pulled into Station Three's parking lot rehearsing what he would say to Hamilton. He would go to him as soon as he stowed his bunk gear, before he could lose his nerve. Then he would turn his attention to his father. He had no idea how much it would take to bail him out, but he would come up with the money somehow. They needed him on the outside. *Andrew* needed him. For the first time since he was a boy, he had no problem admitting that. Andrew needed his father at his side. Would that make them a pair of crazy Tates? Fine. Good. Great. Crazy might be the only way any of them were going to survive what came next.

The common room was empty. He heard voices from the kitchen and gave a wave as he made his way to the locker room. He was actually a few minutes early today, something so rare it apparently quieted the room. They would have to get used to it. His days of being late were over as well. Even Sid would have to concede the change sooner or later. Probably later. Provided, of course, there *was* a later.

Andrew made his way to his locker. There would be a later. The voices echoing at the bottom of his mind were a little more manageable this morning. Not quieter. If anything, they were closer than before. But less intimidating, less authoritative, more like the racket of children shouting in a playground. Evil, homicidal children pulling the wings off butterflies, but children nevertheless.

As Andrew removed the combination lock, he heard someone enter the room and turned to find Hamilton standing in the threshold.

"Morning, Captain. I was just about to drop by your office. There's something we need to discuss." He tossed the lock on the bench and yanked the door open.

"Andy. Could you do me a favor and step back from the locker."

"Captain?"

"Step away from the locker, Andy. Now."

Andrew retreated to the far wall as the captain moved into the room, followed by a man he recognized as a union rep and two uniformed police officers.

"What's going on?" His sense of clarity and purpose vanished in a puff, replaced by the far more familiar feeling of impending doom.

"Just stay over there."

"He needs to give you verbal permission before any search," the rep advised. "If you want this to go smoothly."

The captain turned to Andrew. "Do I have your permission to search your locker?"

"Search it for what?" His breath caught as he remembered the flask of Royal Crown secreted behind the loose panel. He'd forgotten all about it until this moment. Could that be what this was all about?

"Just yes or no. Do I have your permission to search your locker?"

"Yes," he said through a mouthful of wood shavings.

182

"Permission given and witness by union representative Jacob Cass," Hamilton said.

Andrew pressed his back against the wall to remain upright and the officers positioned themselves at his elbows. Were they here to keep the peace as he was escorted from the building? What did they think he was going to do? This was all a misunderstanding. Had to be. How could anyone know about the panel? He'd always been so careful.

Not careful enough, obviously. Hamilton reached into the locker and there came the faint squeak of a bolt being unscrewed, followed by a clank as it fell to the metal shelf. The captain's body blocked Andrew's view, but the scrape of the back panel being slid aside was unmistakable. It was the sound of his career ending.

In the seconds it took Hamilton to rummage around the revealed piping alcove, Andrew wondered how he could have been so monumentally stupid. What would Grace say once she heard the news? Escorted from the building by cops, having to endure a walk of shame past fellow firefighters, all their worst suspicions about him confirmed. *At least have the decency to take me out the back bay*, he thought. *For the love of god, don't parade me through the front door.*

Hamilton sighed, a defeated hiss that bowed his head.

"Captain, I know how this looks, but I swear..." Andrew sucked the rest of his words back down his throat with a ragged gasp. Hamilton turned toward him with disbelieving eyes, clutching not the flask of Crown Royal but a handful of morphine vials.

"Jesus, Andy. I would never have believed you capable of this."

"Captain, you have got to believe me. I've never seen those before. I swear on my mother's grave."

The rep stepped between him and the captain. "My advice to you, Mr. Tate, is to stop talking now. The union will provide a lawyer. He should be the one you plead your case to."

One of the cops handcuffed Andrew and together they lead him to the door.

"Can they take me out the back?" he managed. The officers paused and Hamilton gave a nod. They turned down the hall and passed through the vehicle bay, where the men and women of Station Three had gathered to watch him go.

Part 3: Breach

Fourteen

John Tate stood outside the cell, wondering how long it had been since he had last watched his son sleep. Twenty years? Twenty-five? He'd been such a skinny kid. A wisp of a boy, all knees and elbows and healing scrapes, too bold for his own good.

When he would check on Andrew in the middle of the night on his way back from the bathroom, it appeared as if the covers had swallowed him. His body barely raised a hummock amid all the folds. Only his mussed head on the pillow gave proof the boy was there, snoring softly, and John would sometimes smooth a cowlick or brush the hair from his forehead, still amazed he had played a role in such an astonishing act of creation. If Andrew began to rouse at his touch he would shush him back to sleep before checking to make sure the windows were locked, the blinds pulled. His night patrol, Lindsay called it, asking more than once if he thought she went around unlocking things after he fell asleep? But John couldn't help himself. There would be no return to slumber until he reassured himself the house was secure. Even before his discovery of the *bilantu offalate,* he had known there were monsters out there, the two-legged kind that disguised themselves as men and slouched in the near-dark, searching for a way inside.

Andrew lay stretched across the bottom bunk, one arm thrown over his eyes, the other dangling to the floor. There was no blanket to burrow under, no pillow, just a bare mattress. The beddings for new arrivals didn't arrive until just before lights-out. A box of toiletries sat unopened on the floor next to him. His scrubs were at least two sizes too large, an orange tangle from which arms, head and feet emerged like poles from a collapsed tent.

John saw the man in the top bunk lean over to say something to Andrew. When his cellmate didn't respond the man dug in his nose for a moment and flicked what he'd produced at him.

"He's not alone," John said quietly, edging away from the open door. "Any way you can change that?"

"Absolutely," Hector said. "Can never have too many delousings. I'm I right, Book?"

The other guard snorted. "Long as I don't have to go poking around his asshole I'm good."

Booker Lamont, one of the twelve officers involved in the infirmary debacle, was what John was beginning to think of as a Recent Convert, someone, like Emily Cho and Hector Salvador, who'd joined the cause after having the veil pulled from his or her eyes. That the other eleven officers hadn't followed suit was worrisome. It meant they had either convinced themselves what had happened was a mass hallucination, or they had allied with other forces, a possibility that kept John up most of the night, listening for the approach of footsteps outside his cell.

"Wait here," Hector said, and the two guards went inside. John still hadn't figured out how Hector managed to spend so much time at his side. Since the infirmary attack, he'd essentially become his bodyguard, escorting him whenever he left his cell and spending the rest of his shift parked on a chair outside his door. When he'd asked if such duties were authorized, Hector had simply given him a wink.

After a few moments, raised voices erupted inside the cell, followed by a thump. The box of toiletries came skidding into the hall, accompanied by the unmistakable buzz of a taser. A howl of pain. A series of curses. He could imagine Andrew curled up at the back of his bunk, watching the commotion in groggy confusion.

"That's a lawsuit, motherfucker. You can't drag me out of my bunk and tase me for no reason. I know my goddamn rights."

"Tase you? Nobody here has a taser. Book, you got a taser hiding somewhere?"

"Not me."

"Well, I sure as hell don't. This is what happens when you fall out of your bunk and hit your head. Start seeing tasers everywhere."

"Ah shit, man. You fuckers crack me up."

Hector and Booker emerged dragging the inmate between them.

"Take your time," Hector said as they passed. "This one's going to be occupied for the next hour."

John returned the scattered toiletries to the box and stepped into the cell. Andrew sat at the edge of his bunk, elbows on his knees, fingerprint-inked fingers interlaced. When he saw John, his head sank.

"Who told?" he asked the floor.

"Guard said you were booked on a narcotics charge."

"Word travels fast."

"Mind if I sit?"

John eased down next to him and set the box between their feet. "Am I the only one who finds it ironic they give you travel-sized toothpaste and soap in a place designed to keep you from traveling?" Andrew continued to stare at his feet. John could faintly smell the anti-lice shampoo he had used after booking. "How you holding up, Andy?"

"Everyone at the station thinks I'm a junkie, Dad. A morphine addict. When they search my car, and they will once they get a warrant, they'll find a box of explosives in the trunk. And that will be that. Andrew Tate: terrorist junkie. Who would believe anything else?"

"Me, for one. Look, I'm not going to sit here and claim to know you like a father should know his son. But just because I moved out doesn't mean I stopped paying attention.

"I've been watching all these years, watching you grow into a man who chose a career dedicated to helping others, a man who puts himself on the line every day trying to make a difference, willing to do whatever it takes to save people, even the ones who don't want saving.

"From where I'm sitting, that makes you a damn fine human being, one I'm proud to call my son."

Andrew slowly shook his head. "I may not be as bad as the evidence suggests, but I deserve to be here. This morning, when the captain reached into my locker, I knew my career was over. I thought he was going to find the flask of whiskey I'd hidden behind a panel. But that's not what he found. Instead of Crown Royal, he pulls out a handful of morphine vials."

"You were set up."

"Pretty sure I know by who, although how he got into my locker's a mystery. Even I can't remember my lock combination half the time."

"They told him."

"They who?"

"You know."

Andrew cleared his throat. "Yeah. Guess they didn't appreciate us trying to..." John held up a hand to silence him, put a finger to his lips and motioned him to wait. Had that been the squeak of a heel in the hallway?

Edging to the cell door, he poked his head around the corner. Nothing. He lingered a moment, listening. The voices in his mind were a low static of guttural snivelings, unchanged for nearly twenty-four hours.

A possibility had occurred to him the previous night, one he had pondered briefly as he hovered on the edge of sleep. Could the *vetro offalate* block their thoughts from him? In the morning, with Hector stationed outside his cell, it seemed more a product of paranoia and exhaustion than a real possibility.

Now, however, it wasn't as easy to dismiss. The cells on either side of his son's were empty. Most inmates were in the common area, watching television or playing cards. He considered checking all the cells on the block to make sure they were indeed alone, then decided against it, not wanting to be away from Andrew that long.

"Nerves, I guess," he said on his return. "I heard what you did the other night at the cemetery. Impressive."

"Not impressive enough. Little Billy fill you in on the details?"

"Talked to him yesterday."

"Then you know we're almost out of time."

John glanced up. Had that been a shadow? Goddamnit, now he would have to check again. He motioned Andrew silent and crept to the door. He should have asked Hector or Booker to remain behind. What the hell had he been thinking?

"You going to be doing that the whole time we're talking?"

"I have reasons to be skittish. Did you call anyone when you were booked?"

"Who would I call, Little Billy? My bail's been set at seventy-five hundred. He doesn't have that kind of money."

"Grace."

"No." Andrew's head swiveled back and forth continuously as he spoke. "I'm not calling her from here. She can't see me like this, an accused junkie in an orange monkey suit. She'd be filing divorce papers within the hour."

"She knows you're not a junkie."

"Does she? I've screwed up a lot lately. Her brother's ready to string me up by my balls."

"Andy, listen to me carefully. You've been lucky." Andrew turned incredulous eyes toward him. "You have. Somebody at your station set you up and now you're here. They could just as easily have slit your throat while you slept or cut the brake lines on your car. They've been trying to kill *me* ever since I got here."

"Christ, Dad. Why didn't you say something?"

John waved him off. "Maybe they figure as long as you're here you're not a threat. They're right. I need you on the outside. Call Grace and convince her to post your bail. You said you still had some explosives?"

"A lot, actually. I was planning to get even more, before this happened."

"All the more reason to get you out."

"What about you?"

"Don't worry about him, sunshine." The man at the threshold ran his shiv casually down the size of his face, drawing a thin line of blood from forehead to chin. "He's not going nowhere. Neither of you are."

They sprang up, but there was no place to retreat. The inmate was massive, well over two hundred and eighty pounds, most of the weight packed around his shoulders and upper chest. The girth of his neck made his head seem a microcephalic afterthought, a softball balanced atop a barstool.

He took a step into the cell and paused, one ear tilted up as if listening to instructions. At least he wasn't wearing a suit of *bilantu*, as Brutrelli had been. The shiv, however, was larger than any John had faced, a honed wedge of metal as long as his hand secured to twelve inches of broom handle. How in god's name had he managed to keep *that* hidden?

"The guards will be back any second," John said. When the inmate made no response, he reached down and yanked the mattress off Andrew's bunk. It was unwieldy, hard to grip and flimsy, just a foam pad encased in a slipcover, but it would provide some protection.

"Here." He passed it to Andrew. "Try and keep this between you and him."

And since the man at the door still appeared to be preoccupied, John pulled the other mattress off the top bunk. If they charged him now they might be able to make it into the hall and break for the rec center, where there would be guards.

Before he could whisper the suggestion to Andrew however, the inmate emerged from his fugue, rousing himself with a full-body shudder that reminded John of a bear waking from hibernation.

"They want me to do this quick. Chop, chop!" He brought the shiv down in a slicing arc. "All business, those guys. *Ph'nglui mglw'nafh s'ruque! Kalata binto Yog-Sothoth!* But I got some ideas of my own."

191

He made a pelvic thrust and John notice with a cold shiver the bulge at his crotch. "Promised me all the pussy I could ever want if I diced you. And I will. Oh, I will. But I figure why wait? One hole is as good as the next, and I bet yours, princess," he said, pointing the blade at Andrew, "is as pretty as a button."

Father and son charged.

After only a few steps, Andrew tripped over the trailing edged of his mattress and went sprawling just as John plowed into the inmate. It was like hitting a wall of flesh. Rebounding, he stumbled over Andrew's legs and went down himself.

"Like pickin' daisies. Guess I'll do you first, old man."

John raised the mattress in time to meet the weapon, but the force of the blow pushed two inches of metal through the foam and tore the pad from his grip. He twisted in time to prevent the blade from piercing his sternum and felt a sting across his flank instead. When their attacker yanked the shiv back for a second swing, the impaled mattress went with it.

John sprang. The inmate toppled forward, landed on top of him and pinned him face down beneath the mattress. He tried to shimmy out from under, but the guy was too heavy.

"Where you think you're going? I'll squash you flat, you fucking bug." His weight lifted—too short a respite to even take a breath—and came crashing back. John's ribs creaked under the assault.

"How you like that, bug? You squished yet?" The weight lifted and fell again. This time something did crack. Even if John could have inhaled, the pain was so intense he wouldn't have managed more than a low moan.

"You feel a little flatter. When you pop, your guts are... AAAHHHH!"

From under the mattress, John saw Andrew clamped to the inmate's leg, his teeth sunk into the flesh of his calf.

"You want to play too, princess? That's just a love bite." The pressure lifted once again as the inmate kicked Andrew off, grabbed him by the hair and landed a jackhammer series of blows to his face. "Didn't want to mess up that sweet mug before I got my fill, but that's fine. Blood's the best lubricant anyway."

John took a sip of air and scuttled to the wall. Where the hell were the guards? There were cameras everywhere. Someone should have seen the fight by now and sent in the troops. Could the *vetro* have infiltrated the guards in the control room? Or shorted out the monitors?

He scanned the room, looking for anything he could use as a weapon. The shiv! It was still embedded in the center of the mattress.

John slid the pad around the struggling men, wedged it under his foot and pulled the weapon free. As he did the inmate lunged and clamped a hand round the blade. John yanked back, hoping to slice off several fingers. Instead, the head separated from the shaft, leaving John holding a foot of boomstick.

Their attacker spun toward Andrew blandishing the naked blade and John pounced on his back, trying to garrote him with the broken handle. Had Andrew not struck at the same instant, John would likely have been stabbed repeatedly, but his son managed to backhand the metal out of his grip. John planted his feet and reared back with all his weight. *Go down, goddamn you. Go down!*

Instead, the inmate rose with a roar, pulling John up with him.

"Bug! You die now!"

He could still talk? Impossible! They staggered across the room and John was smashed against the wall. His head bounced off the concrete, sparking a cascade of lights that momentarily blinded him. *Don't let go,* he told himself. *Whatever you do, don't let go.*

Andrew threw himself into the fray, slamming everyone against the wall a second time.

"Go for the eyes!" John's grip was weakening. In another moment, he'd be on the floor.

Andrew dug his thumb into an eye socket and their assailant retreated into the hall. John jumped from his back an instant before he hit the balcony rail, beyond which yawned the atrium and the floor ten feet below.

His son retreated into the cell, grabbed a mattress and charged forward intending, perhaps, to bulldoze the inmate over the edge. But he was too slow. The other man ducked and instead of plowing into his chest, Andrew landed across his shoulders. With a tremendous heave, the inmate straightened, sending his son arching over the rail.

"No!"

Incredibly, the guy turned in time to grab Andrew by an ankle before he plunged out of reach.

"Where you think you're going, princess? Ain't done with you yet."

As he hoisted his catch higher John landed on his shoulders, clubbed him across the back of his head with the broken handle and held on as the world inverted.

Unbalanced at last, everyone went cascading over the side, exchanging blows all the way to the floor.

"OH, MY GOD!"

Andrew didn't need the phone to know what Grace had said. He could have read her shock through a foot of tinted glass. Gingerly, he eased into the plastic chair and raised the receiver to his ear.

"Should see the other guy." He smiled and winced, his swollen lips tasting once more of blood.

Grace's hand remained clamped over her mouth as tears welled.

"I'm okay," he tried to assure her. "Looks worse than it is."

"What *happened?*"

"I fell."

She covered her eyes, quivering with silent sobs.

"Grace, I know how hard this is for you." Dear god, could he say anything more absurd? But absurd was all he had left. He couldn't stand the thought of what she must be seeing on the other side of the divider, a broken and bandaged man, eyes swelled nearly shut, one cheek a yellow and purple bouquet of bruises, lips like gorged leeches about to burst. A mess. A goddamn walking disaster. But one who had a job to do on the outside, and if that meant groveling before this woman whose heart he was breaking yet again, so be it. Pride was a luxury he could no longer afford.

"I don't know what we're doing here, Andy. How did we end up in this place? Can you tell me?"

"Grace, you need to bail me out of here."

"They said they found morphine packets in your locker. Drugs intended for suffering people."

"I was set up. You think I'd do something like that?"

"You keep asking the same things over and over: 'You think I'm capable of this?', 'Would I do that?' It gets harder to say 'no' each time."

"I need your help, Grace. Something very bad is coming, and whether you believe me or not, I'm one of the few who has any chance of stopping it."

"I hate this. I hate what you've done to Anna and me. I hate having to come to this hellhole. I hate looking at your broken face. Every time I think we've reached rock bottom, you pull out a shovel and start digging."

Grace's gaze fell to the shelf upon which the telephone rested, a look of dazed hopelessness giving her features a strangely childlike quality.

"Grace, I need you."

She continued staring at the shelf as if waiting for someone, anyone, to throw a blanket over her shoulders and lead her by the elbow back to safety. Eventually, her eyes lifted to his in an unwavering stare that lasted long enough to convince Andrew she was focused not on him, but rather her own reflection in the divider.

"How much?"

"Seven thousand, five hundred."

"So, ten percent of that? Seven hundred and fifty dollars?"

"No. Seventy-five hundred *is* ten percent. They set my bail at seventy-five thousand."

Grace stared, and this time he knew she was seeing him and not something between them. When his bail had been read out during his initial court appearance, he thought he'd misheard. Seventy-five thousand dollars for a first offense? But the judge, taking into account his position as someone entrusted with the public good and his alleged betrayal of that trust, bumped his offense up to a drug trafficking charge and declared him a disgrace to every first responder in the city.

"Just write a check, Grace. It's not like I'm going to skip town."

"You want me to deplete our savings?"

"I'll take a loan out on my 401(k) as soon as I'm out of here."

"Will you? The very second you get out of here?"

"As soon as I can. As soon as I do what needs to be done."

A mirthless smile touched her lips. "Not that long ago, I would have asked what those things might be, those important jobs that can't wait. I know they have nothing to do me or Anna. That's obvious. Still, I would have been curious."

"They have everything to do with you and Anna, with saving you and a hell of a lot of other people."

"Your lip's bleeding."

"Grace."

"I'm not doing it, Andy. If you want out of here, call a bail bondsman." She made to set the receiver on its cradle and Andrew pounded the divider with a fist.

"Then leave! If you're not going to bail me out, take Anna and get away, drive as far north as you can. Pack a few things and go today and don't stop until you reach the mountains."

"Goodbye, Andy."

"Grace, for the love of god look around. Open your eyes. You know something's wrong, you have to. Haven't you been hearing the voices? Haven't you caught glimpses of things that shouldn't be there, things out of your nightmares?"

His wife's features pulled to one side in a brief contortion of distaste, as if catching a whiff of decay.

"You see a lot of strange things when your world is falling apart around you."

Periphery

She cradled the receiver, wrung her hands, stood, and walked slowly out the far door, and if she heard his fist pounding against the divider, she gave no indication. The last thing he saw as the guard pulled him from the window was his wife's wedding ring gleaming dulling on the ledge next to the phone.

Fifteen

ob Sanderson shuffled behind the John Deere, his head bowed
against the midday heat, watching sourly as the machine snarled
minced hay across his sweat-soaked legs. Hay was all that remained
of the lawn, hay and briers. But his wife still kept bugging him to cut it.
After weeks of hounding, he had finally dragged the mower out of the
shed and aimed it toward the withered remains of St. Augustine that had
somehow managed a few inches of strangled growth during April and
May.

Sanderson cut a meandering trail through the yard and doubled back,
making no attempt to keep the rows parallel. When he finally looked up
he saw islands of tall stems amid the shorn grass, giving the lawn a mangy,
patchwork appearance. Good enough for him, but Margaret would bitch
and moan until he came back and did it right. Better to deal with it now
than endure this sauna a second time.

Sanderson grabbed the mower as if to throttle it, and as he did his eyes
drifted across the fence. Something was there. At first, he thought it might
be a child's toy, some elaborate, mechanical thing that transformed from
tractor to dinosaur and back again. It was nestled among a thicket of dried

weeds, a long, low shape, both smooth and complex, a jumble of overlapping plates assembled into some sort of crustacean or bug. His neighbor had grandchildren who sometimes visited. Maybe one of them had chucked his toy over the fence and into his yard.

Sanderson took a step toward the toy.

The toy took a step toward him, moving with a fluid grace he would not have expected from something made of plastic and running on half-a-dozen C-cells. It moved like it was alive. He took a step to the left and the thing near the fence took a crablike sidestep, tracking him perfectly. It had shifted orientation slightly, showing off more of its shape, and he noticed the upward sweep of something that looked like a long horn or stinger protruding from the creature's posterior.

A flutter of panic seized him. That thing was real. It was real and it was stalking him. But just as he felt the first tightening in his chest, the first tingle of adrenaline, he remembered something he had seen years ago, a television show in which unwitting participants were set up by friends for the scare of their lives.

Sanderson smiled and ran a hand through his thinning hair. Sure, that's what this was. A prank. There must be a hidden camera crew somewhere nearby. But they weren't going to make a fool out of Bob Sanderson. He scanned the line of magnolias, looking for the tell-tale glint from a hidden camera lens and took a confident step forward. The thing by the fence skittered forward, halving the distance between them. It was amazing what they could do with servomotors and gears these days.

"I have to admit, you almost look real." He smiled and shook his head. "Still think mechanical effects look better onscreen than CGI." He considered for a moment, then repeated: "CGI sucks. Guess I'm pretty old-school when it comes to the flash."

Old-school? Was that phrase still in vogue? He didn't want to come across as a crony trying too hard to be hip. He turned quickly to his left, toward the shed. Was that an arm poking out from behind the open door?

When he turned back, the robot was less than four feet away. It rose up on a dozen legs, its tail swaying back and forth like the arm of a metronome. He could actually see something that looked like gills opening and closing along its flank.

"Outstanding work guys. You all deserve Oscars." What was that over there beneath the crape myrtle? Just a pile of leaves? It looked almost too ordinary, too perfectly irregular. Just the place for a cameraman to hide.

Bob Sanderson was still smiling toward the crape myrtle when the stinger pierced his brain.

MRS. YORK SAT BEFORE THE CANVAS, HEAD TITLED quizzically, one finger tapped her upper lip. The finger was smeared with dried paint and so was her cheek. She was an intentionally messy artist. Although she would never admit it to anyone, Mrs. York enjoyed looking at herself in the mirror after a long session. The smears on her skin and smock were confirmations of the intensity she brought to her work, her passion and tireless dedication to the highest level of achievement.

After several minutes, she plucked her brush from the bowl of murky water, slathered the broad head in dark vermilion and with five brisk strokes added the beginnings of a fan palm in the bottom right corner next to the fountain. She had spent most of the afternoon getting the details of the fountain just right. The texture was tricky. It was hard to make aged cement look realistic and now she was covering half of it in a big frond, but it couldn't be helped. That corner needed something big and simple to balance out the fountain's intricate contours.

When she had shaded the foliage to her satisfaction, Mrs. York sat back and took a deep breath. The smell of the wildfire was stronger with every passing hour.

"We've offended the gods," she said aloud. "Damn global warming."

Mrs. York—Abbie to her friends—pulled a cleaning rag from a nook in the easel and dabbed at her neck. She wanted to incorporate Mr. Bigglesby into this painting, a secret presence that would be a sort of gift to the careful viewer. Mrs. York wasn't entirely sure how she was going to manage that. She suspected the necessary technique to render something both there and not-there was beyond her current abilities, but she was determined to make the attempt. Mr. Bigglesby himself was lobbying for it. Why else had he been making so many recent appearances?

As she patted her cheeks with the cloth, a familiar trill drew her attention to the branches overhead. Well, speak of the devil!

"Hello, my dear! What brings you out on such a hot afternoon?"

Another, lower trill in response. Above her, Mr. Bigglesby scuttled a few feet closer, his feathers rising and falling the way they did when he became excited.

"Have you come to pose for my painting?" She wouldn't be surprised if he had. Mr. Bigglesby was very clever. Mrs. York had first met her friend shortly after moving into her townhome. That was two years ago and she still didn't know what he was.

At first, she had thought him a phantom, a trick of shadows and light, something conjured up by her artistic temperament. But he had continued to appear, growing more distinct every time, until she became convinced what she was seeing was real.

What marvelous camouflage! When motionless he merged into his surroundings, melting into the background like a fading afterimage. She doubted more than one in a thousand people would realize Mr. Bigglesby was sitting next to them on a park bench if he remained perfectly still. She, however, had learned how to see him, had trained her eyes to look in a new, more thoughtful way.

Mrs. York knew he was real, but what was he? A bird? He was covered in what she called feathers, but she didn't think they were feathers. They were too fleshy, somehow, too ... what? Alive?

Was he a mammal, then? Some sort of exotic arboreal with strange fur? But mammals had four limbs. Mr. Bigglesby had six. And those eyes! What on earth had eyes like that? They were indescribable and so, so beautiful, like gems from the most distant kingdom. She loved looking into them, the way they changed color and luster, first flat and depthless, then hard and brilliant.

It didn't really matter what Mr. Bigglesby was. He was her secret. He was her treasure. And he had come to pay her a visit.

To her amazement, Mr. Bigglesby dropped from the branch onto her patio with a graceful leap. He had never done that before! And a new sound as well, a lower warble that shook his entire frame, not as musical as his trill. Almost guttural. Almost a growl.

"You definitely want to be in my picture. Do you want to pose for me?"

Mr. Bigglesby said nothing, but his "feathers" rose and fell, rose and fell. And were they changing color? Yes, yes they were! They were brighter, flushing from a brownish lavender to a deep crimson.

"And you're excited, aren't you? I've never seen you like this before." She would have to make a quick sketch, but her pad and charcoals were inside.

She stood and backed away, making little patting gestures in the air. "Stay. Stay." Her leg bumped the canvas chair and she turned to catch it before it fell, fearing the noise would scare her treasure away. When she turned back Mr. Bigglesby was no longer where he had been.

A little moan of despair escaped her before she felt the brush of something against her leg, something that was not soft or pliant or featherlike in any way. Mrs. York—Abbie to her friends and two ex-husbands—reached out to grab the paintbrush off the table, but her fingers instead closed around something slick and muscular. Mr. Bigglesby's eyes were brilliant orbs of swirling colors inches from her own. She could lose herself in those colors if she wasn't careful. She could let go and just fall and fall and fall forever. And why not? It would be like entering a living painting, becoming part of an exquisitely sublime arrangement. She liked the notion. It appealed to her artistic side.

Mrs. York gazed into her treasure's eyes and let go.

AMANDA SILVERTON CHECKED HER CELL A THIRD TIME, confirming what she already knew: no new messages. She had missed no calls in the last ten minutes. No calls. No texts. Nothing. She stared at the screen for several seconds, willing it to change. It did not.

She'd been fanning herself under the tree for nearly thirty minutes, her anger peculating like the sweat running down her back and armpits and the crack of her ass. She fanned herself with the handful of fliers she was supposed to turn over to Mark Legosi for the open house, and as her anger deepened her fanning quickened. After another ten minutes, the papers were a fluttering blur.

This was the last time she was ever doing that man a favor. Four-thirty he said. He promised he'd be here no later than four-thirty. Now it was— she checked the clock on her phone—5:10! And he was nowhere to be found. He was probably sitting in his nice, cool office, shooting the shit with some old high school buddy while she was stuck out here. Why couldn't he have gone to Kinko's on his own lunch hour? And who scheduled open-houses for five-thirty on a weekday anyway? Who did he think was going to show up? No one wanted to house hunt after a long day at work.

A strand of Spanish moss brushed her cheek and she swatted it away. She noticed an ant on her arm and she swatted that, too. The tree was a bug magnet, but it was the only shade on the site.

Mark hadn't even bothered to give her the combination for the lockbox. *Oh, I'll be there precisely at four-thirty,* he promised. *You won't even have to get out of your car.* Four-thirty my ass. What had possessed her to wear pants today? She was broiling alive in these wool slacks. The first thing she was going to do when she got home was jump in an ice-cold shower and stay there until her teeth chattered.

She reached back, flicked another strand of moss off her shoulder and adjusted her bra strap. She should have just stayed in her car. Her clothes were plastered to her. And she still had to get ready for tonight. If she had to keep Jimmy waiting there would be hell to pay. She checked the time again. Nearly quarter past five.

This was absolutely the last favor she was ever going to do for that prick. The last. The fliers were disintegrating in her sweating palm. And she was being harassed by every bug in the neighborhood. She swatted a beetle from her leg. Two more minutes and she was out of here. She'd leave the fliers on the front steps and if they blew away, too bad. Nobody was going to show up for this stupid thing anyway.

Something tickled the back of her neck, slipping down her blouse. Damn it! She had to get away from this freaking tree.

She took a step forward, yanking at the tendril-like thing under her collar and was yanked back to the trunk. Amanda let out an outraged squawk and dropped the fliers. She spun, one hand still at her neck, the other sweeping the air above her as if clearing cobwebs from her hair. Her reaching fingers strummed across half-a-dozen more strands before encountering something that felt like an enormous, lolling tongue.

With a cry of revulsion, she tried to pull her arm back, but it was caught. She felt more tendrils brushing across her face and the one down her back looping around to encircle her waist. A shirt button popped loose, then a second. She saw it arc to the ground trailing a wispy piece of thread. Within seconds she was covered in tendrils. The sensation was like being caught in a net.

Despite all this, it wasn't until she looked up and saw what was in the branches above her that she began to scream. In response, the net tightened, heaving her several inches off the ground. The more she flailed, the more constricting it became. She kicked against the trunk as she was pulled higher, knocking off both shoes and sending herself into a momentary spin.

In her struggles, she hit the automatic redial on the phone she was still clutching. The number it dialed before falling from her suddenly relaxing grip was Mark Legosi's. Mark had fallen asleep on his office couch after a long, liquored lunch with investment partners. Although he had slept through the previous three phone calls from Amanda, the last one woke him just moments before Mr. Goldman charged through the door looking for the assessments he had been promised the day before, thus avoiding a rather embarrassing situation.

It was the last favor Amanda Silverton would ever do for him.

Sixteen

They showed him what they would do. Even as he struggled to free himself from the restraints pinning him to the chamber wall, Andrew understood this wasn't a dream; it was a vision of the future, the *near* future, a black spike of premonition pounded into the center of his mind.

They took Grace first. He heard her screams long before he caught sight of the glistening thing approaching through the gloom, dragging his struggling wife by her hair through its own slime trail. Ringing the chamber in a semicircle were the Mechanisms of Nil, humming in anticipation of their next meal.

Andrew tried to call out to her, let her know she wasn't alone in this nightmare, for he understood, somehow, that this was her premonition as well. He and Grace were both trapped in the same web, trashing against wills of immense malevolence. But the sinuous loop around his neck tightened in response to his efforts, choking off his breath. All he could do was watch as the creature glided into the center of the room, swept the husk of a previous victim off the black slab and positioned Grace in its place.

Her arms and legs were clamped; her head immobilized. The rig pivoted to vertical and now Grace *did* see him. What he saw in her eyes was what he had seen in Katie's as he handed her the water bottle in the intersection, a plea to pull her out of this nightmare. But he could do nothing. He bucked and thrashed against the wall, accomplished nothing, sagged in exhaustion.

The Mechanisms had already harvested thousands, but their appetites were bottomless. The remains of prior subjects littered the floor in a charnel house jumble of human wreckage, hollowed out vessels still technically alive, twitching occasionally as the lower brain functions flickered out. The Mechanisms' collectors unfurled toward Grace, tapeworm heads swelling and smacking in anticipation.

Andrew tried to turn away. The restraints held him fast. He tried to shut his eyes, but the lids were suddenly gone, flayed off with a precision honed by endless repetition. The collectors positioned themselves around his wife with a lover's intimacy, nuzzling up to temple and throat, breast, belly and upper thigh, pausing inches from her flesh as if to inhale her scent.

Within this poised moment, a new sound arose and his distress crescendoed into something Andrew had no words for, an anguish so encompassing it seemed to crystallize out of his very bones, sending shards of torment exploding from every inch of skin. The screams approaching down the hall were high and piercing, a child's terrified wails.

Anna clawed uselessly at the floor as the beast dragged her by one leg into the room. Her nails were already bloody ruins. The instant she entered the chamber her eyes found his.

"Daddy!" She stretched her ruined hands toward him. "Daddy, help meee!!"

He would have gone mad then—the white glare of insanity a final refuge from his impotent desperation—had the *vetro offalate* allowed it. They did not. He could feel their will pressed against his lucidity, keeping it constrained and intact. He saw everything they would do to his wife and daughter. He could not look away. And when they were done with him, when they had temporarily satisfied their malice, they flung him back into consciousness with a careless toss.

Andrew tumbled out of the cot, hit the floor gulping air and began swatting the space around his head in an attempt to dispel what he had seen, as if the images were a swarm of hornets skittering into his nose and mouth and ears.

Never. Never would he allow such a violation. Better to smother them both in their sleep than risk an end like that. Better to take their lives with a bullet than allow their essence, their *souls*, to be absorbed by those parasitic machines. Dear god, might some part of them survive the transition? Might their last moments of awareness be from inside a storage tank, awaiting a final consumption at the *vetro's* leisure?

Andrew's breath returned in hitches, not enough to scream, barely enough to keep from passing out once again.

Grace! Had she really shared the premonition? Was she even now convulsing on the bed as consciousness crept back on timid mouse feet? What time was it? What day? The vision had scrambled everything.

Facts then: he was in jail. Andrew touched his battered face. He and his father had been attacked by a man named Theodore Hillsdale, a low-level drug mule and muscle-for-hire. Hillsdale was now strapped to a bed at Tampa General, recovering from a fractured skull and broken collarbone. His father was there as well, his injuries severe but not life-threatening, at least according to Dr. Cho. And his wife and daughter were dead. They had died screaming.

No!

Andrew curled into a ball and hammered the back of his head against the floor. The blow sent a clarifying jolt reverberating through his skull. That hadn't happened. Andrew reached out, grabbed the leg of the cot and tried to pull himself off the floor. He struggled into a sitting position and rested his swollen, sweat-slicked face on the mattress.

The *vetro* wanted to convince him he was nothing, not an insect, not a gnat, not even a germ. But if they were confident of victory, why expend so much energy swatting at him? A lion wouldn't stalk a worm. A shark wouldn't menace a sea sponge. Was it simply a sadistic desire to torment? Then why recruit agents to kill them? Hillsdale said the *vetro offalate* wanted him to do it quickly. That kind of urgency suggested only one thing.

"Scared," he croaked into the sheet. "Scared, scared, scared."

"Andy?"

"Fuck off."

"Mr. Tate."

Andrew eased his head off the mattress. He was facing away from the cell door but did not turn to verify the voice was real. Instead, he simply waited, staring numbly at the wall. If they had sent another of their disciples to finish him off, there would be no escape. He tried to sniff indifferently, but his nose was clogged with dried blood.

"Andy, you need to get up."

With a series of awkward shuffles, Andrew pivoted around. One of the guards who had dragged his cellmate out prior to his father's visit stood in the doorway with another guard he did not recognize.

"Here to kill me?"

The officers exchanged looks.

"Look at his face," Booker explained to the second guard, then, addressing Andrew: "No, sir. You don't need to worry about Reece here. He's joined the forces of light."

Booker paused, clearly expecting a word of gratitude or at least relief from Andrew, but all he could do was stare.

"Anyway," Booker resumed after a second glance at Reece, "we're here to escort you to booking. You're out of here."

"What?" Andrew looked from face to face, searching for some hint of deception.

"You're being released."

"Someone posted my bail?"

"Apparently. Come on, man," he offered Andrew his hand. "We're not going to throw you off the roof. Promise."

Andrew grasped the offered hand and together he and Reece pulled him to his feet.

"Do you know who?" he asked.

"They don't tell us that. All I know is that you're being processed out." Booker held Andrew at arm's length and examined him, his eyes roving from head to foot. "Reece," he said quietly, "go down and grab him some clean scrubs."

The other guard nodded and disappeared into the hall.

"You'll be alright," Booker said in a tone of almost fatherly solace. "This place can take its toll on anyone. Nothing to be ashamed of."

It was only after Booker had settled him on the edge of the cot that he realized his crotch was a sodden mass of darkened fabric. At some point during his nightmare premonition, Andrew had pissed himself.

AN HOUR LATER HE STOOD SQUINTING AND BLINKING into the mid-morning glare, the caustic stench of burning vegetation causing him to gulp and swallow.

"This can't be good."

"It isn't." The escorting officer covered his nose and mouth with a cloth pulled from his belt. "Lutz is under a mandatory evacuation. Fire's grown to thirty thousand acres. They closed a three-mile segment of I-75 a few hours ago. Zero visibility. Local news has gone to wall-to-wall coverage."

"What are they saying?"

"If the wind picks up, we're screwed. But don't panic. Reinforcements are on the way."

"Comforting."

"You say so." He turned and reentered the jail.

Andrew had been incarcerated for just twenty-six hours but the world he returned to was not the one he had left. The oppressive haze hanging in the air bleached the sky a featureless white, draining the color from even nearby objects and giving the cars at the far end of the parking lot the gray vagueness of vast distance. Tampa Fire Rescue would be in full crisis mode by now and getting their marching orders from the Department of Forestry.

How many firefighters were battling the blaze? Hundreds, certainly. Maybe even a thousand. And more on the way. He wasn't sure how that would affect his plan. If all eyes were focused on the wildfire, making a second, bigger attempt to blow up a *coil* might be easier. The police would have their hands full with evacuations, traffic control, logistical support for the various agencies pouring into the area. Calls about suspicious characters digging holes near old property markers might be dismissed as too trivial to investigate.

Maybe.

Of course, he was assuming the box of Trenchrite was still in his trunk. Since he hadn't been charged with possession of explosives it was a reasonable assumption, but he could take nothing for granted. What had once been the foundation of his life had narrowed to a cable swaying over the abyss. All he could do was pinwheel his arms wildly in an attempt to remain centered.

Andrew shaded his eyes with a hand and scanned the parking lot, wondering who had bailed him out. Grace? He doubted she would have changed her mind so quickly, even if she had shared his nightmare. Little Billy? Where would he get the money? Katie Fife? How would she have known he was in jail?

Andrew removed his phone and saw he had a dozen missed texts from Little Billy. He'd read them later. Right now, he needed a ride to the impound lot. He scrolled through his contacts, found Katie's number and dialed. The smoke was stinging his swollen eyes and he dabbed at them gingerly with the sleeve of his shirt.

"Boo."

He spun, heart in his mouth. Katie stood behind him with her vibrating phone in one hand. When she saw his face, her smile stretched into a rictus of appalled shock.

"Oh!" Her free hand rose as if to touch his cheek and Andrew pulled back.

"I'm fine," he said, re-pocketing his phone. "I guess you're the one who bailed me out? How'd you know?"

After a moment, she shook her head. "Not me. We didn't know where you'd disappeared to. Will was afraid it was the *bilantu*. Or someone working for the *vetro*." Her eyes raked his face. "Is that what happened? Did someone try to kill you?"

"Yeah. Charming fellow. They promised him seventy-two virgins if he chopped me and my dad up. Or maybe it was seventy-two ewes. He didn't seem too picky."

"Seventy-two mes?"

"Never mind."

"Your dad, is he…"

"In the hospital, but he should pull through. Little Billy with you?"

"Waiting at the car."

"I need a ride to the impound lot to get my car. The rest of the Trenchrite's still in the trunk."

They set off across the parking lot with Katie in the lead. After a few steps, she said, "It's starting, Andy. The convergence or whatever you want to call it. The *xalantracoils*, they're birthing."

"Birthing?"

"We don't know what else to call it. You'll understand once you see it."

"If you didn't bail me out, how did you know I was here?"

"He told us."

They were approaching Katie's CRV. Leaning against one door was Little Billy, his head inclined in apparent conversation toward a second man also leaning against the vehicle. When they saw him approaching they took a step forward. Andrew stopped, mouth agape, debating whether to bolt or stand his ground. If he was fast he might make it back to the jail's entrance before the other man was on him.

"That's right," Sid Langston said. "I sprang your ass." He appraised Andrew's condition with professional detachment. "Just in time, from the looks of it."

Andrew took a sliding step back. "Why?"

"Because it's all gone to shit out here, and I'm not talking about the wildfire. People are dying in ways none of us have ever seen before.

211

Wounds like something out of a National Geographic special, bites and slashes and who the fuck knows what else.

"Survivors claim monsters sprang out of their hedges and tried to tear them to pieces. I believe them. So do a lot of others, especially the ones who've seen these things for themselves. If you have a plan to fight them—and your partners here say you do—I want in."

"How did you know to call Katie?"

"See, you think I'm just another dumb beefcake, but I actually have a brain in this pretty little head. Her name was in the newspaper article and her number's listed. When she came to see you at the station, I figured it might have something to do with what the homeless guy was ranting about that day. After these attacks began, I decided maybe he really was seeing monsters.

"Which means your old man might not be off his rocker after all. Been debating whether to bail you out ever since. She convinced me it was worth it."

He pointed his chin toward Katie.

"They both did. So," Langston clapped his hands, rubbed his palms, "what's the plan, boss? How we gonna to make things right?"

Andrew didn't trust him. His sudden change-of-heart felt like a ruse to lure them all to some secluded spot where he could do what he wanted without interference. Physically, no one could match Langston and Andrew's recent encounter with a hulking opponent had left him skittish and paranoid.

Still, he couldn't spend all his time looking over his shoulder, second-guessing every person he met. If he was to die, it would be on his feet facing the inevitable, not curled into a ball, waiting for the final blow to strike.

"I trust him," Katie offered without prompt. "If that's worth anything."

"Not me," Little Billy said. Langston turned and gave him a small smile. The smile appeared genuine to Andrew.

"Nothing personal, you could be on the up-and-up, but I've been on the street long enough to know that sooner or later trust will get you killed. Too many things are working against us and we don't have time to figure out who's playing for who. If we asked you to back off and leave this to us, what would you do?"

"Will," Katie chided.

Langston shrugged. "Guess I'd back off and leave this to you. Seems to me, though, you can use all the help you can get. You don't want another recruit?"

"How much do you know about what's going on?" Andrew asked.

"Everything these two have told me, plus what I've heard through the grapevine.

"Look, we've had our issues in the past. Don't expect me to apologize for any of it. But I don't think you stole morphine. I've watched you from day one. You may be an alcoholic, but you're not a junkie. Somebody wanted you out of the way. Now I've put you back into play. Don't want my help, fine. But a lot of first responders know something's up. That includes the TPD and the sheriff's department. They're scared and they're ready to listen to anyone who knows what the fuck is going on."

He gave the others a collective nod and turned away. After several paces, Langston turned back.

"One last thing: there's a big meeting in two hours with all the crisis management coordinators. It's supposed to be about the wildfire, but I think there might be more important things to discuss."

He turned his back to them.

"But what do I know? I'm just the guy who put his condo up as collateral to bail you out."

"I guess he's going to walk home," Katie said after a moment, her tone one of brittle neutrality.

"He came with you two?"

"Of course."

"Your call, Andy." Little Billy offered.

Andrew sighed. "Sid!" he called out. "You never told me where this meeting is going to be held!"

JOHN FINISHED HIS CONVERSATION WITH ANDREW AND HANDED the phone back to Emily.

"I hope this doesn't become a habit. I'm getting tired of being your answering service." When he said nothing she prompted, "So your son's out of jail?"

Booker and Hector had ceased their restless pacing and were watching him from the foot of his bed.

"Somebody bailed him out," he said finally. "A firefighter from his station."

The *vetro offalate* were pick, pick, picking at his thoughts, poking, probing, trying to pry loose anything they could. It took a constant effort to keep them out. He was afraid to sleep or take any of the painkillers various doctors kept offering. The ache of his broken ribs kept him focused and clear-headed. Whenever John felt himself drifting toward sleep, he would press a hand against his side, just under his right armpit, and the bright jolt of agony would catapult him back to full wakefulness.

They were getting stronger with each passing hour. Louder. The confluence had begun. He sensed the two realities pressing and sliding across one another like tectonic plates. Was he the only one, or had others begun to realize the ground was tilting beneath their feet and it was only a matter of time before everything went tumbling over the edge?

"Water?" Emily asked.

John nodded.

She plucked the cup off the table and held the straw to his lips. He drained it and nodded his appreciation.

"Better be careful," he said, "or I may start to suspect you're a big softie under all that gruff."

"It's probably just a phase."

Emily had arrived an hour after his admittance to Tampa General and hadn't left his side since, spending the night in the room's vacant bed. The first thing she'd done was remove the restraints securing his wrists to the side rails. When asked if she'd gotten official permission to do so, she told him to mind his own goddamn business. Once his arms were free, she pulled his chart, flipped through the pages, made a brief notation on the last and slammed it back in its slot.

"Anything you want to share?"

"They were going to put you to sleep later today. Now you'll just be neutered, tagged and released back into the wild. You're welcome."

Later, she'd given him a thorough examination, conferring with a striking redhead she introduced as Dr. Janet Cantall, her "better half."

"I've heard a lot about you," John offered as Cantall's hands roved his bandaged chest.

"Have you, now?" She gave Emily a lopsided grin.

"Yeah. She's tired of you leaving the toilet seat up. Ow!"

"So sorry. Tender spot?"

Hector and Booker had shown up twenty minutes ago, driving to the hospital as soon as their shift ended. Wired and restless, they'd taken turns asking if there was anything they could do.

He understood their agitation, their need to counter a looming threat in some proactive way. Staying centered in the hours before an engagement was often a matter of simple kinetics. Keep moving. Keep pushing back. Keep doing something. *Anything.* Now, as Emily refilled his cup, the pair drifted to the head of his bed.

"I thought I heard you say something to your son about a device," Hector said. "Something you've been working on as a last resort?"

The remark had taken John himself by surprise, prompted as it was by a sudden urge to comfort his son, to offer him the small relief of knowing the fate of humankind didn't rest on his shoulders alone. It was an impulsive act of compassion, one he instantly regretted. But looking into the hungry, desperate faces of Hector and Booker a notion dawned so fully formed it must have been there all along, lurking just under his awareness, waiting for the right moment to emerge.

"You two up for a little recon mission?"

"What you have in mind?" Booker said.

215

John asked them to find a securable location a mile or two outside the circle of *xalantracoils*, something a few motivated protectors could defend.

"Defend from what?" Hector asked.

"Think Brutrelli times ten."

"You kidding me?"

"Ideally, something with a single way in or out, with thick walls and a view of the surrounding landscape."

"So basically, a castle," Booker said.

"Basically. With a moat. If possible."

"No problem. Tell you what, we'll scrounge up a couple dozen knights while we're at it. A wizard, too."

"What are you planning, John?" Emily gave him a puzzled yet hopeful look. She trusted him. They all did. Despite Booker's quip, he knew the two men would take their assignment seriously.

"Less you know, the better." He shielded his head in both hands, then raised a finger to his lips in a shushing gesture. The *vetro* were always listening.

Hector and Booker promised to get in touch the moment they found something. As the door eased shut behind them, Emily removed the lid from a dish on the overbed table tray.

"Hungry?" She made a face at the plate of green beans and gray meat. "I can get you something better than this. I'll send Janet."

"You don't need to stand guard over me twenty-four seven. Nobody's tried to kill me since I got here."

"You need sleep. I'm on to your little trick, poking your sore spot to stay awake. That's got to stop. I could put a sedative into your IV."

"You wouldn't."

"Put you so far under, those slimy bastard wouldn't hear a thing inside your head, no matter how hard they strained. And when you woke, you'd feel a thousand times better."

John shook his head. "We don't know what they're capable of. Maybe it would work, and maybe they'd just reach in and yank out my entire cerebral cortex, read it like a ticker tape."

"A ticker tape?" Emily laughed. "What century are you living in?"

"You get my point."

"And what are you afraid of anyway? What do you have rattling around in that head of yours that's so important? The device Hector was asking about?"

John weighed the consequences of his next words for a long moment. He'd put so many in harm's way already: William, the homeless men he'd enlisted to be his eyes and ears, Andrew, even his own granddaughter. He'd sent Hector and Booker out on a fool's errand to bolster their belief they were doing something of consequence, something vital and urgent.

Their success was irrelevant. It was their belief he needed. If *they* believed, so would the *vetro offalate* once they pried their way into their thoughts. Was he willing to put this woman in danger as well, make her a lure to draw the *vetro* to the flame of her false hope? She would believe what he told her, maybe not as unquestioningly as Hector and Booker, but enough. And the more who believed, the more unshakeable their faith, the better the odds his charade would work.

He had to try. If Andrew managed to sound the alarm at this meeting of emergency officials, there'd be a spike of activity around the *xalantracoils*. The night would provide safety as the *bilantu* slumbered. At dawn, however, anyone near a *coil* would become a target. If he could draw at least a few of them off it might make a difference, give someone the extra minutes needed to finish setting a charge, connect a cord, press the big red button.

Perhaps it was idiotic to think anything he did would make a goddamn bit of difference, but *they* were paying attention. Oh yes: pick, pick, picking. Always. They might be ninety-eight percent certain he could do them no harm, but there was still a sliver of doubt. He could feel that, too. He and the *vetro* were becoming as intimate as lovers.

Belief and doubt. Hers. Ours. Theirs. In the end, it might all come down to who was better at fooling themselves.

"I have something I've been working on for the last fifteen years," he said finally. "A device, yes, of last resort if everything else fails."

"And this whatever can stop the invasion?"

"It might be able to collapse the passage from their world to ours. I won't know until the time comes."

Emily's eyes roamed over his face. John held her gaze.

"And the place you sent Hector and Booker to find. That's where you want to set it up?"

"Yes."

Emily unholstered her phone.

"Who you texting?"

"Janet. She can buy you some clothes before she picks up dinner. There's no way I'll be able to sneak you out of here wearing nothing but a hospital gown."

Seventeen

"What am I seeing?" Andrew asked in a hoarse whisper. Little Billy exchanged a glance with Katie and she offered him a small, strained grin. There were dark circles under her eyes; her hair hung limply around her sweat-sheened face; her lips were cracked; her skin blotchy. Their prolonged exposure to the *xalantracoils* was taking its toll. Little Billy could feel his vitality leeching away a little more each time they ventured too close, a creeping weariness that settled in his bones and lingered long after retreating to a safer distance.

"We think it's little bits of their world emerging into ours."

The *coil* appeared to quiver in the roiling air. Its pulsing was faster than before, brighter, a kiln door opening and closing. Opening and closing. Yet there was no heat. If anything, the temperature around the device was a few degrees cooler than anywhere else. Maybe it was absorbing heat the same way it was absorbing their strength, using it as an additional source of power.

From the *coil's* tip, the bubble swelled. Its surface was semi-reflective, but there was no mistaking the scorched plain shimmering inside. Little Billy had woken from countless nightmares with that hellish landscape fading into the surrounding night.

The excretion elongated to nearly four feet before separating. As it floated up, Little Billy began to count. One Mississippi, two Mississippi, three Mississippi. He reached seven Mississippi before it imploded with a low whoosh. Yesterday, none of the orbs had lasted longer than five seconds.

"They're all doing this?" Andrew's lip was seeping blood. He absentmindedly swiped the back of his hand across it, leaving a red smear to his jawline.

"All the ones we've seen."

"For how long?"

"Two days. But not at night. They shut down after sunset."

"Why aren't people screaming about this on the news?"

"You don't feel it?" Katie asked. She had edged up to Little Billy as he spoke. Now she rested her head on his shoulder, and at her touch a small surge of energy thrummed in his chest. He tucked a lock of hair behind her ear, ignoring the quick lift of Andrew's brow.

"That repulser vibe they give off is stronger," she continued. "We never see people around them anymore, no matter where they are. Never. Traffic will actually swerve from the ones next to a street. Ever see what pepper flakes in a bowl of water do when you dip in a bar of soap? It's like that."

"How much time do we have left?"

"I think maybe all the smoke haze has slowed them," Little Billy offered. "Light seems to be their main source of energy and the light's been a little less intense lately."

"That's just wishful thinking," Katie chided. "They're getting stronger by the minute. The bubbles are forming quicker and lasting longer once they birth. I think we have until dawn. At most."

Another bubble began forming. There was something revolting in the way it grew, twisting and swaying and eager somehow. It reminded Little Billy of an enormous worm emerging from a dog's anus. It broke free and condensed into a misshapen sphere.

One Mississippi, two Mississippi, three Mississippi...

When Little Billy reached eight the orb shrank to the size of a baseball, quivered on the verge of implosion, then appeared to stabilize. He watched, mesmerized, as it drifted toward a nearby telephone pole. When he was certain a collision was inevitable, he exhaled. Thank god. But they wouldn't be able to count on...

"Oh." Katie pressed her face against his chest. "It hurts my head to watch."

The disturbance did not implode upon contact with the pole. Instead, the pole distorted around the sphere, bulging outward at the point of contact like rising dough. The rising became an inflation, the inflation a rupture and then, impossibly, the top of the pole was floating unsupported as the bubble passed through.

"Tell me when it's over," Katie pleaded. She was shielding her eyes with both hands.

Little Billy wanted to turn away himself. Not just turn away, *run* away, take Katie by the hand and make a mad dash to safety, wherever that might be. What hope did they have against creatures capable of *this*? Inhale, he told himself. Exhale. That's it. In. Out. In. A tendril materialized from the top half of the pole and reached out for another rising from the bottom. A moment later they merged and thickened, clumped with a third strand. A fourth.

"It's through."

She lifted her head cautiously. "You could go mad watching that. Why is the pole still standing? Why wasn't it cut in half?"

"Oil and water," Andrew answered.

"What?"

"That's what it looked like to me. A glob of oil in a lava lamp, with our reality being the water. The pole just flowed around it."

"For now." Little Billy took a step forward.

"Will, don't," Katie warned, but he had already pressed his hand over the place where the disturbance had passed through. The wood was cold, but otherwise unaltered.

"I don't know what you're planning, Andy, but whatever it is, it better be damn big." He glanced at the *xalantracoil* over his shoulder, already birthing a new glob. "And it better be fast."

ANDREW'S KEY NO LONGER OPENED THE FRONT DOOR. HE knew it wouldn't before he tried. The new lock was a flat, brushed-steel gray and the old one had been polished brass. But Andrew tried to shove and shimmy his house key into the slot, willing it to fit. The metal grew slick in his fingers and finally slipped from his grip. It landed on the concrete stoop with a faint clink.

"What's the problem?" Sid asked.

"She changed the locks." Andrew snatched up the fallen key.

"Ouch."

He rang the doorbell, waited, rang it again then knocked loudly. The blinds were mostly down. He shielded his eyes and peered through anyway, seeing little more than a sliver of living room floor.

"Maybe no one's home." Sid glanced at his watch. The department-heads meeting was in less than forty-five minutes and he obviously had no intention of being late.

They should have taken separate cars and met at Station One where the conference was taking place, but Sid had insisted they rendezvous early and go together. Andrew suspected the move was partly so Langston could act as his bodyguard should anyone try to kill him again, and partly to lessen the chances of Andrew getting snookered in the meantime. Before agreeing to the arrangement, however, Andrew had made Sid promise to stop at the house so he could check up on Grace and Anna.

"She's home. Her car's still in the driveway."

Andrew knocked again, trying to tamp down the panic. Maybe this morning's vision had been too much for her. Maybe she was lying on the bedroom floor, bleeding from her eyes and ears and nose. Maybe Anna was cowering in some upstairs closet, rocking and wondering what to do.

Or worse, maybe the *bilantu* had come pouring through an open window, an unlocked door.

"Grace!" Andrew hollered up to the bedroom window. "Grace, it's me! It's Andy! Grace? Anna?"

"Neighbors," Sid muttered under his breath.

Andrew ignored him and pounded the door again. "Grace!"

This time he heard a faint thud and a single word: "shit." Even though the afternoon was still bright, the porch light flicked on. A moment later the door opened.

"Did you fall?" Andrew stepped inside without waiting to be invited.

Grace blinked up at him in groggy confusion. "What?"

"I heard a thud."

"I bumped the table and knocked over a picture. Are you really here?" Her hands rose, not to his face but to her own, and as they did Andrew noticed the heavy bandages covering both of her forearms. His wife's fingers roved her cheeks in a tentative, probing manner, tapping and sliding, inching this way and that like spider legs searching for purchase on a slick wall. "Am I here?"

Unnerved, he reached up and clasped her hands.

"Jesus, Grace, what happened?" He turned her arms outward. "Were you attacked? Where's Anna, is she alright?"

"Anna?"

The urge to slap her was instantaneous and overwhelming. Andrew took a long, shuddering breath.

"Our daughter, Grace. Where's Anna?"

"You're hurting me."

He released her hands and cupped her cheeks in his palms. "Is she here?"

"No. She spent the night at my sister's, thank god. My dreams. Andy, they were horrible. So horrible. I woke up screaming, covered in sweat. If Anna had been here she would have been terrified."

He slid his hands down to her shoulders and pulled her close. Grace returned the gesture as best she could, with only the tips of her fingers

223

touching his back. "Andy," she whispered into his chest, "I think I'm going crazy."

"You're not." He stroked her hair, aware that Sid was lingering just outside the still-open front door.

"I can't shake it. All day I've been slapping myself, pinching myself. I, I..." She was shaking so violently her body thrummed like a current in his arms. "Andy, I cut myself today. Intentionally. I haven't done that since I was a teenager. I thought it would snap me out of it. It didn't. I feel like I'm stuck between awake and dreaming and any second I'll slip back into the nightmare."

Andrew eased her off his chest. "You can't shake the dream because it wasn't a dream. It was a vision, jammed into your head. I know because I had the same one this morning. You, on a slab, surrounded by horrible machines."

"The Mechanisms of Nil."

Andrew nodded. "Me strapped to a wall forced to watch, and then something drags Anna into the room, something despicable."

It was Grace's turn to cup his battered face in her hands. She wasted no time expressing astonishment or doubt, demanding an explanation or retreating into denial. "We can't let that happen."

"No, we can't."

"What do we have to do to keep her safe?"

Andrew pointed toward the upstairs bedroom. "Start packing."

FROM JOHN'S HOSPITAL WINDOW, LITTLE BILLY HAD A view across the Hillsborough River to Bayshore Boulevard and its many condo towers. The buildings were blushed in a way Little Billy had never seen before, radiant with an infectious glow not unlike the pulse of the *xalantracoils*. The lowering sun was a blood boil over the bay, a swelling blister in the smoke haze. A few blocks beyond Bayshore lay the southernmost edge of the circle formed the by *coils*. Little Billy scanned the scene, straining to catch a glimpse of something that had no right to be there, something like a misshapen child's balloon drifting through or above the tree canopy.

"Anything?" Katie asked.

Little Billy rubbed his eyes with the heels of his palms. "I thought I might have seen something a few minutes ago, but I can't be certain. The buildings are blocking most of the view."

"What kind of timeframe are we talking about?" Dr. Cho asked.

Little Billy retreated from the window and sunk into a chair near the wall. He hadn't expected to just stroll into John's room, despite the reassurances Dr. Cho had given him over the phone. He assumed there'd be a guard stationed in the hall, maybe two, but when the elevator doors had opened on the fifth floor, he'd seen only Cho chatting with a nurse at the station. She escorted them inside John's room without opposition, saying only "I know people here" in way of explanation.

The doctor wasn't what Little Billy had been expecting. For some reason, he'd pictured a petite, bespectacled, bird-like woman who flitted about from one urgent task to the next. This woman was statuesque and brusque, but instead of intimidating or severe, her direct, no-bullshit manner came off as reassuring, approachable.

"You're the second person to ask me that today."

"We have until dawn," Katie answered, cocking her head at Little Billy, challenging him to contradict her. He did not.

The bathroom door opened. "Something's sticking me in the neck," John said as he emerged. He tried to reach for it with his right hand, winced, tried again with the left and fumbled fruitlessly until Dr. Cho reached over to yank the price tag off his collar.

He thanked her with a grunt. "Your girlfriend dresses me funny. I look like a gay cowboy."

Little Billy squinted. Plaid shirt, creased blue jeans. He gave Katie a glance and she rolled her eyes in response.

"Don't forget the pink ascot. She had to go to four stores to find one."

John pointed to his bare feet.

"Don't suppose you'd like to help me get the shoes on? Thought of bending over makes me want to cry."

"Can't have that."

John eased himself to the bed and while Cho slipped on his new socks and sneakers he turned to Little Billy. "This firefighter that bailed Andrew out, this Langston. You think he's on the up-and-up?"

Little Billy shot Katie another look, one John did not miss this time, before answering. "You mean do I think he's going to take Andrew somewhere and bury a fire ax in his skull? No. Otherwise, I wouldn't have left them alone together."

"And the meeting? He told you where it was going to be?"

"Fire Station One. Only six or seven blocks from here."

"Good." John held out his hand and Dr. Cho eased him up. Little Billy liked watching the way the two interacted. They'd only known each other a few weeks, but he saw in their easy exchange of mild barbs true camaraderie. There was nothing flirtatious or sexual about any of it. "Buddies," came closest to what he sensed.

"Why good?" Little Billy asked.

"Because you're going, too. You and..." he pointed a finger at Katie.

"Katie," she answered, although she had introduced herself shortly after entering the room. "Katie Fife."

"You and Katie, Katie Fife. He's going to need someone there with an in-depth knowledge of the *coils*. Still have my map?"

"Yes. What about you? You're not going?"

John hobbled to the sink and ran water over a comb.

"My being there won't make any difference. Besides," he said, drawing the comb slowly through his shoulder-length hair, "I have a few errands of my own."

"Errands?"

Dr. Cho's cell began to ring.

"That's all you need to know for now."

"This better be good news," the doctor said in way of greeting. As they waited for her, Katie nudged him with an elbow.

"What's up?" she mouthed.

He shook his head.

"You're going to love this," Cho said as she re-pocketed the phone.

Little Billy thought he saw something flit across John's face, a twitch of raised eyebrows, a widening of the eyes, a tug at the corner of his mouth. Surprise, maybe?

"They found something?" he asked.

"Said it's exactly what you're looking for. They're there now, awaiting further orders."

"Don't ask," John said, pointing at Little Billy preemptively. "Go to the meeting. Both of you." He turned back to Cho. "You sure I'll be able to just waltz out of here without getting shot?"

"I'm sure."

"Then let's move. I need to pick up something from my apartment first. Call Hector back and find out if they're armed."

"Don't have to. He assured me they'd be able to defend this place against the hordes of hell. That's exactly what he said, I kid you not: 'hordes of hell.' "

John made his way gingerly to the door. Little Billy thought he would offer some parting word of encouragement, but he simply pushed through the door without a backward glance. Cho at least gave them a nod before following.

Once alone, an impulse seized Little Billy and he jumped up, poked his head out the door and snapped a photo of John Tate and Emily Cho walking elbow-to-elbow to the elevator doors. Katie came up behind him and glanced at the phone's screen.

"Don't know why I did that," he said. "All I got was their backs."

"You know why."

They stood in silence for a moment, staring at the image.

"Take my picture," Katie said. "Over here where the light's better."

Little Billy shook his head.

She fluffed her hair with her fingers, tilted her head in what might have been an attempt at a jaunty, carefree pose and pulled her lips up in an unconvincing smile. "Don't you want something to remember me by?"

Little Billy was across the room before realizing he was in motion.

"I'm not going to take your damn picture, you hear me?" He grasped her shoulders and shook loose a sob. "I don't need to. I'll never need to. If I want to remember what you look like I'll just track you down and look at you."

Katie pushed him away. "You're such a jackass. 'I'll just track you down and look at you,'" she mocked. "So, you'll come back from wherever the hell you drift off to after this is over and look me up sometime? Gee, thanks. Mighty big of you, William."

"That's not what I meant."

A flash of light, a click. "There, now I have a picture of you. Least I won't have to track you down if I want to remember what you look like."

She marched to the door, leaving Little Billy rooted to the spot and wishing, for the first time, the *vetro offalate* would start clamoring in his head once more. He needed something to drown out the other voice chanting *stupid, stupid, stupid*, over and over again.

Katie shot him a glance over her shoulder. "You coming or what?"

Eighteen

Tampa Fire Chief Alonzo Rodriguez sat hunched over the conference table, his gaze roving among the scattered documents and half-empty coffee cups as if verification of the outlandish claims he'd just heard might be found amid the clutter. Across from him, nearly eighty unanticipated attendees waited, crammed shoulder-to-shoulder inside the room.

Andrew was stunned at the turnout. Sid had mentioned that other firefighters planned to "crash the party," but the crowd milling around Station One's front doors had been so large Andrew's first assumption was that something had happened inside to force an evacuation. Most of Station Three's B shift was here, as well as Captain Hamilton sitting at the far end of the conference table with the other station captains.

Daryl Cleeves was here. Sidney Sinclair. Jane Tremonte. He saw Clare Humbert and Terrance Jackson standing together near the opposite wall. Andrew hadn't noticed his partner Gary among the attendees, but his old partner Max was here, milling near the front with a half-dozen firefighters from Station Twelve. The two had shaken hands earlier outside the station.

"I heard what happened," Max said, scrutinizing his face for a moment. "You actually look better than I expected. Word on the street is you lost an eye in the fight and had all your front teeth knocked out."

Andrew laughed, displaying his still intact incisors. "You know how 'the street' likes to exaggerate." His smile withered. "Seriously, though. Thanks for the heads-up the other day. Didn't make a damn bit of difference, but I appreciated the warning."

"Wish I could have given you more specifics. No one back at the station believes you're a junkie. At least none of the ones who worked with you. And I know for a fact your captain doesn't believe it either. Whole thing was a fucking setup."

Rodriguez's heavy sign drew Andrew's attention back to the front of the room.

"Alright." The fire chief drummed his fingers on the top of the conference table. "Let's say, just for the sake of argument, that what you people are claiming is true."

"It's true," Sid broke in. "You think this is a joke? We're all risking our careers coming here." Andrew placed a hand on the big lieutenant's shoulder and raised the other when Langston spun on him.

"Calm down," he hissed.

"We don't have time for this shit."

"Calm. Down."

"Let's say I believe your claims about a rash of animal attacks," Rodriguez continued. The comment elicited a smattering of contemptuous snorts, Sid's being the loudest. Andrew ground his molars and gripped the back of the chair he was standing behind until his hands quivered. "Why storm in here tonight? In case you haven't noticed, we have a bigger problem right now. This could have waited."

"No, it couldn't."

Heads turned. From the back of the room two people pushed forward, one defiantly, the other reluctantly.

"And you are?" Rodriguez asked.

"Katie Fife. My brother was killed by these things."

"Ms. Fife, are you a firefighter?"

"No. I'm a second-grade teacher. I'm here with Andrew Tate." She pointed. "And if you want to prevent a catastrophe like this city has never seen, you'll do exactly what he says. He and Will." She placed a hand on Little Billy. "They know more about what's going on than anyone else in this room."

Rodriguez pushed his chair back from the conference table. "I'm not about to start taking orders from an elementary school teacher who shouldn't be here to begin with. Now I'm only going to say this once, so..."

On the fire chief's right sat a woman in a TPD uniform. Andrew recognized her as Chief Samuels. Before Rodriguez could say more, she leaned over and began whispering in his ear. Except for the crackle and hiss of various personal radios, the room was silent. Rodriguez murmured something back and she nodded. One by one, the fire chief surveyed the rest of the men and women at the table. Some returned his glace with a puzzled frown. Most, however, gave their own small nods in return.

Rodriguez sighed. "Alright, Mr..."

"Andrew Tate, sir."

Rodriguez appeared to do a double-take after picking Andrew from the crowd. It was only later, catching a glimpse of his battered reflection in an office window, than Andrew realized why.

"Mr. Tate. The young lady says we're facing some sort of catastrophe. Do you agree?"

"I do."

"Then please, explain how these incidents are a bigger threat to the city than the largest wildfire in a century."

A calm descended over Andrew as all eyes turned to him. His career was already over. It had ended long before Captain Hamilton had reached into his locker and pulled out a handful of morphine tabs. Even before taking a swing at Max. It had died the day Anna reached for a pot of boiling water while he snored on the couch. So be it. He had a new job now, one passed down from father to son. It was time he accepted that. *Quintaloch, quintaloch, hiding in a tree.*

"These attacks are just the beginning of something far worse. If we don't act now, tonight, a hole will be torn through the heart of this city, and what will come pouring out will make our worse nightmares seem like sugar plum fairies."

The silence was absolute. Even the radios were quiet. Slowly, Chief Rodriguez straightened, his eyes never leaving Andrew's as the two men regarded each other across a gulf that expand and contract with every breath.

"Are you suggesting we're on the verge of some sort of terrorist attack?"

Andrew licked his swollen lips. "Worse."

Rodriguez surveyed his colleagues once again, seeking someone who shared his incredulity. No one met his glance. They were all watching Andrew. In addition to Tampa's fire and police chiefs and the city's station captains, those wedged around the conference table included the sheriffs of Pasco and Hillsborough counties, representatives from both counties' fire departments and several officials wearing the brown and green uniforms of the Department of Forestry.

"Then what, Mr. Tate? What are you suggesting?"

"We're facing an invasion."

Rodriguez slammed his fist against the table. "Goddamn it! You *are* wasting our time. I don't know what you're trying to pull here, Mr. Tate, but I think I can safely say this stunt is going to cost you your career."

Andrew smiled. "Sir, my career was over before I ever stepped foot in here."

"We should hear him out." Captain Hamilton rose and circled around to the front of the table, positioning himself between the emergency response managers and the audience of firefighters. "I've seen these things myself. Thought I was losing my mind. It's good to know I'm not. If Andy knows what the hell is going on I want to hear him out."

"My people have been reporting some pretty strange things themselves." The police chief rose. "I haven't seen anything myself, but I trust the people who've come forward. These aren't rookies. We're talking vets with twenty, thirty years of law enforcement under their belts. If they say they're seeing monsters, I can't just dismiss it as a bunch of overactive imaginations."

"You guys are coming to the party late." A bearded DOF official tossed his pen on the table and rubbed his eyes. "We've been seeing these things for over a month now. I don't like this talk of invasion any more than you do, Chief, but I've seen things I can't explain. Unnatural things. I'm willing to listen to what this man has to say for at least a little while longer."

Attention shifted back to Rodriguez. He sat motionless, only his eyes sweeping back and forth as he gauged the mood of the room.

"Okay, Mr. Tate," he said with a wave. "I guess we're all listening. Tell us about this invasion of yours and what you think we should do about it."

JOHN REALIZED WHERE THEY WERE GOING WHILE THEY were still blocks away. Emily refused to tell him the site Booker and Hector had selected, insisting with a grin it would be "obvious" once they got there. She was right. As they turned south on Florida Avenue he slapped the dashboard.

"Of course."

"You have to admit," she said as she turned into the parking lot, "it's exactly what you asked for. It even has a moat, if you count the river."

The Sulfur Springs water tower was a white finger of weathered concrete poking two hundred and twenty feet into the air. John knew a little about its history. During the '20s land boom, a local developer had built a resort on the site. Hoping to make a dramatic statement, something worthy of postcards sent back to the frozen north by sunburned tourists, he'd commissioned this edifice to ostentation. Instead of a bulbous tank perched on metal legs, this water tower looked like a cross between a lighthouse and a castle turret. Most locals had no idea what it was or why it existed, only that it had been there for a long time and served no discernible purpose. The resort was long gone, victim of the '30s real estate bust. Only this alabaster spike remained.

"We do good or what?" Hector asked as they stepped from the car.

"Can we get inside?"

"We can now," Booker said, rocking on the balls of his feet.

John leaned back, taking in the grime-and-rust-streaked walls. Small windows staggered up the tower, starting ten feet from the base and ending well below the crenelated balcony ringing what would have been the lantern room in an actual lighthouse. The lower windows appeared boarded over. The upper ones, however, were open, black rectangles in the fading light. Hector and Booker might not consider a few unblocked openings twenty or more feet above the ground a vulnerability, but John knew better. Height was no obstacle for some of the *bilantu*.

"You did good."

"Thing is," Hector said, "we drove past it four or five times before slapping our heads. For something so big, it's pretty much invisible. You get so used to it you sort of erase it from view. Weird, huh?"

"You'd be amazed what you can erase from view."

"So, you going to tell us what this is all about now?"

John circled around to the back of Emily's car and double-tapped the trunk with a fingertip. She popped it and John reached inside.

"I needed a secure place to use this."

"You're going to stop the monster apocalypse with a guitar?" Booker asked.

John eased the hard-shell case to the ground.

"It's not a guitar, although it does produce harmonics of a sort. Interference patterns to be precise."

The case was secured around the neck and base with two cable bicycle locks and padded on one side with folded bath towels. Slowly, with great apparent care, he ran his palm across the top, frowning in concentration.

The others gathered around in a silent semicircle. Believe, he thought. *Believe.*

When his hand reached the center of the case he stopped, gazing unfocused into the middle distance. After a moment he removed his palm and lowered his ear to the case, growling in pain.

"Something wrong?" Hector whispered.

"Shush!"

He kept his ear against the surface, watching Booker's feet until they began to shuffle.

"Try this." Emily dangled a stethoscope in front of him and he glanced up at her with raised brows. "I always have a medical kit in my car. That's how we doctors roll."

He accepted the stethoscope with a nod, placed the bulbs in his ears and the drum on the case, shifting it here and there every few seconds before finally giving a satisfied grunt. John raised his hands. Emily and Hector eased him to his feet.

"Thing about padding, it's hard to hear through." He passed the stethoscope back to the doctor.

"We copasetic?" Booker asked.

"We are indeed copasetic."

"And this harmonic thing will stop those bastards from kicking down the front door?"

"That's the plan." He hefted the case with a grunt. "Let's get inside before we lose the light."

With Booker and Hector leading the way, they crossed the grassy swath encircling the tower. The base, John noticed, was finned with a dozen ten-foot-tall buttresses capped with oyster shell friezes. Gaud almighty.

"Fifteen years ago, we never would have been able to get inside," Hector explained as they walked. "The door was bricked over back in the '70s I think. Too many teenagers sneaking in to smoke dope and have sex. Then the city bought it, declared it a historic landmark and decided to have a look inside, make sure it was still structurally sound. Took a whole afternoon of jack-hammering to break in."

"And inside?"

"Shit. Lots and lots of shit. Pigeon droppings. Bat guano. Cockroach pellets. Basically, the whole place was a tower of petrified poop."

"Thank god the city had the good sense to preserve this treasure." Emily patted the curving wall.

They came to an open threshold blocked by what appeared to be a rusted metal plate. The plate had been pushed back a few inches, creating a seam on the left. A length of chain lay heaped on the ground in front of it.

"Good news is they cleaned up the inside and replaced the ladders to the catwalks."

John pressed his hand against the plate. Despite the late afternoon warmth, the metal was cool and damp. He gave a push and it swung inward another two or three inches. The interior was a black crevasse smelling of wet stone, rotting vegetation and a sort of mineral musk that reminded him of his grandmother's root cellar.

"And the bad news?"

"Why does there have to be any bad news?" Emily held her hand over her mouth, closed one eye and brought her head close to the opening. "I'm sure it's delightful in there. Ah!"

She darted back, stamping her foot. John saw something dark fly off her thigh and scamper into the grass. Emily tracked it, took a step, brought her shoe down. There was a crackle.

"That would be the bad news," Hector said, drawing out the first word so that it lengthened into a smug knell of warning.

"Lots?" John asked.

"Depends on your definition of 'lots.' More than a dozen, less than..." he stuck out his lower lip and wagged his head. "Let's say a hundred million. Definitely less than a hundred million. I think."

"You've been inside?"

"Just around the bottom." Booker pushed his shoulder into the plate. With a squeal of rusted hinges and scraping concrete, it swung back another foot. "We stashed our supplies inside." He reached in and removed first one, then two and eventually four duffel bags.

"You've been busy," John said with genuine admiration. "Safe to assume these aren't filled with beach balls and sunscreen."

Hector knelt and unzipped the bag at his feet.

"Flashlight," he said, producing a large, yellow and black model that resembled a handheld spotlight. "LED. Bright as shit. One for each of us. Batteries, of course. Lots of flares. Some glow sticks. Bug spray. Bottled water. Blanket. Gloves. Emergency med kit. Rope."

"What are those for?" John asked, pointing to a tangle of thick rubber bands.

"These?" Hector plucked one up, held out his arm and wrapped the band around the cuff of his shirt sleeve until it was tight. "These are to keep the bugs from crawling up the inside of our sleeves."

"This keeps getting better and better," Emily sighed. "What about things dropping down on our heads?"

He raised his hands. "We had an hour to do this. They don't sell beekeeper hats at Home Depot." He pulled out a roll of mosquito netting. "We'll have to make do with this. Figure we can cut squares, drape it over our heads and tuck it into our collars."

"And then there's these." Booker reached inside the door and removed a bolt-action rifle. "Three of these and two semi-automatic pistols, a .38 and a .45. For anything bigger than a pigeon."

John held out his hand and Booker handed him the rifle. Turning away toward the river, he sighted down the scope, getting a feel for the weapon's weight and balance. "It's light."

"Careful now," Booker said behind him. "There's a round chambered."

John handed it back and nudged the link of chain with his shoe. "Did you shoot off the lock to get in?"

"Course," Hector said. "One shot from the hip. Bam!" He rolled his eyes and turned to Booker. "You believe this guy?"

"Bolt cutters," Booker said. "Less dangerous. Lot quieter."

"Don't suppose you thought to buy a new lock while you were getting supplies? Otherwise, anyone will be able to walk in behind us."

"Book, I'm beginning to think he thinks we're idiots." From the duffel bag, Hector removed an enormous padlock, still in its plastic packaging. "This is twice the size of the one we cut off."

John surveyed the equipment and supplies spread out at his feet. "I hope you didn't break the bank buying all this."

Hector cocked his head. "I'm willing to spend a couple hundred bucks to prevent the monster apocalypse, doc. Long as you think this gizmo of yours will work, that's good enough for me."

"Me, too," Booker added. An instant later his face crumpled. "Damn," he said, clutching his forehead.

Something like a band tightened around John's own head, pressed, relented, pressed again. Hector felt it as well. He and Booker were both massaging their temples, Booker with his left hand, Hector with his right. Dressed as they were in their uniforms, they looked like mirror negatives of each other, one pale face, one dark, both furrowed in pain.

Emily snorted and spat. "They're trying to get inside my head," she said. "Is this what you deal with all the time?"

"Don't fight it. If you resist too much it might cause an aneurysm. Besides, it doesn't matter now. They won't be able to do much once we're inside."

"I hope you're right," Hector said, shaking his head. "I didn't think Brutrelli could break through the infirmary door." He ran his fingers thoughtfully over the metal plate serving as a door. "If they send twenty more like him..."

"It'll hold."

"What if it doesn't?"

"We'll have the high ground. And the guns." John placed a hand on the other man's shoulder and searched his face. "You don't have to do this, you know. You've saved my life once already. None of you have to go in there. I can take it from here."

"You can barely shuffle, professor," Booker said, dipping to collect a duffel bag. "How you gonna get all the way to the top of this thing by yourself? Carrying that?" He pointed to the guitar case. "Enough talk. We doing this or what?"

John's throat tightened. He was their prophet now; there was no other word for it. Their false prophet, leading the people who trusted him most to their possible (likely?) deaths in an act of monumental betrayal. That wasn't the worst of it, though. Three lives, three sparks of faith, three sacrifices. Was it enough? Could the belief of three people draw the *vetro's* focus from Andrew, who, if successful, would soon be mobilizing dozens, if not hundreds, to his own cause?

"Emily, I need to borrow your phone again."

"Goddamn it," she said with feigned annoyance. "You're using up all my minutes."

John dialed William Phipps number, rehearsing what he would say as the call connected and began to ring. "Believe," he chanted under his breath. "*Believe.*"

IN THE HALLWAY OUTSIDE THE CONFERENCE ROOM, Little Billy re-pocketed his phone with a frown and gazed blankly at the wall until Katie raised her hands.

"Well?"

"I have a message for Andrew."

"From John? Why didn't he call him directly?"

"Didn't want to bother him while he's in the middle of his... whatever it is he's doing in there. Rallying the troops, I guess."

"What's the message?"

Little Billy looked through the door's window into the room. Andrew was still at the front, apparently fielding questions from various officials. Two large sweat stains had spread under the armpits of his Tampa Fire Rescue shirt, but he didn't appear to be fatigued or hesitant in his replies. If anything, his confidence had grown during the meeting as it became apparent the rank-and-file were already solidly in his camp. They didn't need any more convincing. They'd seen enough.

Katie touched his arm. "What's wrong?"

Little Billy had known John Tate for twenty-three years. During that time, he couldn't remember a single instance of deception on the part of his former professor. All their phone conversations, the occasional meetings in motel rooms to compare notes and share discoveries, the Skype chats over public library computers, had been open, often urgent exchanges of information, two men pooling their hard-earned knowledge in an effort to understand first the *bilantu offalate*, then the *xalantracoils* and finally the malevolence lurking behind both, the *vetro offalate*.

And yet never once in those two decades had John mentioned a machine capable of disrupting the *coils*. "Didn't want to get your hopes up," was all he offered when Little Billy pointed this out. Now John wanted him to tell Andrew about it.

"John has some sort of device he's been working on in secret, a last-ditch effort in case everything else fails. They're about to set it up at the top of the Sulfur Springs water tower."

"The what?"

"That lighthouse-looking thing you can see from the interstate."

One of Katie's eyebrows rose quizzically. "Do you believe him?"

Did he? Little Billy tried to recall any clues, however small, that would allow his opinion to snap with a satisfying click into one slot or another, belief/disbelief.

A memory surfaced: a face swimming into focus above him. John's face. It was 2008. Maybe '09. Little Billy was on a cot in a room that looked like a school gymnasium. He did not know how he had gotten there or where this place was. Presumably, somewhere in Jacksonville where he'd been conducting field research for most of the month.

He was on a cot and John was standing above him. But John was in Tampa, wasn't he? How could he be here, dabbing the sweat from his face with a towel and assuring him everything would be all right?

The next thing he knew men were lifting him onto a gurney. The rocking ambulance made him nauseous. Then he was in a room with clean sheets and monitors and women in scrubs who took his temperature and blood pressure and replaced the bag on his IV drip.

Eventually, he recovered enough to ask what had happened and was told he was recovering from a very bad infection, one that had sent him into septic shock.

Then he remembered. The downpour had been cold and pelting as he ran down an alley between industrial buildings, searching for an overhang to shelter under. He'd found an open, ground-floor window in a warehouse of some sort and shimmied through.

The drop had been father than expected and he landed on a stack of crates, smashing through the top one. A hot bite across his thigh as something cut him. But how had he gotten to the cot in the gymnasium? Unknown. And how had John known where to find him? Apparently, Little Billy had called. His former professor made sure he was admitted to a hospital. But the cost?

Don't worry about that shit, John said. *Concentrate on getting better.*

Little Billy still had no idea how the man had covered the bill. Did he believe him now? Irrelevant. The real question was whether or not he *trusted* him.

"If John wanted me to go in there and tell everyone giant pink elephants were stampeding to our rescue, I would."

"Out of loyalty?"

"He wouldn't have asked me to do this if it wasn't important. That's good enough for me."

"Well, if it's good enough for William Phipps." Katie pantomimed pushing up her sleeves and straightening the brim of a hat. She motioned toward the door.

"After you."

***

ANDREW TOOK A LONG GULP OF WATER, TRYING TO READ chief Rodriguez's expression as he huddled with the others. He almost felt sorry for him. An hour ago, the biggest threat in his world was a wildfire, a formidable enemy to be sure, but familiar, understandable, combatable. Now he was grappling with an enemy of tooth and claw, intent and malice. It was a difficult transition to make, but it had to be done and done quickly.

Andrew checked his watch. Five after eight. At least it would be dark soon. In the darkness, the *bilantu* would sleep, if sleep was the right word. The *xalantracoils* would shut down, maybe for the last time. And the bubbles? Would those floating globs of other-space evaporate in the dark or would they simply drift silently through the trees until dawn?

"You're sure about all these locations?" Sid Langston asked, inspecting the large, wall-mounted map of the city and the eighteen black dots forming a perfect circle just west of the downtown core.

"Every one is accurate down to the square foot," Little Billy said.

Langston clicked his tongue. "One is practically in the parking lot of my mother's townhouse. Probably parked within twenty feet of it a hundred times. Totally oblivious."

"They're designed to go unnoticed," Andrew said. "That's why Little... why William and I," he raised his hand to an already protesting Katie, "*and* Katie are going out with the demolition crews. We know how to see them for what they really are."

At the conference table, the voice of one of the DOF representatives rose momentarily above the rest.

"I don't see how we have a choice." One of his colleagues placed a hand on his forearm and he shook it off. "Mr. Tate," he said over the heads of the others. "How big did you say these things are? The things I'm hearing in my head?"

Andrew turned to Little Billy, remembering the shadow that had engulfed him under the monstrous hemorrhage of a sun, the flailing appendages, the sonorous, nearly subsonic howl.

"Big," he and Little Billy said in unison.

"Can you be any more specific?"

"Think mid-sized dinosaur," Little Billy offered. "Maybe twice the mass of a hippo. But that's just a guess."

The DOF officer swept his hand out in a "there-you-go" gesture and continued his debate in a lower tone.

"Shit's getting real," Langston said. "Me, I say we call the army, let them handle this. One hit from an 88mm tank shell and those *coils* would be dust."

"Probably," Andrew said as another pang of gratitude shuddered through him. Sid believed him. Max believed him. The firefighters milling in the hallway believed him. And despite their initial skepticism, the men and women at the conference table believed him, with the possible exception of Chief Rodriguez.

Team Tate(the name brought an embarrassed heat to his cheeks, but he couldn't help thinking of them in any other way) had grown from four people to nearly a hundred. He had set something in motion, and the building momentum was becoming a thing of its own. The relief was intoxicating.

And yet in the field of that relief, a nagging concern remained. The *vetro offalate* knew what he was up to. He had no doubt of that. To speak aloud about explosive charges and demolition teams was the same as broadcasting it into the minds (or was it just one Mind?) of the enemy. There was no getting around it. Hopefully, if they completed their work under cover of night, the *vetro* would be powerless to stop them. On the other hand, if dawn found them still dicking around, Andrew suspected even a full-scale military response would be too little too late.

That, however, wasn't the reason for his misgivings. What he'd sensed from the *vetro offalate* after laying out his plan to the others wasn't alarm. And it wasn't anger. It was the equivalent of a vast mental shrug, as if they had instantly evaluated the scheme and judged it irrelevant.

At least his father had something up his sleeve, a Hail Mary from the top of that old tower. And there was the other thing, the thing he was keeping buried at the bottom of his awareness: not the knowledge of some mysterious machine or the location of a secret arsenal of anti-*offalate* weapons, only an unlikely possibility born in darkness and nurtured in drought.

"Thing about the military," Andrew said after a long pause, "kind of hard to imagine them mobilizing anything for this. First, who do you call, the base commander at MacDill? The only thing flying out of there are refueling tankers. The governor? And tell her what, her state's about to be invaded by creatures from another universe? See where that gets you. Even if you manage to get someone to commit to a countermeasure, it has to be in place by dawn. You think that's going to happen?"

"Are we even sure this shit's going down at dawn?" Sid asked.

"Yes." Katie's tone left no room for argument. She was staring at the city map, her head slowly cocking toward her left shoulder. A vertical line ran between her brows from her forehead to the bridge of her nose. "Will," she began but was silenced by Chief Rodriguez's call for attention. The room quickly filled with the firefighters who had been milling in the hall.

"Okay, people." He waited, arms raised, until the room quieted. "We're going to tackle this on a number of fronts. Mr. Tate says our best option is to take out the pylons he described earlier, the *coils*, so that's what we're going to focus on. I understand an attempt to pull one down with a vehicle some years ago was unsuccessful, as was a recent attempt to blow one up. We're going to try to yank them down again, this time with heavy equipment.

"As most of you know, the DOF has some dozers they've been using to create firebreaks up at the wildfire. We can bring two down on a flatbed. Be here in an hour. Mr. Tate's friend," he indicated Little Billy, "thinks destroying even one might be enough to stop this. We're going to be systematic, start with the first and move on to the next if we can't budge it, work through all eighteen if we have to."

A murmur of discontent rippled through the audience as Andrew began calculating how long such a process would take.

Rodriguez raised his arms again, looking like a man wading into steadily deepening water.

"If we can't pull any down, then and only then will we turn to explosives. We already know from Mr. Tate's first attempt how much Trenchrite is too little. I'll be conferring with our explosive experts over the next few hours to determine how much bigger we can go without risking property or lives.

"These things aren't in a field somewhere in the middle of nowhere. They're in backyards. They're in parking lots. In many cases, they're next to utility poles and sewer lines. We have to take all that into account."

"Bullshit." Although Katie's voice was low, several people glanced her way. Little Billy whispered something in her ear. "What difference does it make if they take out a streetlight?" Her volume rose to a stage whisper. "Those things are going to swallow this city whole. Go big or go home, otherwise what's the point?"

Low grunts of agreement, a single "damn right" from Sid, and then a fizz of agitation until someone near the back of the room asked, "What about the National Guard? Shouldn't they be involved in this?"

Rodriguez waited for the room to settle.

"We're going to attempt to contact all possible military channels. But let's face it, other than the Coast Guard, we really don't have a hotline to the top brass. It's going to take time to work our way up to the right people. That's going to take time. Hell, *I'm* still not fully convinced and I'm surrounded by true believers."

"True believers?" Katie huffed. Andrew wiped sweat from his forehead with the sleeve of his shirt. The room had grown stifling with so many closely-packed bodies.

"Now comes the part that will directly affect most of you." Rodriguez nodded to the DOF representative who had asked about the size of the *vetro offalate*. He circled the table and displaced Rodriguez at the center of the room.

"Hello. Not a lot of you know me. My name is Frank Leanza and I'm the Withlacoochee Field Operations Bureau Chief for the Florida

Department of Forestry. Now that we've got that out of the way, the chief has been talking about how we're going to play offense. But as all of you know, any plan is incomplete without a defensive component. You don't fight wildfires without firebreaks, whether they're backburns or burnouts or whatever.

"The way I see it, this situation is no different. Worst comes to worst, we're going to need a containment line around this thing. If those creatures manage to break into our world, I'm not about to let them stroll past us, are you?"

A smattering of agreement. Andrew didn't need to survey the room to know puzzled glances were being exchanged. Leanza felt it as well. He appeared to deflate as the assembled firefighters held their collective breath.

"Hell no," Andrew said. He caught Sid's eye. "*Hell* no."

"Hell no," Sid echo. "Hell no."

Behind him, Max took up the chant. "Hell no. Hell no."

A few more voices joined in. Then a dozen. Soon the entire room was chanting. Hell no, Andrew thought. The war cry of a thousand generations.

"So, here's what we're going to do," Leanza said. Too timid. The chant continued unabated, feeding on itself. Behind the DOF chief, the rest of the committee officials watched the crowd with varying mixtures of amusement, satisfaction and embarrassment.

"Here's what we're going to do," he repeated, nearly shouting to be heard. "We're going to form a perimeter around that circle." Leanza pointed to the city map. "A perimeter of firefighters and police officers. The officers will be armed with guns. The firefighters will be armed with fire hoses."

The chanting continued for another second, maybe two, diminished to a series of isolated voices, then evaporated altogether on a final 'hell.'

"Fire hoses?" someone asked.

"We're going to use them as water cannons," Leanza said.

The room filled with a static charge of incredulity. Andrew knew why. Fire hoses were for fighting fires. The thought of repurposing them, of *weaponizing* them, wouldn't sit well with most firefighters. Besides, how effective could they possibly be against such creatures? What was the phrase? Never bring a knife to a gunfight. Or a squirt gun to the apocalypse.

"I like it." Every head in the room swiveled toward Max. "Think about it. I was a nozzleman for five years. We've all seen what a hundred p.s.i can do. I've knocked down walls with water jets. I've blown out windows. Blasted off roofs. Hell, you could peel the skin off an elephant with a hose at close range."

At the front of the room, Leanza looked as if he were resisting the urge to jump into Max's arms.

"Now if I had a choice," Max continued, "I'd take a howitzer over a fire hose any day. But if something big is charging my way, I'd rather be behind a hose than a pistol."

Max's words were enough to fan the crowd's enthusiasm back into life. It returned in a combustive whoosh as a dozen comments about nozzlemen and pump operators, bore preference and water pressure began to simultaneously snap and pop. As Leanza tried unenthusiastically to reign in the commotion, a single voice gradually rose to cut through the static.

"Is that it?" Katie repeated. The room began to settle once more. "Is that it?"

Chief Rodriguez returned to the center of the room, Leanza retreating gratefully back to the other side of the table.

"Is what it, Ms..."

"Katie Fife. Is that your entire plan?"

Rodriguez leaned his rear against the edge of the table and folded his arms across his chest. "You think it's inadequate."

"Yes."

"Sorry you feel that way, Ms. Fife. We had an hour to cobble this together. It's not perfect." When he saw she was not going to accept that as an answer he sighed. "What? What have we forgotten?"

Katie pointed to the city map. "May I? Will." She motioned Little Billy to follow. The crowd parted as the two made their way to the wall map. "Okay. Let's say worst comes to worst and we can't stop the *xalanthracoils* from ripping us a new one. That means what, exactly? That a piece of their world pops into this circle?"

Little Billy nodded. "That's what we think. Everything inside the circle will be their world."

"That's a hell of a perimeter," someone in the crowd remarked. "Got to be two miles across, at least. We going to have enough hoses to surround it?"

The audience began to chatter again and Katie held up both arms. "Wait! I'm not done yet. If the *vetro's* world appears inside the circle, what happens to everything that's already in there? What happens to the part of our world that's inside the circle?"

"I guess it..." Little Billy's eyes slid shut as his fist shot up to rap his forehead. "Augh! How did we miss that?" He looked at the map with dawning horror. "Oh, Christ. All those people."

"What's going on?" Sid asked. "What's the issue?"

"The issue," Katie said, "is that if their world comes here, our world must go there, to the *vetro's* planet."

For a moment, the crowd seemed to rear back in stunned silence. Then they exploded into chatter. "Evacuation teams..." "At least twenty thousand...," "Never get everyone out...," "Top priority...," "Clusterfuck is what it is...," "Oh god, my brother's house is in there..."

Sid was pushing through the crowd toward Andrew, shouting something he couldn't hear above the din. Little Billy and Katie were close behind. Sid pointed to the door and together all four shimmied out into the hallway.

"If you want to go back," Sid said, moving to the far end of the corridor where conversation was once more possible, "I'll take you."

Andrew checked his watch again. "She should be gone by now. She was just going to pack a few things and pick up Anna."

"What's going on?" Katie asked, glancing from Andrew to Sid and back again.

"My house is inside the circle. Just barely, but yeah, it's in there."

"Then what are you waiting for?" She made a shooing motion with her fingertips. "Go. Go. Family first. Will and I can handle the rest."

"She should be halfway to Ocala by now."

"*If* they haven't closed the more of the interstate because of the fire."

Katie shot Sid a withering look.

"It's getting pretty bad near the fire. Visibility's dropping every hour. Last update, they were considering expanding the I-75 closure all the way to the I-275 juncture."

Andrew reached for his phone. "Let me call her first."

Before he could dial, the phone began to chime "Love Will Keep Us Together," his wife's ringtone. Later, he would remember the black certainty of catastrophe sending an icy spike of panic through the hollow of his throat even before he brought the cell to his ear. He would remember Katie's face, her hands rising to cover her mouth, her eyes widening in fear.

What did she read in his expression to provoke such a reaction? He would remember the red and white "no exit" sign above her shoulder and the fire extinguisher mounted on the wall beneath.

What he would never remember were the exact words spoken by the almost apologetic voice on the other end of the line, one that was not Grace's or Anna's, but familiar nevertheless.

Andrew listened for nearly a minute, saying nothing. When the voice stopped, he stood staring at the screen until Katie whispered, "What?"

"I need to borrow your car," he told Sid.

"What?" Katie repeated.

"They have my family."

Sid tossed him his car keys. "Go," he urged. "Go."

Andrew went.

Nineteen

She was gone again. Gary Wyatt saw the awareness flicker from his mother's eyes as her face contracted into the puzzled frown that had become her default expression. Loretta Wyatt turned as if catching the faint peal of an alarm and Gary placed the bowl of ice cream on the bedside table, knowing what would come next. He had hoped she would stay with him a least to the end of her treat. Ice cream was one of the few things she still enjoyed. Certainly, the only thing she sat still for. Perched on the edge of her bed, she would open her mouth for each new spoonful like an infant in a highchair, and as he fed her he would talk about his day, or exchange some trivial snippet of gossip he'd overheard on the ward, or recite a favorite childhood memory, presenting it like a bauble retrieved from a display case. Remember the time you took me to the zoo and we got stuck on the sky chair ride for thirty minutes? You had a pack of cards in your purse and we just sat up there swaying and playing rummy until the chairs started moving again. Remember that, Mom? Just you and me way up there over the aviary, listing to all the birds and playing cards? That was a fun day, wasn't it?

And with the ice cream glistening on her lips, her eyes would find his and he would see his mother behind them, her startled recognition as if he had suddenly stepped from behind a living room curtain. Not long ago, she might even have said his name. His response was always the same: a loud, bright, casual "Hi, Mom!," the greeting of a boy sliding into a mother's waiting car after school.

Today, however, there had been only the briefest glimmer of recognition amid the bovine contentment of her eager chewing. Now she stood, smoothed her sweater, gave a businesslike sniff and shuffled into the hall. This was how his mother spent her hours: pacing endlessly from one end of the ward to the other, never slowing, never tiring, a tin toy whose clockwork mechanisms were always wound tight.

At first, Gary had wondered where she thought she was going. There was nothing leisurely in her motion. She didn't stroll. She marched with the purpose of someone late for an appointment. When she reached the bay window at the ward's east end, she would pivot and stride with equal purpose to the west end. He didn't wonder about her motivations anymore. He knew she paced because it was one of the few neural loops still firing in her plaque-snarled brain.

But not for long. His mother would only have to endure this hell one more night. Tomorrow a new era would dawn, and when it did everyone evaporating under Alzheimer's relentless, pestilent sun would be refreshed. The *vetro offalate* had promised him this, and he knew they spoke the truth.

Loretta Wyatt turned left out of the room. Gary followed, his hand resting lightly on her forearm although she had no need for his assistance. Except for her rotting brain, she was in perfect health.

His mother was all he had. His father had skipped town when Gary was three and he had no siblings. He wasn't a mama's boy, one of those sheltered, timid, overly-dependent apron-clingers who couldn't decide what to eat for breakfast without consulting mommy first. Growing up, he'd always been athletic and popular. Plenty of friends. Plenty of girls. Still, his mother was his best friend, more pal than parent. Watching her slow deconstruction was like having a limb sawed off with a butter knife.

251

Had he lost her quickly, in a car accident for instance, he would have mourned and eventually moved on.

But he hadn't lost her. Not yet. She was still there, sinking slowly out of sight but visible beneath murky waters. He would do anything to save her. Anything at all. What good were doctors and hospitals if all they could do was stand at his mother's bedside, offering platitudes and false sympathy? Useless fuckers. Every one.

Six months ago, Gary had been on the verge of despondency. He could admit that now. The thought of one more afternoon spent prattling at his mother's side as she ignored him—it was too much to bear. Too much for anyone to bear.

And then the *vetro* had whispered to him, faintly at first, so faintly he thought he might be going mad with grief. Their language was, initially, nothing but gibberish, syllables spiraling round and round at the bottom of his head like particles of grit circling a drain. He tried to ignore them, tried to convince himself he was willfully conjuring up the utterances in an attempt to distract himself from his mother's tragedy.

But they would not be ignored. The more he tried to push them away, the more insistent they became until one night, sweating and thrashing in his bed under the assault, something in his head seemed to dilate and a single word, *ng'al'calu*, suddenly made sense. *Ng'al'calu*: restore. Restore? Restore what? *Knelgulig*. Understanding. By the first gray smear of dawn, he understood the meaning of one more word: *pi'vak*. *Pi'vak* meant mother. After that, Gary listened very closely to everything the *vetro offalate* had to say.

Loretta Wyatt reached the east end of the ward and turned without glancing out the window. "Glad we're not out there, right Mom?"

Gary noted the smoke haze with indifference. A year ago, he would have reported to the station by now, bunk gear in hand, ready for deployment wherever they needed him. But Gary knew something only a selected few were aware of. The wildfire was of no importance. Let it burn. The *vetro offalate* would extinguish it once they were here. All they had to do was *think* the flames into submission. Just as they would *think* the plaque from his mother's brain. Be gone! Puff. Such was the power of gods. Why anyone would oppose their return was beyond Gary.

A television at the nurses' station was showing an aerial view of a vast, white plume rising like steam from a volcanic fissure. Cindy, the nurse on duty, smiled at him as they passed.

"We on high-alert yet?" he asked.

"Don't think so. But you'd know more than me. Don't they keep you guys in the loop?"

"They said they would."

"Then as long as you're still here, things can't be that bad."

"Long as I'm here," Gary agreed. He liked Cindy. She was young and cute and despite her scrubs, he could tell she had a lithe, sinuous body under there somewhere. After the dust settled he intended to ask her out. New era, new girlfriend. He was fairly certain she would say yes. Women, especially nurses, tended to find his devotion to his mother a turn-on. And if she hesitated, well, he could always ask the *vetro* to give her a gentle nudge. He knew they could do that, as well. Really, there was almost nothing they couldn't do.

Except stop John and Andrew Tate on their own.

Gary paused, frowning, as Loretta Wyatt marched on without him. He didn't like thinking about this part. He much preferred dwelling on his mother's full recovery, so close now. But something small and terrier-like refused to let go of his doubt. It growled softly at night and whipped its head, teeth sunk deep into a question he could not shake. It was odd such omnipotent beings would concern themselves with the triflings of a few individuals. What could John and Andrew and their cohorts do to prevent the *vetro offalate's* inevitable triumph? Gnats. That's all they were. Not worth their attention.

And yet the *vetro* had demanded Gary kill his partner. They had even shown him how and when. The motel. The unlocked window. The gun he would find in a box on the top shelf of his mother's bedroom closet (a .22 revolver he'd had no prior knowledge of). It would have been so easy.

With the *vetro* guiding him, Gary would have been a leaf in an updraft, carried along and deposited in exactly the right place at the right time.

And his response to their demand?

No.

Of course, no. He wasn't a killer. It wasn't in his makeup. Gods, however, saw things differently. There was no sentimentality in the *vetro offalate*. Gary had sensed that from the beginning. They were concerned with the Big Picture. The life of one individual was insignificant. In that regard, they were no different than the god of the Old Testament. *He* certainly had no problem commanding thousands to slaughter thousands more. He was a Big Picture kind of guy as well. It didn't bother Gary *his* gods demanded the shedding of blood. It was simply that he was no Abraham, willing to slit his own son's throat at the Almighty's behest. He was composed of weaker stuff.

Gary hastened to the west end of the ward and met his mother on her way back. Falling in step, he draped an arm over her shoulder. "Still can't keep up with you, Mom. You're like the Energizer Bunny."

The *vetro offalate* had been disappointed by his refusal. That was the word he chose to use—*disappointed*—although on some unspoken level he knew it would have been more accurate to say *enraged*. But even enraged wasn't right. What he had sensed heaving and writing just beyond his awareness, held in check by a titanic effort of restraint, was something beyond the capacity of human comprehension, an apoplectic fury that could burn entire worlds to ash.

So, he had offered an alternative. Gary wouldn't kill Andrew Tate, but he would remove him as a threat. His new partner was already viewed with suspicion at the fire station. It wouldn't be hard to push that suspicion into outright animosity. It was only a matter of arranging things. If the *vetro* could distract certain individuals at the right time, he would be able to assure Tate's downfall. Once he was tucked safely away in a jail cell, what harm could he do?

Not only had the *vetro offalate* agreed, they'd shown him exactly how to accomplish this alternative plan. Andrew's locker combination bloomed in his mind with such clarity Gary was certain he'd be able to recite it on his deathbed. They revealed the panel at the back of Andrew's locker as well, the recess it concealed. And look here! A bottle of hooch. When Gary discovered Andrew *deserved* his fate he nearly swooned in relief. His partner was indeed a drunk, just as Sid Langston warned. Putting him behind bars wasn't a betrayal. It was justice.

The morphine vials had been Gary's idea. Schedule II narcotics were strictly monitored of course, with daily inventory checks and disposal of unused portions requiring a third-party witness, usually an attending emergency room nurse. In theory, every milliliter of the station's opiates was documented and accounted for. But when nurses "witnessed" and signed off on Gary disposing Tubex vials he was actually pocketing, it didn't take long to accumulate a considerable stash. A few changes in the log book, two or three hushed conversations with other EMTs about possible irregularities, a confidential meeting with Captain Hamilton regarding something odd Gary had glimpsed as Andrew fiddled in his locker was all it took.

The night before the surprise inspection he slipped out of his bunk, removed the baggie of vials from his own locker and transfer it to the alcove behind Andrew's. And what had he felt as he did this? Not anxiety. There was no danger of discovery. The *vetro* would make sure he was undisturbed. Guilt? Hardly. Shame? When he had written the words, "HOW ABOUT A GAME OF CRAZY TATES?" in lipstick across his partner's locker he'd experienced a twinge of shame, true, mostly at trying to implicate Clare and Sid for something they had nothing to do with. But he needed to create the illusion he and Andrew were on the same side, united against those plotting his ruin.

What Gary *had* felt planting the vials was magnanimity. He was, after all, saving the man's life. If it wasn't for his intervention, his mercy, his willingness to displease the gods, Andrew Tate would likely have died at the hands of one of the *vetro's* more fervent followers. Gary returned to his bunk that night and drifted off to sleep in the afterglow of the most charitable thing he'd ever done in his life.

And now his reward was nearly at hand. He did nothing for himself. It was all for others. It didn't matter that the multitude soon to be restored to their senses would never know he was the catalyst of their salvation. Well, not much. A little recognition would be nice, but Gary was prepared to live in contented anonymity so long as he and his mother could...

"Gary."

Loretta Wyatt's endless parade stopped at the bay window. For the first time in months, she stood motionless in the hallway, staring out at the hazy afternoon. At first, he wasn't sure if she had actually said his name or if he'd only imagined it, so lost in his own thoughts had he been.

"Mom?"

"Gary." She turned, her head tilting in that old way she had of making him feel as if he was the one staring up at her instead of the other way around. "Gary, how did I get here?"

It was his mother, not just a flickering afterimage. She was here with him once again, all of her. The *vetro offalate* had granted his wish early! What glorious creatures!

"Hi, Mom! Welcome back." He clasped her hand and raised it to his cheek.

"Gary." She cupped his chin and rubbed her thumb over his lips. "I had such a strange dream. I was in a room and couldn't find my way out. Every door I opened led back to the same place. I kept opening door after door but I couldn't find a way out. It was so frustrating."

"Don't think about that anymore. You were sick for a little while, but now you're better. You'll never be in that room again."

"You look different, somehow. Older." With her hand still on his cheek, she glanced around. "Where did you say I was, again?"

"You were sick. Your sickness made you confused. This is a place that takes care of people who are... confused."

"A home?"

"It was just to keep you safe until you were better."

"You put me in a home?"

"Mom, that's all over."

"But it's not. I'm still in the room." Her voice began to fade in an unsettling way, not dropping to a whisper so much as growing distant, receding down a corridor of echoing stone. "I remember a day spent sitting in the sky. Playing cards in the sky. Did that happen? The birds were..."

"Come back, Mom. Look at me. Just keep looking at me."

Loretta Wyatt turned her face to him and Gary's breath caught. At the same instant, her hand clamped his jaw hard enough for her nails to draw blood. What he saw in her eyes was terrifying. The old vacancy was gone, replaced by an awareness of blast furnace intensity, so hotly focused he thought he could feel his cheeks beginning to blister.

"We have a new task for you," the thing wearing his mother's face said. It spoke the language of the *vetro offalate*, but such enunciations could not be reproduced by a human larynx. The effort rent flesh and snapped vocal cords.

"Stop," he pleaded. "Talk in my head."

The hand clamped around his jaw turned Gary's head first one way, then the other. He could have broken her grip, pushed her from him, but he didn't want to hurt her. His mother was still in there, he was certain of it, her consciousness crushed up against the inner lining of her skull.

"Go to this place." A house and its location were crammed into his mind. "Take the woman and child you find there to this place." Another image. "When it's done, call him; tell him to come or they will die."

"You're hurting her!" A bloody foam was accumulating in the corners of his mother's mouth. "You don't need to do this."

Loretta Wyatt lips parted in a monstrously inaccurate approximation of a smile, revealing bloody gums.

"Do not fail us again. There will be no further opportunities to prove your worth."

"Yes, yes. Whatever you want. Just let her go!"

The hand dropped from his face, but the creature before him lingered a moment longer. "One more thing, *son*." It drew the last word out, hissing red spittle across his face. "Make sure you bring the gun this time."

HER RIGHT FOREARM WAS BLEEDING AGAIN. SHE'D BANGED it pulling the big suitcase from the hall closet and now the bandages were blooming scarlet blotches from wrist to elbow. Even after all the years of being good, of resisting the increasingly rare urge to draw blood, the sting of her cuts was still comforting. Soothing, even. Delicious. She considered intentionally banging her left forearm to give her pain the eloquence of symmetry.

It wouldn't take much. The wounds were deeper than she had intended, deep enough that she should probably drop by an ER to get herself stitched back together. But there was no time. Andy had told her to go and that was exactly what she would do, putting as much distance as possible between Anna and the abominations Grace had beheld in her nightmare. She would run all the way to Alaska if she had to, then hop a boat and sail over the horizon.

And the images that kept rearing behind her eyes, the terrible machines, Anna screaming and struggling, her fingers, her poor little fingers ruined from trying to claw her way from the dastardly creature dragging her by one leg into the center of the room? Would she ever be able to outrun those images? She didn't think so. The world wasn't big enough. She would have to learn to live with them somehow. *If* they lived.

No! That's what *they* wanted, the things muttering at the back of her head. They wanted her to despair. To give up. To bury herself under the covers and wait for the end. She wouldn't give them the satisfaction. She was leaving, and she was taking Anna with her.

But first.

Periphery

Grace rapped her left forearm against the closet doorframe. The pristine gauze began to discolor. The pain was clarifying and a surge of renewed purpose propelled her down the hall toward Anna's bedroom.

She had worn a long-sleeved Cardigan when she dropped by her sister's house to pick up Anna, hoping to conceal the bandages. It would have worked with her brother, James. James had always been oblivious to nearly all of his younger sisters' "dramas." Not so with Deborah. It's impossible to keep secrets from someone you shared a room with for seventeen years. Knowing what to look for, she had immediately seen the rim of white poking from beneath Grace's cuff.

"Oh, Gracie," she said, her eyes widening in reproach before closing in exasperation.

"Anna ready?" So much for chit-chat. In a way, she had been relieved. She doubted she would ever be able to engage in small, polite conversation with anyone ever again.

"Hi, Mommy." Anna's head appeared from behind her aunt's leg, a pale balloon floating in the relative darkness of the foyer. She tried to give Grace a smile, but it was a feeble effort that withered as she settled against Deborah's thigh.

"Is she alright?" Grace sank to her knees and held out her arms.

"Are *you*?" her sister countered.

Anna nearly collapsed against Grace's chest. "Don't start, Deb."

"We've both been feeling a little under the weather," her sister said, leapfrogging back to Grace's initial question. "There must be a thing going 'round. Stephen has it, too. He's upstairs right now with a towel over his eyes."

"The music can't be helping." As her sister spoke, Grace had become aware of the *bouff-bouff-bouff* of a snare drum pounding down from the second story. She thought it might be Marc Broussard's "Home," but she couldn't be sure. The melody was stuck somewhere between the walls.

"Actually, it does seem to help some. Makes us all feel a little better, doesn't it Anna?"

Grace felt her daughter's nod. She was nearly asleep. "It pushes the voices out a little," she said in a tiny voice.

Pinpricks of pain raced up and down her forearms as her skin erupted in gooseflesh. "What did you say, honey?" She eased her daughter's head from her shoulder and brushed a strand of brown hair from her eyes.

"She said she's been hearing voices in her head since this morning." Deborah made a low coughing sound that was supposed to be a dismissive chuckle. "You know how kids are; don't get worked up. She probably has a song lyric stuck on repeat."

"They can't hear them yet," Anna whispered in her ear. "The voices are still too small. But I have small ears and I can hear them."

Grace choked back a sob as she hugged Anna close. Bastards! She's just a little girl. Leave her the hell alone!

"But it's making their heads hurt anyway," Anna continued. "In a little bit, they'll be louder. Then they'll hear. Then everybody will hear."

That had been an hour ago, and now the voices *were* louder. No, that wasn't quite right. They weren't louder. How could something inside your head be loud or soft? What they were, with each passing minute, was closer. More distinct. More… comprehensible. Before long, the jumble of syllables would assemble themselves into understandable words. She didn't know how she knew this, but she did. And when that happened, she was afraid what remained of her sanity would crumble like old paint over termite damage when a finger punches through to the hollow beneath.

Grace turned into Anna's room and had a momentary burst of alarm when she didn't immediately see her. "Anna?"

"*Hum.*"

"Honey?"

Directed by her daughter's voice, Grace noticed a tangle of chestnut hair poking from the other side of her bed. Anna was stretched out on the floor, drawing and humming a simple tune, "*Frere Jacques*," perhaps, with an odd intensity.

"Anna, I need you to help me pack, okay? We're going to take a little trip. How would you like to visit Grandma and Grandpa?"

"*Hum-hum-HUM.* In Virginia? *Hum-hum-HUM.*"

"Yeah. It'll be fun."

"*Hum-hum-hum-hum-HUM-hum.* Is Daddy going?"

Grace tossed the suitcase on her daughter's bed and sat next to her on the floor. Crayons were scattered about, along with loose sheets of paper and several completed drawings. "Maybe, when he gets off work. There's the wildfire, remember? They need everybody to help put it out."

"Is that why we're running away? *Hum-hum-hum.*"

"We're not running away. It's a vacation." Grace brought her head close to her daughter's and began aligning the finished pictures into rows, seven drawings completed in thirty minutes, hastily scrawled sketches of suburban/pastoral bliss: purple houses topped with squat chimneys spewing curly-cues of smoke, a field of chartreuse flowers smiling under a blue and white sky, a horse, a kite, all bordered in a tangle of swirling loops.

It wasn't until she slowly exhaled that Grace realized she'd been holding her breath. What had she expected to see? A stick man labeled "Daddy" suspended against a wall? A row of living machines? Mommy sprawled naked on a dark slab, surrounded by *collectors,* their bulbous heads rendered in spirals of black crayon so forcefully applied the paper had shredded under the assault?

But no. Thank god, no. Anna was still drawing the things little girls were supposed to draw, even if they did seem a little... what? Rushed? Desperate? Intense in the same way she was humming "*Frere Jacques*" over and over again.

"The artist at work," Grace said, running her hand over Anna's hair. "So focused."

Her daughter was holding a green nub of crayon, filling the border of her latest drawing with doodles resembling a snarl of vines. Just a profusion of random whorls, a little frenetic perhaps, and yet there was something about the overall effect that suggested purpose and intent. The borders were quite interesting, actually, more intriguing than the scenes they framed.

Grace ran her finger over one, feeling the waxy marks. Her initial assessment might have been overly dismissive. There was too much control displayed in the borders to call them doodles. Designs would be a better description.

"You really went to town on the frames. They're lovely, honey, but I need you to..."

Grace frowned. She'd been absentmindedly shuffling the pictures into one pile when she noticed a particularly thick sweep of green arching off the right edge of the kite drawing. She's seen a mark of identical thickness curving off the picture of the houses, exiting from the left of the page. She rifled through the sheets until she found the drawing and carefully adjusted both until their borders fell into alignment. They were a perfect match. Every line from one sheet continued on to the other. It took only a moment to arrange all seven into a single image. Assembled, the individual scenes became islands of tranquility nestled within a briar of green snarls.

"You like it, Mommy?"

"Honey, it's absolutely..."

"Absolutely what?"

Terrifying. That was what she had nearly said. It was the green tangles. Something about them unnerved her. Viewed in their near-entirety (seven pictures of what was obviously intended to be a series of nine), the borders had become the real subject of the drawings, not the quaint images they framed. There were things inside the briars. She could almost make them out, low, twisted shapes holding perfectly still, watching with eyes shaped like beer bottles, coiled and ready to strike. Was that a leg? An antenna? Was that a claw? If she squinted and turned her head just so...

"Okay, crayons down." She swept the drawings into a pile and flipped them over. "I mean it, Anna. We need to pack and go."

"But you never finished. All you said was that my drawings were 'absolutely.' Absolutely what, Mommy?"

"Absolutely delightful."

Something in her head had screamed as the shapes wavered on the verge of cohesion. Turn away before it's too late. Don't look! Don't ever look too closely. She could feel her heart's pounding telegraphed in the cuts across her arms. It was as if she had stepped blindly into a busy street, heard the blare of a horn and jumped back as the speeding truck churned the hot air inches from her nose. Something had been avoided. Something very bad. But only just. Another second and it would have been too late. Too late for what? She didn't want to know.

The ring of the doorbell sent her slowing heart galloping again. "Jesus," she gasped. "Who could that be?"

"Daddy?" Anna was still drawing green knots. With a low growl of revulsion, Grace plucked the sheet from under her crayon and stuffed it in among the others.

"Hey!" Anna protested.

"I said no more drawing," she scolded, more harshly than intended. Anna's eyes widened. "I'm going to see who's at the door. Why don't you pick out some nice outfits to take with us? And your bathing suit."

"We're going swimming at Grandma and Grandpa's?" There was a liquid quiver at the edge of her words as she teetered on the verge of tears, but Grace noticed she was still humming under her breath. Was it helping her keep the voices out? Maybe she should...

The doorbell rang again, accompanied by the brisk rap of the knocker.

"Why not? It'll be fun. Now get busy, I want to leave as soon as we're packed."

Grace resisted the urge to race down the stairs. She wanted to fling the door open and throw herself into Andy's arms, beg him to come with them. She didn't want to face this alone. She would if she had to, of course, but it would be so much better with her husband at her side.

Her husband! Her thumb worried the base of her empty third finger. Why had she left her wedding ring on the partition at the jail's visiting

263

room? She'd let her emotions carry her up and out of the room without so much as a backward glance, giving in to the urge to heap new pain on a man already swollen and bruised, a man she had once loved with such intensity she would sometimes wake gasping in the middle of the night, panties already damp, and yank Andy from sleep with hands and mouth and thrusting pelvis. She'd always been the more sexually aggressive of the two. Andy never complained.

Those were what she now thought of as the "good times," before Andy's drinking became something more than an occasional beer in the evening or cocktail at a Christmas party. Before Anna's accident. But was all that gone forever? Andy moving out had been a mistake. *His* mistake. Hers, she saw now, was letting him go. If she had made even a feeble protest he would have stayed.

Instead, she had let it happen with a shrug. Go then, if that's what you have to do to get your head together. But in that god-awful motel room all he'd done was brood and drink. Isolation was the last thing he needed. Why hadn't she realized that before?

Grace didn't bother looking through the peephole. She unlocked the door and flung it open with a small, welcoming cry that clogged in her throat. The man facing her across the threshold was not Andy. He was not Max, although he was wearing a Tampa Fire Rescue tee-shirt. Nor was he the firefighter that had been with Andy early. This man was a stranger, and although he bobbed his head sheepishly and took a step back as she hitched out her feeble gasp, she knew he wouldn't hesitate to strike her if she tried to slam the door.

"I'm sorry about this, ma'am. Truly, I am." The gun rose slightly until it was pointing directly at her chest. "But I'm going to have to ask you and your little girl to come with me. We're going to have us a little family reunion. You and Anna, Andy and your father-in-law." The gun's muzzle jerked twice to the left. "Get the girl."

Twenty

The ascent was excruciating. By the time they reached the third-level catwalk, John was trembling in pain and Emily insisted they all take a break until his agony subsided into something more tolerable. When it became obvious that wasn't going to happen on its own she sent Hector back down to retrieve her medical kit from the car.

"I should have brought the damn thing to begin with," she said. "I was afraid this would happen."

"Just give me another ten minutes," John said through clamped teeth. "I'll be fine."

"You have two broken ribs. You're not going to be fine. You should be in bed pumped full of painkillers and watching cartoons."

"I can't..."

Emily waved him off. "We've been through all this. It's completely dark now; we're safe inside this godforsaken tower, and the *vetro* can't sic their nasty little pets on us until dawn, now can they? I'm not going to give you anything that will make you loopy. A couple of codeine-laced ibuprofen to take the edge off. Otherwise, you'll never make it to the next level let alone all the way to the top. Now quit your damn bitching."

John wanted desperately to stretch out on the concrete, use one of the duffel bags as a pillow and drift off into the red haze of pain-tinged sleep. But he was afraid if he did that he would never get back up again, with or without Emily's little white helpers.

What was he hoping to accomplish here? He had to keep reminding himself as the futility of his scheme oppressed him more with each passing minute. Come first light, how much of the *vetro offalate's* attention could he realistically hope to draw from the *xalanthracoils*? Enough to make any difference? *Look at me! Look at me! Hey, over here you sons-of-bitches. Don't worry about the little men scratching around your* coils. *They're of no consequence. I'm the one you need to worry about.* It was laughable, really.

Pathetic.

"Hey." Emily surprised him by pressing both palms against his cheeks and leaning forward until they were nearly nose-to-nose. "Don't."

"What?"

"Look that way. It's the pain. It's messing with your head as much as the sleep deprivation and the *vetro* trying to claw their way inside our skulls. Don't start second-guessing yourself. We're going to finish this even if I have to strap you on my back and carry you and your harmonic blaster all the way to the top myself. Got it?"

"Sir, yes sir!" Despite the pain of raising his arm, John saluted her crisply. He tried to reassure himself Andrew and William would get the job done before dawn and make this sorry excuse of a diversionary tactic unnecessary. They had all night to destroy a *coil*—just one!—and if they did he was almost certain the entire circuit would short out like a strand of Christmas lights after the failure of a single bulb. God, he hoped it worked that way. It *felt* right, a little unintended insight after years of exposure to the *xalantracoils*, but maybe it was all just wishful thinking.

"Better. Now if you'll excuse me, I literally have a bug crawling up my ass." Emily stood and without a shred of modesty dropped her pants around her thighs, shaking and shimmying and swatting until something fell to the floor and skittered away.

Around the curve of the catwalk, blocked from view by the tower's central core, Booker could be heard talking quietly on the phone, his voice distorted by the tower's odd acoustics. The beam from his flashlight cast his shadow across the outer wall, a top-heavy distortion drifting to-and-fro as he fidgeted through his conversation.

John didn't know much about the man. Was he married? Did he have kids? He thought he heard a name repeated: Marlene. A wife? A daughter? Girlfriend? What had prompted Booker to risk so much for a virtual stranger? It had taken Andrew twenty years to reach the same place.

A flash of resentment flared and faded as quickly as heat lighting. He had no reason to feel anything other than satisfaction in the way things had turned out between Andrew and himself. Their relationship had unfolded precisely as John had orchestrated from the periphery of his son's life. Once he'd been infected with the ability to perceive the true nature of reality, John's only recourse had been isolation. The risk of contagion was too great. And if that meant leaving a confused, resentful twelve-year-old behind, so be it. Resentments might fade. Death was permanent.

And forgiveness? He'd never asked for it. What was there to forgive? But if he ever saw his son again he would tell him he was sorry. Sorry for the way things had to be. Sorry for all the things that couldn't be. Sorry for the unavoidable pain of a truly shitty situation. Sorry, sorry, sorry.

The soft clang of Hector climbing the wall-mounted ladder prompted Booker to end his conversation with a terse, "Gotta go."

"I tell you what," Hector said, tossing the medical kit to Emily. "I'm tempted to shoot out those fucking floodlights." He leaned out the nearest window for a moment, waved a fluttering insect from his face and yanked his head back with a huff of disgust. "They're drawing every goddamn bug known to man, and if Book and I need to shoot at something out there we won't be able to see shit because of the glare."

The floodlights ringing the base of the water tower had been added during renovations, along with the aluminum ladder ascending to the observation platform seven levels up. Other than giving the interior a cleaning, no other work had been done. John understood why. The foot-thick walls did indeed hearken to the battlements of a medieval castle. *Solid*, he had thought as they entered. Built to last. Nothing short of a dozen surface-to-surface missiles was going to breach this defense, and as Hector and Booker had swung the metal entrance plate closed behind them, he'd experienced a profound sense of fortified isolation similar to what he imagined NORAD's military brass felt when the enormous vault door sealed behind them.

The tower's ground-level chamber was ringed by a concrete catwalk encircling a dark pool smelling strongly of minerals. While Booker chained and padlocked the entrance, John had passed the beam of his flashlight over the glassy surface.

The water—still seeping up from the artesian spring below despite the drought—was surprisingly clear. He could follow the spear of light all the way to the sandy bottom where rusted piping from fallen banisters laid twisted among green beer bottles. What looked like an ancient, muck-covered Igloo cooler was down there as well, a few broken cinderblocks, and something else, something inside one of the blocks, a black coil of cable, thick as his wrist.

As John's light played over the crevice, the coil swayed, contracted and shot across the bottom, trailing a plume of muddy sand.

"Shit!" It wasn't like any *bilantu* he'd ever seen. An aquatic species? He had William had always speculated about the possibility, of course, but neither of them was certified divers. Why hadn't they at least slipped on a snorkel mask and stuck their heads underwater? This opened an entirely new avenue of research. What if the thing in the water was amphibious? If it posed a threat they would have to rethink...

"Easy, professor. Don't get your panties in a wad." Hector gripped his shoulder. "They're just freshwater eels. Not everything that slithers is one of your creepy-crawlies."

"How the hell did they get in here?" John asked, trying to pass the slightly breathless quality of his question off as simple zoological curiosity. What the hell was wrong with him? Spooked by a damn eel.

"You're the one with the Ph.D. You tell me."

After that, John had restricted his attention to the floor in front of him where insects and geckos scattered at their approach, disappearing over the side. Overhead, the occasional flap of wings announced a pigeon startled from its roost. The wings of the bats were silent, but their small black bodies would sometimes streak through the flashlight beams and be gone before their presence fully registered.

Standing at the foot of the ladder, staring up at what his flashlight could reveal of the two-hundred-foot climb, John realized he would never be able to carry the guitar case up even a single flight. Too bulky. Too heavy. One of the others would have to manage it for him, something he was loath to do but saw no way around. Even the much lighter duffel bag was too much for him. It'd be a miracle if he could drag his own sorry ass to the top.

"Me and Book will haul up the gear." John touched the guitar case propped against his knees. "No choice, professor. You're just going to have to trust us. We promise not to drop it out a window or jump on it or smash bugs with it."

Hector handed John a sizable square of mosquito netting and a Rays baseball cap. "Netting goes first. Make sure you cover all your face and the back of your neck down to your shoulders. Use the cap to hold it in place."

John did as told while the others toted the gear and guns up to the second level. When Hector carefully lifted the guitar case, something inside shifted, producing the dull clank of metal against metal. Hector's face crumpled.

"No, no." John reassured him. "It's disassembled. You're good."

Now, as they huddled on the tower's third level waiting for the painkillers to blur the edges of his anguish, John fought the urge to toss the case out the window himself and be done with it. They were only three levels up and still had a hundred-and-forty feet to climb. *Quit,* a voice inside chanted. *Quit, quit, quit.* Only it wasn't a single-syllable word looping through his thoughts. It was longer, three distinct syllables. Not

269

even syllables. Gurgles, hisses, pops, an utterance that could only emerge from a throat like a boiling mud pot. *Ghnphss d' pak. Ghnphss d' pak.*

Despair.

"Hold hands!" Emily commanded. "Booker, Hector. Link up."

"Doc, what's the point?" Hector slid down the wall into a sitting position. "What are we doing here, anyway? This is pointless."

"Grab Booker's hand. Now, goddamn it!" With a roll of his eyes, Hector extended his arm and Booker grasped his hand like a man teetering over a precipice. "Now John's."

Emily already held John's right hand. When Hector clasped his left, he experienced a subtle reevaluation, as if realizing an assumed porch light was actually the moon reflected in a window.

Emily settled against the core wall facing the other three and grabbed Booker's free hand, completing the loop. John expected something profound to happen as the circuit closed. He was disappointed. There was no surge of power, no sudden barrier shielding them from the *vetro's* mental barrage. Maybe things didn't seem quite as hopeless as they had a minute before. They had the *vetro offalate's* attention, after all. John supposed that was something. Then again, this minor lifting of spirits might simply be a side effect of the painkillers starting to kick in.

"Now what?" Hector asked. "Should we all start singing 'Kumbaya'?"

Later, on his descent from the top, John would have the fleeting realization that if they had done exactly that, things might not have turned out as they did.

"Now we pray." Booker's tone left no room for debate. John's eyes found Emily's. She smiled and lifted a shoulder.

"Can't hurt, although I have to tell you, I'm agnostic."

"No atheists in a foxhole," John said.

"And no agnostics in a water tower," Hector quipped. John wondered fleetingly if the man knew what the word meant.

Booker led the impromptu prayer group into "The Lord's Prayer" before launching into an impassioned plea for Jesus' protection against whatever evils the night and morning might bring. John found himself not so much following Booker's words as being engulfed in the man's sonorous baritone. The sing-song quality of his prayers, the regular prompt of "can I get an Amen" and their compliance gradually filled a place in his head, a balloon of human (and perhaps divide) interaction that counterbalanced just enough of the *vetro offalate's* relentless inward pressure to allow John to view the top of the tower as a distinct possibility rather than an impossible fantasy.

"I feel better," John said after Booker concluded with a final, definitive "Praise *Jesus*." And because John meant what he said, he added, "Thank you, Booker. Really."

"Jesus is our co-pilot," Hector added, but he too appeared to have shaken off much of his malaise. "Hell, I may just start going to church again if we get through this. Can white people go to your church, Book?"

"So you're white now?"

"Whiter than you."

Booker smiled. "We don't turn anyone away, even your sorry, blasphemous Hispanic ass." Pulling a bottle of water from one of the duffel bags, he took a long swig. John watched his Adam's apple bob and wondered what it would be like to drop by Booker's church to testify and sing boisterous hymns and listen raptly as a charismatic preacher put Satan in his place, to be wrapped warmly in a community of shared fervor and goodwill. Nice, probably, like a flannel hug on a cold winter's night. "So, we doing this or what?"

John's modest feeling of renewed purpose lasted to the fifth-level catwalk. The painkillers got him that far. But as he stood waiting for Booker and Hector to finish bringing up the supplies, his legs began quivering uncontrollably. Sweat stung his eyes and the mosquito netting around his face made him claustrophobic. It irritated the back of his neck where he had tucked it under his collar, and the air beneath the gauze seemed to be steadily thickening to a vapor too hot and caustic to breathe. John ripped the cap off and flung the netting away with a gasp.

"I'll take my chances with the bugs."

Emily took his pulse from a clammy wrist and shook her head. "You're on the verge of passing out."

"You can tell that from my pulse?"

"I can tell that from your white face, glassy eyes and shaking legs. Take a few sips of water. You two," she said, indicating Hector and Booker, "take everything up to the observation deck. No more of this floor-by-floor crap. Once that's done, come back and we'll figure out how to get John to the top."

He made the final ascent perched on Hector's shoulders, helping as best he could by lifting rung by agonizing rung. His pain became a purple current pulsing with every laborious step. Six levels up. Seven. Finally, his head emerged through a trapdoor into an open space dimly illuminated by the glow of the floodlights below. A circle of large, barred windows gave the observation deck a startlingly open feel after the confines of the lower levels. A breeze washed over him, warm and humid and carrying the scent of the approaching wildfire. Compared to the mausoleum atmosphere below, it was an alpine kiss.

"Easy, easy, easy." Emily helped him into the room and eased him to the floor of the deck. "Stretch out for a spell." A bag was positioned beneath his head.

"Don't let me fall asleep."

"Never."

But she must have, for when he turned his head after blinking up at the ceiling for what felt like no more than a minute or two, he found Booker, Hector and Emily standing with their backs to him, staring out one of the windows. All the supplies had been unpacked and arranged neatly along a wall of the deck, along with one of the rifles. The other two rifles, John saw, were slung over the men's shoulders. He couldn't tell if they were also carrying the pistols.

"Nice view?" John asked.

"Very," Emily said without turning. "You can see all the way across the bay to St. Petersburg from here."

"See the fire, too," Hector added.

272

"How bad?" John tried to sit up, groaned, fell back and brought his knees up, trying to find a position that would ease the strain on his ribs. He was a turtle on its back. A turtle skewered through the chest with a molten wire.

"The glow stretches for miles. Thing is, there's been a lot of fire engines going down the interstate into town. You'd think they'd be headed in the opposite direction, toward the fire, not away from it."

"How long have I been out?"

"Not long." Emily returned to kneel at his side. "Twenty minutes, maybe. I don't want to say you swooned, 'cause that's what little girls do. But you swooned. Pure and simple."

"There's that bedside manner again. Can you help me up?"

Emily whistled. "Stargazing's over for now, gentlemen. Do either of you have a wallet?"

Both assured her they did.

"Let me see."

Hector's "wallet" was actually a credit card holder. Emily made a face and told him to put it back. Booker's, on the other hand, was an overstuffed billfold thick as a filet mignon.

"That'll do." She held out her hand and after a moment's hesitation, Booker passed it to her.

"I'm going to get that back, right?"

"If you're good. Here," she gave the wallet to John.

"What I'm I supposed to do with that?"

"Bite it."

"That bad?"

"Probably."

"Do it fast," John said, slipping the wallet between his teeth, tasting the sweat-salted leather and having just enough time to wonder if maybe he should ask for something a little stronger than codeine-laced ibuprofen before Booker and Hector hoisted him to his feet in a single motion. When Emily handed the wallet back to its owner, the imprint of John's bicuspids was deep enough to take a mold from.

"Tell him about the car," Hector said once he was certain John could stand on his own.

"Car?"

"A car pulled into the parking lot about fifteen minutes ago," Emily said, riffling through her medical bag. "It's been down there ever since."

"Anybody get out?"

"Not yet." She removed a blister pack containing two large, red tables. Horse pills. "No arguments. Take them."

He didn't argue. Booker drifted back to the windows, and while John gulped water and swallowed painkillers, the correctional officer moved from opening to opening. "Uh-huh. Here comes another one."

The other three approached and Booker pointed. A car was creeping down the path from the park entrance, its headlights throwing twin cones of illumination across the ground in front of it. From this height, the vehicle was an unidentifiable block of motion, no bigger than a postage stamp. After a moment, it disappeared below the rim of the crenelated balcony outside the windows. There was a way out there—John saw a rusted door off to the right—but the thought of standing at the edge and peering over caused a stomach-dropping jolt of vertigo.

"Maybe it's just a carload of teenagers," Booker said doubtfully.

"Maybe." Hector tried the balcony door. The knob turned, but the hinges were fused with rust. He threw his weight against it, widening the opening only a few inches each time. "Worry about that later."

He returned to the others, reached behind his back and pulled one of the pistols from his waistband. "Doc." He held the weapon out grip-first. "For you."

"I've never fired a gun in my life."

"It ain't brain surgery. Use your non-shooting hand as a platform, aim and squeeze, gently. But leave the safety on for now. No use taking chances."

He nodded at Booker and the guard produced the second gun. "Same deal, professor. Hopefully, we won't have to use them."

Kids, John told himself. Just a few kids smoking weed in the empty parking lot. Probably hear music from a radio soon, faint laughter. Nothing to be alarmed about. No one knew they were here.

As the minutes passed, however, the relative calm became the weighted hush that fills an examination room after the doctor enters with the test results. John thought he heard a car door open and shut. He heard the wail of distant sirens, nearly constant now. A plane overhead. The smell of burning seemed to seep up from his own flesh as he sweated out his pain and the big red pills starting snuffing out the burning places in his chest.

"Maybe we should think about..." Hector began. Emily's phone cut him short. No one spoke, but the four gathered in a tight circle as if preparing to link hands once more in prayer. Each face reflected some mixture of anxiety, dread and resolve. *I guess we're all psychic now*, John thought grimly. *Nothing good will come of this.*

"Here we go," Hector said.

John nodded. "Answer it."

Emily unclipped the phone and read the display. Her glace was all John needed to confirm what he already knew. It was Andrew.

"Hello?" she said cautiously. Three heartbeats later she handed the cell to John. He put it to his ear.

"Andrew."

"Dad." His son swallowed. "Dad, I know you're up there. We need you to come down, okay. We're right outside the door. We have to talk."

"Who's 'we'?"

"It's important." John heard a muffled exchange between Andrew and another male voice. "Bring the device with you."

"Andrew, what's going on?"

"You need to surrender. If you don't, they're going to shoot Grace and Anna. Jesus Christ, Dad. They're going to kill my family."

LITTLE BILLY WATCHED THE DOZER'S TREADS CLAW TRENCHES into the dirt. The roar of the diesel seemed an exclamation of pure frustration. After a moment, the operator—a DOF firefighter named Sam—eased the vehicle back, allowing the cable to go slack, then plowed forward once again. Little Billy imagined a metallic *twang* as the dozer reached the end of its tether and jerked to a stop, the cable behind oscillating in a blur.

Just like all the others. The *xalantracoil* remained fixed in place, a curving finger of stone awaiting the dawn. Christ, how far down did they go? Miles? Sam and the other firefighters on the demolition crew had scoffed when Little Billy pointed out the first *coil*. *That*, they asked, suddenly jovial with relief. *That broken property marker? We can probably dig it out with a shovel. It's already leaning.*

Their confidence evaporated even before the dozer was unloaded from the flatbed. As Little Billy and the others watched Sam ease the machine down the ramp, one of the Hillsborough County firefighters had sauntered over to what he perceived to be a crumbling concrete pylon and given the thing a dismissive pat. When he regained consciousness, all he could do was thrash and scream. "They're coming," he reassured the rest. "Oh god, they're coming."

They were one less now, the stricken firefighter having been transported to St. Joe's under heavy sedation. The crew went about their prep work quietly, speaking only when they had to and then only in the hushed, expectant tones of relatives summoned suddenly to a hospital room to pay their last respects.

Occasionally, one of the undulating bubbles of *otherspace* would float overhead and the men and women would pause to watch, transfixed. In the darkness, the orbs glowed with infernal light. It wasn't night *over there*. Little Billy was beginning to suspect it might never be night on the *vetro offalate's* homeworld. Too many suns, the sky a constellation of ancient, swollen stars on the verge of extinction. No wonder the bastards wanted out. They knew their time was almost up.

Sam gave a final tug, black smoke billowing from the dozer's exhaust pipe like the plume from an underwater thermal vent. Little Billy thought the *coil* shifted every-so-slightly, maybe a degree or two from its original position, but he couldn't be sure. After another ten seconds of the treads deepening their grooves, Sam eased off and cut the engine.

In the relative silence, the sounds of the evacuation efforts sprang up around them once more, megaphones and vehicle-mounted bullhorns calling their warnings out into the night: *Attention, attention, a mandatory evacuation has been ordered. Under penalty of incarceration, all residents of this neighborhood are required to evacuate the area within the next thirty minutes. This is not a request. Attention, attention...*

Leading a slow parade of flashing patrol cars, the point vehicles would pause at each intersection as officers dashed across lawns and up stoops to pound on every door. Terrance Jackson, a Tampa firefighter in Little Billy's crew who had introduced himself as one of Andrew's station-mates, told him thirty evacuation squads were canvassing every neighborhood within the *xalantracoil* circle, telling anyone who demanded an explanation that the wildfire had jumped the I-75 firebreak and was now an imminent threat. It was an audacious lie, one that made little sense considering how far south the evacuation zone was from the actual conflagration.

Still, Little Billy supposed they had to tell residents *something*, and the flood of firefighting equipment pouring into the area likely convinced many the situation was indeed dire. At least that's what the heavy traffic heading out of the target zone suggested. Then there were the chittering voices building steadily to a roar. They had to be contributing to the exodus. Who wouldn't run from that muttering madness?

But all those doors to knock on. All those people! How could they hope to alert everyone in the—Little Billy checked his watch—in the six hours left before sunup? And what about Andrew? Half-a-dozen times he had found himself dialing his number and each time something inside him seized up and he aborted the call. He'd never met Andrew's wife, but he remembered the sweet little girl from the park, the one with the burned arm. He desperately wanted to know she was safe, that they were all safe, but he couldn't face the alternative.

Three hours since Andrew's departure, and with each passing minute Little Billy became more convinced something terrible had happened. Images of Laura's backyard—strewn with a confetti of bloody remains—kept flashing in a nightmare marquee across the black sky, leaving him sick with dread. But he had a job to do here, the most important job of his life. He couldn't let Andrew's fate, whatever it might be, distract him from that.

"I would have bet a month's salary that at least one of these fuckers would snap off." Sam slammed the back heel of his boot into the dusty soil as if punishing the ground for its stubborn refusal to release the *coil*. The other firefighters gathered around in a loose semi-circle, their heads bowed in weariness or defeat. "The tensile strength of these things must be off the charts. I don't want to be a Negative Nelly here, but I'm beginning to wonder if we're going to be any more successful with explosives."

Little Billy had been wondering the same. Their attempt at the cemetery the other night had failed, but he had fallen back on his ignorance of high explosives to nurture a frail sense of naïve optimism about their chances tonight. It was all a matter of scale. Bigger. Deeper. The *xalantracoils* weren't indestructible. The *vetro offalate* weren't omnipotent. Everything had its limits. He'd learned that much over the years.

"Is that you talking," Little Billy asked, "or the voices in your head?"

The other man examined his shoes. "Hard to say, but we need to finish this fast. I don't know how much longer I can hold out. They get any louder, I won't be able to hear my own thoughts anymore."

From the other firefighters, rumbles of agreement.

"I'm all for fast," Little Billy massaged his temples in a futile effort to ease the *vetro's* clamp around his head. Six hours to dawn.

God.

A walkie-talkie crackled to life and Terrance answered. "Status report," a voice on the other end asked.

"Just finished trying to yank down the last one. No go. No go with any of them. How 'bout with you guys?"

"Same. It's like trying to uproot a sequoia with sewing thread. We're moving on to phase two." A second voice erupted from the background. The connection broke for a moment and as they waited Terrace gave Little Billy a small smile.

"I think someone wants to talk to you."

"Demo team one."

"We're here."

"Terrance, can you hand the walkie-talkie to your spotter there. Someone here wants... needs... to talk to him."

Terrance handed him the radio.

"Will?"

The firefighter pointed out the push-to-talk button and Little Billy pressed it. "I'm here, Katie." He paused a heartbeat, then added "over," feeling like a boy playing soldier. He released the button a half-second too late and caught Katie's response mid-sentence.

"...telling me they're only going to bump up the charges in stages, using a little more if the last blast is unsuccessful. Hello? Goddamn it. OVER."

"That's the plan. You heard Chief Rodriguez."

"He's a dumbass. What?" she asked someone on her end. "Is he going to fire me? Will, we've just wasted three hours yanking on these things. Let's just pack all the explosives we've got around the one in front of us and blow the fucker sky high."

Making sure his finger was off the call button, Little Billy turned to Sam. "You said fast. That would be fast. All or nothing."

Sam ran his hand up the back of his head and back down his neck. "Yeah, but I also want to do it right."

Terrance cleared his throat. "There's a couple of things to remember. First, we have our orders. I can radio in and ask if we can change things up, but I already know they'll say no.

"Second, say we say 'fuck it' and use everything we got on this one here and when the smoke clears it's still standing. All we've managed to do is knock out every window in the neighborhood, take down four or five utility poles, cut the electricity for everyone trying to get the hell out of dodge, scatter live wires all over the road and maybe blow a hole through the water main for good measure. No water main, no water pressure for the guys setting up their perimeter of fire hoses. And no explosives left for any other target.

"I say we stick to the plan. Start big here. Big, not massive. Keep the surrounding infrastructure intact. Assess the results. Move on to the next if we have to and go a little bigger there."

"Hello? Anybody still on the other end of this thing or am I talking to myself? Over. Over. OVER, WILL!"

Terrance could have simply dismissed his question, reminding him he was a civilian who held no authority over the rest of the crew. Instead, he had given him a thoughtful response, and for that Little Billy was grateful. He pressed the talk button.

"Katie, I hear you. We all hear you." He gave Terrance a nod. "But our role in this is over. Now we need to step back, let these guys do their job and not interfere."

The silence on the other end stretched out for seven or eight seconds. Little Billy could picture the other demolition team leader trying to wrest the walkie-talkie away from Katie and the ensuing tussle. He was just about to hand his own radio back to Terrance when she responded.

"How much longer do you think they'll be able to do their jobs, Will? I don't know about you, but my head is clogged with *vetro* snot."

"Long as we have to," Sam said. Little Billy wished the firefighter could have been a little more convincing, but under the circumstances, his quiet attempt at defiance was the most valiant display of resolve Little Billy had seen all night. He pressed the talk button.

"These guys aren't going to quit until they're twitching and drooling on the ground, and I don't see that happening anytime soon. Katie, I know you're scared." Across the street, the corner of a two-story Mediterranean was swelling like blown glass as a bubble drifted through it. Little Billy hoped the occupants had already fled.

"We're all scared. But nobody's panicking." Not wanting to end the conversation on a tired and insincere note about staying positive, he tried something he hadn't attempted since college, a tactic that had always made Laura smile on the rare occasions when the stress of finals threatened to overwhelm her. He went for the absurd.

Pitching his tone into a syrupy exaggeration of polished salesmanship, he slipped into what he had once thought of as his game show host voice. "So pack away those blues, grab yourself a big bowl of can-do and turn that frown upside down."

Little Billy made a face and held the walkie-talkie out as if it might explode.

"Where. Are. You." Katie said in a voice lacking all inflection. Little Billy gave her their location.

"I'll be there in fifteen minutes. Over and OUT."

"Oh, you in trouble now," Terrance assured him as he passed the radio back. "If I were you, I'd start running."

"And miss all the fun?"

Terrance grew somber. "Seriously, man, it's like you told your girlfriend: Your job here is done. Be honest, you think we'll be able to blast these things out of the ground?"

"We have to try."

"No, we have to try." Terrance swept his finger around in a circle, indicating the firefighters while excluding Little Billy. "And that's not an answer."

"It's as much as I can give."

"That's what I thought. You want to stay, stay. Nobody's going to chase you off. But what about her? You want her here when the sun comes up?"

281

Little Billy slowly shook his head, unsure what he was negating. All he knew was that the last twenty years of his life had led up to this event and he would not turn from whatever fate awaited him. If Katie insisted on staying—and he knew she would—he wouldn't try to send her away. God help him, if he was to die in the morning, he wanted her face to be the last thing he saw.

"She can decide that for herself."

Terrance shook his head. "I hope she has a hell of a lot more sense than you do."

On that, they could agree.

Twenty-one

It was all a dream. As they stood waiting for the metal door at the base of the water tower to open, a voice in Andrew's head kept chanting the mantra over and over again. This is a dream. It's a dream. This is all a dream. Trouble was, he didn't believe a word of it. This was as real as things got, and the frantic repetition of his thoughts was nothing more than a sort of mental shivering, an uncontrollable reflex that warmed his faculties just enough to keep from slipping into a hypothermic daze of terror.

As he had driven Sid's car north up the interstate, the steady traffic of emergency vehicles heading in the opposite direction had given Andrew the sensation of fleeing disaster rather than racing toward it. If there was a moment of surrealism and dislocation, it was then, weaving around slower vehicles in a car that wasn't his. He had recognized the voice on the other end of the call, the voice that had instructed him where to go, but it was a puzzle piece he couldn't fit into any conceivable configuration of reality.

Gary Wyatt holding his family hostage, pointing a gun at Grace, demanding he rendezvous with them at the Sulfur Springs water tower, threatening to kill her and then Anna if he didn't. Gary Wyatt? His partner of eight weeks? What was he missing here? This couldn't be right.

Some vital piece of information had been omitted, some detail that would realign the situation, affording him a perspective in which everything shifted back into some semblance of normalcy.

Maybe he'd been wrong about the male voice. Maybe it hadn't been Gary's. But the other voice, the one that concluded the conversation? It had been Grace's, no doubt.

"Do what he says," she pleaded, her voice quivering in fear. "This is for real."

He understood how real as he pulled up to the tower. There they were, bathed in the stage glow of the upward-angled floodlights ringing the base of the tower. Grace was still wearing the same clothes he had seen her in earlier, her bandaged arms wrapped protectively around Anna. And yes, Gary was with them, the same man who only a few days ago had scrubbed an insult from his locker door. He was standing arm-in-arm with Grace as if they were about to walk up the aisle together.

Then he saw the gun pointed at her right breast and reality crashed over him with a leaden oppression that reminded Andrew of the extra gravity he'd experienced on the *vetro offalate's* world.

That was when his mantra began. Not real. Not real. At least it competed with the other voices in his head. *Their* voices. But not by much.

Almost immediately Andrew had sensed something like embarrassment from his former partner. The tilt of his head, the apologetic way he told him "that's close enough," as he approached with his hands in the air, Gary's refusal to make eye contact, it all suggested a man reluctantly performing a disagreeable task he could no longer avoid. The first thing Gary had done was volunteer the reasons for his actions in a rushed explanation flung out between them like a shield, and when Andrew was certain he had heard the man correctly he nearly laughed in despair.

"They're not going to keep their promise," he said now as they waited outside the tower's door. He wanted to direct Gary's attention away from Anna, who was obviously starting to annoy him. His daughter had been singing throughout the standoff, a simple, repetitive melody intoned with the same fervor as the prayer of a pilot trying to land his sputtering Cessna on a stretch of busy highway. It was heartbreaking, his little angel trying to comfort herself during the ordeal. The only thing that had kept Andrew from lunging at Gary with a howl of anguish was the fear the gun would go off and hit either his wife or daughter.

Gary's head wobbled. "So you say. But I've seen what they can do."

"Me, too," Andrew suddenly remembered the man he and Gary had transported earlier in the week, the one blaring hip-hop music into the neighborhood and screaming about the voices in his head.

"No, you haven't. They're gods, Andy. Returning gods. This was their world long before it was ours. They can heal us, if we just let them. That's all they really want: to make us better. Make us whole."

"And kill anyone who stands in their way."

Gary's mouth tightened. "The only reason you're still alive is because of me. Me, Andy. I could have shot you coming out of that fleabag motel you've been holed up in at any time. That's what *they* wanted. But I said no. I said getting you thrown in jail would be enough and they agreed. Now here I am again, trying to keep people from dying. So, if you don't mind... Hey, little girl! How about giving the *Row, Row, Row Your Boat* a rest, okay? You've been looping it for an hour now."

Andrew took a step forward, he couldn't help it, and Gary shifted the muzzle of the gun until it was only inches from Grace's chest.

"Stay." He drew the word out, turning it into a canine command.

"Honey," Grace said in a watery voice. "Can you sing in your head for a little?"

Before his daughter could answer, the tower door began to swing inward with the squeal of metal and scrape of concrete. Gary yanked Grace in front of him and bent his knees so that only the top of his head was exposed to whoever was about to emerge. At the same time, Andrew was vaguely aware of motion behind them, a wash of headlights as another vehicle turned into the park entrance. Not real, not real, not real, the voice in his head insisted, faster now, ever faster as the call of the *vetro* grew more insistent.

"Show your hands," Gary demanded. "Just your hands. Nothing else."

A pair of hands reached from the opening. They were not his father's. Even from the shadows, it was obvious the individual on the other side was black.

"You're not John Tate."

"Name's Booker Lamont. John Tate's hurt. He's in too much pain to make it back down here anytime soon."

"Bullshit. Come all the way out of there. Slowly." Booker edged out with his hands over his head. Andrew had not recognized the name, but he knew the face. Mr. Lamont was the guard who had cleaned him up before his release from jail.

"Take off the jacket and do a three-sixty."

Booker did as he was told, turning slowly. If he was armed, the weapon was well concealed.

"I have what you want. Tate sent it down with me. It's in a bag just inside the door. Do I have your permission to fetch it?"

"Send the old man down. We'll wait."

"I told you, he's in bad shape. Someone tried to kill him yesterday and he should be in the hospital. Same guy who did that to Andy." He motioned with his head, but Gary didn't bother turning. "It'll take half-an-hour or more to lower him down and he'll probably pass out before he gets to the bottom. It's the device you want anyway. Take it and leave these poor people be."

Gary all but vanished behind Grace. Only his arms and eyes were visible as he peered over her shoulder. Christ, Andrew thought, haven't we done this hostage thing before?

"If you're planning to reach for a weapon this is going to end badly for everyone," Gary said.

"No, sir. No way I'd risk the safety of the woman and little girl. Or myself, for that matter."

Gary appeared to listen for a moment, his head cocked.

"Do it slowly," he said after a pause.

Booker back-stepped through the opening, leaned to his right while keeping his left hand raised, and groped for a moment. When he straightened he held a duffel bag clenched in his fist.

"Bring it out."

Booker walked forward until ordered to stop halfway between the tower and the hostage taker.

"Open it," Gary—or rather the *vetro*—ordered.

Booker set the bag on the ground and unzipped it.

"Pull it open so I can see inside."

Booker yanked the sides apart.

"Now back off. Back to the door."

Although it was too dark to make out details, the thing in the bag appeared to be two shoebox-sized objects wrapped in gauze and secured by rope. Something drew Andrew's attention up the wall of the tower, the suggestion of motion. A bat maybe? His eyes settled on a black rectangle of window. *No*, he thought even before realizing what he was opposing. *Too dangerous. Don't even think about it.* His cognition caught up with his instinct and a vision of the sniper's errant bullet punching out one of Grace's eyes began repeating as unrelentingly as Anna's song which, despite Gary's order, hadn't skipped a beat.

A new mantra replaced the previous one: *Don't shoot. Don't shoot. Christ, don't shoot.*

"We did what you asked," Booker said. "You have what you came for. Now let the hostages go."

"Not until I see what's in the bag."

"So, look. It's right in front of you."

Andrew couldn't take his eyes off the window. Slowly, like a viper rising from its hiding place, the long barrel of a rifle emerged from the blackness. If Gary happened to look up and to the left, he would see. *Don't look. Don't shoot. Don't move. Don't breathe.*

"Little girl," Gary said. "Do something useful. Grab the bag and bring it over here."

Anna lifted desperate eyes to her mother.

287

"Do it." Gary's voice was boulders rolling down a volcanic slope. "Mom, tell your daughter to get the bag."

First Grace, then Anna turned to Andrew. In their expressions was something he could not bear, the expectation that he knew what to do to keep them safe. His head moved, up, down, but all he could think was *no, no, no.*

"Go ahead, honey," Grace instructed. Anna reached for her mother's hand and their fingers intertwined. After taking a moment to muster her courage, she began slowly edging away. In five steps, she was at the bag. When she bent to pick it up the nearest floodlight exploded. It went out with a percussive whoosh. The resulting column of darkness was a charcoal streak up the side of the tower.

Andrew clutched his head and hunched his shoulders, rooted in place with dread, but when a second floodlight winked out his paralysis broke. Booker darted forward, scooped Anna into his arms and spun back toward the tower as Andrew plowed into Gary's right shoulder, sending him pirouetting backward. Hostage and hostage-taker parted. Andrew grabbed Gary's forearm and yanked it up, intending at the very least to keep the weapon pointed away from his wife. They pivoted around one another, but instead of going down in a tangle of legs and compromised balance, Gary added his own weight into the spin and thrust out his hip. Andrew was sling-shotted around and flung to the ground.

"Bn'nalagor cantala!" *Die now!*

Gary centered the gun on Andrew's forehead, but before he could pull the trigger Grace landed on his shoulders as if she'd dropped from an overhead branch. Her teeth found his neck, her nails his face. He staggered forward, sinking to his knees. Andrew sprang up and pulled Grace off. "Get inside!"

"Not without you."

"Go! I'll hold him off."

"Together!"

He was about to push her toward the door when a voice, a *human* voice, hollered from above, "Give me a clear shot, damn it!"

Good enough. Andrew wrapped his arms around his wife and together they ran toward the entrance where Booker stood frantically waving them on. The sniper fired another round as Grace reached the door. Booker pulled her inside. An instant later something blindsided Andrew hard enough to send him hurtling through the air. He landed in a sprawl, gasping for breath and scissoring his legs like a toppled windup toy.

"Miss me, darlin'?"

The feet in front of him were large and bare and protruded from what appeared to be a hospital gown. The gown was drenched in something dark. Andrew took a sip of air.

"We have unfinished business. Didn't think throwing me over a railing was going to keep me down, did you?"

Andrew rolled onto his back. Theodore Hillsdale. He was horrible with names, but his scrambled brain produced the words like slices of charred bread popping up from a smoking toaster. Ping. Theodore Hillsdale, the convict who had attacked him and his father. He took another sip of air.

"The big guys have plans for me. Nothing's gonna stop that. Not these handcuffs," he held up his left arm, displaying a shackle around his wrist dangling a segment of broken chain. "Not the guard keeping me company at the hospital. He gushed like a fountain when I chewed through his jugular."

Hillsdale reached down and stroked his erection through the gore-splattered gown. "Too bad I had an appointment to keep. Could have had some fun."

A smile, one-third beatific and two-thirds lunacy, split his face like an incision. "But now I got you, precious. And I have this." Hillsdale raised his other hand. "I won't shoot you. At least not yet. First, I'm going to see how far up your ass I can shove the barrel. I figure…"

The *vetro offalate's* warning was loud enough to curl Andrew to a ball. Less than a dozen feet away, Booker sank to the ground with one hand pressed against his temple, the other trembling to keep its tenuous grip on the handgun he'd been aiming at Hillsdale's back.

"Just the big guys clearing their throats!" Hillsdale said with manic good cheer. "Did they..."

Andrew kicked out and heard the kneecap shatter.

"Motherfucker!"

Andrew stood, barely avoiding his attacker's lunge, and pulled Booker to his feet. A bullet knocked a chunk of concrete from the tower wall in front of them, its trajectory passing so close to Andrew's ear he felt the rush of hot air. Was that from Gary's gun or Hillsdale's?

They ran.

Answering gunshots erupted in rapid succession, the sniper's window flashing with each round. At the door, Booker jerked suddenly and stumbled through.

The bag! It was still back there. Andrew turned in time to see Gary snatch it up, and as their eyes met two hands slammed down on Andrew's shoulders. He was jerked inside. A figure circled in front of him and shouldered the door closed. The last thing he saw was Gary's puzzled face peering into the bag before a final howl—either of triumph or frustration—exploded inside his skull, sending a cascade of sparks spiraling down to a pool of dark water smelling strongly of earth and rot.

LITTLE BILLY PEERED THROUGH THE THINNING SMOKE AND thought, *better*. The blast had thrown debris a hundred yards in every direction, splintered pieces of cheap furniture, ancient toys and the twisted remains of obsolete electronics splashing into swimming pools and punching holes through the screened porches of nearby houses. A soiled mattress was balanced in the upper reaches of one of the trees screening the far side of the culvert. More satisfyingly, the detonation had scooped out a crater twenty yards across and just as deep. And yet. And yet! There, materializing in the center of the depression was the *xalanthracoil* that had looked like a pot-bellied stove to Andrew.

Little Billy removed his earplugs. Next to him, Katie did the same.

"You have to admit, that was impressive."

Katie said nothing. The dark circles under her eyes gave her expression a feral quality, feverish, nearly rabid. She leaned her head against his arm and closed her eyes and he wouldn't have been surprised if, a moment later, she had begun sliding to the ground in exhaustion. The voices were wearing them down, relentlessly sandblasting away their sanity. A claustrophobic panic was closing an invisible fist around his throat. Each breath took more effort than the last and they still had one target to go, the *xalantracoil* in the cemetery. It was all or nothing now.

But the voices. If they stopped, even for a moment, he might be able to regain his balance, muster his resistance.

"Thought this one would be different." The demolition chief was a DOF firefighter named Jason, a barrel-chested man with the deep tan and weathered face of someone who had spent most of his life outdoors. "Ground's been changing as we've moved north. Softer here. Sandier. Less clay." Little Billy forced his head up. He had to repeat Jason's words several times to himself before he understood their meaning.

"Bigger crater," he managed.

"Not big enough, I guess. I half expected..." Jason stared distractedly at the result of his carefully orchestrated explosion, swaying slightly, his mouth ajar. His hand rose halfway to his chin and sank again. After another moment, he roused himself. "Sorry, I forgot what I was going to say."

"One last chance," Little Billy offered. "We already tried to blow the next one up. Maybe we loosened it."

Jason turned glassy eyes toward him. "Ground's different up here."

"You already said that," Katie said without opening her eyes or raising her head from Little Billy's arm.

"Did I?"

"Oh, god."

Little Billy realized he was stroking Katie's head like a cat's. If she complained he'd stop. She didn't complain. Slowly, like deep-sea divers trudging along the bottom of the ocean in bulky pressure suits, the men and women around him began gathering up the demolition equipment in preparation for their final move.

"Why don't we try again with this one?" he asked in a pain-slurred voice. "Why drag everything to the next *coil*?"

A diesel engine began cranking in slow revs and fell silent. After a pause, it cranked again, died again. The industrial auger they had been using to drill holes for the explosives was at the end of a hydraulic pivot arm mounted on the back of a converted bucket truck. It was an impressive piece of machinery, the kind of thing you'd expect to see at a construction site or maybe a strip mine. It drilled through forty feet of sandy soil faster than the explosives crew could unload their gear, and when Little Billy saw it in action for the first time he had allowed himself a small luxury: a few moments of cautious optimism. Amateur hour was over. The professionals had arrived.

But when the smoke cleared after that first explosion, the *coil* remained and each successive attempt accomplished nothing more than making larger and larger craters around the targets. After the sixth failure, Little Billy had a chilling thought. What if they were all projections of one thing? What if deep below the surface every *xalanthracoil* curved into a single, massive, indestructible mechanism?

No, that's what *they* wanted him to think. They had forced the idea into his mind with all the finesse of an ice pick punching through his cranium. Ironically, it was this attempt to demoralize that kept his flickering hope alive. Although the enemy's primary focus was northward, efforts to destroy the *coils* had finally provoked something more than their contemptuous indifference. The *vetro offalate* might be more interested with what John was up to, but they were at least a little concerned with events down here. It wasn't much to pin hope to, but it was all he had.

"Stick with the plan," Jason answered after a pause so lengthy Little Billy had early forgotten his question. "One in the cemetery is the most..." The man swayed for a moment, teetering on the verge of collapse.

"The most?" Little Billy managed.

"Isolated. Away from... stuff... infer... struck."

"Infrastructure," Katie coughed up.

"That," Jason agreed. "Big blast. Biggest."

"Plan sucks," Katie grumbled. "Should of started at the cemetery and just kept trying. No moving. More efficient." She swallowed. "Done by now."

The truck engine cranked again, slowed, then caught with a tired sputter. The driver sat staring blankly out the windshield long enough for Little Billy to wonder if she had fallen asleep with her eyes open, or worse, if something inside her head had burst and her final act was starting the engine. Finally, the truck began to ease forward. Little Billy had to assume she was still alive since her slack, expressionless face never displayed a flicker of animation.

"Guess we should make our way... hey." Touching his fingertips to the bottom of her chin, Little Billy slowly raised Katie's head from his arm. "Still with us?"

Her eyes fluttered but did not open. "Still here," she said in a syrupy voice. Her head began to tilt back.

"Katie." He caught the back of her neck. "Honey."

Honey? The word slipped out with an ease that would have surprised and embarrassed him if he'd had the energy, but it drew Katie out of her stupor. She opened her eyes with a sigh of bottomless exhaustion.

"Will, I don't know how much longer I'm going to be able to hold out. I feel like a stranger's inside my head. It's mostly them in there now."

"You need to get away from here." Little Billy scanned the area, looking for someone he could ask to drive her from danger. Small stones and sandy soil continued to slide down the slope of the blast crater. One of the dumpsite's larger pieces of trash, a particleboard dresser spared in the initial blast but left teetering on the lip of the declivity, began an incremental tilt that would eventually send it over the edge. The crater was continuing to widen, but it was a slow, weary process.

"Get out." Katie took a deep breath and slapped herself across the face. "You hear me, you bastards? Get out. Get out!"

"Don't." He tried to grab her hand and failed. The smack of flesh striking flesh was muted in the weighted air.

"I'm staying." She stepped from the circle of Little Billy's arms. "See, I'm fine. Go big or go home. You boneheads finally have to listen to me on this last one and I'm not going to miss my chance to say 'I told you so.' " She rolled her head on her shoulders. "What time is it?"

Little Billy held up his watch and moved it forward and back until the dial swam into reluctant focus. "Five to five."

"Then we better get moving. Dawn is what, an hour-and-a-half away?"

Little Billy thought that was about right. Ninety minutes until another Great Divide, quite possibly the final one everybody comes to sooner or later. He made an "after you" gesture, and as the demolition crew gathered up the last of the gear, Little Billy and Katie began their trudge to the cemetery where the final *xalantracoil* waited.

Twenty-two

The bubble floated above the sputtering streetlight, drifting on sulfurous, otherworldly currents. It rose, parted a hole through a billboard promising good times for those adventurous enough to drink blackberry-flavored vodka, and emerged on the other side, swelling like a boil. Once through, the billboard reconstituted and the spheroid continued on, growing, contracting, reaching out pseudopodium-like projections which elongated and split and merged again before retracting back into the center.

The bubble drifted above an intersection that had been clogged with outbound traffic earlier. Occasional vehicles still moved through the streets—patrol cars and emergency vehicles mostly—but the majority of those who intended to leave were gone. Only the defiant or infirmed remained.

The intersection's traffic signals were dark, as were the lights of the corner Shell station and the Walgreens next to it. Across the street stretched a line of utility poles. Before the demotion crews arrived, the poles had stood in perfect alignment, each jutting from the sidewalk with perpendicular precision. When the boom sounded from the blast site four blocks away, it wasn't loud enough to rattle windows or stir birds into alarmed flight. An hour later, however, the tilt of the utility poles would have been enough for any pedestrian strolling by to notice with a curious frown.

Now, two hours beyond that, they reclined by as much as forty-five degrees, some held up by nothing more than the tenuous support of their overstrained wires. Occasionally, a line would break and spark and hum with electricity before falling limp.

As the orb glided over the staggered poles, the traffic lights at the next intersection went dark. Continuing on a meandering course above newly cracked sidewalks and backyards no longer separated by upright fences, it soon reached the perimeter of the circle defined by the *xalantracoils* and there it bobbed, nosing the edge of its range like a dog testing the strength of its leash.

The airspace within the circle was awhirl with monstrous embers. The bubbles' molten radiance had been steady and unvarying throughout the night. Now each began to dim as something blocked its internal light. What emerged into our world moments later was unlike anything John Tate or William Phipps had ever seen: compact, armored, with heads like jackhammers and mouths like studded roller balls, they dropped to the ground, righted themselves and grew still as the early-morning darkness induced dormancy. They fell by the dozens, each one as big as a Holstein calf, and although their distribution was random, their last act before sleep was to orient themselves with heads pointed toward a single location, a rust-streaked white tower a few miles to the north.

IN ANDREW'S DREAM, PEOPLE WERE SINGING, BUT NOT very well. Voices overlapped. Melodies clashed. Who were they singing to? They were singing to him. They were singing to him and asking him to sing back. Andrew tried to shoo them away. Can't you see I'm resting? But why was he resting? He had work to do. Something important.

A single voice rose about the others. *Daddy, daddy,* it sang, *please wake up. You have to put music in your head. You have to sing.* Odd lyrics accompanying a simplistic melody barely more than a chant. In his dream, something tugged at his collar.

Enough!

He had work to do. The work was… the work was… stopping the *vetro offalate*. Ah, yes. That explained the voices. The *vetro* had changed tactics and were now imitating human speech. Trying to confuse him. This one sounded just like Anna. *Like Anna*, he sang, just a little two-word ditty to show he was in on the joke. Go to hell, you bastards, or rather: *Go to hell, you bastards*. Like it? I call that one the "Fuck You" song.

Andy. Grace's voice this time. *Andy, you have to sing. Sing in your head if you can. It blocks them out.*

Sing, sing a song. In your head. Don't get it wrong. Wait, was that out loud? Hands were on him again, gentle hands easing him into a sitting position.

"*That's right,*" a baritone crooned. "*You just keep on singing. Like shutting a window on a windy day. Works right away.*"

Andrew opened his eyes. "What?"

"*Sing,*" Grace and Anna chorused.

And although he felt ridiculous, Andrew answered in a cracked warble, "*Is this for real?*"

"*Can't you feel?*" Grace responded, pointing to her head.

Andrew blinked. What was he supposed to be feeling? *What am I supposed to be feeling?* he repeated to himself, this time paired with an impromptu melody. Then he understood. The voices stopped when he sang! No, not stopped. They raged on and on, but their volume fell to a bare whisper.

Is this possible? he thought/sang. *Something so simple?* He remembered once more the stereo blaster from the other day. Hadn't the man said something about music drowning out the voices? But he hadn't taken it far enough. Listening to music was a passive, receptive experience. Apparently, to dampen the *vetro's* call the mind had to engage in an active act of resistance. It couldn't just listen to music. It had to create it.

"*I feel it,*" Andrew assured her. "*Why does it work?*"

"*They don't know what singing is,*" Anna explained. She had a lovely voice, a sweet, clear alto as out of place in the tower's dank interior as the jingle of chimes in a mausoleum. "*They've never heard music before. It's like bees in their ears. They hate it.*"

"*How do you know?*" Already, he was beginning to acclimate to this new way of communicating. It was just talking with rhythm and pitch.

His daughter shook her head. "*I just do.*"

"*Anna saved us,*" Grace sang. "*We were all passed out or senseless. She sang to each of us until we responded.*" His wife pulled Anna into a hug, her cheek pressed against the top of their daughter's head, her eyes meeting Andrew's in an invitation. He closed his arms around their trembling bodies and tried to still the shivers with nothing more than the strength of his embrace.

"*I thought an angel was singing to me,*" Booker offered. "*I was sure I was dead.*" He was sitting a few feet away with his back pressed against the outer wall, holding a large flashlight in his lap. When he shifted position, his face contorted in pain and Andrew noticed the blood caking his shirt collar.

"*You're hurt.*"

"*Bastard shot me. Bullet's inside. Since I'm still breathing, figure he didn't hit anything too important.*"

"*I don't know about that.*" Andrew kissed Grace's forehead and edged over to the injured guard, peering through the dark toward the entrance.

Noticing the direction of his gaze, Booker played the flashlight's beam over the door's heavy chain and padlock. "*Nothing's getting in here less we want it to.*" He patted the concrete behind him with his free hand. "*Walls thick. Built to last.*"

Andrew probed Booker's chest, confirming the lack of an exit wound. Depending on the trajectory, the bullet could have lodged in a rib, a vertebra, the breastbone, even the pelvis if it had ricocheted. If by not hitting anything "too important" Booker meant his heart, he was probably right. He'd be dead by now if that had been the case. When his roving fingers slid down the guard's neck and shoulder he discovered most of the blood near the entrance wound had already dried to a tacky paste.

"*How long was I out?*" Andrew asked.

"*According to Anna, hours,*" Grace was rocking the girl in her lap. "*All alone in this horrible place with a bunch of unconscious adults. Singing and singing. Trying to wake us.*" Her unshed tears shimmered faintly in the dim light. "*So brave.*"

Andrew brought his watch close to the flashlight. Christ, it was five to six. Sunrise was less than an hour away. There should have been news about the defense efforts by now. Why hadn't Little Billy called with an update? Then again, maybe he had.

"*Did my phone ring while I was out?*" he asked, reaching into his pocket and feeling the iPhone's shattered face.

"*No calls,*" Anna assured him.

Before Andrew could check if the thing still worked, the clattering ladder announced the decent from above of first Hector, then a woman Andrew had never met. The woman was carrying a medical bag. She knelt next to Booker, slipped on a pair of latex gloves and checked his pulse at the carotid artery.

"*Help me get his shirt off.*"

Andrew set his phone aside and fell into the old routine of triaging a gunshot victim, the ABCDE assessment of checking the patient's airway, his breathing, circulation, etc. The woman picked up Booker's flashlight and aimed the beam at his face. She and Andrew leaned in close. They were both checking for the same thing: bloody froth at the corners of the patient's mouth. There was nothing, making it unlikely a bullet was lodged in a lung. Of course, it wasn't definitive. A blood clot could prevent hemoptysis for hours. The woman worked quickly, her hands moving expertly from location to location as she dismissed possible internal injuries under her breath in a tuneful chant.

"*Diaphragmatic rupture unlikely, no indication of subcutaneous emphysema, ribs good, hallelujah, possible thoracic wall laceration and/or sterna fracture.*"

It was all familiar and remarkably comforting, this unexpected return of professional routine. The doctor (for that's what she obviously was, not a nurse, not a home healthcare aide, a doctor) finished with a dilation check and a declaration. "*You are one lucky son-of-a-bitch. You'll probably live if we can get you to a hospital relatively soon.*"

"*He was just jealous because I was shot the other day,*" Hector sang, the relief in his voice obvious despite his unfortunate decision to sing several octaves above his range. "*Now we'll both have battle scars.*"

Laughter, genuine and infectious, the first Andrew had heard in longer than he could remember, echoed through the tower. It was Grace. Anna joined in with a tentative giggle.

"*This is the weirdest musical I've ever seen.*" His wife sang.

Anna's laughter intensified. "*Can I be Orphan Annie! I like her dog.*"

A pounding on the door extinguished her mirth with a gasp.

"Having fun in there, muffin?" Even muffled by steel, Theodore Hillsdale's voice was a rake of yellowed nails across slate. Anna buried her head in her mother's chest as Hector drew a pistol from his waistband. He approached the entrance, waving the others back, an ineffectual gesture since they were already as far from the door as possible.

"I got some news all of you might want to hear. You think you're safe? You think we can't get to you? Sun's gonna come out real soon and when it does, you're going to get such a surprise." Hillsdale pitched his voice to the coo of a parent mooning over an infant. "Yes you are, oh yes you are." No singing from his side, Andrew noted. And why would there be? The lunatic had probably been hearing voices in his head his entire life. The more the merrier.

Hector put his finger to his lips. Another unnecessary gesture. No one had any intention of engaging Hillsdale in conversation.

"I don't want to give anything away. That would ruin the surprise. But could you do me a favor? Stick your heads out a window when you realize you're about to die. I want to see the looks on your faces. It'll give me something to jerk off to later. Okay. Bye for now. See you real soon."

Hector waited a full two minutes before moving quietly back to the others. During the interim Grace sang softly to Anna: "*Hush little baby, don't say a word.*"

"*Let's move up.*" Hector pointed to the ladder. "*I'll feel better when we have the high ground.*"

"*You go. I'm going to put a compression bandage on Booker first.*" The doctor began rummaging through her kit and Andrew was torn between assisting her and ushering his family up, up and away. When she saw his hesitation, she waved him off. "*I'll get this. If I need help pulling him to his feet, I'll holler for Hector.*"

Andrew nodded and picked his phone off the floor as Hector positioned himself at the ladder, ready to assist the others in their ascent. Andrew held up an index finger.

"*One thing first.*" He touched the shattered screen, saw the number pad spring up, and exhaled in relief. "*Need to spread the word about Anna's discovery.*"

Andrew unlocked the phone and began dialing, praying to the melody of "Oh Come All Ye Faithful," that he wasn't too late.

THE EFFECT WAS DECOMPRESSIVE. LITTLE BILLY'S SKULL seemed to creak in relief as the relentless inward pressure dissipated. He worked his jaw as he sang, ears popping, the outside world rushing back in with an oceanic whoosh that drowned out the last of the *vetro's* howl. He pulled the phone from his ear and stared at the screen as if it were a talisman ablaze with St. Elmo's fire. At first, all he could do was repeat the commercial jingle over and over, marveling at how spacious his mind felt without intruders, how orderly his unscrambled thoughts. How keen.

It had taken a supreme act of concentration to answer his buzzing phone. Like some of the firefighters around them, he and Katie were on their hands and knees by then, crawling the last hundred yards to the final *xalantracoil*. Little Billy's sense of balance was so decimated, when he lifted an arm to retrieve the cell he toppled onto his back in a slow roll, unable to do anything more than stare up at the spinning, lurching sky as Andrew's instructions slowly sank in.

"*Florida orange juice, a glassful of sunshine.*"

The world stopped spinning.

"*Florida orange juice, a glassful of sunshine.*"

The voices fizzled to a distant murmur.

"*Florida orange juice, a glassful of sunshine.*"

Little Billy regained his feet.

"*Florida orange juice, a glassful of sunshine*," he sang to Katie, who was peering up at him through sweat-tangled hair. He made a rolling motion with his hand, trying to convey that she should join him in song.

"*You don't have to keep repeating the lyrics*," Andrew told him through the phone. "*Say whatever you need to say. Just use the melody. Any melody. As long as you sing.*"

Katie caught on immediately. Before he could relay Andrew's message, she was already croaking out an unfamiliar song about someone wearing sneakers instead of high-heels. With each word her voice strengthened, and by the time she reached the chorus, Katie was also back on her feet.

The cemetery was scattered with a dozen stricken firefighters doggedly struggling toward their goal. Those still on their feet stood with bowed heads and slack jaws, shuffling past gravestones in a zombie-like procession toward the southwest corner, where the *xalanthracoil* stood at the center of the crater left after the previous detonation. Behind them at the gates, the auger truck and hazardous materials vehicle idled, their drivers no longer capable of operating the rigs.

"*You guys still with me?*" Andrew asked.

Little Bill brought the phone back to his ear. "*Here and singing.*"

"*The coils?*"

"*Intact for now, but we still have one to go. Gonna give it all we got. Go big or go home, right?*" He gave Katie a wink. She flipped him off with a smile.

"*What about the perimeter defenses?*"

Little Billy turned toward the street. A fire engine was parked at the nearest intersection, a chartreuse Hillsborough County vehicle with a crew of six or seven. Unlike the demolition teams, the firefighters manning the engine were in full gear, helmets, coats, boots. They were moving with a little more life than those closer to the *coil*. Maybe the *vetro's* call wasn't as intense back there. They had already run a yellow hose from a nearby hydrant to the engine and were unfurling three additional lines from the vehicle. Although their preparations continued, they worked without urgency, often pausing with hands on knees to pant and gulp before shuddering back into motion.

Throughout the night, Little Billy had passed fifty or more fire engines as his demolition crew worked its way from *coil* to *coil*, pumpers mostly, from three counties, dozens of municipalities and the Department of Forestry. He'd seen hoses run to hydrants, water tankers, ponds, the river, even swimming pools. His thoughts had been too muddled at the time to appreciate the monumental efforts required to establish these defenses or to evaluate their potential effectiveness. The circle of *xalanthracoils* was nearly two miles across, requiring each truck to be separated by a gap of fifty yards, sometimes more. If the *vetro* came pouring across the breach, the defenders might be spread too thin to contain them for long. And then there was the question of water pressure. The drought had probably...

"*Will, you still there?*"

"*Still here, Andy. Perimeter defenses are ongoing, although they've slowed down a bit due to the vetro's mindfuck. Once I pass on the tip about singing they should be able to finish quickly. If we need them, they'll be ready.*"

"*And the military?*"

"*No clue.*"

Katie stood on tiptoe and sang into the phone, "*What about you? Are you safe? Is your family safe?*" She shot Little Billy a look of exasperation, as if this should have been his first question. He tilted the cell so she could hear Andy's response.

"*We're safe and inside the water tower. Long story. I'm about to go up and see Dad. Sounds like we're going to need his backup.*"

A cold lump lodged in Little Billy's throat. As the *vetro's* call had intensified, all thoughts of John's alleged device had been squeezed into the dark creases of his brain. Now they welled up again, black and oozing.

"*We're not finished yet,*" he sang, trying to outrun his apprehension. "*You'll be able to hear the boom all the way up there.*"

"*I'll be listening.*"

Little Billy looked to the east and a small, unsung 'oh' of dismay slipped from his lips. The sky behind them had begun to pale. He could make out the edges of black treetops silhouetted against an indigo ribbon already snuffing out the faintest stars. Three irregular shapes floated off to his right, casting their own campfire glow and bobbing like flotsam in a ship's wake. A fourth appeared, rising through the camphors and live oaks and sable palms as if percolating up from a methane chamber at the bottom of a pond. He scrutinized the *coil*, expecting to see the first glint of pulsing inner light seeping from its latticework of intricate fissures. It was still dark, but for how much longer?

"*Good luck. Call me once it's done.*" Andrew hesitated an instant before adding: "*If you still can.*"

And on that note, Little Billy thought, re-examining the *coil* as he pocketed his phone. Was that a shimmer along its upper edge, or just the wink of reflected light? The sky was already brighter. He could imagine himself standing here mesmerized until dawn broke, watching the *xalantracoil* power up as his world faded and a new world emerged around him. There was something darkly seductive about having a front-row seat to it all. There! A shimmer. Now gone. Now back. Not his imagination this time. Subtle but definitely cyclical. Fascinating, actually. Almost beautiful.

"*Hey!*" Katie yanked him around and gave him a hard push toward Jason, the DOF demolition chief poised in midstride as if suspended in amber. "*Don't stop singing. We have work to do.*"

Florida orange juice, a glassful of sunshine. Little Billy shuddered. The music in his head had only paused for a moment, but it was long enough to get swept into some sort of debilitating glamour the *coil* had begun broadcasting. How many defensive systems did these things have?

He grabbed Jason by the shoulders and bellowed, "*Florida orange juice, a glassful of sunshine,*" into his confounded face.

"*Oh, for the love of Christ.*" Katie yanked him back. "*I'll handle this. Get your own head straight, then do the same for the drivers back at the gate. We'll need them first. And don't stop singing.*"

Little Billy gave her a thumbs-up and trotted off. As long as he didn't look at the *xalantracoil* again he should be fine. In the meantime, he would sing, sing, sing as the demolition team prepped the last charge, and when the smoke cleared amid a rain of debris, the *coil* would be gone, the circuit broken, the future restored. There was still time, *still time for us, my dear, to save the world*. Lyrics worth remembering.

At the cemetery gates, Little Billy looked east, intending to gauge how quickly night was fading. The indigo band had expanded to a wide swath, swallowing more stars and revealing the presence of a few distant cumulous flickering with heat lighting.

That, however, was not what gave him pause. It was the bubbles. There were more of them, six now, and they were larger than before. More energetic. The biggest began to convulse and heave. A seam developed near the middle and cleaved it in half and now there were seven. Disconcerting as this was, it was how they were moving that jolted Little Billy back into motion and sent him scurrying to the nearest driver. The bubbles were no longer drifting haphazardly. They were all moving in the same direction, north, north-west around the circle's inner curve, following the counterclockwise rotation typical of all developing hurricanes.

Twenty-three

Gary Wyatt was going to kill the beast. The *vetro offalate* probably wouldn't like it. The creature was, presumably, one of their agents. At least that's what it claimed in a rare moment of lucidity. But Gary understood something his psychopathic companion apparently did not: they'd been dismissed. Their task had been relatively straightforward: stop John Tate from using his... his what? The *vetro* didn't know and so Gary didn't know. Not that it mattered. What mattered was that both man and man-beast had failed their gods and were now, at best, nothing more than bystanders at the grand and dark parade.

Something was coming. The beast had been telling the truth when it informed those inside the tower they were in for a surprise. Gary wasn't sure how it would happen, but he was certain the tower before him would soon topple, killing everyone inside. He hated the thought of Andrew and the woman and the little girl dying, but they had brought it on themselves. Why couldn't the old man have simply given the *vetro* what they wanted? Were they all so blind? The human race was sick. It was dying from the cancer of pettiness and cruelty and spite and hatred. Tumors, all. And how were tumors destroyed? Radiation. Chemo. If that didn't work, they had to be cut from the living flesh. It hurt. Hurt like hell. But it was necessary for the healing to begin.

The *vetro offalate* weren't indifferent. They cared. They cared so much they had sent a beast-man to keep him company. Gary watched the lunatic out of the corner of his eye and absentmindedly fretted the bite on his neck. Bitch had turned into a fucking banshee at the end, all gnashing teeth and clawing nails. Had to admire her grit, he supposed, willing to fight for her man like that. Good thing she'd gotten inside without drawing his compatriot's attention. At least her death would be quick. That wouldn't have been the case had the beast scooped her up.

"Ollie, ollie in free," it bellowed happily toward the tower. "The king is in his counting house, counting all his money. I see London, I see France. *Gurty'll lith ulm il tacka.* Gesundheit, motherfucker. Turn your head next time."

How could it still be on its feet? Its left knee was a swollen purple knot about twice the size of a softball speckled with bright scarlet hemorrhages, the calf a discolored mass streaked with tendrils of yellow and brown descending steadily toward the ankle, a sure sign of a deepening infection.

The pain must be excruciating, and yet it paced about with only the slightest limp, sometimes laughing, sometimes howling, the gun in its right hand, its dick in the left. The thing had already ejaculated three times. Its erection never softened. Was that the *vetro's* doing? Were they pumping their snarling attack dog full of endorphins and hormones, keeping it primed for the kill? Or was its behavior simply the product of madness?

Gary Wyatt pulled his mother's .22 from his pocket, flipped the safety back. He'd shot one man already. Granted, he hadn't exactly been himself at the time. The *vetro* had reached their will into the fibers of his muscles and manipulated him like a sock puppet, but he had welcomed their invasion, happy to relinquish the responsibility of collusion and conscious thought. Now that they had tossed him aside, he would shoot the beast. The *vetro* no longer had a need for it. Something new was on the way, something far better suited to the job. It was close, moving faster and faster as the sky brightened, swarming up from the south. The tower would fall, and this beast's usefulness was at an end.

Gary approached. He didn't want to miss. Why would the *vetro* enlist such a creature into their service? Maybe if it hadn't interfered, hadn't bulldozed its way into the fight, Gary would have managed to get inside the tower and destroy John Tate's device on his own. No need to swing a club when a scalpel would do. The beast wasn't even a club. It was a boulder crashing down a hillside, mindless and uncontrollable.

Look at it, standing there stroking itself, once again oblivious to everything other than its next gush of semen. A wave of nausea and revulsion rolled up from his belly and crashed against the back of his throat. Killing it would be an act of mercy for both the lunatic and the rest of humanity.

Gary positioned himself behind the brute. Just keep jerking away, he thought as he raised the gun and centered the muzzle at the back of the skull where the parietal and occipital plates fused. Its death would be instantaneous. Good riddance, beast-man.

When he pulled the trigger, something plowed into the back of Gary's legs, toppling him to the ground. He twisted as he fell, landed on his left shoulder and rolled onto his stomach. Something skittered across his back, needles of pain digging into his flesh. He grunted, more in outrage than agony, and contracted into a fetal position. A weight on his hip, clambering up and over. Something landed in the dirt next to him and moved on, its multitude of legs rising and falling in a rolling procession that reminded Gary of tank treads. When it reached the tower wall, it clawed itself upright and began sweeping its angled head back and forth across the concrete. An identical creature joined it a moment later and began doing the same. He heard a grinding noise, like two large stones being rubbed together.

Within seconds they were everywhere, hundreds of creatures marching to the tower in a gray tide of armored backs and clicking appendages, the dust they raised blanketing the ground in a brown fog.

Their mouths were like nothing he had ever seen, wrecking ball spheres of boney studs continually spinning inside oral sockets. A whirring hum began to swell, locus-like and *hungry*. No, not hungry. Famished. They were here to eat, and eat they would. The entire base of the tower was a solid, living mass that continued to creep upward as new arrivals perched upon the heads and shoulders of the vanguard. The grinding became a deafening cacophony, a feeding frenzy. The *vetro offalate* had sent these creatures to devour the tower like termites devouring a block of wood. He wondered what it sounded like from inside.

"Glooorrrioussssssss."

Gary nearly screamed. The thing shambling toward him through the swarm of tower-eaters had to be a hallucination. The last thing he'd seen before his fall was a flap of the beast's skull unhinging like an access hatch, revealing a cavity and the gray folds beneath. The bullet had to have gone straight through its brain. And yet here it was, approaching with arms outstretched, a maniac grin stretched across its shattered face as if the two of them were long-lost brothers about to embrace.

The beast had grown large while Gary had been watching the tower's destruction. It was no longer just a man. It had become festooned with creatures clinging to it in barnacle-like profusion. They covered its chest, its arms and legs, its neck and blasted skull. Only the face remained exposed. The man-beast had been reborn as an amalgamation of nightmare organisms. Sinuous and semi-translucent, they fit together in a Frankenstein mismatch of glistening protuberances and interlocking appendages.

Run, for the love of god!

Gary couldn't run. His legs were useless bags of meat, boneless and numb.

Shoot it then! You still have the gun.

Gary shot it. Something squealed and fell from the chest and was replaced by another. It was almost upon him. Screaming now, Gary emptied the gun into the advancing shape. In the final seconds before it bent to engulf him, Gary understood two things. He had been wrong to assume the *vetro offalate* had cast them aside. Their fate wasn't to be dismissed. It was to be repurposed. The second realization drove a lance of anguish through the contracting remains of his consciousness: his mother wasn't going to be cured after all. What was left of her mind would be siphoned off, stored in a dark place and sipped at leisure long after her physical body had rotted where it fell. That knowledge was his reward for failure.

The creature crouched, wrapped its arms almost gently around the prostrate man at its feet and lifted Gary into a merging embrace.

"Gloorrioousss," said one of the creature's heads.

"Yesssssssss," agreed the other.

THEY FELT IT FIRST, A VIBRATION THAT SEEMED TO resonate from everywhere as if the tower were a tuning fork struck against a tabletop.

"*That can't be good,*" Hector sang in his off-key falsetto. Andrew wasn't sure how much more he could take of his caterwauling. He knew the officer didn't intend to be annoying. He was locked into his vocal delivery as firmly as a regional accent, but Andrew found himself eying Hector's windpipe with increasingly dark intentions.

"*Feels like machinery,*" Booker sang. He was huddled against a wall, eyes glazed in pain. "*Like the pumps just kicked on.*"

"*Pumps haven't worked in this place for seventy-five years,*" Hector countered. "*That's coming from outside.*"

"*Go have a look,*" John nodded toward the crenelated balcony encircling the observation room. "*And be careful. Some of the* bilantu *are airborne. It's getting light, they'll be active again soon.*"

Hector gave a brisk salute and shoulder his way outside through the rusted balcony door.

Andrew and his family were gathered in the center of the room around his father. The climb up had taken twenty minutes. Anna didn't like the ladders. The rungs were spaced for an adult, not a six-year-old. Still, she insisted on climbing by herself, despite Andrew's offer to carry her.

"*Son*." His father's greeting after he and Anna and Grace had emerged through the trapdoor was more a wavering sigh of grief that an attempt at melody, and Andrew had shaken his head, already knowing what would come next.

"*Andy*," he started again. "*I'm so damn sorry you and your family got pulled into this.*"

"*Not your fault, Dad.*" He went to where his father sat reclining against a final ladder ascending through the center of the room to a hole in the roof twenty feet above. "*Don't blame yourself. You may be our last hope.*"

"*Your plan didn't work?*"

Andrew decided to interpret his father's tone as one of pain rather than panic. "*Don't know yet. Will said they had one last chance to destroy a* coil." He glanced at the sky through the barred windows. "*Won't be long before we find out.*" He placed a hand gently on his father's shoulder. "*They said you'd been hurt.*"

"*Ribs are sore from climbing up here. I'll live. Emily's got a bag of magic pills.*" He nodded toward the doctor climbing into the observation room. "*Every time I feel like passing out she gives me another.*"

"*Is grandpa going to be okay?*" Anna had asked from her mother's lap. The concern in her voice was a blue flame of humanity that collapsed all the anxieties of the morning into a simple question of pain and the alleviation of suffering.

His father smiled. "*Don't you worry your pretty little head, darling. Your granddad is one tough old bird.*" His arm rose and fell. "*You've gotten so big.*"

Andrew realized with a pang his father hadn't seen Anna since his mother's funeral two years earlier. He motioned the girl forward and she came without hesitation. He nodded to Grace and she approached as well.

"*You have some of your grandmother in you.*" His father placed a trembling hand on Anna's head. "*Especially around the eyes.*" He raised his gaze to Grace. "*Good to see you again, Grace. Wish it were under different circumstances.*"

"*Dad.*" Her voice cracked as she leaned over Anna and gingerly embraced him. "*You're looking well.*"

His father's laughter evoked a grimace of pain but did not stifle his amusement.

"*You're sweet to say so. Delusional, but sweet.*"

A moment later, the tower had begun to vibrate and now, as the eastern sky turned rosy in a predawn blush, Hector returned from his reconnaissance.

"*Something's definitely going on out there,*" he sang. "*Couldn't get a good look because of the overhang, but the sound is like a million marbles being rattled in a bag.*" He plucked up one of the rifles and moved to the trapdoor. "*I'm going down a couple levels and look out a window. Should be able to see better. Book, mind the fort while I'm gone.*"

"*No problem,*" he warbled unconvincingly.

"*I'll go with you, Hector,*" Cho sang.

"*Still got the gun?*"

"*No.*" Cho retrieved the pistol from one of the duffel bags and with an expression of profound distaste carefully tucked it under her waistband at the small of her back.

"*How long will it take to set up your device?*" Andrew sang after the two were gone. He had been surreptitiously scanning the room since their arrival, looking for something impressive enough to thwart a race of malevolent titans, a bulky piece of machinery perhaps, cobbled together after years of research and covered end-to-end with a profusion of wires and knobs and glowing LED displays, something that would activate with a momentary shower of sparks before humming to life. He saw nothing of the sort. A few weapons, a couple of canvas satchels, what looked like a battered guitar case. *His* guitar case?

"*Not long.*"

"*What can I do to help?*"

"*Nothing. One man job. Designed it that way. Too complicated for anyone but me to operate, anyway. Too dangerous. One wrong setting and...*" His father pressed his fingertips to his temple and spread them outward with a "pifft" of exhaled air.

A sudden, horrible certainty struck Andrew with such force he would have toppled back had his father's next words not yanked the thought from his head like a rotten molar.

"*Has she forgiven you?*"

Grace took a gulp of air, something between a gasp and a sob. Like Andrew, she knew exactly what his father was asking. He drew a deep breath of his own, and in the time it took to fill his lungs, his emotions flickered from indignation to guilt to humiliation to self-loathing and finally bitter resignation. Why not discuss it now? Wouldn't want to face death stubbornly clinging to all their old, threadbare illusions.

"*I don't know,*" he answered.

"*You don't know because you've never asked.*" Grace swiped away her tears with a thumb.

"*I've said I'm sorry a dozen times. Do you want to hear it again? I'm sorry. I'm sorry. If I could take that day back I would.*"

Anna did not look up at her parents, but she drew herself closer into her grandfather's lap and rested her cheek against his chest. Andrew thought he heard his father grunt in pain, but he did not ease her away. Instead, he draped an arm around her shoulder and began stroking her arm. Anna reached her scarred hand up and patted his cheek.

"Saying you're sorry isn't the same as asking forgiveness. Oh." Caught up in her emotions, she had spoken rather than sung the words. Now she clutched her head and slumped to the floor.

"*Don't stop singing!*" Anna cried, scampering to her mother.

"Honey! Grace!" Andrew eased her up, terrified he would see a slack face and eyes rolled to the whites. Instead, he witnessed something almost as bad: his wife hitching with laughter.

"Yes," she chortled. "*Let's all keep singing. Let's sing our troubles away. Why not? La, la, la. You drank yourself into a stupor and let Anna get hurt. Tra, la, la. And you've said you're sorry a dozen times but you've never asked for forgiveness. Not once. Oh no, no, no. Not a once. Not a once.*"

"*Grace*," he sang, and yes, wasn't this the most fucked up musical of all time? Strike up the band and cue the stage lights because here comes the big finale. He cupped her face in his hands and forced her to look at him. "*Grace, will you forgive me?*"

"Yes." she snarled. "*Yes, you selfish bastard. And goddamn you for making me wait this long to tell you. I forgive you.*" She ran her hand lightly down Anna's scarred arm. "*But I don't trust you. Maybe someday if you're serious about getting sober. Maybe. It's the best I can do for now.*"

"*All I've wanted is a chance to prove it.*"

"*I trust you, Daddy.*" Anna leaped into his arms, nearly bowling him over. "*You saved me from the dragon at the park.*"

"*That's right.*" Over his daughter's head, he mouthed, "I wasn't drinking that day," to Grace.

Maybe she would have snorted in disbelief, the distance between them widening into something unbridgeable. Maybe she would have recognized his sincerity and given him some indication things could still be reset between them. Hell, maybe she would have started singing the "National Anthem". Andrew would never know. Before Grace could respond, the shooting started below.

WHEN LITTLE BILLY CAUGHT SIGHT OF THE *SQUIM* PACK dropping from the trees, the surge of adrenaline tingled through every pore in a wave of prickling heat. He'd been expecting an attack of some sort, but not so soon. He'd never seen *bilantu* active in the muted light of predawn, yet here they were, scampering across the cemetery by the dozens.

Little Billy spun in a desperate circle, looking for anything he could use as a weapon. Nothing but a fallen branch a little thicker than his wrist. He plucked it up and positioned himself between the approaching *squim* and the firefighter he intended to protect. At least he was finally doing something. If he died now it would be a cinematic death, the kind survivors would recount with hushed reverence years later.

The notion was actually quite invigorating. And here was Katie, suddenly at his side. No weapon in her hands, just her fists. She gave him an Amazonian smile of resigned triumph and if he could have thrown her on the ground and fucked her senseless he would have. Instead, he raised his branch and faced the enemy.

They came on.

Little Billy swung.

The *squim* parted around them and continued past the demolition team. In a moment, every last one had skittered over the cemetery's north fence and disappeared, leaving the firefighters unscathed.

"*Where are they going?*" Katie sang in relief and puzzlement.

Little Billy knew. They were headed north to lay siege to the Sulfur Springs water tower.

"*I don't know,*" he lied.

"*Yes, you do. God, please let them stay safe.*"

After the *squim* came the *quintalochs*. The *votasin. Fidelaxes.* A veritable migration of *bilantu* all heading north. If even a few had attacked in some coordinated manner it would have been the end of the demolition team. A single *quintaloch* could have taken out half a dozen. Instead, they surged around the firefighters as if they were nothing more than rocks in a stream.

"*I guess they don't consider us a threat,*" Katie remarked after the initial burst of adrenalin had subsided, leaving them both shaky and deflated.

"*Their mistake,*" he sang, trying to sound confident.

Little Billy slipped into a post-crisis stupor, repeating his idiotic jingle over and over as the men and women of the demolition crew, singing like dwarfs returning from their mine, worked in a frenzy. It was going to be close. Damn close. But the industrial augur sank into the parched earth like a finger through meringue. What had Jason said earlier? The soil was changing the farther north they went. Less clay. More sand. Maybe that would work in their favor. Maybe...

Katie slapped his chest in alarm.

315

"*Wrong side, wrong side!*" she screamed/sang. Little Billy stared at her, the jingle looping endlessly on his lips. He shook his head.

"*They're drilling* inside *the circle!*"

Little Billy chorused the last words without comprehension.

"*We're* all *inside the circle!*" She jabbed upward in desperation and he finally understood.

The bubbles. Christ, there were so many of them now, orbiting ever faster, elongating into capsules as their velocity increased. They filled the air around them in an effervescent swirl, and through their undulating membranes, Little Billy glimpsed shaped gathered and waiting in a heaving, writhing mass. They were inside the circle. The entire demolition team was *inside* the circle! If the breach occurred before they could finish...

Precious minutes ticked away as he and Katie explained the situation to Jason, the demolition chief. The auger was hastily repositioned outside the circle and a new shaft started. But minutes wasted. Dawn was nearly upon them, the sky a pale blue haze of high clouds piling into something more substantial out in the Gulf. For the first time in months, a storm front was approaching, precipitated, perhaps, by the impending breach like water droplets condensing on cold metal.

The auger truck finished drilling and backed away. Then Little Billy glanced over his shoulder and his mounting anxiety evaporated like a puddle under a Saharan sun, replaced by the bottomless calm of total resignation.

They weren't going to make it.

He watched a firefighter feed Trenchrite into the shaft with numb detachment. The charge was massive, at least ten times bigger than what he and Andrew had used the other night and twice as large as the one the demolition team had planted at the previous *coil*. It would have made a good show. But the tempo of the *xalantracoil's* thrumming was now a palpitative flutter, its strobing a film-reel flicker. Through the foliage to the southeast, Little Billy could make out the shine of a neighboring *coil*, a brilliant pillar of light winking between branch and leaf.

"*Get behind the line*," he told Katie, pointing toward the ring of fire engines. The intensely roiling air around the *coil* gave the impression of an over-stoked forge on the point of meltdown, although even now it gave off no heat. At the drill site, a firefighter was struggling to attach the blasting cap while shielding his eyes from the *coil's* blinding glare. A colleague approached and held her coat up as a curtain.

"*What about you?*"

"*I'll be right behind.*"

The firefighter gave Jason a thumbs-up and the demolition chief pulled a wireless detonator from his pocket. Waving his team back, he began tapping buttons.

"*I'm not going without you*," Katie sang as the last of the demolition team darted through the cemetery gates to take up positions behind the nearest fire engine. She tugged his arm hard, nearly yanking him off his feet. "*There's nothing you can do here anyway.*"

"*Jason*," he called. "*Time's up.*" He made a sweeping motion with his arm, pantomiming urgency, but it was all an act. *Too late. Too late. To late for us my dear.*

"*Damn it, Katie, go!*" He pushed her toward the gates with all his strength. She staggered back, tripped over a gravestone and when down.

As the rim of the sun emerged above the horizon, the circulating distortions smeared and merged into a single sheet curving upward in an unbroken white dome. For two seconds, three, the wall remained opaque, and through the fog, a sound emerged, something like giant molars being ground together, enormous teeth gnawing bone. A hot blast of fetid air blew over them and the fog evaporated.

Still on the ground, Katie began to scream. Little Billy decided to join her.

Twenty-four

Emily returned first and his son hoisted her into the room. John tried to rise but the pain was too great and he settled back against the ladder, pounding a fist against the floor in frustration.

"*Help Hector,*" she sang to Booker. "*He's not going to be able to hold it off by himself.*"

"*What is it?*" John demanded.

"*Just like you said, Brutrelli times ten. It climbed in through a window. It must have scaled the outside wall. John,*" Emily's grip was a vice clamped around his bicep. "*It has two heads. It has two goddamn heads!*"

The *vetro* had read someone's mind, Emily's or Booker's or Hector's. Maybe all three. He had told them to expect Brutrelli times ten, and because they believed him and their belief had shined brightly, the *vetro offalate* must have folded the notion into their plans as a mocking tribute to his careless words.

"*Help me to the trapdoor.*" John held out his hand.

"*What can you do?*"

"*Fire a gun.*"

"*Don't worry about that,*" Booker sang. He had dragged himself to the opening, rifle in hand. From below more shots rang out. Something shrieked, chittered, howled, moaned. "*Worry about setting up your gizmo.*" He eased himself onto the ladder with a grimace and began descending. Just before his head disappeared he turned to Andrew. "*If it isn't rusted stuck, close the hatch behind me. Don't open it again until this is over.*"

He was gone. Booker and Hector, two men who had followed him from a jail cell to a water tower, who had put their trust him, sacrificed for him, would now likely die for him. And for what? Nothing? Everything? He'd still didn't know if any of this had or would make a damn bit of difference. At least if the two men perished below they would never learn it was all a ruse.

Andrew had been on the verge of understanding. He'd seen the bleak realization dawning in his eyes. If he hadn't derailed his thoughts with the question about forgiveness it might have ended then, belief collapsing into a vast, black well of betrayal. He'd bought himself a few more minutes, but he would have to open the guitar case soon.

Please, he sang to anything out there that might be listening. He'd never been a man of prayer, at least not until Booker's impromptu worship service. *If you exist and you give a damn about any of this, let these extra minutes count for something.*

"*Help me out, here.*" Andrew was struggling to close the hatch, a rusted square of metal frozen open by decades of corrosion. Straining hard enough to raise the cords on arm and neck, he managed to lift it four or five inches as the hinges howled objections. Grace and Emily joined him, Anna as well despite her mother's warning to stay back. John shimmied his way to a standing position, intending to join them, but the effort left him winded and reeling. What kind of half-assed painkillers was Emily toting around? Their effects were decidedly less than impressive.

"*On the count of three,*" Andrew instructed. He gave the countdown. When they heaved, the hatch rose to perpendicular. Leaning their collective weight against the other side, they managed to force it down across the opening inch by squalling inch, the door's hasp finally slipping over a large staple bolted to the floor.

"*No lock,*" Grace pointed out.

"*Maybe we won't need one,*" Andrew suggested. "*Took all of us to move it.*"

John remembered the way the Brutrelli-thing had pounded through the jail's infirmary door.

"*We'll need one,*" Emily and John sang in unison. Emily bent to examine the staple. "*I have an idea.*" She went to the wall and returned with the remaining rifle held awkwardly across her chest.

"*Make sure it's unloaded,*" John sang.

"*How?*"

He held out his hand and she presented the weapon. He pressed the magazine latch and the chambered bullets ejected, scattering across the floor with a series of metallic pings. She returned to the hatch with the rifle and managed to push the first two inches of the barrel through the staple opening.

"*That's as far as it'll go.*"

Andrew knelt and gave the butt of the rifle a shove.

"*Best we can do.*" He rapped the door's plate with his knuckles. "*Wish this was thicker.*" He pointed to the gridding on the windows. "*Wish those bars were tighter. Wouldn't be hard for one of those floating things to squeeze through.*"

Father and son exchanged looks. Together, they moved toward the balcony door through a cascade of dust and debris drifting down from the ceiling. The vibrations were intensifying, the tower shaking hard enough to bounce the grit on the floor. It was an unnerving escalation, but not physically unpleasant. It reminded John of the foot massager Lindsay had given him one year as a birthday present, used twice in a superficial display of appreciation and then discarded. The vibrations rose through his heels and calves in a warm tingle before dissipating above his knees. Why had he only used the damn thing twice?

They stepped out onto the balcony with the flat, gray-green sprawl of suburban Tampa stretched out before them. The downtown towers were blue-gray and nearly invisible through a milky haze of smoke.

Andrew edged toward the crenelated wall. "*I can see much through this soup.*" He leaned over the lip of the wall and peered down.

"*Well?*" John asked, shuddering through a wave of vicarious vertigo.

"*Overhang's blocking most of the view. There's a cloud of dust down there.*"

"*Like something from a construction site?*"

Andrew rejoined John at the balcony entrance. "*More like a deconstruction site. You think once you crank up your machine, whatever's happening down there will stop?*"

John kept his eyes on the horizon as if scanning for a swarm of approaching *votasin*.

"*I don't think so,*" he sang after a pause. He'd discovered something during the previous hour: everything was less dire when set to music. Hard to take "we're all going to die" seriously when crooned to "*Row, Row, Row Your Boat.*" And so, he sang his son as much of the fairytale as he dared.

"*The harmonizer won't have any effect on whatever's down there. It's designed to interfere with the* coils, *not the* bilantu."

Motion behind them.

"*What are you looking for?*" Grace asked. She blinked into the brightening morning as if emerging from hibernation.

"*Just trying to see what's causing the commotion,*" Andrew assured her.

"*It's getting worse. Feels like something trying to drill its way inside.*"

"*This place was built to last.*" John patted the concrete. "*Walls are a foot thick. At least.*"

"*I don't care if they're eight feet thick. Please, Dad,*" she placed a hand on his forearm. "*Your granddaughter's in there and she's terrified. If there's something you can do, do it now before it's too late.*"

A barrage of gunfire erupted from somewhere below. The volley lasted ten, maybe twelve seconds as the three stood transfixed. Booker called out a warning to watch your left, watch your left. There was a pause, more shots followed by a declaration from Hector: "*They're pouring in too fast.*" Three pops. Inhuman shrieks. "*No, no, no, NO!*" A final shot. And then Booker, in a baritone that seemed to reverberate through the shuddering walls as if the tower itself was singing, began a slow, swelling rendition of "Amazing Grace."

"*Oh, god,*" Grace sobbed. Andrew wrapped his arms around her and she buried her head in his chest. Booker managed to declare that he once was lost before the singing abruptly stopped.

"*Dad.*" Andrew pleaded.

John motioned them back inside, and as Andrew lifted his head from Grace's shoulder his face slackened. John turned to follow his son's gaze out over the balcony.

All for nothing, then. It had all been for nothing. Two miles to the south, a dome of white had materialized like a featureless moon rising over a black sea. Reaching a thousand or more feet into the air, it dwarfed the surrounding topographical features. For the half-dozen seconds it took John's sputtering mind to process what he was seeing, the dome remained opaque. When his thoughts coalesced around a single, idiotic assessment—it's big—the bubble burst, revealing a blasted landscape of shattered, obsidian slabs, twisted spires that may or may not have been constructed and fissures pulsing with crematorial light. Scattered throughout were spherical knots of monstrous tendrils spewing black offal from puckered orifices.

"*So that's what hell looks like,*" Grace sang with a lilt of detached curiosity, as if she had just discovered the inner workings of a carburetor.

"*Inside, inside.*" John tried to block their view with his body. "*For god's sake, don't look at it.*"

"*Why?*" She countered. "*It's our future.*"

"*Not if I can help it.*"

One final lie; one last gift. The only thing he could offer those who remained was the chance to die with hope. It was a pathetic alternative to real salvation and an unforgivable deception, but John, for one, had had his fill of seeing the true nature of things. Let the others take their last breaths believing deliverance was still possible. Such endings were preferable to any alternative, weren't they?

"*You all need to get to the roof,*" John sang as they gathered in the center of the observation room. "*It won't be safe down here after I turn it on.*"

"*You want us to go up there?*" Emily asked, eyeing the ladder with skepticism.

"*No choice.*" He shuffled to the duffel bags. "*Take whatever guns are left with you.*" He guided Andrew to the far side of the room. "*Can Grace or Anna see the* bilantu?" he asked in a low voice.

"*I don't think so.*"

"*Thank god for that, at least. It'll be up to you and Emily to keep watch. She's been seeing them for a while.*"

"*Maybe I should stay here with you. Whatever's downstairs will be knocking soon.*"

"*No. Go up. The concrete and rebar superstructure will help shield out the effects.*" He draped an arm over his son's shoulder and gently pivoted him until he was once more facing Grace and Anna. "*Your family needs you. Be with them now.*"

An insect buzz arose. It was coming from the iron window gratings, the ladder, the hatch, from every piece of metal in the room.

"*Daddy?*" Anna pressed her hands against her ears. "*Is the building coming down?*"

Above her head, the adults entered into a spontaneous conspiracy.

"*Don't worry.*" Andrew settled a hand on her head. "*I'll never let anything bad happen to you. Remember at the park? The dragon was chasing us, but it didn't get us. I scared it away.*"

"*But what if the building does fall? What will you do?*"

He knelt at her feet. "*I'll just call my magic carpet and fly us all away before it does.*"

Anna offered her father a small, conciliatory smile, one that made it clear she wasn't buying a word of it, and gave her father a fierce hug. "*I believe you,*" she sang, and the deception was complete.

A tremendous bang dimpled the hatch, provoking a chorus of startled screams.

"*Daddy!*" Anna cried again.

"*Go, now!*" John brayed. The trapdoor had withstood the initial blow, but the metal plate had risen several inches in the center. Below them, something yammered a cascade of syllables that would have been meaningless a few days ago, but which now held the resonance of a familiar greeting. "WE ARE HERE."

Emily retrieved the .45 from a bag and a box of ammunition for both the .45 and .38. She gave the .45 to Andrew and once again tucked the .38 into the small of her back.

"*Ladies first.*" Andrew touched the ladder. Emily tested its strength with two bobs on the lowest rung and began a quick ascent, her medical bag clutched between her teeth. John would have preferred having only one person at a time on the structure, but a second blow raised a new dimple in the hatch twice as large as the first. More chittering. John was beginning to suspect it was their version of laughter, a lunatic's mad chortle.

Anna went next, followed closely by Grace. When it came Andrew's turn, he faced John with an understanding neither man needed to voice. John extended his hand.

"*Andy.*"

"*Dad,*" he took a step closer, one arm raised, then hesitated. "*I don't what to hurt you,*" he sang with a rueful laugh.

"*Never.*" John pulled his son to him and they embraced. "*I'm so damn proud of you. Always have been. You're a better man than I ever was.*"

"*Bullshit.*"

"*I wish to god things could have been different. I did what I thought I had to, to keep you and your mother safe. Maybe I had it all wrong.*"

"*No, Dad. You had it exactly right.*"

"*I'm just sorry as hell I locked you out of my life.*"

"*Don't keep telling me you're sorry.*" They pulled away.

"*Then say it.*" The thing below pounded against the hatch.

"*There's nothing to forgive.*"

John waited. The beast beneath them croaked, "WE ENGULF."

Andrew raised eyes to the ceiling, his head swaying, Adam's apple rising and falling like the needle on a seismograph. When he dropped his gaze, the face confronting him was that of a twelve-year-old who had just raced from the house to stand at the drivers-side window of his father car as he backed out of the driveway for the final time.

"*I forgive you, Dad.*" The words were a slur of syllables strung on the most rudimentary of melodies. "*Okay? I forgive you.*"

When John thought he could manage his own words, he pointed to the ladder.

"*Now go.*"

Andrew took the rungs. "*See you soon.*"

"*You bet.*"

In a moment, his son was gone. The last thing he saw of Andrew was his feet disappearing through the hole in the ceiling. Once he was alone, John slid the guitar case across the floor with a series of small kicks until it came to rest against the far wall, out of sight of anyone casually scrutinizing the room through the opening above.

Another blow buckled the metal hatch upward by nearly a foot and opened a seam between the plate and frame.

"WE DIGEST."

"*We've been through this all before. Come up with some new material, for Christ's sake.*"

The creature roared from a dozen or more mouths, two of which were once human. The trapdoor was beginning to resemble a Jiffy Pop pan halfway through its cooking cycle. Did they still make those stovetop relics? He and Lindsay and Andrew would cozy up on the couch with a Jiffy Pop steaming on the end table, filling the living room with a popcorn bouquet strong enough to fog the nearest window. On the TV, a Saturday afternoon monster movie, some camp classic from the '50s or '60s with minimal production values and a soundtrack like squealing tires.

John sank to the floor, pulled the guitar case close, opened the bicycle locks, removed the cables around the neck and base.

In December, the popcorn would compliment an evening marathon of Christmas specials, reindeer and snowmen and Grinches with expandable hearts. The big tree glowing in a corner, but John had always preferred the small aluminum one he and Andrew assembled for his son's bedroom dresser. It would turn slowly while chiming "*Silent Night,*" and the stars it would project across the walls and ceiling would go round and round and John would watch as the lights moved across his son's face until the boy waved him off with a groggy, "you can go now."

John unclasped the buckles and eased the lid back. The tower swayed. He removed what was inside and carefully arranged the pieces before him. The seam along the hatch frame opened enough to allow a trio of cable-like flagellum to whip out. They swept the floor clean of debris but could not reach him.

"YOUR FINAL THOUGHTS WILL BE DELECTABLE."

John blew the disintegrating trapdoor a kiss and began the assembly.

THE FIRST ONES THROUGH TRIPPED OVER EACH OTHER IN their eagerness to advance, tangling into a snarl that reminded Little Billy of a monstrous disemboweling, a glistening heap of intestines spewed from a gaping wound. The pileup lasted only a moment—the knot was already unraveling—but it was enough for Little Billy to pull Katie to her feet and begin the dash toward the cemetery gates. Jason was a few feet behind, swallowing air in wheezing gulps as the *vetro offalate* righted themselves. Behind the horde, a blast-crater landscape smoldered.

Hand-in-hand, Little Billy and Katie approached the cemetery entrance as a dozen jets of water arch over their heads and smashed into the living wall. Little Billy didn't turn to see the result, but a tremendous hissing erupted, as if a thousand pressure valves were releasing in unison. A foghorn howl followed, rising from the subsonic to crest in a prolonged moan that settled in the inner lining of his skull.

Something crashed down in front of them, destroying the gate and blocking their exit. Little Billy angled away, weaving through gravestones, his vision a bright tunnel surrounded by swirling black dots. A shape unfurling on their left, big but not massive. It struck a forty-foot segment of fencing and knocked it flat. A way out! But they would have to skirt whatever the hell it was.

No matter, no matter. Katie was still at his side. They stumbled on amid the crack and crash of falling tree limbs, the rending of roots as entire trees were toppled. A new barrier on the right, this one of branches. Don't stop. The flailing thing that had destroyed the fence retracted as if on a reel. Almost out now, feet clattering over metal, the ground shuddering, under assault, the pavement an obstacle course of shattered concrete, and above their heads, the spray of the fire hoses throwing rainbows into the morning air.

They reached the line of firefighters at a dead sprint and ducked under the water jets. Little Billy tripped over a hose, careened through the gap between two pumpers and rolled to a stop somewhere behind the line. Katie was next to him, her hands on his shoulder.

"*Are you alright?*"

"Hell no." He struggled to his bloodied knees. "*Are you?*"

"*I pissed my pants.*" Incredibly, she broke into a smile. "*New number one, baby. 'I pissed my pants at the end of the world and I did it with style.'*" She held out her hand. "*Upsy-daisy. You're getting soaked.*"

The street was awash in runoff from the fire hoses. His legs and shoes were sodden. As he regained his feet a realization struck and he slapped his pockets as if he'd been the one carrying the remote detonator. "*Where's Jason?*"

"*If you mean the guy who was running with you, he didn't make it.*"

Little Billy turned to find Sid Langston on his right, hose in hand, his face beneath his helmet a contorted mixture of revulsion and resolve.

"*What happened?*"

"*What happened? Damn things fell on top of him.*" Sid's singing was like beer bottles breaking when a bar fight turns lethal. "*Don't think they were even trying to smash him. Wrong place. Wrong time.*"

"*Where?*"

Sid nodded to the south. "*What's left of him is next to the downed tree.*"

Little Billy faced the *vetro offalate* for the first time and managed a two-word hymn: "*Dear god,*" before his mind shrank back in loathing. Even so, the biologist in him couldn't help a tittering, mad-scientist analysis of the creatures massed before them.

There was a horrible, parasitic elegance about the *vetro offalate*, a simplicity of design that made it clear theirs was a form derived after countless eons of evolutionary pruning. Sleek as leeches, smooth as tapeworms, with a muscular central trunk and appendages that budded and grew rather than unfolded or extended, they reared up thirty, forty feet into the air and swayed with an odd coordination, like a forest of pale kelp waving in a current. As with the *bilantu*, the *vetro's* epidermis was translucent, revealing inner organs that moved independently, spinning, revolving, pulsating, a collection of interior beings laboring in an emulgent stew.

Or were those the creatures' most recent meals?

Little Billy suppressed a gag.

Repulsive as these aspects were, it was their eyes, their horrid, oversized, pustule eyes that drew a rasping inhalation of absolute repugnance. Dead eyes. Atrophied and filmed with what might have been cataracts, but obviously retaining some functionality, the bowling-ball sized pupils rolled to the inner corners of the lidless orbs, imparting a cross-eyed quality to their inhuman stare. Little Billy was quite certain to gaze into those ulcerated eyes was to invite madness.

"Don't look them in the eye!" he cried, too shaken to shape his warning into a melody. "It's the abyss!"

"*Way ahead of you*," Katie answered, managing something between a song and a scream.

Little Billy lowered his gaze and with eyes slotted nearly shut surveyed the scene once more. The *vetro's* bodies were steaming as the water jets struck them. This was the source of the incessant hissing. Steam rose in vast white plumes, clouds of billowing vapor mercifully obscuring much of the creatures' bulk. Christ, they really had climbed from the pits of hell. He had no idea how they moved, whether their central trunks were supported by legs or pseudopodia or some other unfathomable mechanism of mobility. The steam concealed it all.

Little Billy was amazed at the power of the jets blasting from the hoses. Battering ram columns of water, they struck their targets with enough force to buckle and contort the *vetro's* translucent flesh, creating momentary trenches as the water swept from one individual to the next. He became aware of the perpetual crack of gunfire as officers emptied their service revolvers into the beasts, but he couldn't imagine their tiny bullets inflicting much damage. The hoses, however, were having some effect. They might not be pushing the horde back, but at least they were delaying their advance. For now.

An inhuman bellow of outrage suddenly erupted, prompting Little Billy to clamp hands over ears.

"*Aim for the eyes!*" Sid yelled. "*I just put one out.*"

"*The eyes! The eyes!*" The chant was taken up by others and new bellows arouse, accompanied by the sickening wet, viscous pop of imploding orbs. Little Billy listened.

When he heard the next splat, he darted forward as if it were the crack of a starter's pistol. He was across the street and through the broken fence in seconds, hopefully before Katie had a chance to react or follow. Water fell like rain all around, turning the ground to sandy mud, soaking through his shirt, dripping down his face.

He did not stop. Something whistled past his right ear. Shapes twisted through the disintegrating tree line, rending limbs as thick as oil drums from their trunks.

He did not stop. The head of a stone angle flew past and crashed into the fence.

Little Billy did not stop.

Jason's body was a smear of gore from which an arm and leg protruded like the exposed limbs of someone frozen in a slab of bloody ice. The hand was clutching what looked like a small yellow walkie-talkie. Little Billy pried the fingers open. The light from the *xalantracoil* was a nova off to his left, and as he retrieved the detonator, a shadow fell over him.

He jumped forward. The impact pulped the live oak's trunk and sent a concussive wave blasting through his chest like the bass notes from a gargantuan speaker. He rose from the muck and made the gap in the fence in a dozen unbalanced strides, expecting to be yanked backward or pounded flat at any moment. Was that howl in response to his actions, or had another firefighter hit the mark? This time he managed not to trip over a hose and came to a gasping, gulping halt in front of Katie. She grabbed him by the collar of his jacket and for an instant he wasn't sure if she was going to kiss or slap him. She pulled him forward. Her mouth was over his, her tongue pushing past his lips with an urgency he was more than willing to accommodate.

"*That was fucking amazing*," she sang when they came up for air. "*You almost died like six times.*"

"*Well, I...*"

She pushed him away and slapped him hard across the face. "*Don't ever do that again!*"

"*Yes, ma'am.*" His cheek was hot, but his elation was like nothing he'd experienced before, even during the first, heady days of his and Laura's relationship when every new glimpse of flesh had elicited a jolt of delighted gratitude.

"*Now what? Just push the button?*"

Little Billy raised the detonator, his thumb hovering over the obvious choice for the trigger, a large red button beneath a dial pad.

"*Let's see.*"

A ghastly notion occurred in the same instant his thumb pressed down: what if the explosive charges no longer existed in this world? What if they had been teleported a universe away and now lay buried beneath an alien crust?

The idea was apparently confirmed in the next instant. No explosion. He turned to Katie, stricken, but she pointed to the side of the detonator, drawing his attention to a discrete slide switch he hadn't noticed before.

"*Safety?*"

He slid the switch down and a small light at the top right corner of the detonator blinked on. Katie crouched down and plugged her ears with her fingers.

"*We should warn everyone first,*" Little Billy sang.

"*No time.*"

Little Billy hunkered next to her, raised the device above his head and hit the button a second time.

The explosion was strong enough to hurl the closest firefighters off their feet, rock the pumpers on their axels and shatter windshields. The ground around the *xalanthracoil* rose up in solid brown curtain that continued to expand in a conical wall as dirt and vegetation and headstones and fencing and hopefully ten million tiny pieces of *vetro offalate* rose a hundred yards or more into the air. Despite the upheaval, an odd stillness engulfed the street as debris spiraled in graceful trajectories to distant locations. It took a moment for Little Billy to realize the impression of calm was due to the world falling silent.

Katie was sprawled on her back. Little Billy rolled to her and saw her eyes were open and blinking. He thought he yelled, "Are you alright?" If felt as if he had, but he did not hear the words and Katie did not react. He waved his hand in front of her face and her eyes found his. He pointed to his ears. She shook her head. Something pinged him on the top of the head and he raised an arm, shielding her body with his as debris began to pelt down around them, splashing into the wet street and bouncing off the vehicles. The cascade lasted longer than Little Billy would have thought possible. As he waited to find out if he would be brained by something large enough to kill him or survive relatively intact, his hearing began to return the way sounds will creep back as water drains from a swimmer's ear.

The first words he heard were Katie's. "*Did we do it?*" She'd been repeating them for some time.

Little Billy shook the dirt from his hair and stood, pulling Katie with him. Around them, firefighters and police officers were regaining their feet as the unmanned hoses whipped and snaked in the ruined street.

"*I still hear them,*" he sang, pointing to his temple.

A moment later a blanched appendage groped through the thinning dust cloud. Then another. The light of the *xalantracoil* emerged through the murk, dimly at first, a headlight approaching on a foggy stretch of highway. It brightened steadily in the clearing air until it shone forth in blinding triumph. But the crater around it! Little Billy had no idea how many metric tons of earth the blast had excavated, but it must have been a dozen or more. How could the thing still be standing?

"Hoses, hoses!" Someone was singing. *"You."* Sid yanked Little Billy forward. *"Help me get ahold of this thing."*

Little Billy wanted to ask what was the point? All they could do now was delay the inevitable. But he followed the firefighter to the thrashing hose and fell on it and wormed his way toward the nozzle, the canvass bucking and twisting under him as if it were a living thing.

Sid put the nozzle in a headlock and the flow of water suddenly stopped. The rest of the firefighters were quickly re-establishing their position, closing rank, filling gaps. Little Billy thought of ants beginning the rebuilding immediately after a sneakered foot smashes their mound flat. They would remain until the end, resist until the end. They would die at their assigned positions and they would die singing. It was as good a way to go as any.

"Think I could man a hose?" Katie asked.

Little Billy blinked at her. *"I don't know. It would take some strength."*

Katie pointed to a female firefighter down the line. *"She's doing it."*

"The two of you could, if you worked together," Sid answered. He swept his hose back and forth across the *vetro offalate* now emerging *en masse* from the thinning dust cloud. Little Billy noticed they were no longer steaming. Apparently, the firefighters had doused them enough to significantly lower their temperatures. Were they moving a little slower than before, or was that wishful thinking?

"These hoses are supposed to be manned by two people anyway," Sid continued. *"Just keep the line straight and the nozzle dialed down to a tight jet. Hold on tight, like you see me doing, feet spread wide. When you're ready, pull back on the bale and let her rip."*

"Bale?" Katie asked.

"Handle. Forward to close, backward to open. If you see a firefighter go down, take their place."

Before Little Billy could ask any follow-up questions, his shirt pocket began to vibrate. Retreating further behind the engines, he pulled his phone from his pocket, saw who was calling and touched the screen. For the next two minutes, he stood singing out increasingly perplexed questions as Katie circled him in a decaying orbit, ever closer, ever faster. Finally, he ended the call and looked around as if searching for a familiar face in a crowd of strangers.

"What, what?" Katie demanded.

Little Billy ran back to Sid. *"I need to find someone in charge! Someone with connections to the top."*

"Hamilton's around here somewhere. You remember what he looks like? Work your way south."

"What's going on? That was Andrew, right? What's he need us to do?"

Following the curve of the breach and scanning the face of every firefighter he passed, Little Billy spread his arms as if to embrace everything before him.

"Find a helicopter."

"What?"

"If we don't get a helicopter to the water tower, everyone there is going to die."

Twenty-five

"**W**ell?"

Andrew slipped the phone back into his pocket and turned south, trying to decipher what he was seeing. The smoke haze made it difficult to distinguish anything other than the boldest details, but it appeared the rim of the breach was steaming the way lava steams when it reaches the ocean. There was activity there, flashing lights muted to a watercolor glaze of alternating tints, ephemeral compared to the unwavering burn of the *xalantracoils* shining like a ring of fallen stars.

"*He's on it.*"

"*Does the fire department even have a helicopter?*" Grace's eyes were glassy, her lips bloodless. The only color in her face was the maroon crescents beneath her eyes.

"*No. But the TPD does. The Coast Guard does. Every television station in the city does.*"

"*Andy.*" Her voice broke and Anna reached up from her mother's side to pat her shoulder.

"*Don't cry, Mommy.*"

"*Not me, my brave one.*"

In the room below, another metallic bang sounded. Andrew had to assume the hatch was still holding, but each new blow rang a little differently than the last, the tone becoming looser somehow, more a clang than a thump. Occasionally, something would roar or scream or warble, but these were not the sounds that had prompted Andrew to call Little Billy. It was the grinding, the incessant crunch of stone against stone, or, more likely, tooth against concrete.

He could no longer ignore what his ears were insisting. Grace had been right. Something down there was eating its way through the walls of the tower and it was only a matter of time before the whole thing came crashing down.

Dr. Cho put a gentle arm around Grace. "*I can give you a mild sedative, if you want.*" They were all huddled together in the center of the roof. They had no choice. The circular platform was only twenty feet in diameter and enclosed by nothing more than a low, decorative crenellation of weathered concrete. Although she had tried to be surreptitious about it, Andrew knew Dr. Cho had noticed the bandages on his wife's arms, and he suspected she also understood the implications of those wounds.

Grace shook her head. "*No, I'm fine.*" When the doctor said nothing, she looked Cho in the eye and repeated: "*I. Am. Fine.*"

"*Am I going to ride in a helicopter?*" Anna sang.

"*That's the plan,*" Andrew replied, looking both adults in the eye until each gave a tiny nod. What they had just agreed to Andrew would never be certain, only that it was a wordless contract of defiance rather than deception.

"*When will it get here?*"

"*Soon, honey. Real soon.*"

Andrew cocked his head, his eyes narrowing in puzzlement.

"*What?*" Grace asked.

He shook his head. "*Nothing. Thought I heard something for a second. Just my imagination.*"

"*Something bad, Daddy?*"

Andrew cupped his daughter's cheek. "*Not bad. Something familiar. A little piece of a song. That's all.*"

"*A happy song?*"

Andrew nodded, although the momentary snippet he'd apparently imagined had plucked a cord of melancholy, nostalgia mixed with regret, fondness with loss. He wanted to poke his head through the opening to see what his father was up to. Something was certainly going on below. Even through his song, he could sense a growing desperation in the *vetro offalate's* call, a rapacious gnawing to get in. But he could not look. His earlier realization had returned, the one forgotten when he and Grace had sung to one another the things unsung for too long. If they were all about to die for the sake of some unfathomable deception, he preferred not to know.

"*Something's coming,*" Cho sang, and Andrew's heart bolted into a gallop. "*Can you smell it?*"

He raised his nose to the air—as did Grace and Anna—and inhaled deeply. He'd been smelling the arid tang of the wildfire for so long it no longer registered. To the north, the rising sun blushed the grayish clouds of smoke as they piled into towering heaps, their tops smeared across the heavens by high-altitude currents like a thumb over a charcoal sketch.

The angry sky felt like an accusation. With no one fighting the blaze, how many homes had been lost? How many neighborhoods decimated? He imagined the flames marching unchallenged to the Gulf, leaping highways, consuming the tinder-dry urban canopy until there was nothing left to burn. But then a slight puff of breeze from offshore drifted over them and he smelled it, an aroma so long absent he at first assumed it was an olfactory illusion.

"*Rain!*" Anna cried. "*I smell rain!*"

Andrew scanned south toward the bay. He couldn't make out thunderheads. The haze was too thick. But now that he was scrutinizing the horizon in that direction, he noticed a bruise that had not been there before, a pale blue stain that might have been empty sky or the first hues of an approaching storm.

"*I thought I heard thunder earlier,*" Grace sang, shielding her eyes with a hand.

"Oh, no," Cho whispered. The spoken words were a peal of alarm that caused Andrew, Grace and Anna to start in unison.

"*What?*" Andrew was already motioning Grace and Anna to the floor. Down! Down!

The doctor pointed, and a moment later he saw them: drifting shapes a hundred yards to the southeast, approaching in a leisurely flotilla of lethal pincushions.

"*So many.*" Cho pulled the gun from the small of her back and flicked off the safety.

"*What is it?*" Grace demanded, looking about frantically and pulling Anna to her so tightly his daughter protested she was being squished.

"*Don't look!*" Andrew sang, pulling the .45 revolver from his belt and checking to make sure there was a round in every chamber. "*Just keep your heads down and your eyes closed.*"

"*Is it them?*" She appeared to engulf Anna, arms and legs in constant motion as if she were attempting to spread herself thin enough to cover her child in a living cloak. "*Your father's monsters?*"

"*Just keep your eyes closed until I tell you it's safe. No matter what you hear, keep your eyes closed.*"

"*Daddy, I'm scared.*" Anna's voice was muffled in the folds of her mother's shirt.

"*It's going to be okay. You're going to hear some loud pops, but don't open your eyes. I won't let anything bad happen to you.*"

The ancient lie, repeated from parent to child since the dawn of language. Andrew positioned himself between his family and approaching death and his gaze fell for a moment to the park far below.

Not just an aerial assault. The ground was alive with *bilantu: quintaloch, squim,* others he couldn't remember the names of. They leaped and scampered and slithered and rolled toward the tower to join whatever was already down there.

His throat closed and he licked dry lips with a dry tongue. God, he could use a drink right now. He remembered Katie's hand reaching out to take the water bottle with Comanche's knife at her throat, the way the water had gushed from the open top when she gripped the plastic. That was what he wanted, a cold bottle of water. The realization sparked a crackle of elation that raced down his spine. When was the last time craving a drink prompted thoughts of bottled water? It meant nothing, of course, other than perhaps mild dehydration, but it felt like a victory, maybe the last he would ever claim.

"*Fill your pockets with ammo,*" he advised Dr. Cho. "*We don't want to be groping around when it comes time to reload.*"

As they filled their pockets he caught the faint melody once again. He felt the tower vibrating at an ever-increasing frequency through the soles of his feet. The banging at the hatch below was now an incessant pounding. To the south, the breach was an enormous black, frothing mouth and fifty yards to the southeast the *votasin* were riding a rain-scented breeze toward their prey.

Andrew lifted the revolver, rested his firing hand in the palm of the other and carefully sighted the barrel at the nearest target. He remembered a line of advice from a movie: squeeze the trigger, don't pull it. But not yet. They were still too far away. He and the good doctor would need to make every shot count.

As his finger tightened on the trigger Andrew heard the first faint rumbled of thunder, and for reasons he would never fully understand thought, *Christmas in July.*

"*HOW LONG?*" LITTLE BILLY ASKED. HE WAS FACING Hamilton, but his eyes were on the cell tower behind the captain. What had been a suspicion a few minutes ago was now a certainty. The structure was slowly pitching forward into the breach. Some sort of attractive phenomena maybe, the metal tower responding to the tug of geomagnetic forces emanating from the *vetro's* world?

338

"*Should only be a few minutes,*" the captain said, re-holstering his radio. "*Chopper was already in the air. Only thing left still fighting the fire.*" He saw Little Billy's gaze, turned to the cell tower, and snorted. "*Perfect.*"

"*You need to get everyone out of the way,*" Katie advised, sweeping her hand back and forth through the air.

Hamilton's face hardened. "*Or what? People will die?*"

He understood the man's bitterness. During his frantic search for the captain, he and Katie had witnessed half-a-dozen deaths, men and women disintegrating under the whip of massive flagellum, disemboweled, dismembered, decapitated. Firefighters crushed under hurled projectiles, smeared across the pavement, yanked into hell.

For creatures of such technological supremacy, capable of reaching across entire universes to slaughter their livestock, they fought like schoolyard bullies, swinging at anything within reach. Maybe that's the way they liked it, the satisfaction of getting whatever substituted for their hands nice and dirty. And yet, if their intention was to terrify their opposition into flight, the *vetro offalate* had miscalculated. Hamilton wasn't afraid. He was furious.

The captain sighed and rubbed his eyes. "*You're right, of course.*" The radio was in his hand again. "*Maybe it'll take out some of those fuckers when it falls.*"

"*They're moving slower.*" Little Billy offered. "*Have you noticed?*"

"*Unless a squadron of F-22s is minutes from lighting this place up, I don't see it making much of a difference.*"

Little Billy drifted away as the captain began singing into his radio. The morning's adrenaline was evaporating once again, leaving a residue of fuzzy numbness behind. Dispatching the helicopter felt like the final act in a Herculean list of chores, and with its completion, his usefulness was at an end.

He watched the wall of *vetro* as they swayed and thrashed against the water jets. They were little more than images projected onto an enormous screen. He felt nothing. Maybe he was slipping into shock. Firefighters sang and screamed around him. Police officers reloaded. Fifty yards away, a sheriff's department cruiser lay upended, its hood hanging open and dripping fluids like a lolling tongue. Little Billy wondered if its deputy was still alive and found he didn't care. All he wanted was to curl up in a ball and go to sleep. The ground seemed to tilt and he reached for Katie's hand to steady himself.

"*We all fall down*," he sang, because Katie, too, was swaying on her feet. In fact, most of the firefighters along the line appeared to be struggling to keep their balance. Something was rolling slowly through Little Billy's legs, a battered tennis ball, a chew toy perhaps, from a neighboring yard. It appeared to move reluctantly, pausing after one or two rotations as some small protuberance in its gnawed surface was overcome. Each time the ball stopped, Little Billy expected it to remain still. It did not. It continued on its way across the street. This meant something, he knew, something obvious he should have realized by now, but his thoughts were syrupy. Two plus two. What did that add up to?

Florida orange juice, a glassful of sunshine.

No, that wasn't it.

"*Jesus Christ!*"

The firefighter on his left was backpedaling to his pumper, lips curled in a snarl as he crouched and redirected the hose higher. Little Billy followed the jet and—god help him—his first reaction was a small huff of fascinated admiration.

The two nearest *vetro* had merged into one. The new creature reared above the treetops, its mouths yawning, its surviving eyes rolling in different directions. Little Billy couldn't tell which features were from which individual, so thoroughly had they melded. As he watched, mesmerized, two neighboring *vetro* condensed into one another like globs of oil.

Brilliant.

"*Will!*"

Katie yanked him down as something enormous whooshed over their heads. There was a tremendous crash, shattering glass, the crunch and clang of metal. A fire engine siren began to warble. The blow had pivoted the nearest pumper 180 degrees and split the cab open. The siren seemed to infuriate the mega-*vetro* and it smashed its bulk down again and again until the vehicle was little more than a metal sheet. A firefighter's helmet lay in the grass near the wreck. Little Billy saw no sign of the owner.

"*Come on!*"

Katie raced down the line without a backward glance, and Little Billy followed. An unmanned hose, attached directly to a corner hydrant, flailed across a front yard, swept a row of potted plants off the porch and blew out a living room window before she fell on it. Little Billy joined her and together they wrestled it into submission, turned off the flow at the nozzle and positioned themselves as Sid had shown, with Little Billy in front and Katie bracing him from behind.

"*I don't know how much of a kick this thing is going to have,*" he warned.

"*The bigger, the better.*"

Little Billy pulled back on the bale and the water shot out in a white column. The pushback was strong. It pressed him against Katie, and he leaned forward until he found equilibrium. Katie anchored him from behind.

At least we have a bigger target, he thought as he pulled the nozzle up. The hose wanted to fight him, find its own direction. For a moment, the stream swept back and forth across the ruin of the fire engine as if he were attempting to extinguish its smoldering remains. He pulled the nozzle up and the jet rose, plowing through a wooden fence and the branches of the trees behind before striking the mega-*vetro*, the water pluming around its torso. Little Billy spiraled the jet up the length of its central trunk, hoping to find a vulnerable spot, a hidden seam that would split the beast back into two separate creatures.

"*I guess poking their eyes out isn't enough,*" Katie sang. "*If only we knew where their nut sacks are.*"

"*That'd learn 'em.*" Little Billy agreed.

The *vetro* dodged and weaved, stretched out an appendage that flared into a sort of fleshy catcher's mitt and brought it crashing down. A similar appendage emerged on the other side. It was not an attempt to swat them,

Little Billy quickly realized, but the initial maneuverings for an advancement. The *vetro* was preparing to "step" forward. Already he could see it leaning toward them, shifting its weight onto its arms or legs or whatever those columns of flesh were. He directed the jet at one of them, hoping to sweep it out from under the creature, but it had little effect. The water simply angled off in a blinding spray. He tried the other. No effect.

Katie's arm shot past his shoulder.

"*Aim at that!*" She pointed to the top of a telephone pole a dozen feet to the right of the *vetro*. "*The transformer!*"

Little Billy turned the nozzle and missed the gray drum with his first sweep. The hose wanted to keep going right. He had to struggle to counteract its momentum and reverse direction, but when he dragged the jet back across the pole he struck the transformer dead-center. The incandescent flare blinded him and the boom hit him like an airy fist. It wasn't as loud as the final Trenchrite blast, but it felt sharper, narrower, more a quick jab than a roundhouse punch.

The world was a purple afterimage, but he could smell the ozone, hear the sharp crackle of electricity. And the scream of the *vetro offalate*, a squeal of agony that lifted Little Billy into a near ecstasy of bloodlust. *Fry, fry, fry!* he chanted, sweeping the hose blindly back and forth. *Eat volts and die bastards!*

Blows were raining down all around him. He felt the ground shuddering under the barrage. At the very least, they'd managed to piss the thing off. It was smashing the street to rubble in a temper tantrum. Through the explosion's fading afterimage, he saw a latticework of cracks spreading away in either direction. The ground itself was sagging under the *vetro's* fury. Even the trees were shuddering. The air was filled with a snow of leaves. Little Billy heard a new sound, a vast, deep rending as if an enormous garment was being ripped in half.

He was no longer standing on the sidewalk. The ground had become the deck of a sinking ship and everything was sliding toward the bow. The last thing he saw clearly was the street fracturing into a series of tiers that canted and toppled away from each other.

The hose slipped through his hands and Little Billy began to roll. He couldn't stop himself. He picked up speed, tumbled off the edge of a precipice and landed with a grunt several feet below. The ground tilted and he slid, fell, slid some more. He turned his head and saw a wall of sand and soil. It crumbled over him and the world went dark. He opened his mouth to scream and dirt poured in. The shelf he was lying on was tipping and he was about to plunge into whatever abyss had opened around him.

Blind and suffocating, Little Billy flailed out in a convulsion of white panic. His fingers brushed something like a long, fabric sleeve and he grasped it as everything below disintegrated into nothingness.

THE *VOTASIN* WEREN'T ALL THAT HARD TO KILL. STRUCK with A bullet, they deflated with a whoopee cushion release of gas that sent them spiraling off in random directions. The first time Andrew hit one, he had to suppress a giggle. It was almost cartoonish. But while they were vulnerable and slow moving, they were not defenseless. Fifty feet. That was how far then things could fire their quills. If the projectiles were venomous, both he and Dr. Cho were dead. He'd taken two in the chest, and she one in the arm. The quills had lost most of their velocity by the time they struck, barely breaking the skin and easily swatted out. Of course, the depth of penetration would be irrelevant if the toxin was deadly, but venomous or not, Andrew had little doubt a barb fired within ten feet would do significant damage.

"*How you holding up?*" he asked Cho.

"*Arm's getting tired.*"

"*You're doing great.*"

"*They just keep coming.*"

Andrew reloaded, taking a moment to remind Grace and Anna to keep their eyes closed. The tower swayed minutely in the quickening breeze, a sensation not unlike the bob and drift of his bed after a night of drinking. To the southwest, the sky was cinematic. Branching tributaries of pink lightning leaped from cloud top to cloud top while further out in the Gulf an approaching curtain of rain undulated gracefully. A new gust swept the *votasin* swarm to the east. The creatures reoriented and started closing in once again, but they were fighting the wind and their progress was slower than before, a reprieve that gave Andrew enough time to take careful aim before pulling the trigger. When he did the closest burst open and disappeared below the rim of the tower, shooting quills in every direction as it fell.

They kept coming. Wave after wave. Was something similar happening below, *bilantu* pouring into the tower through newly created openings, scaling the outer walls? Were he and his family only seconds from being overrun from all sides? He shot another *votasin*. It deflated with a satisfying poof.

"*I hear it!*" Anna squirmed out of her mother's grip. "*The helicopter's coming! It's coming!*"

Grace rose to her knees, struggling to keep their daughter under control. "*Anna, stay down!*"

"*But it's right there! It's white with a blue tail!*"

The thumping whir of copter blades swelled to an auditory assault. Andrew managed to empty the .45 with four quick, off-target shots before the rotor wash swept over them in a hurricane blast and he sank into a crouch, an instinctive maneuver intended to keep his head as far from the blades as possible.

"Hold on to Anna!" he hollered into Grace's ear. The downdraft was a cascade of air trying to pound them flat. The copter eased closer. Andrew could see the pilot through the windshield and raised his hand in an absurd gesture of welcome before the rotors' gale forced his head down once again.

The aircraft appeared to be a typical commercial model, something a television station would own, although he saw no logo. It pivoted slightly as it approached to allow passenger access, the sliding cabin door already open. A man in a DOF uniform was perched on the threshold, his feet on the skid. Twenty feet. Ten. Five. The man in the cabin gestured for them to approach. There was no safety gear, no harnesses or tethers. The skid bobbed and swayed a few feet from the roof's edge. It would be a big step up.

"You and Anna first!"

Grace didn't argue, although he could see her scrutinizing the gap between roof and salvation. She grasped Anna's hand and edged to the rim, turning at the last instant back toward him, but in the rotor wash, all he could see of her face was a wild flurry of hair. The DOF man, one hand grasping a straphanger, leaned forward and stretched out the other. Grace said something in their daughter's ear. She reached up. Not close enough.

The firefighter barked something to the pilot and the copter inched closer until the skid touched the crenellations. When Anna reached up Grace grasped her under the arms and nearly hurled her into the cabin. Only after Grace followed did it occur to him to scan for *votasin*. There was nothing in the immediate vicinity. He imagined the entire swarm being sucked in and puréed by the spinning rotors.

"Your turn," he shouted to Dr. Cho.

"What about your father?"

"He's next."

She nodded and stepped to the edge. When she leaped into the cabin, it was as if the tower were a diving board rebounding after a jump. The roof tipped backward. Andrew was tossed onto his back, arms and legs splayed wide. The inclination increased. The duffel bags slid past his head and he suddenly found himself passing over the ladder opening. Twisting onto his belly, he grasped the edges to stop his plunge through the hole.

"Dad!"

The first of the rain hit him, large, cold droplets that felt like a handful of thrown gravel. The tower continued to pitch and he slid from one side of the opening to the other.

"Dad, if you can hear me get to the ladder!"

The tower dipped like a plane hitting turbulence and Andrew's stomach lifted into his throat. Before he could scream, the descent stopped and the tower began to teeter-totter in the opposite direction.

"Dad! For Christ's sake, we have to go!" He'd carry his father to the roof if he had to. Or maybe they could make their way out to the balcony and board the copter from there.

The storm had muted the morning light. Peering down into the now-dim observation room, Andrew could make out slowly rotating colored lights playing across the walls, swelling from sharp circles to fuzzy balls of illumination and back again as they roved the room. Bathed in the colored lights, his father moved into frame and shook his head, a tiny motion that said everything. He raised a hand, closed it into a fist and tapped his chest twice.

Andrew raised his own fist, but he was still on his belly and couldn't complete the gesture. Then he was sliding again, back toward the edge of the roof. He rolled onto his back as his feet struck the crenellations. Here was the helicopter. The tower was falling and the aircraft was following it down. Andrew stood, crouched, jumped. He was in the air. He was reaching out. *Dad*, he thought.

The last thing he heard before sinking into the gloom was the copters' cabin door slamming shut.

JOHN TATE RETURNED TO HIS PLACE IN THE CENTER OF the room just in time to catch the aluminum tree as it topped over. He cradled it in his arms like a dance partner, listening to the music box in its rotating base chime "Silent Night." The hatch gave way with a final shriek. What emerged into the room and kept emerging, roaring in triumph, wasn't "Brutrelli times ten." It was Brutrelli *ad infinitum,* a conga line of fused *bilantu* that, as far as John knew, extended all the way to the base of the tower and beyond. He recognized Theodore Hillsdale's face nestled egg-like in the nest of seeping contours. Another man's face as well. There was nothing human left behind their staring eyes.

346

Outside, the sound of the helicopter grew faint. In the relative quiet it left behind he realized the voices were gone. Not just diminished. Not just muted. Gone. Entirely. The *vetro offalate* were no longer in his head.

"You're alone again," he told the thing in the room. "Castaways, just like before."

The creature shook its many heads, either in negation or in preparation to strike, and John held his son's tree out as if in offering. Lindsay had tsk-tsked him for buying a battery-powered model, predicting the display would run down by the end of the week. But the four D-cells, refreshed annually, lasted all season and now, as he started sliding away from the hatch, his view was filled with the lights of a dozen Christmases past.

"This is what you came for. If you want it, come and get it."

The creature swayed from the now canted opening for an instant and then they were weightless, floating together as the tower plummeted. John Tate let go of the tree and wondered if things would have turned out differently had they all joined together and sung "Kumbaya" when Hector had suggested it.

"Silent Night" played on. His companion opened its many mouths. And in the air between them, the colored lights went round and round.

LITTLE BILLY'S DESCENT CONTINUED AS HIS GRIP SLID DOWN THE FIRE hose. He could breathe again, but there was too much grit in his eyes to see anything other than a watery smear of gray. Debris was raining down, bouncing off his head and arms and shoulders. A slab of concrete tumbled past. He sensed it as a change of pressure in his right ear. It landed a second later with a thick splash and Little Billy kicked out, searching for a foothold along the wall of the precipice he now dangled over. Every kick dislodged more soil. He couldn't find anything solid enough to support his weight. He gave up and decided he would hang there for as long as his strength allowed.

Where was Katie? Had she tumbled into this void with him or had she managed to save herself? There was sand between his teeth, dirt coating the inner lining of his mouth. He tried to call out to her, but couldn't draw a deep enough breath.

His grip began slipping again. In a few seconds, he would fall into whatever awaited below. Hopefully, his death would be as quick as Jason's had been. That wasn't too much to ask, was it? They had done what they could, fought the good fight. It was finally time to let it all go. His arms quivered with exhaustion. Let go.

He willed his hands to relax. They would not. He willed his fingers to unclench. No deal. The process of unbending the digits was beyond the limits of his coordination. Just relax and it will all be over, he reasoned. The muscles of his forearms were jumping. He could not hold on and he could not let go. Little Billy tilted his head back and whimpered.

More dirt began falling around him. He bounced against the wall and cried out. The wall was sliding down. No! He was ascending. Someone was pulling him up. He bumped against the side and kicked his feet into the loose soil, trying to climb the near-vertical slope. He ascended slowly, and with a final heave crested the lip. A hand reached out and grabbed the collar of his jacket. A second hand grabbed his belt. Little Billy shimmied his hips until he felt pavement under his legs. A firefighter and Katie—*Katie!*—dragged him up a shallow inclination before all three collapsed next to the front wheel of a ladder truck.

"What," Little Billy choked out after a moment.

"What happened?" Katie finished for him.

Little Billy nodded.

"Half the city just collapsed."

"What?"

"A sinkhole. Biggest I've ever seen. It's still growing. You must be half cat 'cause you've used up about eight lives in the last fifteen minutes." She bent and kissed him hard, then had to spit the grit from her mouth. "Now the bay's pouring in, flooding the whole thing. There's going to be a new lagoon when this is all over."

"The *vetro?*"

"Haven't you noticed?" She pointed to her temple. "No more voices."

Periphery

The realization sifted slowly into Little Billy's awareness, settling in the dusty folds of his brain. Neither he nor Katie was singing.

"They're gone?"

"Either back to wherever they came from or down to the bottom of the hole. Will, the breach is closed. It's closed!" She threw her head back and raised her hands up to a slate sky. "Thank you, Jesus! At least one *xalantracoil* went into the drink. I saw it. When it did, everything just sort of turned off, there one second, gone the next. See for yourself."

Little Billy was still bleary-eyed. He blinked muddy tears and beheld a panorama nearly as alien as the one he had witnessed when the rift opened. The city he had known all his life was disappearing, crumbling into a vast crater. The opposite rim was already a thousand yards away and retreating in a series of massive landslides that erased entire neighborhoods and filled the air with dust clouds. To the southwest, the bay was flooding in, brown cascades sweeping away or submerging the broken remains of trees and buildings and cars and streetlights. Little Billy saw an overturned hazmat truck, its lights still flashing, lying at the bottom of the sinkhole amid a litter of broken pavement and wondered how many had just lost their lives. How many more were about to die, tipped into their graves like rubbish from a dustpan?

"How could this happen?"

Katie leaned against him, her head on his shoulder.

"I think we did it."

"No."

"With all the blasting. Remember the other night? When we tried to blow up the *coil*? We ended up making a sinkhole."

"But this?" He waved his hand before him. "This would take a nuclear blast."

"Your girlfriend's right."

Little Billy turned to the firefighter who had helped rescue him. He recognized the face, one of the men from Andrew's station he'd met during the night. Terrance Jackson.

"This all started when you set off that last blast. It took a few minutes to really get going, but once it did…" He shook his head in wonder.

"The drought?" Little Billy intended the question as a prompt into whether or not the recent drop in the water table might have contributed to the sinkhole, but Terrance did not interpret it that way.

"Over, I think."

Little Billy struggled to his feet. He felt scooped out, hollow, an empty rind tossed over a shoulder.

"Is it?" There was no misinterpreting Katie's question.

Little Billy was too tired to lie. "We'll have to wait and see." He closed his eyes and inhaled deeply, the scent of approaching rain reminding him of a hundred other storms waited out under highway overpasses and bus shelters, overhangs and public restrooms.

The rain began all at once, a scouring deluge that soaked them in an instant. Little Billy opened his eyes. Nothing was visible beyond the lip of the sinkhole. The torrent had erased it all.

"Andy and his family? John?" Katie's teeth chattered. He took off his sodden jacket and draped it over her shoulder. He didn't bother reaching for his saturated phone. Cell towers poked from the sinkhole's rising water like masts from a dozen shipwrecks.

"We'll have to wait and see."

Twenty-six

It took twelve hours for the sinkhole to fill. By then, news crews from as far away as Australia and China were rushing to the site and the local media—those who still had the capability to broadcast—were camped out around the rim, providing continuing, lurid coverage of "The Big Sink." Officials from the U.S. Geological Survey were quick to provide cutaway graphics of Florida's topography, explaining in grim and knowing voices how a layer of sandy topsoil overlaying a deposit of clay overlying a limestone base was a recipe for disaster. They pointed out the subterranean blue ribbon representing the Florida Aquifer and described its erosive effects on the surrounding rock as "voracious" and "unrelenting". The prolonged drought and the resulting drop in the water table took most of the blame for the massive collapse, with overbuilding and poor water management thrown in for good measure.

Experts had a harder time explaining the collapse of the Sulfur Springs water tower. Despite the structure being several miles north of the sinkhole, the two incidents were assumed to be related. Eventually, a consensus was reached. Tremors from "The Big Sink" were felt as far south as Sarasota, as far north as Port Richie. The water tower had been old and apparently in an advanced state of decay. The shockwaves must have been enough to fracture the foundation and send the entire structure toppling into the Hillsborough River. Inspectors would later conclude the base of the tower had been undermined—"chewed through" more than one would write in his report—but those opinions were quickly dismissed and purged from all official documents.

The governor's approval ratings plunged in the wake of the disaster and the mayor's response was deemed "pathetic," but it was not an election year and both would keep their jobs. The death toll, at first estimated to be as high as thirty-five thousand, quickly dwindled as more and more evacuees were accounted for. The total number of casualties eventually settled at fewer than a thousand, although the exact number would never be known. Most of the bodies of the missing were assumed buried in wreckage at the bottom of what would come to be known as Vetro Bay, a name whose popularity was enhanced by its mystifying origins.

Had it not been for the evacuation, disaster management analysts agreed, the loss of life would have been catastrophic, although no one involved in the decision could offer an explanation as to why so many firefighters had been redeployed to the area. At least no rational explanation. No official mention was made of Chief Rodriguez's early-morning request for a military response to the crisis, an appeal that was met with what could charitably be called a high degree of skepticism.

A secret, bi-partisan commission was established to investigate events just prior to the collapse. Nearly every surviving witness was interviewed, and although their stories were consistent, no physical evidence was ever recovered to verify their outlandish claims and no definitive conclusions were ever reached.

As sightings of bizarre creatures persisted, however, Tampa's reputation as a hotspot for paranormal activities grew to rival Roswell's. The resulting boost in tourism helped finance the city's recovery, and although it was not the sort of recognition local officials would have preferred, when revenues for conventions, tours, specialty shops and niche media outlets were tallied, most grudgingly concluded there were worst things for a city than to be labeled the monster capital of the world.

***

LITTLE BILLY WAITED IN THE HALLWAY, RELISHING THE cool wash of air-conditioning from the overhead vent. St. Joseph's was one of the few places in the city where the power was still on, the emergency generators kept running by a National-Guard-escorted convoy of diesel tankers continually resupplying all surviving hospitals, fire stations, police stations, emergency shelters and government buildings.

He was clean-shaven for the first time in nearly thirty years, and the air blowing across his face lapped his cheeks and upper lip, breathy and intimate. He wasn't sure he could get used to the lack of facial hair. He felt exposed. Maybe not vulnerable—he'd lived on the streets too long to feel that way about anything so pedestrian—but certainly susceptible.

Susceptible to what, though? John was gone. They'd pulled his body from the rubble, along with four other men. His passing was a dull ache in his throat, an occasional clicking when he swallowed, but he'd faced death before. He liked to think he'd been inoculated against the more severe manifestations of grief.

Was it the loss of purpose, then, the threat of an aimless existence now that the *vetro offalate* had been thwarted? He tried to reach back across The Great Divide to remember what he had hoped to accomplish before Laura's family had been slaughtered and his long walk began. Professional recognition? Fame? His name mentioned in the same breath as Darwin, Mendel, Amundsen?

It all seemed as fanciful as a desire to ride unicorns through Oz. He would never publish a paper on the *bilantu*. Even without their masters whipping them into a frenzy, it would be a disservice to humanity to broadcast their existent to the world. Besides, who the hell would believe him? Most of those who'd learned the truth were dead, and those who remained would quickly learn to keep their mouths shut.

Little Billy took a slow sidestep to the left, his back pressed against the wall. Through the open door across the hall, he could see Katie still sitting at her mother's bedside, their hands interlocked, their heads nearly touching. Her father stood on the other side of the bed, a red-faced man in his mid-fifties. Every so often he would shoot Little Billy a coldly impatient look, obviously annoyed some lanky stranger was still lurking in the hall.

This was a mistake. He shouldn't have come. Earlier, as he and Katie lay sprawled on sweat-soaked sheets, she had run a finger down his newly-shaved cheek and asked if he wanted to meet her parents. He had said yes because she had obviously wanted him to, but across her bedroom walls he was already watching the future play out, a dark moment when someone would inevitably stare too long at something they shouldn't, and the loved ones around them would pay in blood for the transgression.

Lying naked and erect under her light strokes, he imagined an arterial spray of blood painting her bedroom wall and began to deflate.

"It's not you," he assured her. "I'm just old."

"You weren't old last night. Or this morning. Or twenty minutes ago."

"We all have our limits."

"We'll see."

Now, in the hospital hallway, Little Billy took another slow step toward the elevator doors. He knew what he was susceptible to. He felt its pull, its false promise. Hope was a disease, and sooner or later it would kill everyone you cared about.

He took another step. One more and he would no longer be able to see Katie, her mother, her disapproving father. Then it would be easy to slink off to the elevator. He closed his eyes and rolled his head back and forth against the wall.

"No."

Katie leaned against him, pinning his shoulders.

"You know I have to."

"I know you think you do, ever since this morning. Men are all the same. Your cocks never lie."

Little Billy glanced across the hall. Mr. Fife had taken a chair next to his wife. He was holding a straw to her lips. If he'd heard his daughter, he was doing a fine job pretending he hadn't.

"Me being around will only put them at risk," he said in a low voice.

"How convenient it must be, to always have an excuse to disappear. What about me? I can see the *bilantu*. How much risk am I putting my mom and dad in?"

"That depends."

"On what?"

"Your ability to ignore the obvious."

Katie pushed off him and looked about as if seeing the hospital hallway for the first time.

"You have me there, Will. I'll never be as good at ignoring what's right under my nose as you are."

"You know what I mean."

"I have a life..." She glanced toward the nurse's station and tugged him around the corner. "I have a life separate from my parents," she resumed in a tone reserved for mothers scolding children just of out earshot from other adults. "I'm not going to sever every connection I have with them just because someday I might slip up and look somewhere I'm not supposed to. I'm not going to live like you. I'm not going to run."

Through the window behind Katie, Little Billy could see the parking garage, the hospital's empty helipad. The sky was a ragged and sodden hem dragged from the Gulf as another line of afternoon thunderheads approached. Four inches of rain in the last three days. At least the wildfire was nearly out. If he left now, he could probably shelter in one of the garage stairwells until the storm was over. No one was going to chase him off. And then where? His instinct was to head north, but maybe this time he'd turn east toward Orlando. Wasn't it traditional to go to Disney World after a big victory?

Hands on his cheeks, gently guiding his face back to hers.

"Will." Little more than a whisper now. "I'm sorry. I know how much you've been through. What you've lost. I shouldn't have said that. You did what you thought was right, but you don't have to leave this time. You don't have to leave *me*. Whatever's going to happen, whatever my fate, I brought it on myself. Willingly. I'm not your responsibility."

"You can take care of yourself." It sounded like a sad admission, even to him.

"Yes, but I don't want to do it alone. I know things will have to change between me and my parents. I won't be able to be as close to them as I was. My dad's already noticed. I see how he watches me, like I'm one more thing about to go wrong. They'll be hurt. Especially Mom. She'll say I'm colder. He'll say I'm distant. They'll blame 'the incident,' and Bobby's death and the sinkhole and god knows what else. Ebola."

Little Billy smiled and she curled her fingers through his. "It's going to be hard. I don't want to spend the rest of my life hovering around the fringe of everybody else's lives, alone. Always alone. And neither do you, William Phipps." She stroked his bare cheek. "Otherwise why would you have shaved off your beard?"

"I thought it would make me look younger."

"It wasn't because you wanted a new start?" Her eyes dropped. She turned his hand palm-up and traced her index finger down his lifeline. "Is it her?" Her voice was a sheet being pulled from a bed, leaves rustling over cracked pavement, a teakettle whistling in a neighbor's kitchen. "The memory of Laura? Are you so eager to leave because you know you could never love anyone else?"

He covered her hand with his free one. "No."

"Then stay. Be with me. And someday, maybe…"

She fell silent, and in that candid pause he found himself back at The Great Divide he had crossed so many years ago. Behind him stretched an endless finger of blacktop shimmering in the heat haze and bridged by a distant overpass.

He knew the place. It was I-10 passing above U.S. 90 just north of Live Oak, Florida. He'd spent a long night there once, shivering through the aftereffects of a *squim* attack. During the height of his hallucinations, Laura and her family had come for a visit. At the time, he'd assumed their presence was an accusation, a rebuke, but now he saw he had been wrong. They had come to forgive him. He'd been absolved years ago, but guilt is a funny thing. Hold it close long enough and you may end up falling in love with it. Clinging to his precious worthlessness had kept him from accepting their gift. Maybe it was time to cling to something else.

The man who had once thought of himself as Little Billy held Katie's hand as she led him back across the Great Divide. In a third-floor hallway of St. Joseph's Hospital, William Phipps turned the corner.

ANDREW HAD HIS FATHER CREMATED. THE URN SAT ON A chair next to him during the funeral. He could see it in his periphery, a squat shape that didn't move, didn't shift, didn't threaten him with its coiled potential to lash out and kill. He could stare at it as long as he wanted and nothing would happen. Nothing at all.

Although the afternoon heat was mitigated somewhat by the blue tent and the steady breeze, he still had to mop his face every minute to keep the sweat from his eyes. July was not a forgiving month for a funeral. Not in Florida. He tried to focus on the pastor's words, tried to keep his head up and his back pressed against the chair, but he was sliding down a sweat-slicked chute and it was only a matter of time before it funneled him to the ground. He only hoped he wouldn't scatter his father's ashes all over hell and back on his way down.

"Drink," Grace whispered in his ear. She placed a bottle in his hand and he gulped half, the water running down his chin to soak the collar of his shirt. The pastor slowed the last few lines of his prayers—giving Andrew a chance to mop his face a final time—then nodded. It was the signal for him to stand and carry the remains to the urn vault excavated next to his mother's grave. Andrew rose with Grace at his side. Her hand was under his elbow, propping him up, and so fortified he managed to place the urn on the platform.

"Your dad drew them away from us," William had assured Andrew two days earlier as they waited for the body to be found amid the tower's rubble. "Gave us enough time to finish setting that last charge. It made all the difference."

If any words had been asked of him, Andrew might have passed that fact on to the few gathered mourners. No words were demanded, however, and Andrew stood at silent attention as a sweating funeral attendant lowered the urn into the ground. Then it was over, his parents reunited. The only thing remaining was to fill in the small pit entombing everything left of John Tate and move on.

Andrew moved on, letting his legs take him where they would. Eventually, he found himself under one of the cemetery's massive live oaks, speaking a few words of gratitude to the firefighters who had attended the funeral while William, Katie and Dr. Cho stood slightly aside, waiting their turn.

"Took a hell of a lot of guts to do what your old man did," Sid rumbled, apparently on the verge of tears. Andrew found his display disconcerting, not because he suspected it was insincere but because it was so out-of-character for the lieutenant. Then again, this was the same man who had stunned him the previous day with the announcement that he was transferring from pumper to ambulance. "Figured you could use a new partner," he confided sheepishly (another first for Sid Langston). "If you're interested."

The offer would have been moot forty-eight hours earlier, but Hamilton called the day after The Big Sink to inform him all charges were being dropped, his record wiped clean. When asked why, his station captain clicked his tongue.

"Seems the lot numbers on those Tubex vials showed they were manufactured twenty years ago. Who knows how long they've been hidden away in that alcove. Since you've only been at the station eight weeks, it's pretty obvious you didn't put them there. It was all a big misunderstanding."

"Amazing they could check the lot numbers so quickly under these circumstances."

"Amazing indeed."

Clare Humbert and Terrance Jackson offered their condolences and Max took Andrew's offered hand, pulled him close and gave him a back-slapping hug. "I expect you to keep your promise about getting together for a beer."

"Let's make it a couple of iced teas. Next week for sure."

Max dipped his head and made for the parking lot, giving Grace a brief hug and a whispered word before departing.

"Hey, Sid," Andrew called to the retreating lieutenant. He turned back. "Sorry a water tower fell on your car."

Sid smiled. "I had insurance. But the loss of my Wu-Tang Clan CD. *That* will take some time to get over."

Andrew rejoined the others, struck once again by William's appearance. He was having trouble reconciling this version of the man with the one he'd met in the park. The suit, the tie, the haircut. He tried not to stare, but he couldn't shake the impression Will was in costume, being fed his next line by the young woman in the short black dress at his side.

"I have something for you," Dr. Cho told Grace. She'd obviously been waiting for Andrew's return and now pulled a folded, letter-sized envelope from her handbag. She passed it over.

"Oh, my god." His wife squeezed the paper with exploratory fingers before ripping it open. "Are you kidding me?"

"I wasn't holding out much hope. But miracles of miracles, someone had turned it in to lost-and-found."

Grace slipped the wedding ring onto her finger and pulled the other woman into an embrace. "I hope they didn't give you too much grief when you asked for it."

"They know better. No one dares incur the wrath of Dr. Doom."

His wife held her left hand out toward him and wiggled her fingers, eyes wide with amazement. "Can you believe it?"

Andrew could only nod and smile. It had been enough for him that she'd asked Cho to make inquiries into her wedding band, especially in the chaotic hours after The Big Sink. Like Dr. Cho, Andrew had assumed the ring was gone for good. Its reappearance at his father's funeral was surreal, dubious even. It held the same portent as a tarot card reading in a dank carnival tent. The Hanged Man? The Five of Cups? A reaction was clearly expected, but he had no idea what any of it meant. He decided to keep smiling and nodding.

"Mommy got her ring back," Anna chirped. "Mommy got her ring back." She pirouetted up to her parents and Andrew gave her a squeeze before kissing Grace. Her lips tasted of salt, but from sweat or tears, he couldn't tell.

"Speaking of miracles." Andrew turned to Cho. "What's this I hear about you finding Jesus?"

"This from Janet?"

"Who else? She mentioned it yesterday when Terrance and I were dropping off a cardiac arrest."

Dr. Cho lifted the hair off the back of her neck and let it slip slowly through her fingers as she spoke.

"When we were in the tower, Booker invited all of us to attend a service at his church. Turns out he was a deacon there. His funeral wasn't what I expected. It was... nice. Jubilant, actually. A real celebration of his life. So, I decided to drop by for a Sunday service. I don't know if I buy into all the halleluiah hype, but I like the people there. They seem to like me. They think I can be salvaged." She laughed. "We'll see.

"Hector's funeral was a lot more formal. The incense made me dizzy, but at least the church had power. Your dad's service was somewhere between the two."

In the wake of her comment, the adults fell silent. A cranking car engine heralded the departure of the hearse. It crept slowly toward the gates, gravel popping under its tires and the small black flag still affixed to its hood.

"Too many funerals," Katie said after a moment. He knew she was thinking of her brother, as did William. He said nothing, but brought his head close to hers. Without raising her eyes, she reached up and touched his cheek. "Well," she sighed, a clear prelude to departure. "I guess we'll see you Saturday, then."

Andrew proposed gathering for lunch at his place first. "We'll call it a house warming."

William rubbed his ear. "You doing okay there?"

"It's creepy," Katie declared, her expression daring anyone to contradict her. "I'm sorry, Andy, but it is. You couldn't find somewhere else to live?"

"All his research is there. It's furnished. And the landlord's agreed to keep the rent the same. At least for now."

"But all those memories," she said shuddering. "I couldn't do it. I'd always feel like I'm being watched."

"I don't believe in ghosts."

"Who's talking about ghosts?"

In the topiary off to Andrew's left, something shifted, fluttered, resettled. He gave Anna a surreptitious tap on the shoulder, prompting her to turn her back on the tree. When she asked 'what?' he gave her a puzzled, 'who me?' look.

"I know it was you, Daddy," she said with exasperation. It was already a tired joke.

"So, noon, Saturday." he said.

William extended his hand and Andrew took it, pumped three times and let go, a brisk, businesslike exchange, the kind of handshake that signified the acceptance of a contract, although Andrew had only the vaguest notion what the terms of the agreement were.

"Saturday." Katie gave him a peck on the cheek and glanced around as if surveying the landscape. Andrew noticed she did not look in the direction of the topiary. "It's weird being in a cemetery and not blowing something up."

Arm-in-arm, she and William began the trek back to her car.

"I hope it works out for them," Cho said once they were out of earshot. "They make a cute couple."

"A little May-December," Andrew noted.

"Don't be mean." Grace gave him a playful slap on the forearm. "Everyone deserves to be happy."

"Hard to believe most of us were strangers three weeks ago," Cho said.

"Or even one week ago," his wife added.

"How are *you* holding up, Emily?" Andrew tapped Anna on the shoulder and she glared at him. But she glared at him in a safe direction. "Still getting questions?"

"Not so much in the last few days. I think they're about to give up and close the book. How about you two?"

"Same," Andrew said after a confirming glance at Grace. "They know we had nothing to do with the tower's collapse. Everything points to a structural failure most likely triggered by seismic activity. That's exactly how it's going to be phrased in their reports. I have it on good authority. As for the rest?" Andrew raised his hands, palms up. "There's nothing to contradict anything we've told them."

"I hope you're right." Dr. Cho removed a small folding fan from her bag and began waving it furiously at her face. "Theodore Hillsdale was a certified lunatic, no one's doubting that. But the detectives who took my statement were having a hard time believing he could break his handcuffs, kill..." she gave Anna a brief glance before resuming. "Do what he did to the guard outside his hospital door, steal his gun and take John and me hostage."

"You said the nurses and orderlies on the floor corroborated everything," Andrew pointed out.

"Except for him kidnapping us."

"Everybody was hiding by then. It's a shame the security recordings were erased," He sighed with saccharin resignation. "Now the police only have your word to go on."

Cho's grin was impish. "Who would have thought a massive power surge could destroy an entire day's worth of tapes? Janet said Lenard was just beside himself when he had to break the news to the detectives."

"Leonard?" Grace asked.

"Head of security at Tampa General. Janet actually saved his wife's life recently. She came into the ER complaining of nausea and a backache. The idiot attending physician diagnosed menstrual pain and prescribed 800 milligrams of Motrin. Turns out she was having a heart attack. If Janet hadn't swung by to check on things, who knows what would have happened. Lenard has been devoted to her ever since."

Grace gave a theatric nod, arms akimbo. "And well he should be. What about Hector and Booker? Why were they at the tower?"

"Hillsdale made me call them. He had a grudge against all of us and was going to shoot everyone once we were inside. How he knew the tower was open..." Cho shook her head. "Total mystery. As for your ex-partner..."

"Hillsdale somehow coerced Gary to do what he did. That's what I told the detectives. They were obviously working together. The hows and whys will probably never get sorted out. The police have bigger issues to deal with right now anyway. The guys who interviewed me looked like they hadn't slept in a week. They just took my statement and left."

"They'll be back."

"Maybe."

Cho slipped the fan back into her bag. "The power's on at my house. I'm going to try and bake a cake. Should be interesting. I'll bring it Saturday."

"You're going, too?" Grace asked in surprise.

"We're all part of something now, whether we want to be or not. I'm going to think of it as the weirdest neighborhood watch in the world."

Grace glanced toward the funeral tent, where two attendants were folding chairs and stacking them on a hand dolly. "For some crazy reason, I assumed all of the bad things would just disappear after this was over."

"Wouldn't that be nice?" Cho checked her watch and gave a small sigh. "Sorry to mourn and run, but my shift starts in less than an hour." She leaned forward and brushed her lips against Grace's cheek, gave Andrew's hand a squeeze, ruffled Anna's hair.

"See you soon," Andrew said to her retreating back. She raised her hand without turning and fluttered her fingers. As he watched her go, a small hand filled his. He ran his thumb lightly over the knuckles, feeling the thickened and folded skin, the irregular topography of scar tissue.

"Daddy?"

"Yes, honey?"

"Can we go home now?"

"You and Mommy can."

"But not you?"

Andrew closed his eyes and exhaled slowly. Sinking to his knees, he ran his hands up his daughter's arms and cupped her shoulders. "We talked about this, remember? Daddy needs to stay away for a little while. He's not feeling well and he doesn't want you and Mommy catching what he's got. Maybe after a little while, I'll get better."

"Then you'll come home?"

"We'll see."

"I know what 'we'll see' means." Her face crumbled. "'We'll see' means 'no.'"

Grace knelt next to them. "Honey, that's not true. Daddy wants to come home. It's just that he can't right now."

"You promised you'd take me to the park again and protect me from the dragons while I ran through the fountains. You promised you'd teach me how to swim and jump off the diving board. You promised to set up my tent so we could eat 'smores and watch *Cinderella* inside."

"We can still do all those things."

"When?" Her voice quivered, but her dry eyes shone with the first hard light of betrayal.

"Soon. Someday soon."

"I know what 'someday' means." She shook his hands off her shoulders and covered her face. "'Someday' means 'never!'"

"Anna."

"Leave me alone! You don't love me! You don't love anybody!"

She darted off toward Grace's Outback. His wife sighed and gave chase. Kneeling in the dirt beneath the sprawling oak, Andrew watched as they passed the *quintaloch* curled around the trunk of a cabbage palm, watched as they swept around the *squim* in the podocarpus and the *volvoxes* drifting lazily above the hood of the groundskeeper's truck. Kneeling on the damp earth, he watched his family survive the gauntlet.

Anna pounded the Outback's fender and Grace said something to her, their heads nearly touching. After a moment his wife looked in his direction and waved, not an invitation to approach but a gesture of farewell. He waved back.

"I see you."

Grace opened the SUV's doors, started the engine, stood talking to Anna as the air-conditioning pushed the worst of the heat from the cab.

Something flat and close to the ground snaked leisurely toward Andrew. He watched his wife buckle his daughter into her car seat, saw Anna reach for something next to her, a plush toy.

The grass next to him rustled softly. It was a furtive, almost timid approach. Probing. He watched Grace climb into the driver's seat and slip on a pair of sunglasses. She closed her door. Thump.

Something brushed the side of his hand so lightly he might have imagined it. Grace backed up, spun the wheel, ease backward.

A brief thrumming, soft as an infant's snore, but he did not turn. He watched as his wife and daughter crept down the lane, rounded a bend, turned right at the gate. They were nearly gone, but he kept watching while Grace slipped into traffic and accelerated toward the presumed safety of the place he had once called home.

Andrew Tate never took his eyes off his family.

After

Berko Obasanjo stood before the yellow wall of spear grass, machete in hand, waiting for his *bibi* to motion him on. She had fallen into one of her spells, motionless, eyes nearly shut, swaying slightly as if in imitation of the rustling stalks all around them. He was thirteen and this was the first time she had allowed him to accompany her on one of her *muda mrefu kutembeas*, her long walks. Some in the village considered his grandmother an *obayifo* because of these bouts of stillness, but Berko knew better. She was not possessed by evil spirits. She was a *mlinzi*, a watcher, and it was her duty to keep the village safe from the unseen ones.

She had tried to explain it to him as best she could, but it was still a puzzle with too many missing pieces. He knew, for instance, that she had slipped into the *subtle stare*, the *seeing-without-looking*. Someday he would learn do the same. But not yet. The unseen ones were too dangerous. More dangerous than a leopard at night. More dangerous than a startled mamba or cornered buffalo.

But why? He did not know. And why did she return again and again to the same termite mounds, the same leadwood stump, the same narrow rock outcroppings that reminded Berko of stone fingers clawing their way from beneath the ground? Yes, he had secretly followed her on many occasions. He suspected she knew he did this. She was a *mlinzi* after all. But she had never spoken of it.

Until today. This morning she had handed him the machete and told him it was time he made himself useful. He was proud of the path he had cut through the tall grass. He was strong and he knew how to use the blade. When he swung the stalks fell before him, the way they did when his father cut sightlines to the river so tourists could take photographs of hippo snouts poking from the water.

Berko wanted to continue cutting his path. He knew where they were going: the termite chimney next to the old mining road. They were almost there. Just a few more swipes and they would emerge into the clearing. He was strong and not tired. He would need a drink soon, though. Path cutting was thirsty work.

Finally, his grandmother roused herself and motioned him to continue. Although she said nothing, Berko sensed her unease. It was not like his bibi to be unsure of herself. Was she second-guessing her decision to bring him along? Was she worried he was too small, too young, too weak? He would show her. Berko swung the machete. The grass parted before him. He was covered in chafe. It made him sneeze, but he continued to swing. Three times, four, six. And then he was through. Now his grandmother would know he was no longer a boy.

He turned as she emerged into the open, expecting a word of appreciation, admiration even. Instead, a queasy knot unraveled in his belly. His grandmother's eyes were wide and unblinking. This was not the *seeing-without-looking*. This was fear. Naked terror. His grandmother, afraid? Never had he witnessed such a thing.

Berko spun, expecting to see a lioness racing toward them. There was no lioness. There was only the rutted mine road and the red dirt and the termite chimney. The machete fell from his hand. The termite chimney had caught fire. It was burning inside, red and pulsing like stoked coals in the blacksmith's forge. The light leaked out from many cracks, as if the mound had been shattered by a great blow.

Berko blinked. Rubbed his eyes. The mound was crying. A great teardrop had formed at its tip, and as he bent to retrieve the fallen blade, the tear lifted and began drifting off toward the river.

"Run," his grandmother hissed. "Run as fast as your legs can carry you. Take the road. Find your father. Bring him here. Tell him the time of the awakening has come. Can you remember that?"

"The time of the awakening has come," Berko repeated.

"Go then. Fly. Faster than you have ever run."

Berko ran. He was young and strong and not tired at all. He ran faster than the hot wind kicking the dust before him, and as he ran, he repeated

what his grandmother had told him: the time of the awakening had come.
It had come. The time of the awakening was finally here.